MINDFUL
OF
MURDER

MINDFUL OF MURDER

SUSAN JUBY

HarperCollins*Publishers*Ltd

Published by HarperCollins Publishers Ltd

First edition

HarperCollins books may be purchased for educational, business,
or sales promotional use through our Special Markets Department.

HarperCollins Publishers Ltd
Bay Adelaide Centre, East Tower
22 Adelaide Street West, 41st Floor
Toronto, Ontario, Canada
M5H 4E3

www.harpercollins.ca

Library and Archives Canada Cataloguing in Publication
Title: Mindful of murder / Susan Juby. Names: Juby, Susan, 1969- author.
Identifiers: Canadiana (print) 20210348755 | Canadiana (ebook) 20210348771 | ISBN
9781443464437 (softcover) | ISBN 9781443464444 (ebook)
Classification: LCC PS8569.U324 M55 2022 | DDC C813/.6—dc23
ISBN 978-1-4434-6443-7

Printed and bound in the United States of America

23 24 25 26 27 LBC 6 5 4 3 2

For James

PROLOGUE

Edna Todd was in love with herself and had been for a long time. Her lavish self-regard was built on a bedrock of appreciation for her good looks, still very much in evidence, her strong, flexible body, and what she considered to be a vivacious and intriguing personality. Having such a warm relationship with herself had made her three-month self-guided retreat not just tolerable, but richly enjoyable. And now that the three months were nearly over, she felt an added satisfaction, bordering on elation, that she'd accomplished her goal. She'd completed Plan A, which meant she'd finally, at long last, decided what to do with the Yatra Institute, her retreat centre, which she loved almost as much as she loved herself.

In the stillness of her office, Edna adjusted her posture at her desk. Posture had always been a major concern. Once she felt aligned, she went about relaxing the various muscles of her face and diaphragm, which aided in breathing, another area of abiding concern. This done, she took three long, intentional breaths, noting where one ended and the next began. It was a routine she performed at least four times a day and a critical part of her extensive self-care regimen. Then she went back to writing in her lovely new journal.

She should have dealt with her estate long ago. If she could be said to have any personal failings, procrastination was certainly one of them. So was a certain level of disorganization when it came to tiresome paperwork.

Edna, toned and lean at seventy-two, considered herself to be in late middle age. She worked hard to stay fit, even when she was in isolation, and took pains to dress becomingly. This evening she wore crisp, line-dried white cotton pyjamas. Her long silver hair, made more dramatic with iron-grey lowlights that she had touched up every six months, fell around her angular face in a way she secretly thought suggested a certain inner depth. With the big decision made, every part of her felt lighter.

She finished the day's journal entry by listing her digestive status (excellent), her blood pressure (that of a relaxed ultramarathoner), and finished with a note that it was nearly time to transplant the lettuce starters. Then she slipped the journal onto the shelf at the end of a long row of similar books. The spines were organized by colour and size rather than by date. Presumably, she'd misfiled the one she had been writing in for the past month. She'd had to start a new one before the old one was complete, but that was nothing new. Should someone wish to write about her life, which had of course been fascinating, after she was gone, they would have all the primary research materials they needed.

Edna laughed at the brazen insistence of her own ego, which she affectionately visualized as a cat that climbed into her lap to demand attention whenever it pleased. She gave it the metaphorical equivalent of a soft pat and gently but firmly placed it on the floor. She could practically see it twitching irritably and stalking off to wait for another opportunity to intrude. Edna Todd was self-satisfied in the extreme and she knew it.

After turning off the lights, she climbed the stairs to the second floor. Around her, the old lodge was quiet, except for the sighs of settling boards and the faint cries of night-calling birds.

The upper floor of the lodge contained two bedrooms, and the rest of the space was wide open and surrounded by windows. A thick yoga mat lay in the middle of the hardwood floor. In front of one window, a meditation cushion faced a short table with an altar arranged on top.

With a somewhat showy grace, Edna knelt in front of the yoga mat, touched her head to the ground, and then unfurled into a headstand, imaging herself opening like an alien flower greeting three suns. Her agile toes, affixed to large feet, flexed up and down as she maintained her inversion for exactly five minutes.

When she was finished infusing her brain with blood, she settled into her meditation nest. On the low altar sat a small, stone statue of Buddha flanked by two small bouquets of fresh flowers and herbs. She lit the beeswax candle, set her meditation timer, rang the silver bell three times, and then sat in silence, noticing thoughts as they arose, along with emotions, bodily sensations, sounds, and scents. When she got lost in thought, which happened often, she thought of Helen, who'd gone off to school in September. When the retreat was over, Edna planned to speak with Helen first, to tell her the good news. Helen would be relieved not to have to execute what they had decided to call Plan B.

Planning. Edna noted about the mental activity. *Planning.*

Then she went back to focusing on sounds as they entered her ears and the feeling of her hands as they lay on her lap. Until her thinking mind took centre stage again.

Planning. Planning. Plan A, Plan A. Complete. Or it would be once she'd informed Lest and Associates of her decision.

After forty-five minutes, the alarm sounded and Edna rang the bell three times and bowed, touching her forehead to the floor, three times. Then she blew out the candle and got to her feet without using her hands, feeling calm, centred, and intensely pleased with herself.

The lodge and the three-hundred-acre property were closed to guests for the off-season. Usually, Edna spent winters visiting other retreat centres and exploring her own curiosity about the world and the many spiritual practices in it. This year, however, she'd undertaken her longest-ever self-retreat to give herself time to consider her future and that of the Institute. And she'd finally come to her conclusion, which had required violating the silence of her retreat. Edna rubbed the tops of her arms in a self-warming gesture since there was no one else to hug.

Inside the modest washroom attached to her bedroom, Edna poured her nightly dose of liquid magnesium and calcium into a small porcelain cup and tossed it back. The supplement was her single concession to age and her post-menopausal status.

She was in the midst of brushing her teeth a minute or so later when the feeling started. Her stomach lurched and a primal alarm sounded deep inside.

Edna gripped the edge of the sink and spit the gritty, baking soda–based toothpaste into the hand-painted blue wash basin. Without rinsing out her mouth, she walked quickly, staggering a little, back to her bedroom, where she climbed into her neatly made bed, trying perhaps to avoid the clanging reality of what was happening inside of her. She reached over to shut off the lamp, but her hand missed and she knocked it over. It fell onto the old wooden plank floor and broke into several pieces.

The sound broke through her denial. She needed help. *Helen!* Where was Helen?

Then she remembered that Helen was in school and she was alone. Horribly and completely alone. She needed to get downstairs to the office, where the landline was located and her cellphone was charging. Edna tried to swing her legs over the side of the bed, but they wouldn't move. She tried to get up, but her arms refused to hold her weight. The logical part of her already-dying brain knew that she wouldn't have been able to use the phone even if she could reach it.

Edna Todd's heartbeat slowed and so did her breath. In its final moments, her brain conjured the image of a cat being put to sleep at the vet's office. It was a perfectly good cat, healthy and sleek. Such a terrible shame. She wasn't ready. She was magnificent! The last noise Edna made was a cry of irritation as she managed, finally, to kick one leg out from under the covers. She was dead before the sound left her throat.

She never noticed the figure standing in her bedroom door, watching.

Part 1

THE PEOPLE

CHAPTER 1

The new butlers stood in a line in front of the gleaming white yacht. They wore dark suits and polished shoes. Their nails were clean and their hair was neat. All but one were drunk.

"Excuse me!" called the photographer, who'd been hired by the North American Butler Academy to take graduation day photos. "You there. Third from the left. The brown-haired gal? Can you please move over one?"

Helen Thorpe, the only sober butler, changed places with a lean, thirty-ish man. She was five feet, ten inches tall, half an inch taller than the man she replaced.

"Better. Better. Okay, that's better," said the photographer, who was a scurrying sort of person. He bent down and aimed the lens of his camera at the row of nine butlers.

"Beautiful! Look at you. So tidy! Show me your best butler faces."

The butlers kept their faces exactly the same as they would do throughout their careers. Pleasant, professional, impassive. Among them, Helen Thorpe somehow seemed extra still, as though her very molecules moved more slowly. She watched the little photographer with clear, thoughtful eyes. She saw that he was darting hither and fro on the dock, not paying the slightest attention to where he was going. She saw that his clothes, though clean, were not new. The heels of his shoes were worn down. He was making a strenuous effort to do a good job. The only expensive thing on him was his camera, which was not brand new, but of exceptional quality. He was, she thought, probably beginning his business as a photographer. Something about the way he strived to keep them amused and to get the best shots suggested an attempt at a fresh start. Honest effort poured off him.

He knelt on a bench bolted to the middle of the dock, and then he climbed up a pole with rungs on it, holding on with one hand and making dramatic attempts to shoot with the other.

The butlers, who had been up all night, watched him work with well-disguised bleariness. They'd kicked off the festivities the night before with a lavish dinner at a fine French restaurant, followed by visits to a series of bars and clubs. After they closed down a speakeasy at 3:30 a.m., they'd gone to the beach for a sunrise bonfire. At five, they headed back to their dorm rooms in the old mansion that housed the North American Butler Academy, which, according to the marketing materials, was in the business of "creating specialists in domestic excellence." They cleaned themselves up for the early morning photo shoot, which would involve group shots and individual portraits to be used for their professional profiles on Butler.com and the school's advertising materials.

Helen didn't drink and had quietly put herself in charge of keeping the rest of the butlers from being roofied or otherwise coming to harm. "No butler left behind," she'd said to the youngest of them, a girl from Virginia by way of Ireland named Murray whom Helen had retrieved from behind a leatherette couch in the "quiet room" of a dance club filled with music that sounded like multiple emergency vehicles converging on a construction site.

"I love you, Helen," Murray had said. "Everyone loves you. You're so relaxing."

All night the other graduates gave versions of the same speech to her. She smiled, enjoying the feeling of caring for them. They were butlers, so they were easy to love. Helen knew not everyone in her new career would be so easy. Her job would be filled with difficult people, the way most jobs were.

"One shot with you all smiling!" said the photographer, who had slicked-back hair and a face that was faintly haggard under his tan. He gave them a strange little smile as though to demonstrate what a smile was. The hungover butlers gave indistinct smiles in return.

"Yes! Yes! That's right! Everyone likes a butler who can smile, am I right?" he muttered as he clicked away.

"Okay now," he said, standing and nearly running backwards to get a new angle. "Beautiful! Beautiful but—" Before he could finish, his heel hit the lip of the dock and he pitched back. His body went rigid and he began to windmill his arms. The camera flew into the air like a brick hurled in a riot.

Helen reacted instantly. She took four giant steps and caught the device before it could smash onto the dock. Then she set it down and stepped over to look at the photographer, who was thrashing around in the oily water.

"Help!" he screamed, coming up for air.

"Can you swim?" she asked, though it was obvious he could. He'd already started churning his way toward a ladder hanging off the side of the dock, moving with all the ease of a pug in a pool, which is to say, without much ease at all.

"What?" he spluttered.

"Are you okay?" said Helen, slowly.

"Yes. Yes." He spit out a mouthful of water. "My goddamned camera. My life is ruined."

"It's here," she said, holding it up. "Don't worry. I've got it. It's safe."

He reached the ladder and scrambled up, trying to catch his breath.

"You saved my camera? Instead of me?" He stared at her. Before Helen could respond, he went on. "You're a goddess!" he said. "I spent the rest of my money on that lens. For this gig. I could kiss you." He gazed up at her calm face and something about it caused him to revise his words. "But I won't, obviously."

"Helen's going to be the best butler since Jeeves," said Gavin Vimukthi, the elegant man who'd come to stand beside Helen. He reached out a hand to help the photographer back onto the dock.

"Someone will get you a towel from the ship," said Helen.

The photographer, whose slick look was even more pronounced now that he was soaked, appeared almost undone by the near disaster, but something about Helen's kind but matter-of-fact manner restored him to himself.

"Yes. Of course," he said. "My bad. I get a little worked up sometimes. Never shot butlers before. To be honest, this is my first corporate gig."

Helen nodded. "You're doing very well."

"I fell in the fucking ocean," said the photographer.

"It's absolutely fine," said Gavin, soothingly. "Helen saved the day."

"Course she did," said Murray Cleary, the young butler who wore her black hair in a neat French braid. She was breathless from her dash up onto the yacht. The Silicon Valley owner rented it to the

Academy so they could train butler candidates in yacht management in exchange for free butler service when he took it out. Murray gave the photographer a fresh monogrammed towel.

He wiped off his hair and face.

"Losing that camera would have been the end of me," he said. "This shoot is the difference between eating and not."

Helen looked at him with such kindness that he wanted to cry, though he couldn't have said why.

Five minutes later, the photographer was once again clicking away, pausing every so often to wipe his wet hair out of his eyes.

When they had finished the shoot, the photographer shook each of the butlers' hands with his, now as damp from sweat as from ocean water.

"In my next life, I want to be a butler," he said when he reached Gavin, who had the kind of good looks that made people stare. "You people are all so calm."

"We merely appear that way," said Gavin. "Helen, on the other hand, actually is calm."

Murray leaned in toward the photographer. "We think she used to be something special. Like maybe a magician or battlefield nurse."

"Possibly with the Canadian version of the CIA," said Gavin. "Something where you have to be cool-headed."

The three of them turned to watch Helen, who had boarded the yacht. She reached for her phone, looked at the screen, and put it to her ear. Even from that distance, there was something compelling about the deliberate way Helen comported herself.

"Helen," said Gavin simply. And they all understood it was a complete thought.

Helen.

Chapter 2

Helen had not been a magician, a combat nurse, or an operative with the Central Intelligence Agency or CSIS. She had been a Buddhist nun who had left her order when her mother became ill and needed her. Her teacher, the twinklingly cheerful and widely revered monk from Burma Sayadaw U Nandisara, was famous for his practice of a challenging corpse meditation. When she told him she had to leave the monastery to go and care for her mother, he graciously told her that she would always be welcome back. But after her mother passed away, Helen found herself employed at a New Age retreat centre on one of British Columbia's Discovery Islands. She started as a meditation teacher and then became the lodge manager, before the owner of the Yatra Institute, Edna Todd, paid for her to go to the North American Butler Academy in Florida.

Helen was not always as suffused with emotional equilibrium as her fellow butler candidates supposed. Just now, she was in fact being buffeted by a welter of feelings as the voice on the phone told her that her former employer and most beloved benefactor, Edna Todd, was dead.

Helen felt the ship beneath her dip slightly and didn't know whether it was from the ocean swelling or her knees buckling.

"Does this news come as a surprise to you, Ms.— ah, is it Ms.?"

"Yes," said Helen. "I'm a Ms. And yes, I am surprised. Edna was death positive, of course."

"Death positive?"

"She believed that people need to get a better relationship with death. They need to spend time thinking about the end of life and what it means to them. She viewed death as a transition between one plane of existence and the next. But I didn't know she was ill."

"You're saying she only planned to transition if she was sick?" asked the lawyer.

"Well, no. She wanted the right to end her own life any time and place she saw fit," she said. "But I always assumed she'd only take that final step if there was a compelling reason."

Below her on the dock, the butlers were loosening ties and relaxing into conversation, while one after another had their headshot taken against the glittering backdrop of wealth that was the marina. Helen wished she was down there with them and not having this conversation. But then she caught herself. *Stay present*, she told herself, as she had countless times before. *This moment will not come again.*

"I'm afraid it looks as though she decided to, uh, go over to the other side three days ago. We have not been advised that she was unwell. I'm very sorry." The lawyer sighed softly into the receiver. "I apologize that it has taken us so long to track you down. Ms. Todd hadn't updated your contact information."

"I'm sorry, too," said Helen. She waited, fearing what was coming next. Had Edna taken care of business as she'd promised to do?

"Ms. Todd left instructions for you to execute something she referred to as Plan B. Are you familiar with it?"

Helen's stomach dropped like a stone. "Yes," she said. She tried to find the quiet place inside herself. A tear ran down her face. She made no move to stop it or the ones that followed.

"You know about the relatives? And the courses?"

"Yes," said Helen. "Edna and I discussed her wishes in some detail. I just didn't think . . . it would be necessary."

"I'm afraid it is," said the lawyer. "This, uh, plan would be hard to explain to someone who wasn't somewhat prepared."

"Quite," said Helen, who felt not at all prepared.

"How soon can you get to the island?"

Helen thought of all she had to do: Tell her new employer she would not be able to take the job after all. Find a flight from Florida to Vancouver and then get a float plane to Sutil Island. And then . . . It didn't bear thinking about.

"Tomorrow or the next day," she said. The morning was getting hot and the sun glinted off the overwhelmingly white surfaces of the yacht, which the Silicon Valley owner had named *Bitcoin Queen*. The butlers and the photographer were gone and the dock was empty. Helen was alone with only the prospect of Plan B in front of her.

BACK IN HER room at the old mansion that housed the North American Butler Academy, Helen sat at her desk, which had always made her feel like an oversized child. Edna was gone. It was like learning that the moon had disappeared. It was going to take some time for the new reality to settle in. Regret pushed at her. Why hadn't she been more insistent that Edna check in with her during her retreat? Edna was not such an accomplished meditator that she could go three months without speaking to anyone, especially not on a self-guided retreat. But Edna hadn't wanted to bother Helen at school and she'd promised she *would* check in with someone. Had she?

There was a knock at her door.

"Helen?" came Murray's soft voice. "Are you there, Helen? It's me, Margaret." She dissolved into giggles, and Helen opened the door to find Murray and Gavin standing there, suit jackets off, ties thrown back over their shoulders.

"We've decided we can't stand for you to leave. We're going to sit in your room and stare at you so you feel bad for us," said Gavin in his posh British accent.

The two butlers came into the room and sat on Helen's bed, as they'd done many times before.

"Helen," said Murray. "I've been asking myself how many times a day I can text you. I'll have my own duties to attend to, naturally, but I can't exist without talking to you at least ten times."

"Shush now," Gavin said to Murray, who fell immediately silent.

Gavin didn't speak. His dark eyes searched Helen's face.

"Is everything all right?" he finally asked.

Helen nodded at her two friends and felt a fresh set of tears begin.

"Oh no," cried Murray. "Oh no. Helen! What is it? And here I was being so silly."

Gavin and Murray gave her such caring looks that she almost couldn't stand to look at them.

"Come and sit down," said Gavin, scooting aside so Helen could sit between them.

She cried until she was done, and then shared her grief at losing her mentor and, being perfectly honest, her sadness at having to let go of the new job.

"I know I shouldn't care about the job, but I do," said Helen.

"Of course you do," said Gavin.

"I'm not sure I follow," said Murray. "What is it you have to do with the estate?"

Helen swallowed. It was too complicated to explain Plan B. "I have to take care of some complex decisions," she said. "I promised Edna a long time ago."

Murray made a sympathetic tsk. "I'm so sorry. It's very bad timing. But I doubt your new employers will look for someone else just because you can't start right away. How long could it take to get things sorted?"

Gavin nodded. "They chose you for a reason."

On the recommendation of the head of the Academy, Helen had been hired to work for two of the wealthiest and most prominent philanthropists in North America before she'd even completed her training. The Levines made their money in shipping and instilled a sense of civic responsibility in their children, who were lawyers for Human Rights Watch and environmental organizations. Now in their late sixties, the Levines had homes in Calgary, Toronto, San Jose, and the South of France. They were secular Jews who had a serious meditation practice. There was a temple on the grounds of one of their estates.

"They are amazing people, Helen. They *rescue* things," added Murray. "No doubt they won't mind waiting a couple of weeks. They'll see that it's very noble and responsible of you to help settle your former employer's estate."

"That level of trust in you is a mark in your favour, I'd say," added Gavin.

Helen didn't think Plan B was noble or even rational, but what they'd said about her new employers was true. They had a greenhouse full of rare heirloom plants they were rescuing from extinction, and they adopted retired racing greyhounds and off-the-track thoroughbreds, and all manner of creatures who would otherwise go to the slaughterhouse. These animals lived in genteel circumstances on beautiful estates. The family's gardens and orchards helped feed underprivileged people in neighbouring communities. They were friends with many of the most powerful and influential people in the world. And they were going to pay her a starting salary of nearly two hundred thousand dollars a year to manage their household affairs.

Or they weren't. And she wasn't.

"What can we do to help?" asked Gavin.

Helen shook her head. She couldn't put her thoughts together clearly.

"How are you getting back to Canada?" he asked. "To Vancouver and then to your island?"

"Flying. I was just about to call."

"Let me take care of it." Before attending butler school, Gavin had worked as a flight attendant on private aircraft. "I'll see if I can get you on a private plane, at least to Vancouver. Maybe I can get you all the way to your island."

"Stud," said Murray, casting him a sidelong glance. "So glamorous."

"Thank you," said Gavin, who really was glamorous.

"We'll take care of you," said Murray. "We're not leaving our Helen to deal with all this trauma alone. She's one of us. A fully trained and certified butler. It's like being a Green Beret, isn't it?"

"Only with much better manners," said Gavin.

Helen put an arm around each of them and had to admit that in the midst of her pain, she felt warmth.

Within an hour, Helen had called her new employers and explained her situation to their current butler, who had planned to retire immediately after he finished training her.

"I understand if you need to choose someone else," she said.

He didn't hesitate.

"I feel confident that Mr. and Mrs. Levine won't mind waiting. They're in France for another month. I'd planned to get you up to speed while they are away, but I'm sure they won't mind having me stay a bit longer. I have been in their employ for nearly thirty years," he said.

"I'm sorry that this will delay your retirement," she said, trying not to sound too relieved.

"I will miss this place. From my condo in Miami," he said, laughing gently. "Mr. and Mrs. Levine and the family and the rest of the household staff are looking forward to meeting you. And Helen, please accept our condolences on your loss. I'm glad there is one more thing you can do for your late employer." He sounded absolutely sincere and she felt a great surge of gratitude.

Moments later, Helen was on her way to the airport, carrying the bag Murray and Gavin had packed perfectly for her, heading not to her future, but to her past.

Chapter 3

After disembarking from the float plane at the Sutil Island dock, Helen breathed deep the mingled scent of decay, salt, and wind-whipped air while the pilot and two other passengers made their way up the dock to the small shack of a terminal building.

The water gently moved the boards under her feet. Seagulls swooped and dove like wind-stolen parasols. The wind pushed at her back, urging her to the shore, but she closed her eyes, braced her legs, and stood firm. When she opened them again, Tanner was gazing into her face.

"Sorry, dude," he said. "Were you praying?"

"Tanner. It's good to see you again."

"You too, Hel. Bummer sitch. Ms. Edna was so awesome. I remember when she'd paddle over here in her kayak and do some moon shit on the dock. Like yoga or witch business or whatever."

Helen nodded.

The Sutil Island public dock was a popular spot for boaters, wiccans, and people who liked to smoke pot under the stars, which meant everyone on the island.

"I'll drive you to the lodge," said Tanner, who was as gloriously beautiful as he was unkempt, with his tousled, dark blond hair and violet-blue eyes. He was Sutil born and raised. He had no lies in him, and no pretensions. His mother grew garlic and his father smoked weed and fished sometimes. They were good people who had raised a fine young man.

They walked to the parking lot together and up to a small, rusted-out truck parked in the gravel lot behind the terminal.

"You need to stop anywhere?" asked Tanner, after they got into the dusty vehicle and fastened their seatbelts. "Before you head to the lodge?"

"I'll go to the Co-op later." She considered for a moment. "Are you looking for more work?"

"Nah. I'm fuelling up boats and planes here at the dock a couple of days a week and taking out the odd fishing charter. I wouldn't want to lose my work–life balance by getting another gig." He said this with no visible sense of irony, which Helen found charming.

He drove them slowly along the narrow roads. Helen wondered if it was possible to drive quickly in the truck. Probably not.

Sutil Island belonged to Discovery Islands, a group located at the northern edge of the Salish Sea and the Johnstone Strait. It was one of the bigger islands in the group, with a year-round population of 512 people. In summertime, the population sometimes swelled to over 537, not including guests at the lodge, which could hold up to sixty. Few residents worked full-time, no matter what the season. They were retirees, freelancers who mostly procrastinated from home, micro-scale farmers who spent their days staring moodily at failing micro crops, meditators, and people who opposed capitalism and most forms of effort. Tanner was practically a workaholic compared to many of Sutil's residents.

"How did you know I was coming?" she asked.

"I've been talking to Edna's lawyer. I helped with the flight for Edna's earthy remains. That's something, eh? Her going off to that place and letting the birds eat her for science."

Helen wouldn't have put it quite that way. "She wanted a sky burial. Donating her body to the forensic centre was as close as we could get."

Helen and Edna had also researched whether Edna could arrange something similar to a Parsi Tower of Silence, to have her body placed in a tower so it could be devoured by vultures, but the representative from the Vancouver Island Health Authority gave them a firm no. They looked into sending her remains out to sea on a raft, but a number of health and safety, environment, and Transport Canada regulations prohibited it, to Edna's disappointment.

Edna had been the president and founding member of the Sutil Island Death Positive Club, which was one of the liveliest clubs on the island. She felt she had to set a creative standard for everyone else when it came to her final resting place.

Tanner shuddered. "Sky burial sounds quite a bit better than letting the buzzards peck your bones clean. That's what happens, right? They leave you in a field?"

"I believe Edna is being left on the mountainside. The birds will take her aloft. She'll be of use to science. That was important to her." Helen didn't mention that she'd always had the distinct impression Edna felt confident she was never going to die, so her avant-garde approach to body disposal would not be necessary.

"Personally, I think I'm going to ask to be planted in the ground under an apple tree when the time comes," said Tanner.

Helen thought that sounded rather nicer than being left naked on a mountainside.

Her initial impression that the island was quiet had shifted as her ears adjusted to the absence of urban noise and awoke to the insistent clamour of nature and the sea under the steady rumble of the truck's labouring engine.

"I'm going to miss her. We all are," said Tanner. He turned to her with a face so sincere that she wanted to reach out and hug him. He'd been only eight or nine when she came to Sutil, and it was strange to see him now as a strong and tall young man. She didn't hug him, obviously, because he was driving.

Fifteen minutes after they left the float plane dock, Tanner pulled up into the gravel parking lot where the Institute van and tiny Smart Car were parked, both painted the distinctive lavender hue that was the official company colour. Helen got out of the truck and stared up at the old cedar lodge.

Even though the woman who had been the beating heart of the place was gone, it appeared unchanged. Helen had half expected the huge trees that covered the property would have shed their needles and leaves in mourning. Of course not. The deciduous trees were covered in new leaves. The evergreens showed fresh, new growth. Many of the trees were over a hundred years old. Some had been standing sentry for two hundred years or more. They'd been watching shorter lives start and end for a long time.

The Yatra Institute had the air of a building that would last forever, barring disaster. Now it was Helen's job to bar those disasters.

The responsibility felt like a bag of cement on her back.

She looked at the big, slightly ungainly lodge. It was not beautiful, but close examination revealed it to be well-built and carefully maintained. It was the right building in the right place, and the sight of it gladdened her. Tanner carried her suitcase up the stairs to the big porch, where she thanked him and then waved him on his way. She turned and sat at one of the built-in wooden tables that looked out over the green lawn, which sloped down to the beach. The tide was out. Black oystercatchers with bright orange bills waded in the shallow water. Seagulls and crows squabbled and flapped over something dead near the driftwood line. A heron stared grimly into a tide pool.

As always, the Yatra Institute affected her in a way not even the monastery had done. She'd never have left if Edna hadn't insisted. She would not have left the monastery if her mother hadn't become ill and needed her care. But after leaving both places, she'd been glad of the change.

Strange undercurrents of energy moved around the place. Edna had thought they came from the transformations yogis experienced while taking courses. Helen wasn't sure that was true, but the slightly hypnotic quality of the place was undeniable.

Helen let her head fall back. How on earth was she going to do what needed to be done in the next couple of weeks? One task at a time, she thought. That's how.

She let her eyes close. She'd only agreed to Plan B because she didn't imagine it would ever come to pass. Edna, like many white western Buddhists, had a tendency to treat various spiritual practices like an all you can eat buffet. The results could be unsettling and even unseemly. Plan B, with its mix of practices, had a bit of that flavour, which made it even less appetizing. Before her thoughts could get any darker, the phone buzzed in her pocket and she answered.

"Did you make it to your lodge all right?" asked Murray.

"Yes," said Helen. "I'm here now."

"Now you can settle your late employer's affairs," said Murray. "We forgot to ask what that entails."

"It's a bit, uh, unusual," said Helen, choosing to go with extreme understatement. She couldn't think of a reason not to tell them, even though she found the whole thing embarrassing. "We called it Plan B."

"What was Plan A?" asked Murray.

"Plan A was that Edna would decide who among certain of her relatives should take over the lodge. It seems she didn't do it before she died, so we're left with Plan B."

"And that is?" said Murray.

"Plan B is I decide who should take over, using Edna's criteria."

"Good lord, that sounds intense," said Murray. "I'm putting Gavin on speaker phone for this." There was a click and Murray continued. "Who's in contention, then? Are they good people? Environmentally minded? Able to take over a New Age retreat centre on a moment's notice?"

Helen watched as one of the seagulls grabbed the dead thing from the crow and went flying wildly away, the crow in pursuit.

"I don't know. I haven't met them yet."

"Who are these people?" said Gavin.

"Edna's great-nephews and a great-niece. She wanted one of them to run the lodge for some complicated reasons having to do with a stipulation in her late husband's will. I'm not entirely clear on the details. I don't think Edna was, either."

"So how will you decide?" Murray asked. "Interview each of them and administer a Rorschach, a lie detector, and a few random drug screens?"

Helen wished. "I have to invite them to the lodge and make them take three of the most popular courses."

"What!" screeched Murray. "No you're not! It's too insane! Like a reality TV program."

She was exactly right, of course. It *was* like reality TV. The thought made Helen feel vaguely nauseous.

"I am. And it is. But that's what I have agreed to do."

"Didn't you say the courses at the lodge are highly eccentric?" asked Gavin.

"Well," said Helen, "they're not for everyone. But they *are* fascinating and eclectic."

"The lodge has been closed, right? While your boss was on retreat? Who's there now to help you?"

"No one," said Helen. "I'll have to get things up and running and there's not a lot of time."

"It sounds unmanageable," said Gavin.

Helen agreed, though her training in right speech meant she didn't say so.

"What exactly do you need to do?" Gavin asked.

"The lawyers said that the teachers are on their way, I think. So are the, uh, students. I just need to get the various accommodations ready. The food. Some staff . . ." She didn't mean to sound so defeated, but there really was a lot to do before the guests arrived and only a few days to pull it together. Normally, the lodge didn't open until June, and it did so with a staff of at least fifteen people. She'd have to track down anyone who'd worked at the lodge in the past. Maybe some would want to come to work on short notice. But she feared they wouldn't. And she couldn't offer people a full season's work. There was no guarantee the lodge would be open for the season. If none of the candidates wanted to run it, Helen had no idea what would happen to the lodge in the short term or the long term. That would be up to the lawyers. She only knew her part of Edna's final wishes. She only knew Plan B.

Gavin said something in the background that Helen couldn't quite hear. "Brilliant," replied Murray. "You took the thought right out of my mind.

"Look, Helen. You're not waiting hand and foot on a whole pack of great-nieces and -nephews by yourself. We're coming. Gav agrees."

There was some muttering and what sounded like scuffling in the background.

"Gavin is already trying out a new packing method. You know how he is. He'll pack a case five times to get it right. It's not just butler precision at this point. It's obsessive compulsion. Full blown. It's like watching a bantamweight fight a cardboard box. Anyway, we're coming. His new job doesn't start for three weeks and I have a bit of time before I start mine."

"I can't ask you to do that," said Helen, so full of gratitude she couldn't put much strength into her protestation.

"Don't try it on with me, Helen. You're a certified butler, not a scullery maid. You'll want our help. We'll help you figure out who's who and what's what in this affair."

More muttering in the background.

"Gav's just done a bit of reconnaissance. We'll arrive at your Sutil Island tomorrow afternoon. Before you know it, you'll have this task completed and the best person will be left in charge and you'll be off to your new position." Pause. "Gav says don't worry. I say it too."

With that, Murray hung up and Helen finally felt ready to go inside.

Chapter 4

The lodge had been built in the late fifties out of cedar that grew on the property. At one end of the main floor was a large dining room with windows on three sides and enough tables and chairs to accommodate up to sixty guests. A doorway on one side of the dining room led into a small sitting room that faced the ocean. That led in turn to the serving area from which meals were served, buffet-style. Beyond that was the large commercial kitchen equipped with a separate baking room, a nook for the dishwasher, glass-fronted refrigerators, and a large walk-in cooler. The doorway on the forest-facing side of the dining room opened into the big foyer with guest bathrooms across from a long coffee and tea station. The foyer looked out over the famous Yatra garden. Edna's office was tucked into a room at the base of the stairs that led up to the second floor.

When the lodge was open, guests checked in via a small building between the parking lot and the garden. They stayed in the variety of mismatched buildings—kutis, A-frame cottages, cob cottages, ocean-front and hillside cabins—that dotted the property and were connected by a maze of trails.

As always, the main lodge smelled of old woodsmoke, sea air, and countless bouquets of flowers from the garden. Helen made a circuit of the main floor. In the dining room the wooden floors and tables were clean. The sitting room was orderly, all the pillows fluffed, and the fireplace neatly swept, the basket of kindling full. The kitchen was spotless and so was the serving room, with its big serving table pushed up against the wall. Other than the hum of the appliances, all was quiet, as though the sounds from outside could not get in. Helen opened a window in the kitchen and the room immediately filled with birdsong.

Then Helen went upstairs to Ms. Edna Todd's bedroom. That's where the lawyer said she'd done it. It looked serene, though the simple double bed was unmade. A plain pine side table sat beside the bed and a single chair with an embroidered seat had been turned to face the window that looked out at the water.

Helen tried to picture Edna lying in the bed, lifeless. The image wouldn't come, perhaps because Edna had always had a vivaciousness bordering on mania. She was famous for her headstands and had gardened like she was in a competition, and loved nothing more than an esoteric self-improvement effort. Edna Todd, seventy-two, had been generous, intensely curious, often unintentionally funny, and, considering her passion for all things spiritual, a startlingly un-self-aware person. She'd loved fiercely and freely admitted her faults—when she noticed them, which didn't happen often. Her impulsiveness had saved Helen's life. After Helen had left the monastery and lost her mother, she'd felt like a rowboat set loose to be dashed on the rocks. She'd been contacted by Edna, who'd been a regular guest at the monastery. Edna had invited her to the Yatra Institute, which lay on the other side of the country. There Helen would guide guests in meditation. From the moment Helen arrived, their bond had been unshakable. Edna treated Helen like a guru and like a daughter, and Helen had basked in the older woman's care. And she'd been helpful to Edna, especially after she took over management of the lodge.

Helen didn't linger in Edna's room. Instead, she did what needed to be done. She made phone calls. Arranged things. Made lists. Bought groceries at the Co-op. And she tried not to let her discomfort with what she had to do or her confusion about Edna's choice to die alone distract her.

Chapter 5

MURRAY CLEARY

The pilot let himself out the front of the plane and then opened the side door to let us off. Not a moment too soon. He was alarmingly youthful, even to a person such as myself, who is also scarcely older than a teenager. The plane was the size of a Toyota sedan and bobbed around in the air like a truck driving over potholes. If I ever get a job, I better make sure they have a proper plane and not some insane little boat with wings.

I thought my legs might collapse from the relief of making it off alive, but then I saw Helen waiting for us at the end of the dock, standing so still, so peaceful, and I felt instantly stronger. Of course, we didn't crash. Nothing so dire could happen on Helen's watch.

Gavin had to stand back from the bobbing wing while we waited for the pilot and a dockhand to retrieve our bags. They were stored in the plane's pontoons, which seemed like tying lead weights to a bird and then asking it to take off.

"There you are," said Gavin when we reached Helen. He gave her a kiss on her cheek. I'd be somewhat jealous if he kissed any other non-hideous woman, but not Helen. Helen deserved all the kisses.

"You've missed us terribly, of course," I said, getting in there to give her my own hug.

Helen smiled at us. "I'm extremely glad to see you both."

She reached to take my suitcase.

"Unhand that," said Gavin. "Murr and I are the butlers in this scenario. *You* are the client."

"At your service, madam," I told her.

Helen gave up my case. She looked windswept and healthy and completely in her element.

"We will be equal branches of butlering," said Helen.

"Any sane person would agree that three butlers are better than one," I said. I was about to go on to make more jokes about our new profession when the dockhand stood up and began to say something to one of the other passengers, an older man in new and expensive-looking outdoors clothing. The dockhand was absurdly handsome. He had on a cable-knit sweater and jeans slung low and oh my god.

"Who's that, then?" I asked Helen. "He's *gorgeous*."

Helen laughed. "I presume you mean the younger one. Does this mean you're *not* on duty just yet?"

"I can't help having eyes, can I. Look at him!"

"That's Tanner," said Helen in a low voice. "He's *nineteen*."

"Oh, he's perfect for Murray then," said Gavin. "She has the soul of a nineteen-year-old."

At least he didn't say I had the maturity of a nineteen-year-old, although that would also be true. I am twenty-four, and I feel sixteen half the time and eighty-six the rest.

Gavin laughed and put his arm around me. "Ah, Miss Murray,

you're going to have to watch you don't get caught in such antics at your next post."

That made me self-conscious about leering at the dockhand, but not so self-conscious that I stopped. But I did make sure to look away before he turned around.

The boy left his conversation and came over to us.

"Tanner," said Helen. "This is Murray Cleary and Gavin Vimukthi. The three of us went to school together. They'll be staying with me at the lodge for the next couple of weeks. We're going to be running the lodge in a limited capacity."

"You're *all* butlers," Tanner said in wonder. Which I appreciated, because it *is* an amazing thing. I am not only the first member of my family to go to college, I'm also the first one to meet a butler, never mind *be* one.

"A veritable band of butlers," said Gavin, grinning.

Tanner shook our hands, and when he let mine go, his cheeks were flushed. I like to think it wasn't just the brisk ocean breeze but rather my charisma, which hasn't had much of a chance to shine lately.

"Come and visit us at the lodge one of these afternoons," said Helen.

"I'll do that," said Tanner, and he gave me a little look and then stared at his shoes. I believe there was a moment between us and nothing can convince me otherwise.

Then Gavin and I followed Helen up the gangplank to a van painted a particularly Easter shade of lavender.

"You can put your tongue back in your mouth now, Mur," said Gavin, taking my arm.

"Did you see how he couldn't focus on anything but me? He's obviously in love. I think it's mutual, to be honest."

I snuck a look at Gavin's face and saw no evidence he was jealous, which was disappointing.

On the drive to the lodge in the big purple van, Helen pointed out various sights along the narrow, twisty road. The hints of fog had cleared and the sky was blue. Trees pressed in on all sides. It was a bit spooky, really. If the weather turned dreary, Sutil must be dark and oppressive. We lived in Ireland until I was seven. Sutil Island reminded me of that.

We passed scrubby fields filled with sheep and goats and strange ramshackle houses made of wood and stone and bits of random metal, all with dirt driveways. There were driftwood sculptures in many yards, and fences made of driftwood surrounding wild, overgrown gardens. Helen said the fences were there to keep out deer. Mostly, they looked to be doing a good job of keeping in the weeds.

"I'd love to see a deer," said Gavin.

"It's a bit like seeing a squirrel or a pigeon in the city," said Helen. "They are delightful until they've eaten everything in your garden."

We went past a house hidden behind an imposing wall composed entirely of stacked tires.

"Reduce, reuse, recycle," said Gavin.

Then Helen turned off the paved road and we drove up a long, well-groomed gravel driveway lined on both sides by forest. After a couple of minutes, we emerged into a clearing and Helen pulled the van into a parking lot in front of a small building marked *Reception*. Behind it was a large building, weathered silver, that looked out over a huge expanse of calm grey ocean.

Helen shut off the engine and turned to smile at us. "Welcome to the Yatra Institute."

I could hear the pride in her voice and was glad we'd come, and not just because I don't really have anywhere else to go—unfortunate, since I have nearly fifty thousand dollars in student loans and am the only graduate from the academy who hasn't gotten a position. I haven't told Gavin or Helen about what happened during my internship. I've made vague noises about having a job at a hotel. Maybe by the time our visit to Sutil Island is over, I'll have figured out what to do about my employment situation. And maybe not.

"It's ravishing," I said, even though I felt a little squeezed on all sides by all the nature.

We got out of the van and retrieved our bags. A patch of wild roses at the corner of the building gave off a heady perfume, and a large lavender bush beside pulsed with bees.

"Stunning," said Gavin.

The three of us stared at the water. In the distance a small boat sped between two islands, while in the foreground a larger boat moved with steady deliberation in the opposite direction.

"If I had to take a few courses in order to inherit this place, I believe I would do so happily." Gavin walked up to the bentwood gate beside the reception building and peered through. "Look at this, Murr."

I joined him and we stared like a couple of Peter Rabbits at a garden that must have been at least an acre or two. It was filled with orderly flower and vegetable beds. There were rows upon rows of young plants and enormous, established bushes. Small espaliered apple trees in full bloom stood sentry against the far fence line. A fountain trickled nearby and an old wooden table surrounded by metal chairs sat at the foot of a gnarled tree covered in white blooms.

It was like something Eve might have planted on her way out of Eden. A bastion against the wilderness.

"The garden is almost fifty years old," said Helen. "Edna designed it when she and her husband took over the Institute. We'll take a tour after I get you settled."

We followed Helen into the lodge, where I found myself exclaiming over everything, from the wooden decks that wrapped around three sides of the building to the mismatched but well-organized kitchen. Nothing was fancy, but it all had a quality of honesty, functionality, and age.

I tuned back into the conversation to hear Helen say that Gavin and I would have our own cabins because the lodge only slept two and she didn't think either of us would care to stay in the room where her old boss had died.

"Correct," I said. "I would not like to do that."

"The cell reception on the island isn't great," said Helen. "But it's more consistent near the lodge."

"We can unplug," said Gavin. "It sounds perfect."

"And while the weather is sometimes ideal, we also sit right in a storm path. It can get quite intense."

"I love a good storm," I lied.

We stood in front of the long refreshment station in the entryway. It was equipped with coffee canisters, stacks of drinking glasses on trays, a single sink, and shelving filled with small teapots, cups, and an assortment of teas.

"Helen," said Gavin in that gentle but insistent way of his, "who will be judging the competitors?"

"I suppose I will," said Helen. She looked uncomfortable at the notion, which didn't surprise me. Helen seemed constitutionally opposed to standing in judgment of other people. It was part of what made her so relaxing to be around, even for someone like me who adores judging others.

"And what are the courses?" asked Gavin.

"Flower arranging, dance, and meditation."

He laughed. "Well," he said, "that sounds like a lot of fun. How does it work?"

Helen leaned against a table. "That part is a bit complicated. Normally, students just take one course at a time. But these students will take all three at the same time over the course of nine days."

Gavin's perfect eyebrows went up. "Is that a challenging proposition?"

Helen sighed. "I think it is. Each course is so different. Each activates a different part of the participant's brain and body and spirit. It's hard to explain."

"You mean they're going to have to be flexible?" I asked. That seemed reasonable.

"The flower-arranging course is aesthetic and symbolic. The dance course is physical and emotional. And the meditation course requires deep stillness and concentration. It's a lot to bring all those things together in a single day. It will be demanding for everyone."

I thought it all sounded quite lovely and said so.

"I hope the students agree. The courses have been taught here for many years. Edna believed that they led students to essential self-knowledge and gave them a sense of their own worth and a sense of purpose and power."

"And how will you decide which student is best at all the things?" asked Gavin.

Helen closed her eyes as though the question exhausted her. "I am not at all sure. I suppose I'll speak to the teachers, and the students. I've also been given another criterion."

"Yes?" I said, spellbound.

For a moment, Helen didn't respond. And then she said, "Edna asked that I assess them using their pāramīs and the brahmavihārās."

"Their what?" I asked.

"Their pāramīs and the brahmavihārās. They're Pali words that describe Buddhist concepts. Pāramīs are sometimes called the perfections. They're things like generosity, equilibrium, discernment."

"Ah," said Gavin. "We don't often talk about the brahmavihārās in the West."

Helen must have noticed the confused expression on my face. "The brahmavihārās are also known as the divine abodes of loving-kindness, empathetic joy, compassion, and equanimity. They were part of Edna's meditation practice," she said.

"So was she wiccan or a Buddhist?" I asked.

"She was a number of things. She liked to mix it up in her spiritual practices," said Helen. "I'm sure it all sounds a little confusing. I'm supposed to assess their perfections—"

"Or lack of," I interjected.

"Right. Specifically, I'm to assess their ability to access the brahmavihārās. It's really not quite . . . right."

Gavin puffed out a breath. "And how exactly are you to do that?"

"Through interviews. By watching. I don't know, to be quite honest. These are profound and nuanced concepts and they're part of an ancient tradition. They aren't meant to be used in this way." She sighed. "I don't know how it's going to work."

"You'll make it work and you'll be fair," I said. "What do you do when you decide?"

"Then I ask the candidate if she or he would like to run the Institute."

"What if they don't want to?" asked Gavin.

"Then I suppose the lawyers for the estate step in. I've no idea about the rest of the will, except that the property is in trust. My only role is to offer Edna's relatives these courses."

"Well," said Gavin. "That is certainly passing strange. Murray and I will do what we can to make sure things run smoothly, come what may, for our floral-arranging dance yogis who are supposed to be calm and kind and generous and emotionally stable and full of joy."

"I am eternally grateful," said Helen and she sounded it.

Chapter 6

Resistance to unpleasant realities had always been one of Helen's challenges, as Sayadaw U Nandisara fondly pointed out to her countless times. When Helen sat down to discuss what needed to be done to prepare for guests, her own resistance was in full flow.

"We got extremely lucky and the dance and floral instructors are available on short notice. And I will guide the candidates in the meditation course."

She felt herself wince as she said the last bit. How was she supposed to judge people who were trying to learn to meditate? Half her task was to convince the new meditators to stop judging themselves. It was a terrible and ironic proposition. Why had she agreed to do this? The answer to that was clear. Edna had been convincing *and* she seemed unlikely to ever die.

"*You* teach meditation?" asked Murray.

"Aha!" said Gavin, as though a long-held suspicion had been confirmed.

"Where did you learn that?" Murray asked, and her sharp interest made Helen uncomfortable.

The three of them were seated in Edna's office. It was a comfort to have Murray and Gavin at the lodge. In the months that they'd been at school together, the three of them had become close. She felt she could tell them anything, but for some reason, she hadn't told them about her time as a monastic.

"At a monastery."

"A monastery! Did you take a course on meditation?" asked Murray.

Helen shifted in her seat. "I lived there."

"You *lived* in a monastery?" said Murray, as though Helen had informed them she'd once spent time colonizing one of Jupiter's moons. "For how long?"

"Three years," said Helen. It had been closer to four, but there was no need to exaggerate.

"Were you, like, a monk?" asked Murray. "Did you wear robes?"

"I was a nun," said Helen.

Gavin and Murray gaped at her.

"Now it all makes sense," said Murray. "It's how you're so calm. You're a Buddhist nun!"

"Just nun," said Helen. "And no, I'm not anymore. I took the robes when I was nineteen. I left a few years later and came here to Yatra to work."

"Was it peaceful living in a monastery? Do you miss it?" said Murray.

Helen missed living as a monastic but she also didn't. It had been as peaceful as her mind and heart and the conditions allowed it to be. There were other people at the monastery, which always complicated things.

"I was born in Ireland. Irish Catholic. But you're still the only real nun I've met," said Murray. "It's very impressive."

Helen wanted to tell her it wasn't, but she didn't want to dampen her enthusiasm.

"Why did you stop being a nun?" asked Murray.

Helen sighed and traced the edge of the teacup with her finger. "My mother got sick and I went home to care for her until she passed."

"I'm sorry about your mom," said Murray. "You didn't want to go back after? Or is that not allowed?"

"Oh yes, I would have been welcome to go back any time. But Edna invited me here to teach and I ended up staying."

"It must have been hard to leave the monastery," said Gavin.

"It was. I was very comfortable there. Maybe too comfortable." Helen smiled. She didn't mention that she hadn't been heartbroken to leave behind some of the more stringent precepts, such as not sleeping in a high or luxurious bed. It was lovely to sleep well off the ground in a well-built bed covered in quality linens.

Helen wanted to tell them that she and her teacher still talked, and that she still practised. She was still Buddhist. Instead, she changed the subject.

"I will teach the meditation course."

"I guess so!" said Murray.

"We'll need to hire a cook for the guests."

Gavin and Murray were skilled in the kitchen, but they would not be able to handle three meals a day for the week and do all the other things that would be required. Edna had clearly specified that she wanted her relatives to have what she called "the full Yatra experience," which meant hiring a professional chef to create exceptional vegetarian meals.

"Just tell us what you need," said Gavin. "If it's household help, we're there. If it's assistance with the programs or judging, we're there."

"Getting this place up and running for guests normally takes at least a couple of weeks, but I've already prepared some of the cabins. It's still going to be a challenge."

"We're highly trained professionals," said Gavin. "We can do anything."

"You are both my favourite," said Helen.

"Obviously," said Murray, "I'm a little bit extra your favourite." She smoothed her glossy black braid with both hands. "One more thing on the household front. I think we need an employee. Why be a butler if you've got no staff to boss about?"

Gavin pointed at Murray and mouthed the words "not my idea."

"I'm serious," said Murray. "It's not *just* the pure pleasure of telling others what to do. We need to keep up our skills. We can teach some newb everything we know and stay sharp."

As soon as Murray said it, Helen liked the idea. She didn't really want Gavin and Murray cleaning toilets and changing beds, and she suspected that she might not have time herself.

"Would you like to be in charge of human resources?" she asked Murray.

"The young man from the dock must need a job. Can we recruit him, please?"

Chapter 7

Helen rode her old bike to the Co-op to post the job advertisement on the bulletin board, while Gavin and Murray got settled in their cabins.

As she was cycling back, her phone rang. She reached into her pocket and pulled it out, and managed, with difficulty, to hit the answer button.

"Helen Thorpe speaking," she said, trying not to pant into the receiver. "How can I help you?"

"Hello? Hello? I'm calling about the job." The woman spoke as though she was talking into a pretend telephone made of a toilet paper roll.

"Oh yes. One moment please," said Helen. She realized it wasn't very mindful or very professional to ride and talk on the phone at the same time, so she slowed to a stop before she rode out of range of cell reception, something that happened every twenty feet on Sutil Island. "We're looking for—"

"The ad says you're offering staff accommodation?"

"That's ri—"

"He'll be there this afternoon at—" The rest of the caller's words were garbled and then the call dropped.

Helen stared at her phone for a few seconds before putting it away and getting back on her bike. She hadn't ridden since she moved off the island, and it felt intensely pleasurable to make her way along the quiet roads with the wind in her face, moving under her own power.

Back at the lodge, she and Gavin and Murray spent a satisfying hour creating an annotated list of what needed to be done and who would do it. In households with a lot of staff, the butler often acted as household manager and scheduled and coordinated everyone's workloads. But with three fully certified butlers on hand, the arrangements were more democratic.

They got busy vacuuming, sweeping, and dusting the lodge and guest cabins, making lists of groceries and other assorted tasks. Gavin and Murray reviewed the lodge management and program binders. There were no more calls about the job.

Helen headed to the office at 1:30, feeling buoyed by their progress. As she passed the small sitting room, a splash of colour caught her eye. She stopped and peered into the room.

A rotund young man with SunnyD orange hair was perched nervously on the sofa, staring fixedly into the empty fireplace.

Helen cleared her throat, and he turned to offer her the sort of smile usually seen on the faces of guilty dogs in viral videos.

"Good afternoon," she said. "Are you—?"

"Here about the job," he confirmed. His hands gripped his knees. "The door was open so I let myself in. I'm early. I hope that's okay. This is a hotel, right? Or like a B&B or something? That's what my friend's mom said? When she told me about it?"

"This is the Yatra Institute. It's a retreat centre. Or rather, it was. It's been closed for several months. We're going to reopen for a small group of important guests."

He didn't respond.

"I'm sorry. What's your name?" Helen prompted.

"Nigel."

"Welcome, Nigel. My name is Helen. I'll be interviewing you."

Nigel struggled to his feet, revealing the full glory of his outfit. He wore checked green pants, a bright-yellow dress shirt, red suspenders, and a black-and-white houndstooth blazer. Every item looked to be at least one or two sizes too small. It would have been the perfect ensemble to wear to an admissions interview for a discount clowning school. He smelled overpoweringly of cologne.

They shook hands and he pumped hers up and down like someone on a losing streak with a slot machine.

She led him into the office and put the kettle on to boil.

"Tea?" she asked.

"Yeah! I mean, yes, please. That would be great."

"Do you have a preference?"

He stared blankly.

"What type of tea would you like?"

More staring, this time with slightly open mouth, suggesting a sinus problem.

"Herbal or caffeinated," she clarified.

"Sorry. I'm sort of nervous. Fear makes me act dumb. I haven't had too many job interviews. To be honest, I'm not even sure I'm employable. Herbal, please."

Helen's nostrils burned as the fragrance came off Nigel in waves. She tried to ignore the olfactory assault as she spooned a blend of dried herbs, all from the Yatra garden, into a tea strainer, placed it in the little Japanese teapot, and added hot water. She carried it over on a tray with two teacups and saucers, small spoons, and honey and set it on the clean wooden desk.

"This is really fancy," he said, sounding morose.

While they waited for the tea to steep, Helen sneezed twice and then asked if he had a résumé.

He handed her a folded piece of what looked like scrap paper. On it, he'd handwritten his name, cell number, and nothing else.

She gave him a quizzical look.

"All I had time for," he explained.

It turned out it was Mrs. Ranier, who lived just down the road, who had called Helen, on Nigel's behalf. Mrs. Ranier was a premature retiree whose hobby was making blobby-looking soaps. Apparently, Nigel had come home about two weeks before with Amy, the Raniers' twenty-two-year-old daughter.

"Mrs. Ranier said this would be the perfect job for me," he said.

"Do you have a background in cooking or hospitality?" she asked.

He scrunched up his face. "I worked at, uh, Smitty's for, like, twelve minutes. Bussing tables. But I cooked at camp. When I was with the troupe."

"The troop? Were you in the military?"

"Not military, exactly. We were a sort of theatrical troupe," he said. "At a summer camp? We called ourselves the Drama Kings. A little on the nose, I know. I was the camp cook, or I would have been. And a counsellor. That's where I met Amy. She was a counsellor there too. Until . . . well, never mind."

Helen did mind.

"Can you tell me a little more about yourself?"

"My parents are okay, I guess. I mean, they're not cheerful people. It's because they live in Port Alberni. Honestly, I think they'd be happier in Victoria or even Nanaimo. In a bigger town they'd see less people that they hate."

"Fewer," corrected Helen, kindly but firmly.

He paused for a moment and then resumed. "My parents hate *everyone*, especially everyone in Port Alberni. They're resentful people. I don't know why."

In response to Helen's appalled expression, he clarified: "They don't hate me. At least, not much."

"Can you tell me about your work history?"

"That's it, really. Smitty's and different jobs at camp. I might go to school in the fall to take culinary arts at Vancouver Island University."

"I see. Would you like to learn more about hospitality? Fine dining? Household management?"

At this, his face brightened. "Oh my god! Yes! I love learning things. Seriously."

She believed him—and found herself liking him for his enthusiasm and apparent inability to dissimulate.

"Can you provide references?"

Another face scrunch. "Amy?"

"Who supervised you at camp?"

"Well, that's just it. There was a thing with me and Amy. It's why we came home. I don't think the camp will be giving me a reference," he said, his voice full of regret.

Helen got up, opened a window, and then sat back down, trying to ignore her watering eyes. Had he taken a bath in his perfume? It had a top note of rotten citrus, a middle note of pressure-treated lumber, and a bottom note of petrochemical slurry.

In her time at the monastery and then at the Institute, she'd met many slightly lost young men like Nigel, who were looking for somewhere to belong and something to do. She didn't hold his lack of experience against him but wanted to be sure he could handle the work.

"Can you tell me more about the 'thing' with you and Amy?"

"We were hosting a weekend for homeschool kids. Kind of a pre-season thing. The regular campers don't show up until the end of June. Anyway, the homeschool kids went out on an overnight owl and bat hike and we were in camp alone, so we cut loose a little. We did some Molly. It didn't seem like a big deal. But one of the owners found out because a few of the campers came back early and we were dancing a lot and I guess it looked suspicious. We got sent home. I guess the technical term is 'fired.' There might have been something else in those drugs. Maybe bath salts? PCP? Anyway, we got pretty, uh, messed up. It wasn't normal dancing, I guess. We couldn't seem to stop."

Helen looked at him, awed by his candour. "Do you do a lot of drugs, Nigel?"

He met her eyes. "I smoke some pot sometimes. Not every day or anything. I've done mushrooms. Smoked some hash. And we take ecstasy once in a while. Never got as f— I mean messed up as with that stuff we took at camp."

"I see. Given your substance use, do you think you're capable of holding a job for a few weeks?"

"To be honest, I use way less drugs than almost anyone I know. And I'll cut it out entirely while I'm here. I don't drink, really. So that's good, right?"

Helen thought this was another case for using the word *fewer*, but she didn't correct him again.

"If I find you high or hungover on the premises, I will have to let you go. Immediately. Would it help if I drug tested you?"

Many addicts and alcoholics had showed up at the monastery in Nova Scotia and also at the Yatra Institute, hoping the new environment would help them quit their addictions. A few had asked to be drug tested to help them remain accountable. It was hard enough for beginners to go through a serious meditation retreat without trying to detox at the same time. But some had managed it.

Nigel nodded seriously. "You know, it might. Good incentive and all that. If they'd had drug testing at camp, me and Amy might not have done what we did. Not that I'm blaming the management. I'm just saying, boundaries are helpful." He sat rigidly forward in his chair.

"Your job here will last about three weeks. We offer live-in accommodation. The hours will be long, but we will pay overtime for anything over eight hours."

"Cool. Will I stay in here with you?" He waved a hand to indicate the lodge.

"You'll stay in staff quarters on the property," she said.

"Right. Okay. Well, this is perfect because Mr. and Mrs. Rainier told me it was time for me to get going. Things really have a way of working out good."

"And I have one more request," said Helen.

"Anything."

"Please don't wear that cologne ever again."

"You don't like it?"

"I do not."

"I got it at Walmart. On sale. Four bucks for a huge bottle. I've been trying to use it up."

He surreptitiously sniffed his shirtfront.

"Not even a little squirt?" he asked.

"Please, no squirts whatsoever," said Helen, firmly.

He sighed. "Okay. I'll see if Mrs. Ranier wants to use it in her soaps. Sass 'em up a little."

"Good idea," said Helen, reflecting that the addition of that scent to the misshapen soaps would mark the end of an already underperforming business. "Are you prepared to start now?"

He inflated slightly. The boy was part balloon. It was charming.

"You bet. How many guests we got tonight, Boss?"

"You may call me Helen in private, but please refer to me as Ms. Thorpe in front of guests."

"Got it."

"No guests tonight. Three arriving in two days and a fourth the following day. Two of my colleagues are already helping out, and there will be a chef and two instructors who will be coming to teach classes. They're due in three days."

He stuck out his bottom lip like a four-star general thinking hard about whether or not to launch an invasion. "Okay. Good ratio of guests to workers. That sounds can-do-able."

She took the shopping list from her notepad and gave it to him along with two hundred dollars in twenties. "Please go to the store and get these items. Bring back all the receipts. And the change."

He looked shocked that she was trusting him with cash, but she felt a deep sense that he would be responsible.

"Is food included in this job?" asked Nigel. "I eat quite a bit. I could tell you I'm an athlete but that would be a lie. I just have a generous appetite."

"Yes," said Helen. "I think you'll find the food here most satisfying."

"Love the name of this place, by the way," said Nigel. "It's really, uh, unusual."

"It's a Sanskrit word meaning pilgrimage to a holy place."

"You mean this place is like a church?" He looked worried at the thought.

"No. The name refers to the concept of a spiritual journey. That's what our guests experience here."

"Oh. That seems pretty good." Nigel said this with the air of someone being offered a platter consisting entirely of things that were not tasty.

"Spiritual evolution is not a job requirement," said Helen.

Murray appeared in the doorway. "Thank god," she said. "I have experienced zero spiritual growth since I've been here."

Nigel turned to look at the young butler with his mouth-open stare, a crush appearing over his head like a thought bubble over a cartoon.

"Sorry?" he said, wonderingly.

Murray laughed, a clear, happy sound. "I'm sorry to interrupt. Helen, I wanted to bring you this." She held up a sealed envelope and then placed it on the bookshelf. "Found it on the little iron table in the garden."

Murray nodded once more and disappeared.

"Does *she* work here?" Nigel asked.

"She does."

"I'll take the job. I mean, I was already taking the job, but now I actually want it."

Again, his inability to dissemble was a wondrous and vaguely alarming thing. Helen wondered if she was going to have to let him go in a day because he wouldn't stop mooning after Murray. Probably. But Murray was more than capable of setting people to rights when necessary. Murray might, in fact, be just the sort of person Nigel needed to learn from.

"I'm glad to hear it," said Helen. "Once you've done the shopping, you can collect your things. Can you drive?"

"Yes," he said. "I'm very cautious and reliable behind the wheel. I once thought I might like to be a school bus driver."

"Is that so?" said Helen. He was a tremendously strange young man and she liked him.

They got up and he shook her hand several more times, until she clasped her hands behind her back so he couldn't do it again. She gave him the keys to the lavender Smart Car and they made their way out of her office. Helen stood in the parking lot and watched him drive carefully down the road. Then she washed the scent off her hands before retrieving the envelope and opening it.

Hello,

I need you to know that Miss Edna's death was not natural nor was it voluntary. I know because I was hired to be her death doula. We'd discussed her plans in some detail and there is no way she took her final trip without me at her side.

I am not able to share this information with the authorities. There is so much they do not understand about our movement and I have too much important work to do to risk arrest, publicity, and even jail time.

I am telling you this because I believe you can help and that you will not bring harm to visionaries who are simply trying to help others.

Yours in sorrow.
Anon.

Helen read it over several more times, as mystified as she was disturbed. Why give this information to her? Why not an anonymous note to the police or the medical examiner? And Helen felt dismay that the message spelled out some of the things about Edna's death that she had been trying not to think about. Why *had* Edna decided to go? Had she been sick? If so, Helen was sure Edna would have told people. Edna liked to make a scene. She was not the sort to slip away quietly.

The style of the note gave her pause. Maybe it was the way the writer had signed off. *Yours in sorrow.* The words felt honest, and the slightly grandiose tone of the letter also felt right. Edna would have wanted someone with deep conviction to help her navigate between this world and the next. Edna adored people who had a high regard for their own skills and influence because she saw herself in them. Helen, who didn't think about herself much, was the exception to the rule. Helen was almost sure that Edna hadn't had a death doula in September, when she'd left, so the person must have been hired recently.

She would call the police and give the note to them. That was the best way she could help.

Chapter 8

Two days later, the first guests arrived at the appointed time in a Land Rover the colour of arterial spray.

Helen waited in the parking area, hands neatly folded behind her back. Beside her stood Gavin, Murray, and Nigel in an orderly row.

A white-blond man in his late twenties got out of the driver's side and looked around, frowning slightly. His eyes, partly hidden under his mop of well-cut hair, looked like they belonged on a sled dog. Or a goat.

Blinking seemed to require a great effort, as though his eyelids weighed two pounds apiece.

"Tad Todd. We're expected," he drawled when he saw her.

Helen approached. "Yes, sir. Welcome. I am truly sorry about the circumstances of your visit."

Confusion froze his facial muscles. Then he remembered.

"Riiiight," he said. "My great-aunt." He pronounced it on-t. "Are we here to attend her services?"

"Edna asked that her service be held on Samhain," said Helen.

"Saturday?"

"Samhain," clarified Helen. "Halloween. This fall. It will be a closed event. The loved ones of wiccans usually hold private rituals to remember the dead."

His mouth hung slightly ajar. Maybe he was a mouth-breather, like Nigel, or he was so suffocated by ennui he couldn't close his mouth. Edna had been a committed foe of mouth breathing. She felt it was the great enemy of physical health and psychological well-being.

Finally, he said, "Wiccan. Riiiiight."

"Well, isn't that just incredibly tedious," said the second man, coming around the vehicle to join his brother. "I'm Wills," he said.

Wills Todd was probably a few years older than his brother and looked many years older due to sun damage. He was heavier and coarser in his features. Wills Todd resembled his handsome, overbred looking brother, but seemed to have been created by an altogether clumsier hand.

"I'm Helen. These are my colleagues." She pointed to Gavin, Murray, and Nigel. "We'll make your stay here as comfortable as possible."

Gavin stepped forward. "May I take your luggage, sirs?"

The brothers ignored him. Tad was the palest sort of white person. Wills was the leathery kind usually found in Florida or Hawaii. Both affected a slouchy, be-linened style.

When Helen looked at them, she had to remind herself to be kind in her thoughts as well as her actions.

Tad rubbed his eyes. "I've *just* come from Berlin. I'm *vastly* tired."

"I was at a sailing regatta in Bermuda when the lawyers called with this mysterious mission," said Wills. "Had to leave to come here. We're *quite* mystified as to what it's all about."

"Of course," said Helen. "Please come in and we'll discuss."

"And *you are*?" asked Tad, as they made their way.

Helen introduced herself again.

"I think my beloved brother is asking *what* are you," said Wills. "Lawyer? Accountant? Housekeeper?"

"I worked here for many years." Helen offered no further explanation as she escorted them up the wide stairs of the lodge while Murray and Gavin and Nigel unloaded their luggage from the Land Rover.

Around them, the birdsong was carried out to sea by the gusting wind.

"I suppose you're unemployed now that the old girl is dead," said Tad.

"Actually, I have been at school for the past year. I just graduated. She left a request asking me to come back and assist with her final wishes."

"Oh," said Tad, thoroughly uninterested. He looked around the lodge. "Well, this place doesn't exactly seem to be booming. Remember visiting when we were kids, Willy?"

"I recall a lot of unfortunately dressed people wandering around with vacant expressions," said Wills. "Always seemed to be completely silent or chanting. I guess they were religious. Terribly creepy thing for a child to see things like that."

Helen led them down the hallway and into the office, where two chairs waited across from her desk.

"The lodge was closed for the season and Ms. Edna had just finished an extended self-guided retreat," said Helen, preparing to tell them about Edna's death. But the Todd brothers weren't listening.

"When is the lodge due to open again?" asked Tad.

"The middle of June."

"So you've cancelled everything?"

"We've put the season on hold," said Helen. Whether or not the season would be cancelled depended on what happened over the next few weeks. If things were not settled, it would be up to the lawyers. Helen didn't say any of this lest it result in more questions.

"She just dropped dead?" said Tad.

"She decided to transition," said Helen, trying not to think of the note.

"On purpose?" said Wills.

"I believe so."

"Was she depressed? Sick?" asked Tad.

"I don't know," said Helen.

"All so very weird," said Wills, by which he clearly meant inconvenient. Then he fixed a noticeably bloodshot gaze on Helen.

"What did you study? At school, I mean?"

"I trained to become a butler," she said. "I've just graduated."

He squinted in surprise. "A *butler*? For *this* place?"

Helen smiled but didn't respond. She didn't mention that Murray and Gavin were also butlers. There might be such a thing as too many butlers, even for people so conspicuously and self-consciously rarefied as these ones.

"Let's cut to it, shall we. Did Edna leave it to us?" asked Tad. "Shouldn't we be talking to her lawyer instead of the help? Or rather, the *former* help."

Helen felt her emotional equilibrium slip. "She asked that I carry out some of her final wishes. That's what her lawyers have instructed me to do. That's all I know."

"Father always said Edna had a terror of being conventional," said Tad. His thin nostrils flared. "She probably gave everything to a foundation for indigent crones."

"In her will, Ms. Edna asked that you visit the lodge and—"

"What *fer*?" interrupted Tad, putting on a fake accent of indeterminate origin. Two bright-red spots had appeared on his cheeks.

"She requested that you each stay at the Institute and—"

"Why, for *god's* sake?" exploded Tad. "We have *things* to do. And *frankly*, being summoned here without explanation is a major hassle. And shouldn't a so-called *institute* have some sort of gravitas?"

Wills shot his brother another glance.

"What on earth is the meaning of all this?" said Tad.

"It *does* seem ridiculous," said Wills.

"I don't know that I care to participate in this folly," continued Tad. "Willy, what do you think?"

Wills cleared his throat. "Well, I've missed the regatta already. And the next one doesn't start for"—he stared into space as though doing a calculation in his head—"several weeks. I suppose I could hang about here. I could use the rest."

"The situation is absurd. The nonsensical whim of some capricious old woman who never lost her taste for self-indulgence," said Tad. "Is the place going broke? Does she expect us to bail it out?"

Wills looked at his brother. "I think it did fairly well."

"It's a *spiritual retreat centre*," said Tad. "A place gullible people go to be relieved of their money. There must be some law of financial gravity at work." He heaved a sigh that expanded his thin chest and some of the anger seemed to leave him. "Fine. I'll stay. But I hope to god there's *something* to do on this island."

Helen steeled herself. "Edna requested that you take three of our most popular courses."

"What?" screeched Tad. "Are you *completely* serious?"

Helen nodded.

"Should have known there'd be some catch," grumbled Wills.

"What kind of courses?" asked Tad in a poisonous voice.

Helen took a moment to find a neutral place in her body, a trick she'd learned at the monastery to calm herself during stressful situations. Ah, there it was. Her left elbow. It was almost always reliably untroubled.

"I think you will enjoy the courses," she said. "Many people have taken them multiple times."

"Why?" asked Tad.

"They enjoy them, find them personally illuminating."

"I *mean*, why do *we* have to take them?" asked Tad. "I can assure you that *I* won't enjoy them."

"You can certainly refuse."

That seemed to stop Tad for a moment. He gave his head an almost imperceptible shake. "What are they?" he demanded. "If there's any nudity or risk of injury—" He was so upset at the thought of what the courses might entail that he couldn't continue.

"Are we taking that one where they teach you not to feel cold?" mused Wills. "Bloody bizarre, but I've met sailors who swear by—"

"The Wim Hof Method," said Helen. "No, we're not really set up for that, but Edna was a great fan of his teachings."

"Thank Christ for small mercies," said Tad.

"The courses are flower arranging, dance, and meditation." She thought it best to keep the names of the courses to herself for now, lest

Arranging Your Inner Flower, Devi Dance, and Meet Yourself, Lose Yourself caused highly strung Tad Todd to have a stroke. They would find out soon enough.

"The courses take six days each. But we've designed it so each of you can take them all at once over nine days."

"Bloody right you did. We're not staying here forever!" seethed Tad.

Wills narrowed his red eyes. "When you say 'each of you,' do you mean both of us?"

"There will be four of you participating."

Tad and Wills suddenly looked like two starved greyhounds who'd just spotted a rabbit.

"You two, your cousin Whitney. And your other cousin."

"Ferdinand is joining us?" said Tad Todd in an incredulous voice.

"No, he has declined the invitation."

"Not surprised. He and that wife of his are lazy as a pair of stuffed ducks," said Wills. "Don't do a damn thing."

"I guess they can afford to live a life of leisure with her money. The lucky bastard," added Tad.

"I mean your other cousin," said Helen.

"We don't have another cousin," said Tad and Wills in tandem.

"You do, according to the lawyers. She's the only child of Edna's late brother-in-law, Topher."

"Why did we not know about this person?" asked Tad, as though Helen had personally kept the information from him.

"I'm afraid I don't know. All I know is that she and Whitney will be joining you. At Edna's request."

Tad flicked his head back so the long part of his white-blond hair fell into place. Then he smoothed it with a hand for good measure.

"I'm not sure I can participate. Perhaps I should give it a miss. I will let you know after I consider. In the meantime, perhaps you could see us to our rooms?"

"Of course," said Helen.

Wills stood. "I suppose it'll be fine for me, even with the courses. Nice of Edna to think of us. It's a damned good thing I was able to get away."

"How nice for you," said Tad. "Some of us have commitments. People who depend on us."

Wills flinched.

Outside, the birds continued to call, and the incoming tide kept up its steady wash against the shoreline.

Helen had trouble imagining the two men across from her embracing the material in the courses, much less demonstrating the sort of values Edna cherished, but it was early yet. The Yatra Institute was a special place. It changed people.

Chapter 9

WILLS TODD

Pain. That's all there is.

The pain of spending hours with my un-fucking-bearable brother. The pain of the ferry ride, which was perfectly fine except for the nausea from my hangover rising and falling and threatening to crest right over my head and drown me. The pain of being back here and completely unable to appreciate the splendour of the place . . .

Of course, it *is* splendid and always has been.

Because of . . . well, because. It does no good to think about what might have happened. Put it in the vault. It's done.

Pain at the thought of executing the plan, even though it shouldn't be that hard. We've been playing our roles for years.

The courses and the mystery cousin are an unexpected twist, but not insurmountable.

Not for fakes like us.

I just hope it works. It's got to, or I am screwed beyond measure. At the moment, I'm the brokest rich person I know, thanks to that goddamned regatta project. The whole thing went sideways as soon as I poured the last of my trust fund into it, which I did only after Vito Ronzetti made the handshake deal to come on board as a sponsor. No one could fault me for it. Ronzetti is one of the best-known luxury-adjacent brands in Europe. They've got sports cars, watches, fashion. None of it top shelf, precisely. Their stuff is more in the mid-tier. But there's a lot of it. Anybody else trying to start a yacht race would have given an arm to get them on board, but I was the one who succeeded. Me. An upstart from West Vancouver.

Who could have predicted that eighteen-year-old Mario Ronzetti, favoured child of his father, Vito, and sole heir to the Ronzetti fortune, would wrap his Lamborghini (not a Ronzetti product, I note) around a telephone pole right after the agreement in principle was struck? Mario, thank fuck, walked out of the wreck and straight into treatment, which is where he is now. How nice for him. And as part of his recovery program, he confessed to his father we sometimes did drugs together. He said that I got the drugs for him. The goddamned unfairness of it. That kid had better hookups than I ever did. He's European. They're very social about drugs over there.

His father instantly forgot all the healthy things I'd done with Mario. How I took him under my wing. Gave him sailing lessons. Brought him around to races. Introduced him to owners and crew. Got him away from that absolutely useless EDM scene. Put him on some more manageable pharmaceuticals. I spent a small fortune on the kid, but it was worth it when he convinced his dad to back my project, which is currently a massive red blotch where my bank balance used to be.

I kept my gaze focused on the butler's head as she drove Tad and me to our cabins in the guest golf cart. Better to look at her skull than Tad's. That bastard. That absolute bastard.

Christ, my head was sore. I should be in treatment with Mario. Not that I was ever as bad as him. But I am finding the taper-off pretty bloody painful. I took my last pill before we got on the ferry, and I'm here on this island with zero chemical assistance. Well, at least I'm taking it like a man.

The reality is, and I say this in all humility, I'm a bit of a throwback to the time when people of means were brave. You could see the quality on display in boardrooms and on racetracks, ski slopes, and high mountain peaks, as well as in wars, obviously. You saw it in the officer class. Not that I've ever been to war. Or in boardrooms. I'm not a business person in the standard sense of having a job and working in an office. But I've had my share of outdoor adventures. The point is that people got rich and stayed that way because they were bold. They had vision and courage.

But now it's all hedge fund and Silicon Valley assholes who spend their time bitching at contractors while they compete to build the most ostentatious house. They get their asses waxed, and give fucking TED Talks or have secret meetings with the Koch brothers and shoot animals trapped in fenced enclosures.

There are no real honest-to-god sportsmen anymore. I'm a dying breed. I might actually *be* dying. Which is fine, since also I'm not rich anymore. And I won't be again unless this goes well.

God, was she intentionally hitting every single pothole? Helen? Is that her name? I thought about speaking up and telling her to be more careful. But Tad's up there beside her, radiating irritation and something else. Menace, maybe. I'm not sure when my brother, who'd always been your garden variety prep school asshole, got so vicious.

My skin, which was already prickling with some strange sort of heat rash, was getting hotter. My stomach cramps snarled inside me. I wished I could peel off my skin. Turn myself inside out.

I'm only thirty-two. Going on three hundred and two. I'm going to have lots of time to miss my money and think about everything else that's wrong with my life for the next week and a bit, in between the flower arranging and dancing and meditating, for the love of sweet Jesus.

It's fine. It's all fine. I can handle this. It's time to press restart. People come back from worse positions. But there's something about that butler that makes me nervous. It's the way she looks at me. At us. Like she can read our thoughts and we make her sad.

Good-looking woman, though. When I get back on my feet, maybe I'll hire her. She could work as a butler at my sailing club. If things work out like I hope, I'm going to have one of those.

God, would those birds please Jesus shut up for five goddamned seconds.

"Mr. Todd?" said Helen. She turned around and looked at me. How long have we been stopped?

"Yes. This is fine," I said, looking at the cabin. At least it is one of the bigger ones. Some of the cabins at Yatra are bathroom-sized. No problem for me because I have spent a lot of time on boats. But Tad won't like small accomodations. Not at all.

The butler climbed out of the golf cart and grabbed my luggage. Tad watched me climb out and his eyes were like coins on a corpse.

I followed her in. Amazing I could still walk in my condition, which was not good. Not good at all, now that sobriety had really started to set in.

"Would you like some assistance unpacking?" she asked.

"No," I said, a little too quickly. "Thank you."

"Can I bring you anything else? We'll be serving cocktails at six tonight, to be followed by dinner."

"I'll be there. Now if you don't mind, I think I'll take a nap. Jet lag."

"Certainly, sir," she said, and left.

I shut the door and slid the wooden bolt latch into place. Wooden bolt. I forgot there are no proper locks in this place. Radical openness, Aunt Edna called it. To hell with that. I'm going to get one. I'm not spending over a week in the woods with my brother without a deadbolt.

Chapter 10

The vehicle that drove slowly up the gravel road to the Yatra Institute was smaller and narrower than a regular van. Its preposterous aesthetic suggested whoever chose it at least had a sense of humour. It contained the third potential heir, Edna's great-niece, Whitney Varga. Ms. Edna's late husband's youngest sister had produced a daughter named Meredith, who became an actress of sorts and married an Eastern European film producer named Boris. Whitney was the only child of that union.

According to the report Helen received from Devon Lest, Edna's lawyer, the Vargas lived in Europe and had a house in Greece. Whitney's mother hadn't broken through as an actress, but it was thought that Boris had made a great deal of money in a way that no non-show-business person could understand.

Helen hoped Whitney would be more down-to-earth than Wills and Tad. The vehicle suggested a sense of whimsy at least.

When the tiny bus pulled into the gravel parking lot, there was a pause of at least two minutes. Then the door on the right side was flung open.

A slim girl with a long fringe in her eyes stood in front of the little bus, keys swinging from her finger. She was accompanied by an older woman who climbed out of the passenger seat on the left side and made a production of smoothing out her voluminous trousers and adjusting what appeared to be a cape or, at minimum, a shawl.

Helen went to meet them, while Gavin, Murray, and Nigel stood in a receiving line near the lodge.

"Hello," she said. "My name is Helen. I'm glad you made it safely."

"I'm Whitney," said the girl. "And this is my mother, Meredith."

"So, *so* pleased to meet you," said Meredith in a breathless voice, like a pop star addressing a massive audience.

Meredith Varga must have been at least sixty but could have passed for six to eight months younger. She exuded drama and not in a good way. Energy, Helen had long ago learned, could be quiet or loud. Meredith had deafening energy.

"It's a pleasure," said Helen.

"Oh, don't worry, I'm not staying. Whitney has informed me that she was told to come alone and that she has some highly mysterious and top-secret thing to do here. I'll be on my way very soon. I just wanted to let *someone* know how sorry I was to hear of Edna's passing. We weren't close, but I *so* approved of how she spent her days."

Meredith spoke in such a portentous and belaboured way that Helen almost had trouble following her meaning.

"She was so *unusual*. Not the same old, same old." Meredith shuddered to show her abhorrence of the same old. "It was just so marvellous that she stayed here at the Harpy Institute casting spells and spending her days with warlocks and hippies. Fantastic."

"We miss her," said Helen.

"Of course. I should have said that. I'm also really *quite* broken up about it. Aren't I, Whitney?" She looked at her daughter, who stared through her hair at the ocean and didn't respond. "Whitney? Did you hear me? Aren't I devastated?"

"Yes, Mother."

"Darling, you sound almost dismissive of my feelings," said Meredith. "What was I saying before I was interrupted. Oh, yes. I'm not staying, of course. Unless you'd like me to. I felt I had to come along with Whitney to support her."

Helen saw the sidelong glance Whitney gave her mother. If the look had been made of hard steel, Meredith would have fallen over dead.

The three of them stood still for several awkward moments.

"So you'll be catching the next ferry?" Helen asked, when Meredith made no move to depart.

Meredith's carefully sculpted eyebrows rose.

"Mmm? Yes, of course. That's what I'll do. Unless you think this business will be concluded right away. If that's the case, I'll find a B&B and Whitney and I will probably leave the island together. But if there's room for me here . . . ?"

"I'm afraid not," said Helen.

"Alone, Mother," said Whitney. "I told you. The lawyer I spoke to said Aunt Edna left clear instructions. I was to come alone and stay for ten days or so. I'll call you when we're done."

"Well, I *am* your mother. I couldn't possibly let you come here and confront god knows what all by yourself."

"Could have fooled me," muttered Whitney.

With evident disappointment, Meredith seemed to accept her

fate. "Alrighty, then. I'll be off. It was nice to meet you," she said to Helen. "And to see this dear old place again. It's *very* special." For a moment the veil of pretension lifted and Helen thought that Meredith might be someone worth knowing, or at least might have been before she was suffocated by her own affectations. But then the act was back into place.

"Ta, darling!" she said. "Do call if you need anything. I'll just manoeuvre this contraption along the way I came and back onto the ferry. I hope no one tries to talk with me on the boat. There's really nothing worse than other people who want to converse with one."

"Goodbye, Mother," said Whitney.

Meredith gave her daughter a distracted air kiss and made her way to the driver's seat of the little van. It reversed neatly and then made its odd, bumblebee-like way back down the gravel drive alongside the ocean.

When it was out of sight, Whitney exhaled. She still wasn't looking at Helen when she spoke. "My mother is"—she paused for effect—"completely insane. But she's not a bad person."

Helen thought that seemed like a wise and accurate assessment.

INSIDE THE OFFICE Helen went through the same routine she'd gone through with Tad and Wills. She offered Whitney tea or coffee and explained that she had no further information about the estate that she could share.

"I'm to stay here for how long, exactly?" Whitney tilted back her head and blew her long bangs out of her eyes. She had none of the furious energy that seemed to charge through her mother's body like electricity through high-voltage wires. Whitney, instead, was notably still. Whether it was the stillness of poise and calm or the stillness of someone trying not to be noticed was hard to determine. "With Tad and Wills?"

"About ten days," said Helen.

"That much time with them will be a challenge," said Whitney. "Our family isn't exactly renowned for togetherness. Did Auntie Edna want us to come here and do one of her rituals?"

Helen described the courses.

To her relief, Whitney brightened.

"Oh," she said. "That sounds quite fascinating."

"I'm glad you feel that way," said Helen. "The courses have been popular over the years." She didn't say that they had always drawn the most peculiar guests, and at the Yatra Institute, that was saying something. "We've prepared a cabin for you." She paused. "And there will be one more guest."

She explained that Ferdinand had sent his regrets but that there was another cousin. Whitney didn't react, not even to ask a question. It was odd, but perhaps she was not easily flustered.

Whitney got to her feet. "One thing," she said. "I think my mom drove away with my luggage."

"We'll have someone drive to the ferry lineup and collect it."

Helen opened the office door and found Nigel standing outside with the sheepish look of the eavesdropper who has been caught. There was a polishing cloth in one hand and a tin of wood wax in the other.

"Hi," he said. "I'm just standing here."

"I see that. Ms. Varga, Nigel is available should you need anything during your stay. You met briefly outside."

Nigel didn't say anything because he was too awkward and Whitney didn't because she was probably too busy taking in the full effect of

Nigel's outfit, which was a horrific conglomeration of stripes going in different directions. He looked like one of the painter Gene Davis's less successful efforts.

"Nigel, we'll need you to drive to the ferry to collect Ms. Varga's things from her mother."

"If she has any questions, tell her to call me," said Whitney. "But whatever you do, don't let her come back here with you. She'll try, so be prepared."

Nigel nodded, like this was exactly the sort of thing he'd been hoping for when he stood listening outside the door.

"Thank you, Nigel. That will be all," said Helen, and pointed him down the corridor.

"Right," he said.

Helen led Whitney out of the lodge.

"This place hasn't changed much since we last visited Auntie," said Whitney, swivelling her head to take in everything. "When we were kids."

The sun shone down on the garden, which was coming up a little late this year. Plants looked healthy but smaller than in Junes past. The annuals, however, were doing their level best to make up for the delays. Massive tulips punctuated the garden with pops of red, yellow, purple, and white.

Three magnolia trees were in full bloom, though Helen had noticed that the youngest was suffering from some sort of blight. Its large pink blossoms were covered in a black shroud-like substance. Many half-opened blossoms had rotted and fallen off the branch before they could open fully. She made a silent note to find out what was wrong with them.

The rows of plantings were lined with a simple but efficient system of drip irrigation. Lettuces, cabbages, herb beds, alliums, massive kale plants, row on row.

The large greenhouse with the attached cold storage housed hundreds of vegetable and flower starters in various stages of maturation.

Once again, she felt the weight of Edna's plan on her shoulders.

Whitney stopped and turned 360 degrees to take it all in.

"I love the new gates," she said.

"They went in about five years ago."

The plain wooden gates on each side of the garden had been replaced, and the new ones had bentwood designs at the top. The bottom halves were solid and went right to the ground, so rabbits and other creatures couldn't get in. Each gate had a sign on either side reminding visitors to please keep them latched to keep deer from destroying the garden.

"You'll be staying in the Eagle's Nest," said Helen.

"Is that the one up on the bluff?"

"That's right."

They turned left out of the garden, and Helen slid the latch to the gate back into place. They walked side by side up the wide cedar-chip path. Salal and shoulder-high ferns lined both sides. The trail rose to the highest point of the property, where a tall, narrow cabin stood in a small clearing, facing the ocean. From the porch one could see down to the beach. Behind the cabin ancient cedars soared skyward.

Whitney stopped on the porch and turned to look to the sea. She didn't say anything. The girl was not easy to read. To Helen, most people felt like books she'd read a long time ago and liked very much. It wasn't that she found them predictable or boring, but most people felt familiar. She could almost always sense their need to be understood and appreciated. This was true even of people who were closed to themselves.

Not so with Whitney. Something about her flashes of honesty and candour made her seem less transparent somehow.

Helen opened the door to the Eagle's Nest.

A hand-hooked rag rug lay on the floor at the entrance. On the main floor was a small living room, a kitchen, and a bathroom. Upstairs was a large bedroom and another bathroom with a deep, old enamel bathtub in front of the upper window, too high for anyone to see in to.

"The cabin has been stocked with coffee, tea, mineral water, juices. We will be serving cocktails at six this evening, followed by a light dinner in the lodge. And if you need anything else at all, we'll gladly get it for you. As soon as we've collected your luggage, I'll have someone bring it up."

Whitney gave Helen the briefest of smiles. "Anything could happen in a place like this," she said.

"Yes, I suppose it could," said Helen, not sure how to interpret such an odd comment. "I hope you enjoy your stay."

Whitney seemed to realize how melodramatic her words had sounded. "I mean, good things seem possible here. You know, clarity. Peace."

"Yes," said Helen. "In fact, we're renowned for helping people achieve those things."

Then she made her way back down the hill.

Chapter 11

When Helen stepped back into the garden, she noticed someone crouched in the far corner.

She drew closer and a man she didn't recognize smiled up at her from under a large straw hat. He held a lettuce starter in a gloved hand.

"Hey," he said. "I'm Leon. From over at the reserve. I guess I sorta broke in here to get the lettuce planted."

"We appreciate it," said Helen.

"Yeah. We t̓oq̓ qaymıxʷ like to do our crime in reverse. Can't stop giving."

Helen laughed.

"I've been gardening for Ms. Edna since you left. She wanted these to go in this week. You're Helen?"

She nodded.

"I hear you went to butler school? Man, we could use you at my house. We got some big-time disorganization over there. We need either you or that Japanese lady. You know, the one who wrote *The Magic Art of Throwing Away All Your Shit*?"

Helen laughed and his face lit up with pleasure.

"Marie Kondo," she said.

"That's her. I'm taking hospitality at Vancouver Island University. Everyone in my class is crazy about that book. Easy for them. They don't have four younger sisters who keep everything they ever get for sentimental reasons."

"Ms. Kondo is popular in butlering circles as well," said Helen, liking Leon and wishing *he* were one of Ms. Edna's relatives. She'd put him in charge in a heartbeat.

"Okay, well, like I said, I don't know if I'm supposed to be here anymore. You can pay me or not. I just didn't want all the little plants dying before things get figured out. I'm making a smaller version of this garden outside the band office because I like the design. A bunch of the kids on the rez are helping. The Elders are showing us some Traditional plants to put in. I think they're worried the new generation is going to plant all kale."

"I'd like to see your garden some time," said Helen. "I suspect we all would."

"We all?" he asked.

"My co-workers and I. Two of my fellow butlers have joined me and we've hired a young man to help out."

He pretended to count to three, using his gloved fingers. "One, two, three butlers. Isn't that a famous kid's book? Or like a crime story?"

Again she laughed and he shone.

"It should be."

"It could also be the beginning of a killer joke about a light bulb," he added.

"The possibilities are endless," she said. "I have to go inside to attend to dinner, but if you'd like to stay and look after the garden until things have been resolved, I'd be grateful and will happily pay you your usual wage."

Leon, who was possessed of a calm and intelligent face, nodded, no longer smiling. "Sorry about Ms. Edna. She was good."

Helen liked the way he put that. "Yes, she was." She considered for a moment. "Did she say anything to you? About her plans?"

"You mean, did she tell me she was going to cross over?"

Helen nodded.

"No. I knew she went to that death club they got here. But that seemed like more of a hobby, you know?"

Helen did know.

"She was retreating for the past few months, so I just got notes from her. If I showed up when she was out here, doing that slow meditation walking, she just waved and went inside. But I wasn't around too much."

"I see. Well, thank you," said Helen.

He nodded. "I'm going to get these planted before I go home."

And with that, Leon turned and seemed to disappear under his sun hat as he hunched over the neat rows of lettuces.

Feeling reassured by Leon's presence, Helen made her way into the lodge, where she found Murray and Gavin stuffing Nigel, who'd returned from his errand, full of information they'd learned at the North American Butler Academy.

"How are things going in here?" she asked.

"Fine," said Murray. "Gav and I have just been telling Nigel here about the principles of room cleaning. He is a tabula rasa, cleaning-wise, so it's a challenge." The way Murray looked at Nigel reminded Helen of a tennis racket looking at a ball.

Nigel looked to Gavin, who explained. "She means you're a blank slate. Luckily, you're a good student."

Gavin polished silver with quick, confident movements. He was the best multi-tasker Helen had ever met. She was a highly competent person, but mindfulness training had made her averse to trying to do too many things at once.

Helen checked to see how Nigel was responding to all the instruction.

"Murray says I don't have any manners," he reported.

Murray nodded. "He's like a young armadillo we picked off the side of the highway. Not versed in the social graces."

"They keep saying I need basic life skills," said Nigel, happily.

"He ate a bag of ketchup chips for breakfast," said Gavin.

"And an Oh Henry! bar. Gav and I got diabetes watching him."

"We're going to teach him about diet and nutrition tomorrow," said Gavin. "Help him live long enough to become a decent domestic."

"It can't be any worse than learning how to clean a room properly," said Nigel.

"You are going to love the lesson on fine rug care," said Murray. "It's beyond gripping."

"Healthy eating is the cornerstone of a healthy life. And you're in excellent hands with these two," said Helen.

"Didn't I say that very thing?" Murray beamed smugly at Nigel.

"What you said was 'Don't you feel like a pig eating that first thing in the morning?'" replied Nigel.

They went on like that, comfortably talking while they prepared the first meal for the guests. Gavin went out to pick greens and herbs for a salad. Helen showed Nigel how to cut up summer squash, carrots, and onions for the soup. Murray prepared the pistou with basil and garlic and freshly grated parmesan, and Helen drained the beans she'd soaked overnight. As dinnertime approached, Helen led the three of them into a walk-in cupboard off the baking room. The cupboard was lined with sturdy shelves that held stacks of dishes.

"Ms. Edna kept these for personal entertaining."

Gavin picked a plate off the top of one of the stacks and showed it to Murray, raising his eyebrows. The plate was decorated with a pink heron contemplating the water in which it stood.

"I don't like to pry, but was your former boss quite well off?" asked Gavin, his accent sounding slightly more British than usual.

Helen paused. "I don't think so."

"These are Gien," explained Gavin. "Hand painted in Faïencerie de Gien in the Loire Valley. The name of the collection is Gien Les Grands Oiseaux. This is exquisite crockery."

"They remind me of my mom's Costco collection," said Nigel. "Only more French."

"They were designed by the French Impressionist Félix Bracquemond." Gavin picked up another plate that featured a pelican taking off from a pond. "I don't want to be crass, but each of these costs at least three hundred dollars."

Nigel quickly replaced the plate he'd been examining like he was handling an explosive.

"Here is another complete set of Gien," said Gavin, moving on to another stack. Each plate was separated by felt discs. "This one is the Safari collection. Utterly stunning." He showed Murray. "Designed by Stéphane Alsac. You see the detail here?"

The dishes were decorated with images of zebras, elephants, cheetahs, and giraffes on the savannah.

"Each of these sets is worth a small fortune," said Gavin. "Even considering the depressed market for dishware. Your employer had exceptional taste."

During her time at Yatra, Helen had inspected and cleaned every item in the lodge many times. She'd learned from Ms. Edna to rotate the dishes so they received equal wear. Each piece gave her a deep sense of pleasure, the same way that flowers and candles and waxed furniture did, and the way that a ringing bell did. But she'd never considered their cost and Edna had never mentioned it.

Gavin surveyed the various sets. "If I had to guess, I'd say there's close to sixty thousand dollars' worth of dishware in here."

"Oh," said Helen, floored.

"This evening let's do the Gien Les Grands Oiseaux," said Gavin, taking three of the bird plates from the stack. "Start this grand adventure with a flourish." Then he picked out dessert plates and serving plates, and white platters, cups, and bowls, each with delicate patterning at the edges. "The Rocaille Blanc will work nicely with the birds," he said.

"We're going to show you how to properly set a table," said Murray to Nigel as they filed out of the pantry.

Helen picked up a package of silverware bundled in felt and followed them.

Gavin and Murray chose a round table in the corner of the lodge. Murray draped it with a freshly ironed white tablecloth. Then she covered that with a smaller pale gray cloth. There was something reverent in the way she and Gavin worked.

They showed Nigel a butler's stick. "A beautifully laid table is a work of art. Precision counts," said Gavin.

Then they had Nigel measure out the distance between each item on the place setting. "If we had more than three guests, the ideal distance between the centre of each plate would be twenty-four inches," he said. "But we will give tonight's guests more room."

"If I ever win the lottery, I'm getting some of these bird dishes," said Nigel. "Why is the cutlery upside down?"

"Silverware," Gavin corrected gently. "Notice anything about it?"

"It came out of that cloth bag," said Nigel. "And there's writing on the back."

"It's monogrammed. In the French setting style, the cutlery is turned over so guests see the initials and know that they are eating with real silver."

All three butlers enjoyed Nigel's dumbfounded expression. Then everyone stood back to admire the table, Nigel mimicking their upright postures, hands lightly clasped behind his back.

"It's gorgeous," said Murray. "But since we're doing self-serve, we need to put the plates in the serving room. Are you sure you want the guests carrying them?"

"I think it will be fine," said Helen.

"But formal service after the chef arrives?"

Helen nodded. She didn't want the talents of her butlers to go to waste.

"We need something for the centrepiece," said Murray. "I'll be right back."

She left the dining room and reappeared a few minutes later with an armful of flowers and greenery. She placed several of the kale stems covered in yellow flowers and red, purple, and yellow tulips around the table. Strewn among the hand-painted dishes, the effect was magical.

"The rest can go on the serving table," said Murray.

"Our dinner table at home never looked like this," said Nigel. "Not even for Super Bowl or the Stanley Cup."

Gavin gently slapped him on the back.

"When we're done with you, you'll be able to create beauty any-where."

In the service room adjoining the open kitchen, they prepped the heavy wooden serving table from which the guests would help themselves.

Helen placed a wooden slab on a riser made from a piece of burled wood. That would hold the big soup tureen.

Gavin wrote out small cards describing each dish and placed each in a wire holder.

Murray laid out the rest of the flowers and added a large bouquet of Solomon's seal, bearded irises, and tulips she'd arranged earlier. The bird plates sat in a row at the end of the table.

Helen glanced at her watch. "They should be here soon," she said.

They put out the sandwich fixings and Murray showed Nigel how to warm the soup bowls. Helen arranged the thinly sliced vegetables and a selection of fine cheeses on a cutting board. She added sliced pickles, lettuce, tomato, and sprouts. The warm olives and roasted fennel slices would go out just before service started.

"Ready?" asked Gavin. He stood with his hands behind his back.

"For anything," said Murray.

Helen hoped that was true.

Chapter 12

Whitney was first inside at five minutes to six. She had changed into a slouchy grey cashmere sweater and dark jeans and had thin leather sandals on her feet. Her hair was brushed but still hung in her face. She carried a book in one hand. Helen was surprised to see that it was Thich Nhat Hanh's *Peace Is Every Step*.

"Welcome," said Helen. "How was your afternoon, Ms. Varga?"

"Please call me Whitney. It was very peaceful."

"May I offer you a cocktail or some other refreshment before dinner?"

"Ohh," said Whitney, moving to peer into the serving room. "What are we having?"

"Italian soup, a selection of fresh breads, and salads," said Helen. "Our chef arrives tomorrow, but I hope you'll find this acceptable."

"Of course," said Whitney. "Will the boys and I be eating together?"

"Ah, Whitney," came an affected voice behind them. "Glad to see your enthusiasm at the prospect of dining with us." The brothers, who must have slipped in a side door, strode toward them. Wills had a rolling gait that revealed how much time he'd spent on a sailboat. Tad managed to look bored by the very act of walking. In spite of their differences, Helen realized she saw them as a unit. She would have to be careful to remember they were two different people, not a single rich-guy entity.

Tad inclined his head to give Whitney an air kiss in the general vicinity of her cheek and then did a double take when he spotted the dining room table.

"Oh *my my*! It seems someone has been studying the food and life-style magazines. And I just got a peek at the food in the kitchen. Very on trend with the butcher's block make-your-own sammies."

Nigel looked crestfallen at Tad's withering comments.

"It's all lovely," said Whitney.

"If you like sandwiches that you have to make yourself," said Tad.

"We will be serving more formal dinners beginning tomorrow. After the chef arrives," said Helen.

"I'm sure she'll be Michelin quality," said Tad.

Wills peered into the serving room. "Any chance of getting a drink? And Tad, stop berating the help. For god's sake. They could spit in your food."

Gavin materialized in front of him and took his order.

Whitney rolled her eyes. "And *this* is how two weeks can be made to feel like two years," she muttered.

All the staff wore dark denim aprons with leather straps. Gavin looked impossibly tall and handsome in his. Nigel less so in his.

The guests moved into the dining room.

"Would you like a cocktail or a glass of wine?" Gavin asked Tad and Whitney.

"That would be nice," said Tad. "Something a little cheeky. Do you have any craft beer? This place seems to call for that. So much wood. I expect men with large, untrimmed beards and their hair in buns to be wandering around."

"We have an excellent oatmeal stout brewed in Powell River. It's called Perfect Storm."

"I don't care what it's called," said Tad.

Gavin's pleasant expression didn't falter. "Coming right up," he said.

"Do you have anything non-alcoholic?" asked Whitney.

"Let me guess," said Wills. "You are *still* a teetotalling vegetarian."

"With an eating disorder," fake-whispered Tad.

"Shut up, you two. You haven't matured since we were kids. It's pathetic."

"Egads," said Wills. "It seems we've been put in our place, brother."

"*Devastating*," said Tad. "And Whit, how's your mother? Still scrounging around, looking for the main chance?"

"We have a lovely shrub with blackberry and ginger. Would you like to try that?" Helen asked Whitney, who seemed about to make an angry retort or burst into tears.

"Yes. Thank you, Helen." She turned back to her marble-eyed cousins. "And you, Tad, are the same dreadful clod you've always been."

The three of them stood awkwardly in the dining room like they were at a poorly attended office party. The brothers affected a bored nonchalance. Whitney stared at the large painting depicting the Institute garden that dominated the wall.

Helen and Gavin headed to the kitchen to get the drinks, indicating that Nigel should join them. Murray was in the kitchen putting the last-minute touches on the food dishes and getting ready to slice the bread.

When they reached the back room where the drinks were kept, Nigel couldn't hold it in any longer. "Oh my god," he said. "What's wrong with those people?"

Gavin held a finger to his lips. "The first rule of domestic service is that we do not gossip about the guests."

"At least not when they're around to hear it," said Murray.

Gavin got a frosted glass from the freezer and fetched the bottle of Perfect Storm. The bottle and glass went on a tray with Wills's vodka martini, which Gavin prepared with an ease that reflected his experience pouring drinks for some of the richest air travellers in the world. Helen poured Whitney's ginger and blackberry shrub mix into a glass filled with ice cubes and added a long toothpick with three small cubes of apple from the orchard, separated by a mint leaf and a basil leaf. She topped it with mineral water from Germany.

When the drinks were ready, Helen showed Nigel how to hold a tray correctly.

The guests had moved into the sitting room, and the pace of the verbal sniping had slowed. Wills read his phone. Tad stared moodily out the window, and Whitney seemed immersed in her book.

"Here we are," said Helen, serving Whitney first.

Whitney tasted her drink. "This is excellent," she said. The smile softened her face and transformed her into a striking woman.

"Huh," said Tad when Helen put the beer and the frosted glass in front of him. It was obvious that he couldn't think of something rude to say and it threw him a little.

Wills grunted a thanks when he took his drink.

"When you're ready, dinner will be served from the big table," said Helen.

"Thanks," said Whitney.

Tad nodded and Wills made another noise.

Twenty minutes later they assembled in the serving room, where Nigel began to explain the menu. Tad ignored him and pushed his way to the table, where he began to fill his plate. Wills followed his brother's lead, disregarding Nigel's increasingly wavery explanation. Only Whitney listened until the end.

"Thank you," she said. "It all sounds very good."

Her cousins had already left the room when she began to select a few low-calorie items.

When Whitney had gone to the dining room, Helen reflected that this might indeed be a very long ten days and that if she was asked to give an assessment now, she'd vote to keep the cousins as far away from the Institute as possible.

Chapter 13

NIGEL OWENS

While the guests were eating, I tried to make myself useful, which I admit doesn't come natural to me. I didn't know what to do, since the butlers were butlering the shit out of the situation. Every dish was whisked away the second the guest finished eating. Every drink was refilled the instant it was empty. It was like the guests only had to think of something and one of the butlers had already done it. I was just getting in the way, so I wandered around waiting for a job to come up that didn't require any skills.

When the heavy, red-faced brother stepped out of the bathroom and called me over to ask if I had any drugs he could buy, I wasn't that shocked. I mean, I *was* a little surprised because no one has ever thought I was a drug dealer before. I'm not cool enough for that. But I was not surprised because I have very bad luck. Yes, I got the job and it seemed cool and I was learning about rich people stuff, such as how you should heat up dishes before you put food on them. But then the guests showed up and they are like cartoon villain wealthy people from *The Simpsons*. They are like that lady who got her head cut off in the French Revolution because she said the thing about cake. It makes sense one of them tried to score off me. Either I'm screwed because the guests think I'm a dealer or I'm screwed because a guest is mad that I'm not a dealer.

"Uh, no sir," I said, remembering to be polite, even when turning down drug requests.

"Come on," said the one, called Wilson, I think. I can't keep the two brothers straight. They're both awful but in slightly different ways. This one is like the teen-movie jock bully. The other one is more like a teen-movie private school bully. A bit more refined about being an asshole. "Nothing?"

I shook my head and wanted to disappear. The last thing I want is to get shitcanned for selling to a guest. Not that I could since I don't have anything here. I'm not even that much of a drug guy and I've always been strictly recreational and non-hardcore.

"I can pay," said Wilson, keeping his voice down and glancing between the dining room doorway to the right and then back at the kitchen to the left. We were in the foyer, which is wide open and the perfect place to get busted.

"Sorry, sir. I'm not, uh, the right person."

"You dress like *that* and you don't get high?" said the guy.

"No, sir."

"Forget it," he said. He pushed his greasy hair off his face. His head looked too small for his body. "Forget I said anything."

He walked over and picked up his drink from where he'd left it on the long coffee station. He tossed it back and left the glass beside the stack of clean teacups.

I was feeling a little freaked out from being in such a nice place and learning so much etiquette, and now being mistaken for a drug dealer, so I rushed over and rubbed the ring of condensation off the wood and carried the glass to the pass-through window to the dish-washing station.

I wondered if I should tell Helen that he asked me for drugs, even though it doesn't look very good on me if the guests automatically *assume* I'm a dealer.

Better to stay quiet and pretend it wouldn't occur to anyone that the fat guy with orange hair knows about anything illegal, even if the truth is that any fifteen-year-old who hangs out at the 7-Eleven knows just as much as I do.

I started heading into the kitchen when Murray blew past me. She smiled and I died a little. That little accent! The black braids! And she's snarky, too. She's a bit of a silky badger. Not that I know anything about badgers. Or butlers. Or anything, really. I should mention that I'm also a little in love with Helen, even though she scares me even worse than the guests. I don't love her in a romantic way, but more like when a younger guy falls for an older woman because he wasn't parented properly. I would just like her to tuck me into bed and tell me everything is going to be okay.

Yes, I know I'm borderline creepy. At least I'm comfortable with my grossness. I figure the real problems happen when you don't even know you're a Flaw King.

After I got over the thrill of Murray going by me, I bustled into the kitchen to start the dishes. No rubber gloves. Where'd Helen say those were kept? I walked out of the kitchen and toward the door that leads down into the basement, where the cleaning supplies are. That's when I noticed the female guest, Whitney, about halfway up the stairs to the second floor.

She spotted me and froze. Like she was afraid I was going to shoot at her.

"Hello?" I said, because I couldn't think of anything else.

"Oh, hi."

She took her hand off the railing as though she had no idea how it got there. "I used to love wandering around this place when we were kids. Thought I'd check things out. See if it's all how I remember it."

"Okay," I said. I didn't know if I was allowed to tell guests where they can and can't go, but I was also sure Helen wouldn't want anyone up there.

"Are you staying in the lodge?" asked Whitney.

She'd started coming down the steps, moving extremely slowly, like she didn't want me to notice.

"I'm in a staff cabin."

"Helen is staying upstairs?"

"I guess so," I said, feeling like every word was a new mistake.

"The washrooms are still in the same place?" she said.

I pointed to a doorway behind her and nodded. She'd nearly oiled her way back down the stairs by this point.

"Good," she said. "It's nice when things stay the same."

She was one weird girl. Or woman. I couldn't really tell which she was. She was so barely here.

I stepped back as she walked quickly past me and into the women's washroom.

Before I could do anything else, Murray came out of the dining room.

"Move, move, move," she said. "Come on, soldier. Let's go."

So I went.

Chapter 14

By the end of the meal, the cousins' animosity had softened somewhat. During her trips to and from the table to drop off and collect things, Helen heard them talking about visiting the Institute as children.

"Do you remember the nude herbalists conference? Left me with a lifelong fear of mint," said Wills.

"I rather enjoyed the drumming conference," said Whitney. "It was quite stirring to hear them drum up there on the bluffs, hour after hour."

"Like *Lord of the Flies* or *Apocalypse Now*," said Tad.

Before dessert was served, Gavin took Nigel outside so they could freshen up the cousins' cabins while Murray and Helen served the final course.

Dessert was a small bowl of locally made vanilla ice cream topped with a berry compote, served with coffee. By the time the three finished, they all looked like different people. Nicer people with softer faces. At least for the moment.

Helen checked the table one last time to see if they needed anything.

"I've got flashlights in case you'd like to go for a walk this evening. I can get a headlamp for anyone who wants one."

"Thank you, Helen," said Tad expansively.

"When does the missing link arrive?" asked Wills. "This secret cousin none of us have met."

"Rayvn will be here tomorrow."

"When is the celebration of life for Auntie Edna?" asked Whitney. "Has that been scheduled for after our courses?"

Helen thought of Nigel's telling her he'd found Whitney sneaking upstairs, presumably to get a look at where Edna had died. Perhaps the girl had been fonder of Edna than Edna had been of her.

Helen explained that Edna's life would be celebrated at Samhain.

"Can non-witches come?" asked Whitney. "I would like to be there."

"I'm afraid I don't know," said Helen. "I don't have those details."

"My mother is not going to like it if we're not included," said Whitney.

"Neither is ours," said Tad. "She's been on the phone to me half a dozen times asking me for details about the memorial."

"Doesn't bode well for any of our parents' receiving an inheritance," said Wills.

They all looked at Helen. Their faces were no longer relaxed.

"So, Helen. What *is* going on with the will? Did Edna leave it all to the nudists? You must have some idea," asked Tad.

"As I've mentioned before, I know nothing about the estate or the will. I've just been asked to carry out Ms. Edna's wishes."

"Don't know or *won't say?*" said Tad.

"She didn't leave this place to *you*, did she?" asked Wills. "That would be outrageous. We'd have to contest it in court."

"I don't believe so," said Helen.

"I've looked up property values on the island," said Tad, already forgetting Helen so completely she might as well have left the room. "They're not bad, considering the lack of amenities and infrastructure. But apparently it's impossible to get any major developments approved." Nervous alarms sounded throughout Helen's body and she briefly closed her eyes.

"And not even the worst philistine would want to develop this property," said Wills. Helen's fear subsided at Wills's reply.

The cousins walked out of the dining room and Helen couldn't hear what they said next.

Only Whitney said thanks on her way out of the lodge.

AFTER THE KITCHEN and lodge were clean and swept and Gavin, Murray, and Nigel had gone to their cabins, Helen's curiosity took hold. She was executing Plan B with so little information. What else was in Edna's will? Yes, Helen could decide which relative would be invited to run the lodge, but who would own it? Edna was an inveterate planner and an ardent list maker, even though she procrastinated about difficult decisions. That's why she'd made the Plan B. She hadn't trusted herself to make the decision quickly.

What were the implications of Helen putting one of these people in charge? Was that *all* she was doing? She felt like Willy Wonka giving the children a tour of the chocolate factory, but in this case, she didn't know what they would get. A lifetime supply of chocolate? A pristine acreage and lodge? A job?

Helen went into the office and, feeling slightly foolish and also like she was betraying a trust, she looked at the bookshelf where Edna had kept her journals. For decades Edna had used a line of journals called Paperblanks. Completed books of many sizes with handsome designs filled a few shelves. In these diaries Edna had written about her days, significant and insignificant events and inspirational quotes, and she'd made notes about the garden and the lodge. She'd been as disciplined about writing in her journal as she was undisciplined about making decisions on matters that vexed her. And she was fond of telling people about her journaling.

The journals were organized by colour and size, which was not a system Helen would have recommended. But surely the most recent would be at the end of the row? She opened the last book on the bottom row, which was bound in an exuberant Hawaiian floral print hardcover. The final entry was dated two years before. Helen checked the second-to-last book. It was dated four years before. Some of the journals were in storage, but there were at least three shelves' worth in the office.

Edna kept a stack of fresh journals on top of a cabinet. Helen checked them. All blank.

After Helen retrieved a piece of paper and pen, she started at the top shelf. She took down each book and flipped it open to check the date and make a note of it in her book. Only a few of the books were consecutive. None of them was recent.

Perhaps the missing journals had been taken by the medical examiner as part of the routine investigation of an unexpected death. They should be returned, if that was the case. They were part of Edna's legacy. It was another thing to ask the authorities about. Not that she wanted to meddle.

Chapter 15

There was a body in the middle of the garden. Well, technically, the body was about a third of the way up the garden and it was sprawled out on the rustic table under an apple tree. But it was very much a body.

Helen, who'd been about to do her early morning walking meditation, took a deep breath and went to investigate. She got close enough to recognize the floral designer, Jenson Kiley, staring up into the apple blossoms.

She approached cautiously so as not to startle him, but she needn't have worried.

"There is a hummingbird nest on this branch," he said. "Can you even?"

Helen could even. She'd been aware of the nest because she had a gift for finding small treasures in the garden and elsewhere. But it hadn't occurred to her to stare up at it in quite the way Jenson was doing.

"From this angle, it looks like it was created by a sea horse in a tree of coral."

Helen looked at the florist and then tried to peer up at the underside of the tiny nest.

"Does it?" she said.

"Or perhaps a tiny asteroid in a field of endless stars."

"Ah," said Helen. She'd forgotten just how artistic Jenson could be.

"I will need to remove this branch," he said.

"There are eggs inside," she said. "So I think we'll leave it for now. I suspect the tree would not care to have a major limb removed."

"If we put a heater on the eggs, that might get things moving," said Jenson, sitting up suddenly. "Get those little hummers up and out. This is an incomparable look. Award winning. I could do a design around that nest and flowering branch that would change the course of floristry."

He wore dark gray trousers, a checked button-down shirt, a green sweater vest, and a blazer. His facial features, small and sharp, had an elvish aspect that suited his neat proportions.

"We're glad you could do this for us, Jenson," said Helen. "I didn't expect you until later this morning. I'm sorry I wasn't here to greet you."

It wasn't the first time he'd arrived at Yatra without her noticing. Jenson Kiley had always moved around like quicksilver on a plate.

"Oh, it's okay," he said. He waved a hand distractedly through the air, as though pointing at a satellite located somewhere above. "I've been here since yesterday."

"Pardon?" said Helen. "Where?"

"Hmmm?" he said.

"Where have you been since yesterday?"

"Sourcing extra flowers and foliage for the course. I know all the gardeners worth knowing on this island. I wanted to see what they have. What they might donate."

"I see. And where have you been staying?" she asked.

"In my van. At the beach. Listening to opera and dreaming of making a bouquet for La Scala."

"Where's your van now?"

"At the campground at the beach. It's a Mercedes. Very comfortable. I rented it for this trip. Though of course, after today, I will move into my usual accommodations on the campus. I walked over from the campground because I need the exercise. The forsythia is in bloom, you know. And it's truly breathtaking against a backdrop of ocean spray and apple blossoms. I must capture the essence of that combination." He put a hand on her forearm and she leaned in to listen. When he said nothing, just stared into space, she gently removed her arm from his grasp.

Yes, time had dulled the memory of just how strange Jenson Kiley was. Helen recalled that Edna had always insisted he be watched carefully, lest he "denude something precious." He was ruthless in the pursuit of floral arrangements, which didn't exactly fit with the Yatra Institute ethos. But he was a gifted designer and a favourite with a certain kind of student. More than one had come to Helen after taking Jenson's Arranging Your Inner Flower course to announce that their lives were forever changed. Not only did they know how to do flower arrangements, but they repeated that they now saw with "the eyes of a flower."

She wondered how his new students would react to the news that their fate could be tied to a man who saw universes in apple blossoms.

"Did you know, Helen," he said, staring now at the patch of irises at the end of one of the rows, "that flowers can hear our thoughts?"

She smiled. Of course it wasn't true. If it were, flowers who encountered humans would never bloom again.

Chapter 16

Later that morning, Helen waited at the ferry terminal with a patience rarely seen outside of former monastics. The few white clouds high overhead moved imperceptibly westward. The spring sun was warm but not hot, and the forest around the ferry terminal seemed to be breathing.

Walk-on passengers and people waiting to collect travellers moved around Helen like tourists around a tree.

The big white-and-blue boat docked and the few foot passengers disembarked ahead of the cars.

Helen watched.

The first few had the look of islanders: strange hats, work pants, old dogs on the ends of frayed strings. The last foot passenger was a young woman in full camouflage gear. But it was not traditional camo. She wore a laced camo bustier under an oversized camo shirt, a wide leather belt, and camo army pants. The camouflage patterns were all different, which caused a bit of a visual disruption when one stared directly at her.

Helen went to greet the new arrival.

"Rayvn?" she said.

The young woman nodded.

"How do you do? I'm Helen Thorpe." She extended her hand.

"Rayvn Wildwood," she said.

They shook and Helen gently ushered Rayvn out of the way so the cars could begin offloading.

Rayvn Wildwood, whose birth name was Rae-Jean Wegman, had extravagant black hair in loose curls, which were held tight to her forehead with a camo headband. She carried a black physician's bag and pulled behind her a huge black vinyl suitcase covered in metal rivets.

"I'm so nervous," said Rayvn, with no preamble. "The lawyer said something about taking life courses so I prepared for, like, a *Survivor*-type thing. But the truth is, if we have to be self-sufficient, I'm probably going to die."

Helen stopped herself from laughing at the notion of this girl, Wills, Tad, and Whitney living rough on Sutil Island.

"I promise we'll take care of you."

"Phew," said Rayvn. She looked around. "Sure is a lot of nature on this island, eh?"

"Yes," Helen said. "There is."

She led the girl to the Institute van and wrestled her enormous suitcase into the back.

"This whole deal is probably the weirdest thing that has ever happened to me," said Rayvn, again without preamble. "It's kind of freaking me out. And I'm pro weirdness in general. So."

"I understand," said Helen.

She pulled out of the parking lot and Rayvn talked. And talked.

"I never even met any people from this part of my family. You know how some families have a—whaddaya call it? Black sheep? Well, I figure I'm more like the rumour of a black sheep. Apparently, my biological dad was married to my mom for, like, twenty-five minutes. They had a little diddle-daddle."

Diddle-daddle. Helen had never heard it put quite that way.

"It happened the one and only time my mom left the country. Her and this other girl from her hairdressing school went to Burning Man. Like, in the desert? I guess my mom and my biological met there and got so high that on the way home, they stopped in Vegas and got married. When they straightened up, they went their separate ways, never to twain up again, if that's the right expression. My mom came back home to Nanaimo, had me, and not long after that, she met and married my proper dad. You know, the one who raised me. Like I said, I have no relationship at all with my biological father or his family, which makes all this super random."

"By the terms of your late aunt's will, you have been asked to take part," Helen explained. Then she told Rayvn what she could about the next days: the courses, the other cousins, the history of the lodge.

"Huh," said Rayvn, when Helen was done speaking. "Guess I didn't need to go full camo. Probably should have gone for tie-dye or just green velvet. I made this outfit myself." She looked down at herself.

"Impressive," said Helen. She could tell that a lot of work had gone into it, particularly the bustier, with its metal grommets and leather laces. For a girl with a lot of cleavage showing, Rayvn also managed to seem quite bundled up. She appeared to sense what Helen was thinking.

"I know my look is a lot to take in," she said. "A little bit medieval, a little bit Ho-ski and Slut."

Helen laughed.

"I LARP and it's made me bold," added Rayvn. "Also whimsical."

"Looks great on you," said Helen kindly.

"Thanks," said Rayvn. "Was she nice?"

Helen glanced at the girl. "I'm sorry?"

"My aunt who died. Ms. Edna. She sounds like a pretty cool lady."

"She was a true original."

"Wish I could have met her. And my dad, I guess."

The lawyer had told Helen that Rayvn's biological father, Edna's brother-in-law, had died many years before. His will had specified that only after the last family member of his generation was dead should Rayvn be told about him.

The girl was quiet for the rest of the trip. When they got to the lodge, Helen invited her into Edna's office and gave her the rest of the spiel.

When she was done, Rayvn placed her hands flat on the desk. Her nails were long, pointy, and black. "I think you should know that I made twenty-seven grand last year. That was my best year by about five grand."

Rayvn, in her early twenties, was younger than the others, and her apparent lack of guile made her seem even younger, even though she dressed like a stripper wearing a hunting blind.

"I see," said Helen.

"What I'm trying to say is that this is all out of my league. People who make less than thirty grand don't come to places like this."

"Not usually," Helen agreed. The Yatra Institute kept its courses and its rates affordable, but most of the clientele was comfortably middle class or better off.

"Did you have trouble getting the time off work?" Helen asked.

"My manager let me take my holidays. I don't want to brag, but

I'm kind of a big deal at Electronics for Less. Top salesperson in small appliances in our region for two months in a row last year. Hope the whole chain doesn't fail without me there to shore up revenues."

Rayvn laughed. So did Helen.

A knock sounded on the office door.

"Come in," said Helen.

Gavin, Murray, and Nigel came in.

Helen introduced each of them, explained who they were. Rayvn made a point of standing up to shake their hands and repeated each of their names. Helen could see how she'd become the top appliance salesperson at her store. She could also see them pointedly not staring at Rayvn's ensemble.

"Would you like me to show you to your cabin?" asked Gavin. "We can give you a tour of the grounds if you're not too tired."

"Oh man, that'd be magical."

Gavin picked up Rayvn's doctor's bag and the whole group of them left the office.

THE CHEF WAS next to arrive. The butlers had met her when she gave a lecture at the North American Butler Academy on how to hire and work with a personal chef. To conclude her two-day workshop at the Academy, the chef, Leticia, had made them all what she called an old-fashion peach cobbler. It was a cake filled with peaches baked in browned butter and studded with apricots and tiny hints of candied ginger. Helen still dreamed about it. Gavin had been the one to suggest they check to see if she was available at short notice. He remembered her saying that she'd decided not to run her own restaurant so she could focus on doing limited-run gigs that interested her. Luckily, she was free.

Leticia had striking almond-shaped eyes, freckles, and hair that she mostly kept hidden inside an intricate headwrap. She had the air of someone who could adapt to any situation, no matter how formal or how laid-back. It was a quality highly prized by the wealthy. She would suit the atmosphere at Yatra perfectly.

Gavin collected her from the float plane dock, and Helen and Murray greeted her with hugs. She was an extremely huggable person.

"Please tell me you'll make us the peach cobbler," said Murray after finally releasing her.

"Hush now," said Gavin. "Wait until she's inside before we begin making demands. Plus, she's already agreed the first peach cobbler will be for me. I might be convinced to share."

They were escorting Leticia into the lodge when a white Escalade came roaring into the parking lot, going much too fast. It stopped, spraying gravel.

"Go ahead," said Helen. "I'll be there in a moment."

The vehicle idled for a long time while its driver looked down at what must have been a cellphone.

Helen was not an easily irritated person, but an idling Escalade was a uniquely irritating thing. She took a calming breath, closed her eyes, and thought about emotional equilibrium.

By the time she'd regained hers, the driver had shut off the vehicle and emerged.

Wayfarer (who cared not that she might be infringing on the sunglasses brand) strode toward Helen, biceps highly defined under her tan, her disconcertingly fat-free and muscular body encased in high-performance athletic wear.

Helen had spent so much time in a monastery that she always found herself taken aback by revealing clothes, whether worn by men or women. She inclined to modesty and thought robes were really the most attractive thing one could wear. They allowed one's inner nature to shine out more naturally.

"Helen," said Wayfarer in her thick Glaswegian accent. "For Christ's sake, aren't you a sight for ma weary eyes."

And in that instant, Helen remembered how much she enjoyed the dance teacher, who was, at least outwardly, the least Yatra person possible.

The two women hugged, and Helen noted how very different it was from hugging Chef Leticia. Hugging Wayfarer was a bit like embracing an oiled-rock statue that had been out in the sun for some time. Not unpleasant, but odd.

Wayfarer, who used only the one name, stood back and looked at Helen. "Ye no been spending every spare minute at the gym, have ye?"

Helen allowed that was true.

"But I expect you have," said Helen. "You look very strong."

"Oh, aye," said Wayfarer. "I've won two Natural Championships. No many dancers can say tha. They're muscle adverse. A person needs to project tremendous strength to succeed in this world."

Wayfarer was in her mid-forties and had jet-black extensions that hung down to her perfectly formed behind, which that she told Helen had once been used in an ad for a Brazilian glute-enhancement specialist, even though her glutes were all natural. Her skin was tanned to the shade of some sort of exotic wood and her large brown eyes were framed with extremely long and thick eyelash extensions that looked like they were an effort to move. Her lips were plumped up with fillers, and Botox injections had lifted her eyebrows in a way that made her seem permanently concerned.

Her black tank top with mesh cut-outs revealed chiselled arms and pecs, and her shiny white-and-black tiger-striped tights showed off thighs and calves that Helen had heard called "epic" more than once.

"Isn't she the most magnificent specimen?" Edna used to say in an awed voice every time Wayfarer showed up to teach the Devi Dance program, which she'd done every year for the past twelve. Helen did not instantly share Edna's appreciation for Wayfarer's physique and self-presentation. In fact, every year Helen had to work through some of her own prejudices about vanity. As a woman who had almost none, she had trouble understanding people who seemed to have a lot. An uncharitable part of her suspected that such devotion to appearances meant the person in question wasn't working on her inner self. That, she learned every year, wasn't true.

Wayfarer had overcome a childhood filled with poverty and violence and, through heroic hard work and unbridled ambition, become a renowned dancer and choreographer. She taught many forms of dance, all around the world, but was best known for the extremely physical combination of dance and martial arts that she'd created and named Way-bo, much to the annoyance of the Tae Bo community. Students in Los Angeles and Miami and Rio de Janeiro and Moscow spent exorbitant sums to attend her Way-bo dance workshops. Thousands of students paid high fees to take her online classes, in which she led them through movements that seemed both aggressive and impressive in equal measure.

Wayfarer had come to the Yatra Institute during a difficult time in her life. The wounds of her past had been catching up to her, and all the money and success had not healed what ailed her inside. She'd met Edna at a conference for cultural innovators in San Francisco and they'd bonded. Edna invited Wayfarer to the lodge to take some healing workshops. Later, they'd agreed that Wayfarer would come every year to teach Devi Dance. The waitlist for her program was long and her students were devoted.

They were also a stark physical contrast to, say, the meditators or people who came to learn about astral projection. And the end of the dance program was always something wondrous to behold. And for almost all of the students, it seemed to be transformative.

Helen had great respect for Wayfarer, in spite of their vast cultural differences.

"I canna believe she's gone," said Wayfarer. Her long sable eyelashes were wet. "Jesus Christ but I loved that woman."

"I know," said Helen. "And she loved you. I think she was your biggest fan, and that's saying something. You have a lot of fans, Wayfarer."

"Aye, she was like the mother I never had because mine was a useless snatch."

Helen nodded sympathetically.

"I mean, I know that my mother did her best, like, but she was utterly fuckin' awful, she was."

"Yes," said Helen, who knew, thanks to meditation interviews, quite a bit about Wayfarer's mother.

"I've got to get back on the meditation so I don't turn into her, you know?" said Wayfarer. "Edna always said it was the key. I just can't stand to sit still on me own. Not unless I'm in residence here on Extra-Sedation Island."

Wayfarer was one of those people who only slowed and calmed down in optimal conditions. She settled almost against her will. Helen had known many like her and admired that they put themselves into situations that challenged their amped-up systems.

"I'm happy to be here but generally fucked, of course. Keep in mind. I'm grieving, like."

"Yes," said Helen, appreciating how forthright Wayfarer was. She also knew from the times Wayfarer had visited that when she wasn't teaching, she'd be theatrically feeling all her feelings all over the property. There would be tears at breakfast, fits of anger in the garden. Wayfarer did not hold back. "I'm so glad you're here," she said, when Wayfarer didn't say anything else. "Let me get someone to bring you to your cabin."

Helen walked Wayfarer into the lodge and, as always, it reminded her of leading a racehorse in the peak of health. Like a racehorse, Wayfarer was the result of the latest discoveries in physical training and scientific nutrition. She was a manifestation of physicality, seeming to be more alive than anyone or anything in any direction.

They entered the dining room, where Nigel was setting the table for lunch, and Helen hesitated, knowing what was coming.

Nigel, wearing white and red trousers and a horrendous brown paisley shirt under his more tasteful dark denim apron, looked over with a cheerful expression that froze on his face when he spotted Wayfarer, who, it should be noted, was close to six feet tall. He seemed to disassemble, the way a Madonna superfan might upon finding the pop star in their apartment bathroom. Helen could practically see the thoughts and emotions chase themselves across his face. *Who? Here? Why?* His mouth dropped open and he sagged to the side ever so slightly. A ridiculous performance, thought Helen, but not unusual. He dropped the cutlery he'd been holding to emphasize his reaction.

Wayfarer was not traditionally beautiful, but she was, as Edna had always said, a specimen. *Just wait*, Helen thought wryly, *until he sees her dance*. Then things will get serious.

"Nigel," she said to the young man who was now scrambling on hands and knees to retrieve the utensils. "This is Wayfarer. Our dance instructor for the course. Can you please help get her settled? As you know, she's in Apple Blossom Cottage."

Nigel leapt to his feet, knives and forks bristling in his hand.

"If you could please get her bags from her vehicle? And perhaps see if she would like a snack before lunch?"

"Yes! Right away, sir!" said Nigel.

"It's fine," said Wayfarer, in her Glaswegian growl. "I can get to the cabin myself and get ma bags there too. There's no much of it. One of the benefits of skimpy outfits." She grinned and her whitened teeth gleamed against her tanned skin and colourless glossed lips.

"Ahhhh," said Nigel in a strangled voice. And then he bravely rallied. "No, of course. I'll show you." He straightened his knees, then his back, like a puppet whose master had finally remembered to pick up the strings. "Let's go!"

Helen suggested he put the cutlery in the wash bin before he went. He did so, then hustled over and took from Wayfarer's large calloused hand what Helen hoped was a fake fur purse so small it looked like a child's toy. The dance instructor looked bemused as she gave it up.

"I love dance," he babbled, looking at Helen because he seemed afraid to look at Wayfarer. "I dance myself. I mean, I have. Danced. At dances. At school mostly. I also once went to a rave. We hardly had any raves in Port Alberni. It was in the woods. Like way out there. The rave, I mean. People were doing meth and getting all, like, violent. It wasn't very rave-y. But I did dance there. Also, once, I played a dancing garbage can in our school performance of *Sesame Street*. But I was, like, seven or something and it wasn't much of a dance. I should take lessons. Maybe from you. Or something."

Wayfarer stared down at the young man with an expression of

tolerant exhaustion only a magnificently fit person can bestow on one who is far less physically impressive.

"Let's go, then," she said. "You can keep telling me your dance stories while we walk."

Helen caught Nigel's eye and inclined her head toward the kitchen to remind him to check whether Wayfarer was hungry.

"Oh my god," he said. "You teach dance, so you must be hungry. If I danced, I'd be so hungry. Although no one really ate at that one rave I went to. Probably because so many people were doing meth. Chef can make you anything. But she just got here, so maybe not right away. But not meat. We don't have meat here. Do you eat meat?"

Helen waved goodbye, knowing Wayfarer would just let Nigel run through his nervous talk until he had gotten over the shock of her. As she left the dining room, Helen heard Wayfarer tell him that all she ate was meat, which wasn't true. Sometimes she ate eggs.

"No way?" breathed Nigel. "Like the Rock. You know, Dwayne Johnson? I heard he eats a lot of meat. Also, fish. Do you eat fish?"

"Oh, aye. I'm like a commercial fishing boat the way I go through the fish," said Wayfarer.

And then they were outside. It was true that Wayfarer ate meat and that the Institute was a vegetarian establishment. When she visited, Wayfarer bought sustainably raised, organic, skinless, boneless chicken and turkey breast and so-called happy lean cuts of pork and beef at the Co-op. The staff in the grocery store's café roasted it for her and she ate it in her Escalade, so as not to draw crowds.

At the lodge, Wayfarer consumed vast quantities of egg whites and made smoothies with her huge collection of protein and vitamin powders. And she took down enormous quantities of fruits and vegetables and a few nuts, all without dressing.

Helen had already laid in extra provisions to accommodate the dancer's appetite. Wayfarer once told Helen that she burned nearly 3,500 calories a day doing her various forms of training, which ranged from weightlifting to running to multiple forms of dance and styles of martial arts. She'd also said something about micronutrients and macros and carbohydrates, which had caused Helen to lose focus.

Everyone was here. The flower-arranging course would start today at two. The dance class would start after dinner, followed by a late-night meditation. At six the next morning, Helen would lead another meditation sit, which would be followed by an intentional movement session, breakfast, then a flower-arranging session. It was on.

WHILE CHEF LETICIA got to know the kitchen and worked on her menu for the evening, Gavin and Murray prepared a light lunch of fresh rye bread from the little bakery in the village, green salad from the garden, paper-thin slices of fennel with garlic-parmesan sauce, roasted eggplant with a balsamic reduction, and an onion tart, also from the village bakery.

Nigel reported that when he'd dropped Rayvn Wildwood at her cabin, she looked around and declared it "cool." She was soon back in the lodge, curled up in the sitting room and reading a Stephen King novel. She hadn't changed out of her camouflage outfit. Nigel was clearly thrilled by everything about Rayvn Wildwood. He declared her "rad" at least four times before Helen reminded him it was best not to discuss guests, even in rapturous whispers.

Just before noon, Tad and Wills came in together through the garden-facing door. Their outfits were just right for a casual lunch at a west coast lodge. Jeans, T-shirts under cashmere sweaters, expensive running shoes. Their hair flopped over just so, and both brothers were freshly shaven.

Wills carried a sailing magazine and Tad held his iPad. It seemed to Helen that Wills's eyes were brighter or at least less bloodshot.

"Hello," said Helen. "I hope you both enjoyed your morning."

"Fine," said Wills, shortly.

Tad didn't answer. He was staring at Rayvn, who had finally left the sitting room and was in the foyer inspecting the tea and coffee station as though she'd never seen anything like it. She clutched the enormous novel to her chest.

"*Who* is *that*?" asked Tad.

"Allow me to introduce you," said Helen.

Whitney entered behind her cousins. She had on a long, unstructured, grey cotton shift with buttons down the length of both sides and a thin white shirt underneath. Her feet were encased in dove-grey flats in soft leather.

"Ms. Varga," said Helen. "Welcome. I'm just making introductions."

By this time, Rayvn had turned around to face them, still holding on to her novel like a child with a favourite stuffy.

The four cousins faced off.

"Ms. Rayvn Wildwood," Helen began.

"At your service," she said cheerfully, but when she saw her cousins' hard expressions, her heavily lined eyes widened with alarm.

"Ms. Whitney Varga," continued Helen.

Whitney briefly took Rayvn's hand before dropping it.

"And Mr. Wills Todd and Mr. Thaddeus Todd."

They, too, shook Rayvn's hand with all the enthusiasm of people asked to take turns holding a dead trout.

"So," said Rayvn, smiling at Tad, "do people call you Tad? Tad Todd?"

"Hilarious," said Tad. "What a fresh and original sense of humour you have."

"Sorry, I was just—"

"Thaddeus was my mother's father's name. It was very important to the family that his name be handed down." His expression remained one of unwavering hostility.

"I sort of like it," said Rayvn. "It's cheerful."

"It's perfectly ridiculous," said Wills to his brother. "Your middle name is Nevin. I don't know why you won't use it. You could avoid these painfully predictable conversations with dull-witted people."

The brothers glared balefully at each other and then at Rayvn.

"I suppose we can't all have tasteful names like Rayvn," said Tad. "With a name like that, if you become an exotic dancer, you won't even need a stage name. Perhaps you're already employed in that field?" His eyes raked up and down his cousin, coming to rest on her bustier.

Rayvn's soft, round face with its pallor and red lips and dark eyeliner and smoky eyeshadow evinced no hurt feelings or shock. She stared steadily at Tad Todd until he looked away.

Helen kept her expression pleasant and neutral and reminded herself that everyone was dying and so was she.

This test would have been simpler if Edna's values had included an appreciation for pettiness and sniping and sarcasm.

"Where on earth did they find *you*?" asked Wills.

One of a butler's main jobs is to make everyone comfortable. A good butler does this by anticipating everyone's needs. A great butler does it by anticipating everyone's needs while remaining so unobtrusive as to be nearly invisible. In this instance, Helen decided to forgo greatness.

"I'm terribly sorry to interrupt," said Helen. "I don't want your lunch to get cold. It's traditional here at the Institute to serve luncheon buffet-style."

Tad rolled his eyes. "Just like we did for dinner last night? Whoopee."

"Let's just do it," said Wills.

"Hope the plates are big," said Rayvn. "It's always so embarrassing to have to go up like four times."

"Oh gawd," said Tad.

"Please come this way." Helen led them into the serving room.

Nigel stood at the end of the butcher block table.

"Nigel will be pleased to answer any questions and explain today's menu," said Helen.

"We can read the cards," said Tad. "Good lord. So formal. Talk about polishing a pig's ass."

"It looks spectac," said Rayvn. "What've you got for us, Nige?"

The three cousins gaped at their strange cousin, apparently shocked at her easy manner with the help.

Then in a repeat of the night before, Nigel attempted to recite the menu, while Wills and Tad ignored him and started serving themselves. Whitney and Rayvn listened until the end.

"Sounds lovely," said Whitney. "Thank you, uh, Nigel, is it?"

He nodded.

"No meat?" asked Rayvn.

"The Yatra Institute is vegetarian," said Helen. "We sometimes serve locally caught seafood or fish."

"Look, they'll get us meat if we request it," said Tad, who stopped on his way back to the dining room. "It's their *job*. If you ask for a hot dog, they have to get you one."

Whitney gave Helen an apologetic look. "I'm vegetarian so this is perfect."

This earned her a foul look from Wills and Tad.

As the guests carried their plates to the dining room, Helen wondered briefly what she should do if they began making requests that violated the Institute's ethos. There would be no pig roasts on the beach. No plastics smouldering in burn barrels. Helen had to hope they would find their way clear to enjoying vegetarian food and healthy living.

And on the plus side, she liked Rayvn, and Whitney was odd, but at least she read Thich Nhat Hanh. Glimmers of hope in the midst of all the strangeness.

Part 2

THE PROGRAMS

Chapter 17

NIGEL OWENS

All of us went into the garden thirty minutes before the first course was to start. We stood there watching while the flower-arranging guy did yoga.

I asked the new chef what was happening, and she said she thought he was doing sun salutations.

The butlers were looking and acting extremely butlerish. They didn't react when the little teacher guy, who had on a super-clean white apron over his shirt and vest, did yoga push-ups right on the chip path. After each push-up, he arched his back, shot up to his feet, touched his toes, touched his knees, then put his hands in the air like he was trying to flag down a cloud. It seemed like a lot of work.

"Do you think he's worried about getting his apron dirty?" I said, but quiet, so he wouldn't hear me and feel embarrassed. Helen gave me this look of, like, extreme kindness that made me want to shut up. Maybe I don't need to point stuff out all the time.

When the flower teacher was finished doing his sun salutes, he pointed his hands in prayer at the sky, then he pointed them at the apple tree with the hummingbird nest in it, like he was doing the *Charlie's Angels* two-handed gun grip.

"This tree, this nest," he said in a voice that was surprisingly loud, "will be our inspiration. May all the work I do with the students of the bloom result in beauty and insight into all dimensions for all beings. Metta, metta, metta."

Gavin and Murray nodded in unison. Helen bowed and clasped her hands like one of those yoga teachers on Instagram. Me and Chef Leticia looked at each other, which was nice. Because it was some weird shit.

The flower teacher came dashing over to us.

"Our work will commence at two. We will break at four."

Everyone nodded. The students were only doing a half day, but it was shaping up to be plenty intense.

The teacher turned and looked at Chef Leticia.

"I must warn you that they may be too excited, too caught up in personal growth, to eat. Perhaps even too excited to sit still for medita-tion or to focus on dance. They may not even be able to sleep. Such is the transformative power of the floral learning journey."

"Of course," said Helen. Something about the way she said it made me think that the students would probably be fine to eat and dance and meditate.

"Please let us know if you need anything," said Gavin, really gra-cious as usual. Man, I would give a lot to be half as elegant as that guy.

Then the flower teacher went sprinting over to the big work table under the apple tree. He looked at all the stuff laid out on it, handouts with illustrations and technical terms, a whole bunch of vases and containers we'd put out for him, gardening gloves for everyone, these vicious-looking spiked things Gavin called flower frogs, clear tape, some kind of putty, wire, a bunch of shears and scissors, and tubes.

He ran his hands over the length of the table as though he was magicking the supplies.

"Yes, I certainly will. This. Is. Marvellous." He turned so his back was to us. He was really using the whole stage. I'm also theatrical, so I appreciated his technique.

"Marvellous!" he said again. "Don't you agree?"

"Yes," we said to his back. "Marvellous."

"And now I will retire to the flower shed until it is time for me to make my entrance. *Avec des fleurs!*"

With that, he went zipping off into the little garden shed like an actor going backstage before the performance.

At eleven, the guests stood around, each looking unhappy in their own way, except for Rayvn, who seemed pretty at ease. She'd changed into a bright-red velvet dress with a full skirt with some kind of padding at the butt, and a massive brown leather belt, which was even more excellent than the camo outfit. I love a woman who knows how to dress.

The four of them turned to stare when the floral guy came striding out of the shed, which is so covered in some kind of flowering vine plant that it looks like it might fall over. It's all very BBC.

The instructor had a white bucket over each arm. One was stuffed with flowers and the other one was full of different kinds of greenery. He looked BBC, too.

The four guests stared at him, probably because he was so energetic that the air around him seemed like it was full of sparks.

"Welcome!" said the flower guy. "Welcome to your journey into bloom. Leave all your preconceptions at the garden gate. Be prepared to shock yourself as you learn that it is possible to arrange your inner flower!"

"Holy Christ on the cross," whispered the guy who'd tried to buy drugs from me. "I need a drink."

I don't think the flower teacher heard him.

Helen, who'd been waiting off to the side in that quiet way of hers, stepped forward. "Good morning, everyone. I am so pleased to introduce your instructor, Jenson Kiley."

Jenson smiled and dipped his head like he was very royal, but also extremely humble about it.

"We are so fortunate to have Jenson here with us. His Arranging Your Inner Flower course has been a favourite here at the Yatra Institute for many years. Students come from all over the world to take his program."

"One might say I'm a perennial favourite?" said Jenson. I'd never heard an actual chortle before, but I'm sure that's the name for the sound he made.

"Yes," agreed Helen. "Exactly."

Tad rolled his eyes. Rayvn gave a big smile. Her lipstick matched her dress exactly. There was also a bit of lipstick on her teeth, which I wanted to mention to her, but I didn't want to embarass her.

"Mr. Kiley has done custom designs for the Kennedy Center for the Performing Arts, the Met Gala, and countless high-profile weddings, including that of Sheikha Mahra bint Mohammed bin Mualla."

"She asked for me by name," said Jenson Kiley. "I was *so* flattered!" He sounded like a cat purring when he spoke.

"In addition, he is the preferred floral designer for several major performing artists and actors."

"But not Madonna. I could never work for someone who loathes hydrangeas. Imagine loathing any flower! We must be inclusive and see the beauty in everything from the dandelion to the orchid."

"He has won national and international floral design awards, including the America's Cup of Floral Design and the Florist World Cup," Helen continued.

"Oh pshaw, Helen. You do go on!" chided Jenson in a happy voice.

As the list of all Jenson Kiley's accomplishments and whatnot got more and more impressive, the guests started to pay attention, even the brothers.

"So please join me in thanking Jenson Kiley for bringing his extraordinary gifts to share with us today."

Helen clapped and so did the rest of us.

The florist looked like he was about to die of pleasure.

"I am *so* thrilled, *so* filled with joy, to be here with you today. Thank you, Helen, for that warm and wonderfully detailed introduction. It's fate that brings us together today and I send my condolences to each of you and to the universe at the loss of Ms. Edna Todd, one of the finest and most gifted, spiritually oriented floral artists I've ever known."

He hung his head for about ten seconds, like a conductor who'd forgotten the song. Then the head came up and he went on. "But it's not fate that will determine the course of your studies in bloom. Oh no."

He swept his arms up from his sides, and now, instead of looking like a conductor, he looked like he could front a death metal band. Like I said, the man is theatrical.

"It's hard work! It's fierce seeking! It's beauty and truth. These are the bywords of the true floral educator."

There was an extremely long pause that went on so long it got awkward. Then he finally let his arms fall back to his sides and continued. "As we teach you to arrange your inner bloom, what we are really doing is asking you to become floral communicators."

Tad and Wilson had these very suspicious looks on their faces.

Whitney looked like she didn't know what was happening, and Rayvn seemed to be enjoying herself enough for all four of them.

"Please, sit down and we will begin," said Jenson, pointing to the work table. "But one moment, please!" The guests paused.

"For this first task, I am going to ask for help from the butlers."

"Butlers?" said Tad. "There's more than one?"

"Gavin? Murray? Helen? May we ask for your help?" asked Jenson.

"You're *all* butlers?" demanded Tad, like they'd been keeping that information from him intentionally.

"Yes, sir," said Gavin.

"Oh, for *god's* sake," said Tad, genuinely outraged for some bizarre reason. I can't think of anything better than multiple butlers. I really can't.

"Can you believe our good fortune!" cried Jenson Kiley. "The only other time I've come across a household with multiple genuine butlers in residence was at the earl's estate in the South of France. And in that instance, the butlers were there with their principals because it was a gathering of the absolutely most exclusive people." He gave this little look at the students like he didn't think they were in that category. At all. "There were four private jets on the private runway. Two private helicopters. Four certified butlers. You have never seen such service." He sighed. "As I was saying, Helen, might we prevail upon you and your colleagues to help us get started?"

"Of course," she said.

"Excellent! Gavin, I assign you to work with Whitney."

At this news, Whitney seemed to stand up taller and straighten her shoulders. It's not surprising. The guy is seriously handsome and chiselled and all that.

"Murray, will you assist Wills?" I made a note to myself that his name wasn't Wilson.

"Of course, sir," said Murray.

"Helen, you will work with Tad."

Tad looked even more butt-faced at the news, if you'll excuse the expression.

"And Nigel, you will help Rayvn."

Obviously, I won the helping lottery, but I'm not a registered butler, so it didn't really seem fair.

"Um, sir?" I said. "I'm not a butler. I'm more of a . . ."

"House boy?" said Tad, who really takes his commitment to being an asshole seriously.

"You are going to be perfect," said Jenson, which I appreciated. I also felt better when Rayvn gave me a warm smile, lipsticked teeth and all.

The students sat in the four chairs around the big table and we stood behind them, and I'll be the first to admit that Jenson Kiley was an exceptional teacher, or as he puts it, floral educator.

It was a perfect day. The sky was blue with a few white clouds chugging along. The sun was warm but not too hot, and if you don't mind me getting a bit poetic, the garden seemed to be caressing us in this pleasant way.

Jenson gave us what he called a potted history of floral design and how it developed in France, the UK, the Netherlands, Asia, and North America and then explained what he called the fundamentals of shape and height and colour.

"A floral arrangement should complement the home and surroundings. It should be designed to fit the space where it will stand, whether it is the centrepiece for a table, a tall arrangement for a vestibule, or a hand-tied bouquet for someone special. Every arrangement is an expression of what is in your heart, and it should take into account the history and nature of the flowers you choose."

While he spoke to us, Jenson Kiley started making a flower arrangement, almost like an afterthought. He told us the names of the stuff he was using: curly willow and Solomon's seal with little white bells hanging down, white tulips, white ranunculus, and what he said were the first white peonies of the season. He cut the stems and organized everything by height and colour. He said the willow gave his arrangement drama, which it totally did.

"Now, you see the shape we've got here?" he said, showing how the Solomon's seal had a "wavelike quality," leading into the "density of beauty" of the flowers, which he said he "intentionally massed in three tiers."

Jenson Kiley worked so quickly and with so much confidence that watching him was a little like being hypnotized.

"*Et voilà*, darlings!" said Jenson when he was done.

It was the most beautiful flower arrangement I ever saw. At first, I wondered if I was so impressed because I don't know anything about flowers, but when I looked around, Tad, Wills, Whitney, and Rayvn looked just as stunned. Even Gavin and Murray stared, also blown away. Helen had this little Cheshire Buddhist smile.

"My god," said Tad.

"That is absolutely breathtaking," said Whitney.

Wills let out a loud breath.

"Egads," whispered Rayvn, which I appreciated for its flair.

"Do you know why I can make such creations so quickly?" asked Jenson.

The students all shook their heads.

"Because I have studied. I have read. I see what is in the raw materials offered to us by each flower, by each stem, by each leaf. If you truly understand what is in your heart, you will create floral design that is a reflection of the deepest parts of you."

Now all the students were nodding. Rayvn, who I was now thinking of as "my" student, looked about ready to levitate. I could relate.

"Please take a dictionary," instructed Jenson.

The butlers slid the nearest books toward their students and I did the same.

"I have provided an assortment of Victorian flower dictionaries, an Asian dictionary, and one from the Netherlands. Every person should own at least one flower dictionary."

"Uh, obviously," whispered Rayvn.

"Now I know you are all dying to make full-length ballgowns out of pink carnations from an English garden and roses grown on the banks of Lake Malawi. In time, children. In time. Today, we will start with a more modest task. We're going to make tussie-mussies. These arrangements date back to the fourteenth century and are composed of flowers and foliage chosen in part for their meaning," said Jenson.

"Can't you just feel yourself getting smarter," whispered Rayvn, putting into words exactly what I was feeling.

"The meanings behind flowers and foliage are taken from mythology, herbal lore, art, and literature, and from the physical aspects of the individual plants. Most have multiple associations. And the Victorians loved to send small bouquets that could express things that could not be said out loud. The tussie-mussie is really a form of cryptological communication. Isn't that just wonderful!"

Jenson picked a bunch of basil from one of the buckets. "Basil, for instance, means 'best wishes' in Italy, 'hatred' in Greece, and 'sacred' in India.

"Traditionally, a tussie-mussie is accompanied by a note describing the meaning of each plant in the arrangement. Such notes were used to avoid misunderstandings.

"Before we break for lunch, I'd like us each to look up the plants we have available here and use them to make a tussie-mussie or two. We will display them around the lodge and cabins with our description cards. The effect will be absolutely charming. You have your butlers to help." Jenson gave me a look. "Or at least you will have a helper. And I am here to consult."

With that, the four students and their helpers began to read the books and look at the plants in the buckets.

I was trying to look useful when Rayvn poked me in the arm.

"I need one that means 'don't kill me in my sleep,'" she said. "For those two."

She glanced at Tad and Wills, who were stuffing little purple flowers—irises, I think—into their bouquets. The way Helen and Murray handed them shears and bits of raffia reminded me of surgical nurses on a battlefield.

"I'll see if I can find something," I told her.

I was leafing through the book when the entry for irises caught my eye. I read it and pushed it over so Rayvn could read.

"It says here that the ancient Greeks used to plant purple irises on the graves of deceased women, so the goddess Iris could lead them to heaven," she said. "That seems appropriate, since we're here due to a lady who died. Good choice."

Before I could say anything else, Jenson Kiley showed up beside us.

"You're deeply witchy," he said to Rayvn. "Show it." Then he went striding off.

Rayvn watched him go. "This situation is completely insane and my cousins are scary. But it's all going to work out, right?"

I nodded quickly. "Definitely." And I handed her a sprig of something that I thought might be parsley.

Chapter 18

Helen took a break after Tad's third demand that she assess the symmetry of his tussie-mussie. She went inside and found a message from Officer Rosedale on her phone. She went to the office and called him right back.

"Thank you for returning my call," Helen said. "As I said in my message, I'm here at the Institute handling some, uh, matters pertaining to Edna Todd's passing."

"Right, right. I'm sorry it's taken me a while to get back to you. I've been in court on another case. Ms. Todd's lawyer, Devon Lest, told me it was fine to speak with you. I'll tell you what I can." Rosedale's voice was guarded but polite.

"As Mr. Lest probably told you, I'm the executor for Ms. Edna's estate. Well, part of her estate."

"Part?"

"It's a bit complicated." Helen waited for him to say that the lawyer had explained what she was doing, but he didn't, so she continued. "I was the lodge manager here at the Institute for several years. Shortly after I arrived back, I received a note."

"Yes?"

"The writer said they were Ms. Edna's death doula."

Officer Rosedale didn't answer.

"Do you know about this?" she asked.

"About death doulas?"

"Yes."

"I've heard of the concept," he said.

"Did you know Ms. Edna had one?" asked Helen, uncomfortable to find herself questioning the officer.

He was so taciturn he could have given some of the most silent monks she'd known competition.

"Perhaps you should tell me exactly what you found," he said.

"It might be fastest to read it to you."

"All right," said Officer Rosedale.

Helen took the note from the desk where she'd stored it and read it to him.

"I see," said Officer Rosedale. "Where did you find it?"

"A colleague brought it inside. It was in the garden."

"Colleague?"

"A student from my graduating class who is helping out here."

"Oh?" he said.

Helen sighed inwardly but not into the receiver.

"Two friends from school are here with me."

"Is that right?"

"Yes."

"What kind of school?"

"Butler school," she said, dreading the commentary sure to follow. But there was none.

"Someone came onto the property to leave you this note?" he said.

"Yes. But that's not unusual. People are quite accustomed to doing that, at least when the lodge is open."

"Hmm," said Officer Rosedale.

"The other thing I wanted to mention is that some of her journals are missing. Specifically, the ones from the last few months."

Rosedale said nothing.

"I'm wondering if you took them. As part of your investigation?"

"We didn't take any journals," he said.

"She wrote in a journal every night for as long as I knew her. She'd done it since she was in her teens."

Officer Rosedale didn't respond.

"If she was planning to take her life, I'm sure she'd have journaled about it."

"We interpreted the death literature and explanatory forms on her side table as the equivalent of a suicide note. Have you looked everywhere for her journals?"

"Just her office."

He heaved a sigh into the receiver. "I'm not due to visit Sutil for another several days. I have six islands to visit before then. But I'll try to get there earlier. Have you read the medical examiner's notes?"

"No," said Helen.

"The M.E. was clear about the factors that led to Ms. Todd's, uh, decision," said Officer Rosedale. "Meditating too much. Being alone for too long. Belonging to the Right to Die group. Means and opportunity. But you're welcome to speak with the M.E. yourself."

"Thank you," said Helen, who wasn't sure she wanted to go that far. She did not relish the role of amateur detective. She had enough to do already, and she knew that she had a tendency to be suspicious. It was a part of herself that she found difficult. But the police officer was already giving her the doctor's name and contact information. Helen wrote it down and then ran a hand over the polished desk. "From what you've said, it seems this doctor has some strong feelings about the rational suicide movement *and* meditation."

"I don't share those prejudices. My dad died of Lou Gehrig's a few years ago. We were grateful he had the choice, even if he didn't take it."

Helen stared at the blank walls of the office.

"Ms. Thorpe, you knew Edna. What do you think? Could she have simply decided to go without telling you or anyone else?" asked Officer Rosedale.

"Transition," said Helen.

Helen considered for a moment before answering. "I don't know," she said. If she was being perfectly honest, she thought it was unlikely and she really, really didn't like the implications of that thought. Right speech, she reminded herself. Right speech was kind, true, and necessary. Her fears about Edna's death were not kind and possibly not true. But maybe they were necessary to speak aloud. "It doesn't make sense to me. Based on what I know of Edna."

"And you knew her well?"

"I was not just her lodge manager. I was also her spiritual adviser in many respects."

"Mr. Lest mentioned that you used to be a nun," said Officer Rosedale.

"Yes. I met Edna at my monastery, and after I left, I came to work for her. We knew each other well enough that she asked me to decide who should take over the lodge if she hadn't made the decision before she died."

Another long pause. "Is that right?" A thin edge of suspicion had crept into his voice.

"I'm in the process of deciding. Using Ms. Edna's criteria."

"And what is that criteria?"

Helen cleared her throat. "Ms. Edna prized a number of spiritual qualities."

"Such as?"

She decided she was not up to explaining the brahmavihāras to him. "Kindness, joy, emotional stability, compassion."

"Those seem like good things," he said. "Can you give the place to anyone?" Pause. "For instance, are you eligible?"

Helen laughed, relieved to be able to say no. "I have to decide between Ms. Edna's great-nieces and -nephews."

"How exactly are you evaluating their kindness and whatnot?"

"It was Edna's wish that they take three educational programs that are aimed at revealing a person's values."

"Who is paying for all this?" asked Rosedale.

"The estate. Via Ms. Edna's lawyers. She had it all set up."

"Do these people, the great-nieces and -nephews, *know* they're being judged?"

"I was asked not to share that part."

Even longer pause.

"That is the strangest thing I've heard all week and I am police for seven different Gulf Islands," said Rosedale. "I will be there as soon as possible. Please call if anything comes up. And Ms. Thorpe?"

"Please call me Helen."

"Helen. I think you should be a bit careful. You've got yourself a highly unusual situation there. Could be a bit of a pressure cooker."

"Yes," she said. "It is."

They hung up and Helen sat still in her chair for a long time.

Chapter 19

By dinnertime, the wind had picked up and a persistent rain began to fall. The temperature dropped ten degrees, putting the run on the young summer. Sudden gusts of wind drove the rain slantwise into the windows, where it trickled down in moody rivulets. Startlingly fast shifts from fine weather to bad were common on the island.

The chill and damp outside made the coziness inside the lodge all the more inviting.

Wills, Tad, and Whitney entered the lodge together. They shook off their umbrellas and pushed back hoods of expensive raincoats.

Murray, Gavin, Nigel, and Helen stood in the foyer with their hands behind their backs, and Gavin stepped forward and offered to take their wet coats.

Tad made a big show of surprise.

"Well, well, well," he said. "A coat check service! Things have gotten so fancy around here at old Yahtzee. Three butlers and a coat check!" He behaved as though he'd never set eyes on Gavin before.

"Do you ever stop?" Whitney looked around. "Where is Jenson?"

"He is taking dinner in his room. I believe he's preparing for tomorrow. He doesn't dine with the guests while he's teaching."

Wills extended his lower lip. "Not a bad teacher, really. Interesting material. Well presented. I was impressed." It was obvious that compliments didn't come easily to him, which made Helen appreciate them even more.

"Agreed," said Tad. "Overall, so far this is not as hideous as I expected."

"You two are ridiculous. We are being taught floral design by a genius," said Whitney, simply. "I don't know when I've ever been so inspired."

The three of them gravitated to the side table where four tussie-mussies were displayed, along with their explanatory cards.

"I see that we all focused on mourning flowers," said Wills.

"We're here for a sad occasion," said Whitney. "It makes sense."

"Yes, but it wasn't until I started working with the plants that I felt a sense of that," said Wills. "I suppose there's a chance I'm not emotionally in touch with myself."

Helen tried not to let the shock show on her face. One hand-held bouquet and they were showing signs of insight and vulnerability? It was a miracle. Once again, she marvelled at how Yatra's offerings had an uncanny ability to tease flexibility out of the rigid and depth out of the shallow.

"It's sad, but it's not a bloody gothic tragedy," said Tad. He was staring at Rayvn's tussie-mussie, which she'd made out of broken tulips, dead leaves, a small dogwood branch, and a single bent anemone. The little bouquet looked ravaged and somehow also ravishing. The card, in Rayvn's uneven hand, read "Mortality, Melancholy, Sacrifice, and Forsakenness."

"Cheery, isn't it?" said Rayvn, entering the lodge and peeling off her drenched camouflage jacket. She'd changed into an outfit that made it look as though she'd just spent three days on the couch watching Netflix. Her stained black track pants were bagged out at the knee and her oversized T-shirt read "Meanness and Spite and Nothing Else Nice."

"Jesus," said Tad. "We're in a rustic setting, but we still have eyes."

Rayvn looked down.

"May I take your coat?" asked Gavin, smoothly pretending he hadn't heard Tad.

"Good evening," said Helen, to the sopping-wet girl. "I hope you enjoyed your afternoon."

"Fell asleep as soon as the class was over. All that fresh air is a shock to the system," said Rayvn, as she handed her camo jacket to Gavin. "I'm a sleeper."

"Would you like me to find you a rain jacket?" asked Helen.

Surprise crossed Rayvn's face. "You'd do that? Wow. Thank you. That would be amazing. I forgot about rain when I was planning my clothes. I don't do the outdoors that much, so . . ."

"Women's medium?" Helen guessed.

"You're good," said Rayvn, as amazed as if Helen had guessed the precise number of jelly beans in a huge jar.

Gavin came back from hanging the jacket and handed her a towel.

"Cool," said Rayvn. "I should have gone back to my cabin for the umbrella, but once I was out the door, I was committed. I hate to walk more steps than I need to. I could wear myself out. You know how it is."

Helen didn't know, but she nodded.

Rayvn wiped the water off her face, briefly towelled her hair, and then draped the towel over her shoulders, as though she was in a sauna. All the while, her cousins stared. There was something compelling about how Rayvn moved. A quality of unselfconsciousness that drew the eye.

"Let me take that for you," said Helen, taking the towel.

With obvious reluctance, Rayvn joined Tad, Wills, and Whitney in front of the tussie-mussies and the four of them stood in silence, until Whitney asked Rayvn where she was from.

"Nanaimo," said Rayvn.

Whitney nodded hesitantly, as though she'd feared as much.

Murray asked Rayvn if she'd like a drink.

"Could I have a Mountain Dew Me?"

Helen could see Murray consulting her mental database of drinks, which was extensive.

"Mountain Dew and triple sec and melon liqueur and pineapple juice," said Gavin.

"You know it?" breathed Rayvn. "Hardly anyone does. I had it at this bar in Kamloops. It's so sweet it makes your teeth fall out but it's awesome."

"Allow me," said Gavin. "It's been some time since I've had the opportunity to make one."

"How old *are* you?" asked Tad, managing to put maximum skepticism into his voice.

"Twenty-two," said Rayvn. "Almost."

Tad turned around and sighed so hard, the broken tulips in Rayvn's tussie-mussie swayed.

Helen was pleased that she'd decided to condense the cocktail hour into a half hour so the cousins wouldn't have to endure each other for any longer than necessary. Too many drinks and they would not be able to dance, much less meditate later. And after today, there would be no more alcohol until the end of the programs.

Despite the signs of introspection before Rayvn entered the room, the cousins went back to being unpleasant. Tad sneered, Wills guzzled his drinks, Whitney moped. Rayvn looked like she wanted to go back to sleep.

Helen thought again of the task. She was supposed to decide which of these four people should take over Edna's life work of caring for a rare and profoundly eccentric place designed to educate peculiar and sensitive people in matters environmental and spiritual. The brahmavihārās, or four divine abodes of loving-kindness, empathetic joy, compassion, and equanimity, were to be her guides. Thus far she could locate little evidence of those qualities in any of the candidates. Instead, they were like embodiments of the hindrances that, in Buddhism, are the things preventing people from growing in their meditation practice and spiritual attainments. The Five Hindrances—greed and sensory desire, ill will, sloth and torpor, restlessness and worry, and doubt—were, Helen knew, experienced by most people, but each of Edna's potential heirs seemed more afflicted with them than your average bear.

Helen reminded herself not to live in the future. Focus on the signs of growth. Still, tension sat across her shoulders like an overbearing man's arm. What was she supposed to do if the potential heirs were all completely unsuitable? Officer Rosedale's words of caution rang around in her head. What if one of them had something to do with Edna's death? It was a thought she hadn't allowed into her head before, but it landed with a thump that suggested it wasn't going anywhere. The situation was making her paranoid.

Gavin returned with the lurid yellow drink and Helen wondered what had possessed him to lay in the ingredients needed to make such a concoction. Helen was strong on many points of butlering, such as being a calming, nearly invisible presence and noticing what needed to be done, but she wasn't good at predicting alcoholic beverages, never having been a drinker or a habitué of drinking establishments.

Murray discreetly ushered the cousins into the small sitting room, where an arbutus log burned bright and fragrant. Helen went to check that all was on track with Chef Leticia, who had been moving about the kitchen in contemplative silence. Chef Leticia would have been a spectacular chef for the long, silent retreats that had always been Helen's favourite part of the programming at the Institute.

After finding everything going smoothly, Helen quietly instructed Nigel to bring Jenson Kiley the evening's menu so the florist could choose his meal. Then she returned to the sitting room, where she found Wills and Tad deep in conversation about what an imposition it was to be at the Institute, while Rayvn read her damp Stephen King novel, and Whitney stared pensively out at the dark evening.

"Incredibly gauche of Great-Aunt Edna to make us do this," said Tad. "Her spirit must be lurking offstage like some sort of twisted . . ." Tad struggled to find a comparison.

"Impresario?" offered Wills.

"Exactly," said Tad. "This entire set-up is like a down-market theatrical production. Agatha Christie put on by an abysmal amateur playhouse."

Gavin entered and gave Wills his drink, which Wills accepted as though he was doing everyone a favour.

"What's that?" Tad asked.

"Johnny Walker Blue, sir," said Gavin.

"For god's sake," said Tad. "That's three hundred dollars a bottle!"

Gavin didn't reply.

"Good to know you butlers are so free with Edna's funds," continued Tad. "Whatever pittance she had left after running this place into the ground." Helen didn't mention that the bar at the Institute had always been stocked with expensive items. Edna wasn't much of a drinker and alcohol wasn't served to guests of the lodge, but Edna sometimes entertained in the off-season and she liked to be able to offer her friends "something decent."

Wills took a sip, while Gavin waited with the small carafe of distilled water at the ready.

Wills finally seemed to notice him again. "You really are a proper butler." He held out his glass and Gavin poured in a small amount of water. Helen had learned at the Academy that some serious whiskey drinkers believe that drinking scotch neat numbs the taste buds, so they added distilled water a bit at a time so the full flavour could be absorbed. She admired Gavin's ability to address the vast spectrum of needs among this peculiar collection of drinkers.

Whitney had a glass of white wine and Tad had a beer.

"Can I offer you another beverage?" Gavin asked Rayvn after her cousins had watched with fascination and suppressed glee as she gulped down the Mountain Dew cocktail like a marathon runner at the Gatorade station.

"Yes. One hundred more, please," she said. "Just kidding. One is enough."

At this the cousins looked disappointed.

Helen felt herself wanting to linger in the sitting room so she could listen to the conversation between the guests, but instead she retreated to the kitchen with the staff, who gathered around to go over the final instructions for service.

When Chef Leticia indicated that it was time, Helen asked Nigel to ring the large bell to announce dinner. The bell was a lodge tradition and it was so loud that Helen asked Nigel to go outside on the porch to ring it so as not to deafen everyone inside.

When Helen entered the sitting room to escort the guests into the dining room, she thought she heard Whitney whisper "thank god."

Inside the dining room, the corner table had been covered with a blue-and-white antique French cloth. Fresh flowers and apple blossom boughs and a handmade blue bowl filled with green crabapples formed the centrepiece. White candles of different heights flickered, illuminating the crystal and silverware.

Murray had created the table design for the evening and chosen Edna's Bernardaud Jardin Indien dinnerware. The dinner and salad plates were decorated with botanical illustrations of rare plants from Mumbai, and platters and jugs and other pieces were covered in graphic patterns. The elaborately set table was arrestingly pretty.

The nieces and nephews were quiet for a long moment as they gazed at the table.

"This is absolutely gorgeous," said Whitney, finally.

"We're so glad you like it," said Helen.

She showed them to their seats, and then Tad broke the spell. "Helen, after we've finished the classes, will we find out who is inheriting this place? Is that the idea here?"

"Shhh," said Whitney. "Not now."

"Why not now?" demanded Tad. "This *is* some sort of bizarre competition, isn't it?"

Wills was distracted by the dinnerware. "Tad? Did you know that the old lady had taste like this?" he asked. "It's *not* half bad."

"That reminds me," said Tad. "When you and your butlers have time, Thorpe, we'd like an inventory of all the dishes and silverware. *S'il vous plaît.*"

Helen saw Murray stiffen when Tad used her last name.

"These plates must cost a boatload, eh," said Rayvn, holding up the yellow-rimmed plate with a rattan trompe l'oeil pattern inspired by Indian furniture design.

"I love the individual menus," said Whitney, drawing a finger over the cardboard card at her place. "So elegant for a private dinner."

"We've brought in a chef who will be creating your dinners for the rest of your stay," said Helen as she and Gavin poured each guest a glass of the very dry champagne Gavin had chosen to accompany the appetizer course. "And for this dinner, we'll be doing table service."

They tasted the champagne and murmured their appreciation.

"Well, since we're here, I suppose I should give a toast," said Tad. "May we all prosper as we deserve."

"Hear, hear," said Wills, staring at his brother with a strange expression. Whitney and Rayvn chimed in, "Hear, hear!" They clinked glasses.

Helen and Murray went back to the kitchen where Nigel and Gavin waited. Each of them took a warm plate that held two Fanny Bay oysters wrapped in thin strings of crispy potatoes. The oysters rested atop a small bed of marinated spiralized apple and kohlrabi and cabbage.

The staff members lined up behind Helen, and they walked single file into the dining room.

"My goodness," said Whitney, when she saw them.

Nigel and the three butlers each stood behind a guest and set down their plates in unison. When Helen put down Rayvn's plate, the girl craned her neck and offered up the thrilled look of a child who's just been offered something she's really, really not supposed to have. Helen resisted the urge to wink at her.

"Nicely done," said Wills, reluctantly. "I don't know when I last saw true French service."

"There was nothing like this when we came here as kids," said Tad.

"God no," said Wills. "It was all graham crackers and dried-out hunks of tofu. Maybe that was just Nanny hogging all the good stuff for herself."

Helen and Gavin moved quickly around the room, pouring each guest more champagne.

When they were done, Helen and the others filed out of the dining room to pick up the next course of individual salads of shredded dark-green wakame marinated in ginger, rice vinegar, soy sauce, and fragrant toasted sesame oil, tossed with scallions and topped with tiny, perfect cubes of crisp green apple.

Helen gazed at the line of four salads on the counter with deep satisfaction. The guests were being given every opportunity to move into a state of gratitude, which Edna felt was a state worth pursuing. Perhaps these optimal conditions would allow the guests to experience spiritual shifts. They would reveal their natures to be pure and noble. Or maybe they would continue to act like demanding, entitled brats, incapable of behaving with integrity or decency. And maybe one or more of them was even worse than that. Whatever happened, Helen would be glad when Officer Rosedale arrived and began investigating.

Chapter 20

NIGEL OWENS

Kalaivaani Hall was a long, rectangular building with a high ceiling. There were a lot of windows along one wall. The other wall was covered with fancy hangings of women with a lot of arms and extra eyes, and elephants, and overall, it looked like if a hippie had decorated a super-nice gym. The hall was empty except for us and the students. They sat on the floor in front of the stage area, and I sat with the butlers in chairs at the back. I admit that I liked seeing Wills and Tad having to sit like kindergartners.

We sat there quietly for a while until Wayfarer came out from behind a curtain. These Yatra teachers like to make an entrance.

I don't want to bring the topic around to me and my thoughts, but I have to say one thing. I know my fashion sense is borderline self-defeating. My taste for bold colours and in-your-face patterns gets me attention and it's never exactly the right kind of attention. But what people don't realize is that when you're a super-bad dresser, people *always*, always underestimate you. And it's a smart move to keep expectations low, especially if you're not a high-performing individual.

To put it another way, I look semi-ridiculous and people are mostly nice to me because of it, the same way they're kind to sad clowns and cats with only one eye and half an ear. Aggro dudes don't come after me because there's no a-hole glory in beating down a fat guy wearing red pants and yellow suspenders.

When I saw the dance teacher come prowling out onto the dance floor, I thought she might be doing something similar. Only her thing wasn't looking like a goof. She was dressed like she was a dancer in some rapper's early-career video or like she's the girlfriend of some uber-douchey YouTuber.

Wayfarer had been pretty polite with me when I brought her smoothies and salads and boiled eggs. She came to the door of her cabin in a long, animal-print dressing gown and always smelled strongly of coconut.

But when she came out on the small stage, her tights were full of cut-outs and her top was a bunch of straps that showed as much skin as fabric. And in spite of how powerful she looked, she also didn't seem quite real. I couldn't imagine anyone bothering her, in the same way like if you saw Batman rolling down the street, you'd probably just let him go, no matter how much you'd like to have his autograph.

Gavin has suggested in that very polite way of his that I should wear what he calls "less flamboyant" clothes, so I've been trying. And the plainer my clothes get, the more exposed I feel. I wonder if the dance teacher feels the same when she covers up. But back to the class, which was pretty fucking amazing.

"So," she said, stopping in front of the four students and putting her fists on her hips. She had on bright-white running shoes. "We're here to dance. No just any dance. Devi Dance."

"Debbie dance?" said Tad, who really is a jackass.

"No," said Wayfarer. "Devi. We will dance like shining gods. Show our truest selves, yeah?"

Tad's skinny little shoulders slumped even more than usual.

"Any of you have dance training?" she asked.

I didn't know whether to hope they did or didn't. All I knew was that I didn't want to miss a minute of this thing.

Rayvn and Wills raised their hands about halfway up.

"Ach, you can forget all of it. What we're doing here is no some square dancing or pop and lock. It's no ballet or tap. It's no style at all. Devi Dance is about learning to tap into your own power. The energies of the ancients, like."

I remembered to take a breath.

Whitney raised her hand.

"Yes?" said Wayfarer, like a drill sergeant being interrupted by a potential enlistee's parents. Like it was too soon to bring down the hammer, but the hammer was definitely in sight.

"Isn't using the word *devi* like appropriation of South Asian culture and kind of copying that famous dancer? The one actually named Devi."

Wayfarer fixed her with a glare. "Regina Devi was an American of Indian descent who studied traditional dance forms. And she *was* a fantastic dancer. But I'm using the word *Devi* to mean divine, yeah? And there's no dancing more divine and more devilish than one inspired by Saturday night in Glasgow, the Spirit of William Wallace, and the fury of a Scottish dancer who's been stood up."

At this Whitney shrank back, looking totally bewildered, which was a reasonable response to the word salad Wayfarer had just unleashed.

"I have a thing with my hip. Some pain. I get physio for it—" said Tad, gesturing with his hand.

Wayfarer stared at him like she couldn't have given less of a shit if there was a million-dollar no-shits-given prize.

Tad let his hand drop.

Then Wills, who is apparently not much for taking a hint, put up *his* hand. "We just ate," he said.

Wayfarer glared at him. "That's yer problem. Eat less next time."

Wills put his hand down.

I snuck a glance at the butlers, but they weren't giving anything away.

"Devi Dance is the work of my lifetime. It will be the work of *your* lifetime. Raw power. Primal rage. Desire. Ye no any idea what it is to be truly in your bodies, do you? To be swept into yer bodies' most powerful energies, yeah?"

There was this single spotlight shining down on her where she stood on the wooden platform, which is about a foot or so high. The rest of the hall was just barely lit with some sconces and what was left of the daylight outside.

"I will no be teaching you Way-bo here. That is the dance I invented and have taught to luminaries around the world."

Earlier I'd heard her tell Helen that she didn't need to be introduced. To be specific, she said, "Ah'll do ma own introductions. Tha way they'll pay close attention."

And it was true that we were all paying attention when she explained how what she would be teaching was not a dance style, but rather a "deep, personal body expression."

Tad put his hand up again.

"Will we be expected to memorize steps?" he asked.

"We're no practising for a flash mob in the Mall of America."

"Will there be a performance element?" asked Rayvn.

"Your every move is a performance. And I have to say it could be a lot more impressive, yeah?" said Wayfarer.

The light from outside had almost all leaked away and the windows had turned into mirrors. The dance teacher was going back and forth like a leopard or maybe more like a motivational speaker, sort of like that guy who came to speak to our tenth-grade class about not doing meth, which was ironic because from the way the guy was grinding his teeth, he was on quite a bit of meth at the time. Wayfarer's long black hair was whipping back and forth as she started to sway to the music, which was getting louder in this very exciting way. Kalaivaani has a sweet sound system, actually.

Wayfarer was sort of swooning in front of the students, and then she clamped her arms down to her sides as though that was some clear instruction, which it wasn't since none of the students moved. "Get up, then," she growled at them.

They got up, looking at each other nervously, which I understood because I was pretty nervous, too, at that point.

Wayfarer waved her arms over her head in a seaweed-y way.

The students followed her lead, but they looked more like balloons at a car dealership than kelp in a king tide.

"Thass it," said Wayfarer. "You are moved by the undercurrent of energies that surround ye," she said, her voice loud over the music. "Plant those feet and feel the earth's support, yeah?"

Planted feet was one thing they all seemed good at. They stood in one spot, doing their half-hearted waves. Except for Rayvn, who was giving it her all. The music got louder. It was some sort of Indian-sounding electronica music with bagpipes, which reminded me that

I've never really travelled anywhere. I felt myself swaying a little.

On the stage, Wayfarer strode back and forth, her ridiculously toned arms going in and out like bellows. The students tried to copy her. Wills and Tad were as stiff as members of the British royal family, Whitney was lethargic, and Rayvn looked a bit like an ostrich trying to take flight.

"Catch the beat," said Wayfarer. "Let the body respond!" She began to bend back and forth. One leg rose into the air, impossibly high, until it was over her head. Then she arched her back until one hand trailed on the floor.

It was awesome.

Then she was off, running and leaping from the low stage.

The students, who'd stopped moving when she did the thing with her leg, started dancing harder. Tad tried a few fist pumps and Wills began doing this weird kicking thing. Interestingly, they did look how I imagined drunk Scottish people look right before they get in a fight outside of a pub.

Whitney began to get loose, or at least her version of loose, which was like a cross between interpretive dance and someone trying sign language. And Rayvn was flinging herself around the hall and definitely going to need a chiropractor after.

"Feel it!" yelled Wayfarer, and then she leapt into the air again. "Use the energies swirling inside!" She spun in place so fast I got dizzy looking at her.

In another minute, the students were racing all over the floor, their inhibitions dumped like backpacks after school. It was all going good until Tad punched Wills, who'd been happily stomping around in circles, right in the stomach during one high-speed pass, and Wills doubled over and puked right on the floor. Then Wills straightened up and kicked Tad so hard in the thigh they both fell down into a big old pile of brother-on-brother mayhem.

"Fucking asshole," yelled Tad.

"Yes!" cried Wayfarer. "Feel the rage!" Then she bent over backwards so far her hands touched the ground.

"Keep MOVING!" she bellowed when she straightened up.

The brothers got to their feet and, still giving each other the death stare, went back to stomping and punching around, trying to avoid the vomit. It was way more devilish than I expected.

The music got louder. The students danced harder. Wayfarer came over to us.

"Ach," she said. "Tha didn't take long."

I guess I must have looked startled because she explained. "No uncommon to see skirmishes among family members. It's a powerful practice."

I could tell that even Gavin and Murray were a little shocked, but they said nothing.

"Be a bit careful, okay," Helen told Wayfarer. "These people might be a bit more volatile than your average student."

"Scratch any human behind the ear and you'll end up with molten lava on your finger. Key is to get the red-hot flowing in the right direction."

And then she was off, leaping back into the action. "Devi Dance!" she yelled. "Earth, air, fire, water! Welcome all the elements!"

Strangely, the students didn't seem too affected by the fight. Whitney did some kind of arm-twisty dance and Rayvn was sprawled on the floor, arms and legs thrashing around like a breakdancer having a nervous breakdown. Tad and Wills stormed around the room in tight, furious little circles, coming close but not quite close enough to lash out again.

Everyone was careful not to dance or roll in the puke, so they hadn't completely lost all sense.

I was torn between loving all of it and being a little bit afraid. I looked at Helen and she smiled at me, which was reassuring.

Helen would not be hot lava if scratched. She would be a cool breeze. Or a soft stone in the early afternoon. And a good thing too, because I'm almost certain that if the students weren't supervised, they'd tear each other to shreds and maybe us, too.

Chapter 21

fter the dance experience (Wayfarer's term for her classes) ended and she'd taken the students through some peculiar-looking Kundalini-inspired stretches, Helen took over from her. The students looked half crazed: sweat soaked and slightly stunned. It was a typical response to Wayfarer's teachings.

"Next," Helen told them, "we will sit together and I will lead you through a meditation. But first, you may go outside and take a short walk. Please stay nearby. We'll ring a bell when it's time to come back into the hall."

This time, none of them raised their hands. Instead, they slowly got to their feet, walked to the back of the hall, put on their shoes, and quietly left.

Helen gestured for Gavin, Murray, and Nigel to help her prepare the space for the sit. Gavin got a mop and bucket, and he made short work of the mess on the floor.

Murray put a low table on the riser where Helen would sit to lead the meditation. Then she put up the items for the altar: a stone statue of Buddha, a candle, and a flower arrangement Jenson had made.

Gavin, Murray, and Nigel put out all the things the students might need for their meditation practice: flat zabuton pillows, bean-filled meditation cushions, foam blocks to prop up knees, cotton blankets, and for those who had trouble sitting on the floor, folding chairs behind their spaces.

When the hall was ready and the candle had been lit, Helen slipped to the back of the hall to wait. Nigel rang the bell and Gavin waited at the front of the stage.

The four students stepped inside and hesitantly approached the items laid out for them.

"What's all this for?" asked Tad, too tired to be as peevish as usual.

"Make yourselves comfortable using the items available," Helen instructed. Then Gavin showed them a few of the different ways people sat during meditation.

"Aren't we just supposed to sit like this?" asked Whitney, who sat on her knees directly on the floor.

"If you like," said Gavin.

"Stop showing off," muttered Tad.

"I'm going for cozy!" said Rayvn, who used all the pillows near her and got up to get some more. Then she wrapped a blanket around her waist and put another over her head so she looked like a larva inside a cocoon.

Tad fussed around trying various postures.

Wills sat in the chair after kicking the props away. Then he seemed to think the better of it and pulled a blanket and a cushion closer. "I might need these if it gets cold in here," he said.

"Is everyone warm enough?" asked Gavin. "We can start a fire in the woodstove."

"I'd like that," said Whitney, who was still on her knees without so much as a mat under her and had taken no blanket.

"Even more snuggly!" said Rayvn. "I love meditation so far."

Gavin nodded at Murray, who walked over and quickly lit a match for the stove, which was already prepared. Soon the crackle of the fire filled in the silence of the hall.

Jenson and Wayfarer quietly entered the hall. For once, the two teachers were not emitting the high-pitched frequency of high-flying performers. They took their seats on the cushions they carried inside with zero fanfare. Jenson wore a sweater and Wayfarer had changed into sweats and a hoody and she pulled a large orange scarf over her shoulders.

It was time.

Helen walked to the stage, turned to the Buddha, and bowed three times. Then she settled onto her cushion, took a drink of water, and began.

"Tonight, we will begin our meditations together. We will sit twice a day—each morning before breakfast and once again before bed. We've placed schedules for the rest of our days together in each of your rooms. You will also have a series of interviews with me."

Tad's hand went up. "Why?"

"To see how your meditation practice is going."

He puffed out a breath but didn't say anything else.

"Our sessions together will include dhamma talks and guided meditations," she continued. "Have any of you meditated before?"

Wills and Tad shook their heads. Whitney and Rayvn raised their hands.

"I did Headspace a few times," said Rayvn. "An online meditation app. Gives you guided meditations," she explained.

"I've read a lot about meditation. But I don't really do it," said Whitney.

"I think you'll all find it easier to start with the help of each other. We will work to create supportive conditions for you."

The students didn't look convinced. Helen reminded herself that these were not seekers who had come here wanting to learn meditation. They were here under duress.

"We are going to explore the brahmavihārās," she said. "But first, let's go over the basics."

Helen sat cross-legged, relaxed but upright, and spoke in a calm but authoritative voice.

She instructed them to close their eyes or leave them open just a bit and then to set an intention for their sit.

"It can be anything," she said. "To be aware of your body, to be in touch with your feelings, to be more peaceful."

"To get better returns on your investments," said Tad.

Helen did not respond and her measured tone didn't change.

"Once you have set your intention, we'll do a body scan. Feel where your body touches the earth or the chair. Feel your sit bones, your feet. Allow the earth to hold you."

She could see the students' faces change and soften as they followed her instructions.

"Now, starting at your feet, feel your way up your body. Start with your toes, the tops of your feet, the soles."

She took them all the way through their bodies and then instructed them on how to find and use an anchor.

"An anchor is a place to rest the attention. Some people use the breath. They watch each breath rise and fall and make a note of the pause when one breath ends and another begins. Other people anchor and stabilize their awareness with the hands or with hearing. Pick one and rest your attention there."

"Can we think?" said Rayvn. "I'm worried I won't be able to stop thinking."

Helen smiled, appreciating the honesty of the question.

"Human beings are storytelling machines and so it is natural for us to think. When you catch yourself lost in thought, gently bring the attention back to the anchor. Each time you catch yourself and come back is precious."

"What's the point?" asked Tad.

"Let's try it and maybe we'll find out," said Helen. "For now, please just close your eyes."

Silence fell over the hall. After about ten minutes, the twitching started. Whitney was clearly in pain on the floor.

"If you need to adjust your posture, please do so," said Helen to everyone.

There was some shifting around. Whitney pulled a meditation cushion closer and sat on it.

Helen continued to speak into the warm silence and encourage them to go gently back to their focal objects when she sensed their attention drifting.

Twenty minutes into the sit, Wills was fast asleep, mouth open wide, breath whistling in and out.

Tad and Rayvn went out next. The energy in the room shifted again, leaving a blank where they had been. They all had good reason to be tired, and lethargy was often the first hindrance to meditation. It was all as Helen expected. Whitney continued to shift uncomfortably, but when she was still, she was still in the manner of a branch about to break.

"When you feel yourself drifting off or thinking, make a gentle note about what is happening. You may say to yourself, very quietly, *thinking*. Or perhaps, *sleepy*. If a pain is happening, examine it with curiosity and kindness. Is the sensation warm or cold? Is it moving? If a feeling gets to be too much, find a place in your body that is neutral and turn the attention there."

Wills let out a snore. Tad's head bobbed up and down. Rayvn's blanket cocoon sagged to the side. Whitney fidgeted.

Behind them, Wayfarer and Jenson sat, emanating calm. Stabilizing the space around them.

And behind them, Nigel, Gavin, and Murray also sat quietly in their chairs, eyes closed. Waiting.

Chapter 22

NIGEL OWENS

The next morning, our first full day, things really got rocking, if by rocking you mean I had to get people up to meditate at the ass crack of dawn.

At 5:30 a.m., I had to go all over the property ringing this enormous gong. If I tried something like that at home, someone probably would shoot me.

We should have just let the students sleep in the hall. I'm pretty sure they all slept through the first meditation session anyway.

By the time I got all the way over to the cabins closest to the hall, the guests who were staying at the other end of the property had started shuffling down the path. Except for Rayvn. Her cabin stayed dark.

At first, I thought the gig at the Institute was going to be easy, but yesterday Helen came down with the final schedule and it's a beast.

Schedule

First sit: 6:15–7:30 a.m. (Kalaivaani Hall)

Breakfast: 8:00–9:00 a.m. (Lodge)

Flower Arranging: 9:30–11:30 a.m. (Garden)

Movement: 11:45–12:30 p.m. (Garden)

Lunch: 12: 30–1:30 p.m. (Lodge)

Rest: 1:30–2:30 p.m.

Interviews/Meditative Time: 2:30–3:30 p.m. (Dauber Cottage)*

Personal Reflection: 3:30–5:00 p.m.

Dinner: 5:00–6:00 p.m. (Lodge)

Rest: 6:00–7:30 p.m.

Devi Dance: 7:30–9:00 p.m. (Kalaivaani Hall)

Evening sit: 9:00–10:00 p.m. (Kalaivaani Hall)

See bulletin board for your interview schedule

That is a long-ass day even if it's not exactly chipping rocks in a quarry. For the students, there's only two and a half hours for rest, unless you sleep during the personal reflection time, which I would. I do most of my best personal reflection while I'm asleep. Also, it doesn't seem very spiritual to overwork us like this. But the butlers don't seem to mind.

When Wills and Tad and Whitney had headed for the hall and Rayvn's cabin was still dark, I decided to knock on her door. Nothing. I got on the gong and started banging it. I hit it ten times before a light went on and the door opened a crack.

"What?" she said.

"Meditation in five minutes," I said.

"Oh shit." She shut the door and there was a lot of commotion in her cabin. I retreated off her porch when she came boiling out of there in her pyjamas and slippers, camo coat flapping in the wind as she ran for the hall. I felt pretty good about helping her out since she's the only one I really like.

I didn't get to watch the morning meditation because I was helping Chef in the kitchen. Gavin prepped the dining room and Murray was helping Jenson get ready for the flower class. But whatever happened in the hall seemed to put the guests in a good mood.

They hardly said any shitty stuff to each other at breakfast, even though Tad hates oatmeal and Whitney wished we had this brand of hemp milk that she prefers. I didn't even know you could milk hemp.

At 9:30 sharp, Jenson Kiley started the second flower class. He was dressed exactly the same as the day before and he looked even tidier, which I wouldn't have thought was possible.

"Today," he said. Then he stared toward the ocean, which he couldn't see because of the garden fence.

We watched him. And watched him.

"Today," he continued, finally, "you shall learn what it is that *you* need to communicate through blooms. In our last learning journey, we explored some traditional meanings of flowers and foliage. Now we explore *you*. Not just what you want to say, but who you are and who you want to be."

"Who I am is a person who is on the verge of dying from exhaustion," Rayvn whispered loudly.

Jenson Kiley ignored her. "This morning, you will complete a profound *dharmacize*." He drew out the word so that it sounded like dhaaaaarmaSIIIIIZE. At least, I think that's what he was saying.

"Today we will abide in the realm of the four desires." Jenson started walking back and forth behind the table. He had this huge cedar branch in his hand and he was swishing it back and forth, like he was working himself up for a sword fight that he was for sure going to lose because he only had a cedar branch.

He stopped at one end of the table. He held up his cedar wand, leaned forward, and stared at the students, who were sitting in chairs, watching. "Who among you knows what dharma is?" Jenson snapped his head around to look at Helen as though she'd been trying to get his attention, not standing totally still in that Helenish way of hers. "Don't answer, Helen. You're a ringer."

Whitney put her hand halfway up. Then put it down. Too late. Jenson saw her.

"Yes?" said Jenson. "And allow me to say that I do *love* your outfit. Salwar kameez meets Audrey Hepburn. Absolutely fetching on you. You look like a stock."

She had on this light-yellow tunic kind of thing. It went all the way to her feet, and the sides were open to show that she had on light green pants and silver sandals. It was a very garden-y looking outfit.

"A stock?" said Whitney.

"*Matthiola incana*," he said. "Commonly known as night-scented stock. Heavenly in fragrance and unutterably soft in pastel hue."

Whitney looked happy until she remembered she was supposed to be answering the question.

"Dharma means fate, I think."

"Wrong!" cried Jenson. He seemed overjoyed that she got it wrong. "Wrong, wrong, wrong."

Whitney stopped looking happy.

"We are discussing dharma in the context of the four desires, which are—?"

He waited for someone else to answer and when no one did, he went on. "Oh, for heaven's sake, this is a spiritual retreat centre! I'd think one of you would know."

Tad looked back at us and glared, as though he wanted someone to give him the answer so he could get the lecture over with.

"Let me guess," said Wills. "The four desires refer to a stiff drink, a good meal, a long massage, and . . . well, you know."

"My first desire is for a nap," said Rayvn.

Jenson didn't bother to answer them. Instead, he explained. "The four desires are the dharma, the artha, the kama, and moksha." He listed the words off on his fingers while sweeping his branch through the air with his other hand to emphasize each one. "Dharma is also known as dhamma in Pali. Do not get hung up on terminology. Instead, you must focus on the *spirit* of the words."

He sure wasn't a boring teacher even though I had no idea what he was talking about. If my high school teachers had been half as good as him, I might have graduated with better than a B– average.

"All of these desires help you to fulfill your individual destinies, and the first of them is dharma. I put the question to you again: what is dharma?"

This time, Rayvn put up her hand.

"Yes, my dear witchy one in need of a nap?" said Jenson.

At his words, Rayvn blushed, but continued. "I think dharma is more along the lines of who you're meant to be."

"YES!" shouted Jenson. "That's it! That's it! Your dharma is your deepest purpose *and* your desire to fulfill that purpose. Our dharma is our sacred duty, and it influences all our other desires. If you follow your dharma, you will bring good into the world."

"What about the other ones? Army and karma and all that?" asked Tad.

Jenson got this look on his face that made me wonder if he didn't actually know the other ones or at least couldn't explain them. "Helen, perhaps you can elaborate on the other three?" he said.

Helen explained that artha is what people need in the way of material resources to fulfill their dharma.

"If my dharma is to be a successful hedge fund manager, my artha means I need a house in midtown Manhattan?" said Tad, who seemed to think he was being incredibly funny.

"Perhaps," said Helen. "Or it might mean skills with math and the ability to see patterns."

"Oh," said Tad.

She went on. "Kama describes our more intimate desires."

"Sex," said Wills, like he'd been waiting for his chance to say the word.

"It means all sorts of pleasures," said Helen. "Friendship, intimacy, appreciation of beauty, and yes, physical pleasures."

"Kama is *the* major driver of achievement in the floral design field, I can tell you," said Jenson. "We're sensualists to a person."

"Moksha refers to the desire for freedom," said Helen. "The freedom from the wheel of suffering."

"You mean wanting to die and whatnot," said Wills. "Buddhists are always wanting to die, I think. They want to die so they can stop feeling bad."

Helen didn't tell him he was an idiot, which must have been hard for her. "Buddhists seek awareness of what it is to be free of desire. They want to be at peace with what is."

"What is?" said Tad. "What do you mean 'what is'? I'm pretty sure only inanimate objects have no desires."

"I mean to be aware of what is actually happening from moment to moment. Not lost in our memories or projections of the future. Or endless stories."

"I fail to see how any of this is related to flowers anyways," said Tad.

"Everything is related to flowers," said Jenson. "Listen carefully. What we are teaching you is absolutely critical to arranging your inner flower."

"I still don't get it," said Wills. "Yesterday was easier."

"You're living in the past, dear one," said Jenson. "Let's dive into your dharma and more will be revealed! First, using a brilliant exercise from Rod Stryker's classic book, *The Four Desires*, as our inspiration, I'd like you to write your own eulogy. Write it from the perspective of someone who loves you."

The four students leaned forward like he'd just informed them that the public streaking part of the course would begin in five minutes.

"The rest of you may go," he said, waving at us. "This is very deep work. The students must do it alone."

I was sad I couldn't stick around to see them write their own eulogies. It'd probably take about three minutes for each of them to say they had been an asshole and no one really missed them. Except Rayvn. She deserved better.

"Can we just write about the kinds of flowers we'd like at our funeral when we die?" asked Tad. "Because the answer is none of the usual varieties. I loathe all those smelly lilies and carnations one sees at funerals."

Jenson gave him a fierce look.

"Sorry," said Tad, which surprised me. Tad didn't seem like the kind of person who apologized for anything.

"Students may spread out around the garden."

I followed Helen and Murray and Gavin out of the garden and into the lodge.

No one said anything until we got inside. And then all Helen said was that she had to go to her office and make a phone call and we should get to work. I had to clean Rayvn's and Tad's cabins. I decided to go through the garden to get to the trails. Who knew flower arranging could be so intense?

Chapter 23

Feeling somewhat foolish and reluctant, Helen went to the office to call the medical examiner. She was surprised when the doctor picked up after one ring.

"Dekker," said a brusque female voice.

"Hello, Dr. Dekker. My name is Helen Thorpe. Officer Rosedale may have told you I would be calling?"

"Nope," said Dekker.

"Okay. Yes, well, I'm wrapping up Ms. Edna Todd's affairs and I have a couple of questions."

"Go ahead."

"I'm not sure if you will be comfortable answering, but did you do a blood test? And did you happen to take any of her journals for evidence?"

Dekker's voice grew chilly. "Let me call Officer Rosedale. I can't disclose any specifics without permission."

"Of course. Perhaps you could just let me know whether you saw anything that might be a cause for concern."

"If I did, then I would not have deemed Ms. Todd's death a suicide. Obviously. Perhaps you should ask Ms. Todd's lawyers or the police to see the report."

Helen was enjoying her time as a detective less each second.

"I understand that the deceased belonged to some sort of death club. She took the medications they recommend," said Dekker.

"Were there any signs of . . . a struggle?"

"What are you suggesting, Ms. Thorpe?"

"A number of us are surprised that she took her own life," said Helen.

"I gather you do not belong to the same suicide club? Perhaps the ugly reality of what it means to kill yourself comes as a shock."

Dr. Dekker was clearly not a woman who approved of people choosing the time and manner of their passing.

"You don't believe any concern is warranted?"

"I do not. She took drugs that killed her. Drugs she had procured god only knows where. There were no signs of a struggle. To be candid, Ms. Thorpe, there are those of us who believe that membership in one of these death organizations is itself a form of suicidal ideation. It makes it too easy. I also understand that she had been on a months-long silent retreat. The literature suggests that a certain percentage of people who undertake such retreats experience severe mental-health side effects, especially if they are not supervised by an experienced teacher. One of those side effects is suicidal depression. Ms. Todd created a lethal combination of factors for herself. Isolation, easy access to drugs, suicidal ideation."

Helen guessed that Dr. Dekker wasn't much of a meditator. She wondered what she would think of the life Helen had lived in the monastery. She hadn't spoken to anyone for an entire year. She'd undergone purification practices that laypeople would likely find appalling. Helen regretted none of it.

"As to your other question, no," continued Dr. Dekker. "There were no journals found near her body. Nor was there a note. But her Right to Die booklet was on her bedstand with some forms she'd completed about her wish to be in control of her own death. Right beside the medications."

"I see. Thank you for answering my questions."

Dr. Dekker's voice thawed. "I'm sorry about Ms. Todd. I'm sure her friends miss her. If I could suggest something, it's that they disband their death club and focus on living. To do otherwise is to squander the gift of life. Such a shame to focus on death and isolation while surrounded with such beauty and friends who care."

That was just it, wasn't it, thought Helen. In the midst of life, death. It was hard to fully appreciate one without being constantly aware of the other.

That's the point Dr. Dekker was missing.

So far, Helen's sleuthing seemed pointless. But her questions remained.

She got up and went into the foyer and looked out into the garden. The students were all busily writing. She wondered how much of what they wrote would be true. Years of interviewing meditation students had taught her that even when people tried to lie about themselves and their experiences, they told the truth.

Sayadaw U Nandisara had told Helen that she had the gift of clear seeing married with compassion and that she also had a pronounced aversion to unpleasantness. This was, Helen knew, not a bad psychological set-up for a butler. It was not, however, the best psychological profile for an investigator.

As Helen gazed out the window, a garden gate opened and a young man stepped into the garden.

"Who's that?" asked Murray, who had come up behind her with a dishtowel neatly folded in her hands.

The young man, who had tousled brown hair, was dressed in a sport jacket and tie. He peered around as though he was supposed to meet someone.

One of the three cousins at the far side of the garden said something to the others and all three heads snapped up. The young man spotted them in turn and he also seemed to come to attention.

"Jared Weintraub," said Helen.

"And who is he?" asked Murray.

"He's an exceptionally fine painter. He's also the only realtor on the island. Please excuse me," she said. "I'd better go and see him."

INSIDE THE GARDEN, Jared greeted Helen just as Jenson Kiley strode over to them.

"Hello," said the young painter.

"We're in the midst of deep work here," said the floral educator. "I'm afraid we can't have civilians wandering through."

"I'm sorry, Jenson," said Jared. "When I saw you at the pub two days ago, you forgot to mention that you were going to put the lodge on lockdown."

Jenson Kiley smiled ever so briefly. "I was in a different frame of mind then," he said. "You should know that. You're also an artist. You've taken the course. I like to think it made you a better painter AND a better real estate agent."

"Absolutely," said Jared. "I apologize for interrupting. And hello, Helen. It's good to see you again. After all the . . . sadness."

Helen kept her voice low, aware that Tad, Wills, and Whitney were watching them from their position near the compost heap and Rayvn was staring at them from the bench near the pond. "Let's go inside," she said.

As they walked back to the lodge, Jared kept glancing over at the cousins.

"Working on their obituaries?" he asked in a whisper.

Helen nodded.

"It's such a weird, self-involved thing to do, but it was strangely illuminating," he said. "I learned that I need to get successful enough to paint full-time or people are going to have to lie about my life satisfaction at my funeral."

"That's a lot of pressure to put on yourself," said Helen.

She'd known Jared since he was a teenager. He'd worked all over the island starting when he was fourteen years old: packing groceries at the Co-op, bussing tables at local restaurants, renting kayaks to tourists in the summer. He was one of the hardest-working people on Sutil, which was admittedly an easy title to capture. Jared was the only child of a single mother who had always been on social assistance and who spent whatever small amount of money she brought in to buy weed and have drinks with whatever loggers or sailors might be in town. She still had her special stool at the pub, though fewer men came around it now that her looks, once striking, had faded.

Helen had seen Jared and his mother interact only a few times over the years and had always been struck by their implacable mutual resentment. Jared treated his mother like a local curiosity, even though they had lived on the same property until he made enough money to buy his own small cottage across the island from her. Before that he'd lived in a tiny cabin he'd built mostly by himself while his mother lived in a small, badly maintained house left to her by her parents.

Jared's mother liked to criticize him for being uptight. "Oh, here's the President and Vice President and Secretary at Arms for the local Chamber of Commerce," she'd say when he came into the pub, where she spent most of her time.

"Ah, Gina. Nice to see you in your office again today," he'd respond. And after the initial barbed greeting, they ignored each other.

The two of them seemed tightly bound by old scars and hard feelings. It was a knot that would take many years of effort to loosen. It was work neither of them seemed interested in doing.

"How are things going with your painting?" Helen asked.

"Good. Thanks for asking. I've been invited to take part in a Gulf Islands artists show in Vancouver in the fall. Good gallery. My agent says it could be a turning point. But I'm working in watercolours lately. Not very on trend these days."

"I think your work is exquisite," said Helen. He painted scenes from Sutil Island and managed to infuse every picture with a compelling mix of moodiness and what Helen always felt was longing. She understood she was probably projecting what she knew of his personal life into his artwork. Hard not to.

One of Jared's large paintings hung over the piano in the dining room. He'd painted the garden and lodge but included planning sketches complete with notes. He used a drone to get the angles, and the effect created a strange sense of vertigo. It defamiliarized a place Helen knew well. There was something distant and calculating in the painting that reminded her that the garden and grounds had been designed by people trying to create an impression.

Inside the lodge, Helen offered Jared tea.

"Oh, no thanks," he said. "I just stopped in to say hello. And to follow up on something. I spoke to Edna not long before she died."

"Oh?" said Helen, surprised. Edna had been on silent retreat, which meant she shouldn't have been speaking to anyone.

"I contacted her because I need to borrow the painting. For the show."

"Did you drop by?" Helen asked.

"No. I called. She picked up."

Helen found herself disturbed to learn that Edna had been answering phone calls on her retreat. On the other hand, Edna had never done such a long self retreat. She was a woman who enjoyed pleasurable distractions, which is why she pursued so many different spiritual traditions.

"Did you see her?" Helen asked.

"Just briefly. I dropped off some information about the show. In Vancouver."

"How did she seem?"

"Fine. She wasn't talking much because she was on retreat."

"When was this?"

Jared leaned against the long side counter, crossed his arms, and looked up. "Maybe a month ago?"

"Really," said Helen. Edna had weeks left in her retreat then. People did not usually break their silence until the last day or so except to speak to a teacher. This was all very strange. It was something else to share with Officer Rosedale.

"Did she seem well?" asked Helen.

"Oh, yeah. You know, crazy healthy and, I don't know, alive. Kind of jacked up, to be honest. You know Edna. Her light bulb always had more wattage than anyone else's."

That was a good way to describe Edna.

Helen wanted to ask him if Edna had seemed like a woman on the verge of taking her own life, but she already knew the answer.

"Anyway, Helen, the reason I'm here is that on top of wanting to say I'm sorry about Edna, I'm still hoping I can take the painting away for the show. I'll need your written permission."

Helen nodded. "Of course."

"Are you taking over here permanently?" he asked. "People are saying you are. People think you inherited this place."

"No," she said simply. And gave no further details.

Jared gave her a sharp look that didn't totally suit his normally pleasant face. Maybe that was his real estate face, she thought. The business-y part of him that was going to make enough money so he could paint full-time. In her experience, artists were just as tightly attached to the endlessly turning and painful Wheel of Becoming as everyone else. Ambition was everywhere, and more often than not, it was ruinous.

They made arrangements for Jared to pick up his painting before the show, and she walked him to his car, a seven-year-old Lexus, which he'd told her a couple of years before that he was still paying for. Jared's business consisted mostly of facilitating real estate transactions within families, as few people sold their properties outright on Sutil. She guessed it wasn't terribly lucrative.

After they said goodbye and his car was out of sight, she found herself replaying their conversation, though she couldn't have said why.

Chapter 24

WILLS TODD

Jenson Kiley asked us to arrange our chairs in a semicircle.

"It is not possible to arrange one's inner flower if one doesn't know what it is!" he said. "One must consider the flower's essence, its shape, colour, form. What other flowers look well with it? Is it a hardy fall flower or a simple spring daisy? An extravagant summer beauty or winter's bare branch? We must do deep work to understand this."

Tad, Rayvn, and Whitney were looking at their sheets of paper like they regretted having written anything on them. I certainly bloody regretted every word I'd put down. The task was deviously effective at making one reveal at least a few shreds of truth.

While the florist did one of his long pauses for effect, Rayvn looked around like she was expecting a helicopter to land and extract her from the situation. Whitney kept shifting her skinny butt around in her seat, and Tad wore that expression he always gets when he feels like his dignity is being impinged on. Tad has always been very committed to his dignity, even if he doesn't give a rat's ass about other people's.

"All right," said Jenson. "Which of you would like to go first?"

I found myself staring at my hands, which are still calloused, thank god. I never trust a man with soft hands. And my nails were clean, which was more than the new cousin could say. Those barbaric talons of hers looked incredibly unhygienic.

Finally, Tad put his hand up.

"Wonderful. Thaddeus, are you ready?"

Tad got to his feet. He had on brand-new Sperry sailing shoes, which was ironic, since he can't sail for shit. Then he sat back down. "Maybe I could read it from my seat?"

Kiley shook his head. "It won't be as impactful." The word *impactful* made my head hurt. It reminded me of all the business analysts I had talked to about the regatta. A bunch of useless naysayers and assholes.

"I would prefer not to read mine out loud," said Whitney. "What I wrote feels private."

Jenson Kiley put his hands on his apron, which made me wonder why we didn't all get aprons. Maybe it was some floral educator power play, like making people in meetings sit in small chairs. A few of those business analysts I spoke to did that to me. Humiliating.

"Why?" asked Jenson.

"Because it's personal," said Whitney.

"Why?" demanded Jenson again.

Whit's face flushed. "Because what I wrote is what I *wish* were true about me. Right now, it's not. No one is going to say any of this about me when I die unless I make some big changes."

Her performance was impressive and a little too convincing. For the thousandth time, I wondered why I'd agreed to the plan, which was dreamed up by Tad and Whitney. It was too complicated. There were too many ways for it to go wrong.

Whitney, usually so pale and droopy, stayed red in the face. Clearly upset. For some reason, this made the florist happy. He clapped his hands together. "Yes!" he cried. "How many of you are the person you'd like to see in the eulogy you wrote for yourself?"

Rayvn's hand went up, went down, and then stayed up.

"What's this?" said Jenson. "You are already self-actualized?"

Rayvn shrugged. "I thought we were supposed to be honest," she said.

"Let's have you go first, then," he said. "Do not worry about a thing! You are perfect and you are among friends."

She was manifestly neither of those things, but I guess he was trying to be encouraging.

Rayvn got to her feet. I couldn't help finding her both bizarrely fascinating and a serious worry. It was hard to believe that Uncle Topher, who was aggressively boring, could have hatched a child like her.

Today the girl had on a big green skirt that reached her ankles, high-heeled leather lace-up boots, a wide leather belt that cinched in her middle, and a poufy white blouse. Also, some sort of leather choker that looked like a dog collar. I assume she's a goth, but I'm not sure. She looks like she just failed an audition for a *Princess Bride* reboot. And the thing that really gets me is how she's not self-conscious about her poor dress sense at all. Quite bizarre, really.

"I need to read this?" she said.

"Radical openness is required for the fully actualized life. True dharma means bravery. Please face the group. Like you're delivering a eulogy."

"I thought dharma meant desires," I whispered, confused. Whitney ignored me.

"Seems like the term means whatever that guy says it means," whispered Tad.

Rayvn got to her feet and walked in front of us.

"Fearless," instructed Jenson.

"If you say so," said Rayvn. She wore a side ponytail that she must have put in before she combed her hair. There was a large tangled lump at the back of her head. I'm pretty sure I saw a leaf stuck in there, too. I hoped Helen had noticed. Edna always liked people to be neat. She thought it was a sign of being spiritually evolved. Tad, Whitney, and I were always tidy and we'd made sure to be even more so since we'd arrived at the Institute. Rayvn's slobby costumes and general demeanour had to count against her. But she was dressed to the nines compared to how she rolled into meditation this morning. Late and slovenly—not a winning combo.

I found myself holding my breath as Rayvn cleared her throat like a two-packs-a-day smoker and shifted around. Then she snapped the pages out in front of her face a few times. Incredibly irritating.

"Rayvn Wildwood is perhaps best known for being one of the top small-appliance salespeople in the mid-island region," she began.

Tad looked like he had just been asked to open an airplane door at 10,000 feet. Whitney stared straight ahead, a pleasant but frozen expression on her face.

"But there was much more to her than that."

Another throat clear. Rayvn held the paper so close to her face I wondered if she had some form of extreme close-sightedness.

"Rayvn," interrupted Jenson. "Do you need spectacles?"

"No," she said. "I'm fine." Then she continued with her summary of her life, read from a distance of about three inches.

"She will be fondly remembered by the members of the mid-island LARPing community, where she excelled at swordplay and bringing a sense of urgency and commitment to her roles.

"In addition, she had an excellent sense of humour and a loving relationship with her friends, most of whom were just as untanned and unfit as her.

"She had an unconventional approach to fashion and took pride in not dressing for success because the fashion industrial complex is a scam that tries to make everyone fit one model of beauty. Also, fashion is terrible for the environment. Rayvn made a lot of her costumes out of used clothes and also old curtains.

"Rayvn usually played either a troll wench or blacksmith apprentice wench in the games. She loved the work of Stephen King and other horror writers and has written fan fiction in a variety of worlds.

"No one ever thought she would accomplish much in the way of standard success, but she rose quickly in the field of small appliance sales and seemed to have a knack for figuring out what people need. She slept too much and ate too many chips. But she was always fairly happy, which is more than most people can say."

She lowered the page and looked at us and at Jenson Kiley.

"I'm nearly done," she said.

"You are doing beautifully," said Jenson, with obvious sincerity, which made my stomach clench up.

I tried not to think about what I'd written.

Up went the pages and her face disappeared again. "Rayvn believed in being straightforward and in telling the truth, even if it was uncomfortable. She helped people as much as she could. She was not a pretentious asshole."

The papers came down and her dark eyes appeared. She stared right at me and Tad and Whitney.

"Okay, that's it," she said. "It's not poetic or anything, but that's what my friends and family would probably say."

"Loved it," said Jenson. "You certainly know who you are. It's most admirable, particularly in one so young."

"Not sure what any of it means for my inner flower," said Rayvn.

Jenson Kiley was obviously still cogitating over the words of her statement and he didn't answer her directly.

"LARPing," he mused. "Authenticity. Straightforwardness. Small appliances. Trolls and blacksmiths. Not being pretentious or an asshole." He put air quotes around the word *asshole*. "Very, very interesting."

"Can I sit down?" said Rayvn. "That was sort of strange and now I feel dumb and embarrassed."

"Oh yes, of course," said Jenson Kiley. "Sit down." He made notes in a small book and continued to mutter to himself. "Fairly happy," he muttered. "I like this. We can work with this."

When he finished reading, he pointed to Tad. "Thaddeus? Are you ready?"

Tad sighed and got up with his sheets of paper. I gave some serious thought to running out of the garden and straight down to the ocean and swimming until I drowned. Or reached Japan.

Chapter 25

WHITNEY VARGA

felt sweat dampen my pages as Tad took his place in front of us. If I'd known we would have to take courses, I would have done more research into the Yatra Institute's programming. But even if I'd looked more carefully at the catalogue when Aunt Edna shared it with me, who could possibly have imagined that a flower-arranging course would involve something as ghoulish as writing one's own personal eulogy.

Rayvn's testimony had been frighteningly forthright. As a person raised by two fantasists, I know how stark the truth sounds against lies, no matter how good the liar, at least to anyone who is listening carefully. And Helen and the florist were listening carefully to us.

Tad is so emotionally shut down that I wondered if he'd just read off his CV, which wouldn't take long, not with his paltry work history. But by this point, we should've all been showing some growth.

I forced myself to focus on what Tad was saying.

At first, he sounded so clinical he might have been reading some stranger's CV rather than his own.

"Thaddeus Todd was a good person. I enjoyed his sharp sense of humour and his ability to cut through nonsense.

"He was also an exceptional driver and he had fine taste in cars. In fact, he was one of the first in line to buy the Mercedes AMG GT R, which is something of a throwback to the Mercedes Gullwing SL. Very cool car in a custom midnight blue."

I couldn't believe what I was hearing. Tad is many things, but insane isn't one of them. What was he doing?

"He took good care of himself and maintained the same weight from the time he was nineteen until the time of his death. Not easy to do unless you have tremendous self-discipline, which he had in spades. Not like some members of his family who have let themselves get a little chunky."

He chortled stupidly and Wills let out a loud sigh. I closed my eyes. Tad's glib recital sounded terrible after Rayvn's candour and vulnerability.

"Not only that, but his tennis game was near professional quality and he had a golf handicap of . . . well, he'd be too modest to want me to give you the number. Let's just say he was really very close to a scratch golfer."

Then Tad stopped reading for a long moment and took a deep breath before continuing.

"He was a good son. Helped his parents. And his brother. And even if he wasn't Mr. Soft-and-Fuzzy, personal-relations-wise, he did the right thing. Usually. And he gave to charity and supported many good causes."

With that, Tad practically ran back to his chair.

Jenson Kiley kept up his nodding. "Sporty, an appreciation for aesthetics. Family-oriented. Duty, discipline, kindness. Yes, I see." He'd gotten up and was pacing back and forth, holding his elbows with opposite hands and staring into the sky. "I know a number of Scandinavian floral designers who might be described exactly that way."

"William? It's your turn."

Wills's already grim expression grew even more unpleasant. "Wills," he corrected.

"Ha! Of course," said Jenson. "I must remember that. As in, last wills and testament. Please, go ahead."

Wills got to his feet and stumped up to the front. He was already looking a bit stockier than he had when he'd arrived, which is to say his stomach was straining against his shirt. He also looked broad and powerful, at least in his body.

I happen to know that Wills is softer than he looks. He's never been as naturally mean-spirited and untrustworthy as Tad, but he is manifestly unspiritual. What is it the Buddhists call people who can never get enough of anything? Hungry ghosts? Edna mentioned the concept the last time I spoke to her and it perfectly describes Wills. Never enough food, drink, money, or, I suspect, drugs. I've dated a few druggies and they all have that glassy gleam to the eye, even when they're clean.

Wills shifted from side to side and rubbed his thick hands on his pants. "I don't know about this," he said. "It's like we're tempting fate or something. Asking God to smite us. And I still don't get what any of this has to do with flower arranging."

"Oh ye of little faith," said Jenson. "Read away. All will become clear."

"Wills Todd, survived by his younger brother, Tad, and predeceased by his parents"—he snuck a glance at Tad, who frowned back—"was frequently misunderstood. He often followed a value system that he knew was bullshit, even if he had trouble admitting that. He eventually learned that helping others is the road to freedom. That was tough and sort of against the grain because he was basically a selfish guy who drank too much. But he eventually pulled it together and became fairly useful. He loved the ocean and helped many people learn to sail and appreciate the water. His wife and kids loved him and he provided for them generously before he died. While sailing. Or maybe having sex," he added, defiantly. "Okay. That's it." He bolted for his seat as though he expected a lot of questions from the press.

"Thank you so much, Wills," said Jenson. "I found that quite moving."

Rayvn and Tad nodded. I felt sick. Wills's words had been powerful and they sounded true. I had not expected that.

"Here is what I'm hearing, dharma-wise," said Jenson. "I hear misunderstood but useful. I hear resilient. And I hear water."

Wills gave a half shrug.

"I hear an entirely imaginary wife and kids," said Tad.

"The search for deepest meaning is no laughing matter," said Jenson.

To my surprise, Tad had the good grace to look ashamed.

"Whitney, are you ready?" asked Jenson.

"No," I said, folding and refolding my pages. I wondered if the waves of discomfort coming off me were visible to the naked eye. "I really would prefer not to do this. I'm quite uncomfortable with public speaking."

"You need some beta blockers," said Wills. "Took 'em by the handful when I was in university."

"Not just beta blockers," said Tad.

Jenson Kiley ignored my cousins and looked at me with deep concern. "Why? Is your deepest desire one that you dare not speak aloud?"

I looked up. "No, of course not. I just don't understand what any of this has to do with flower arranging."

"More than you can imagine," he said, mysteriously.

I couldn't make myself do it.

"I think I'll pass on this part of the exercise. I've written down my answers and I will share what I've written with you," I said. "But I'm not going to read it out loud."

Jenson stared at me like he was trying to figure out a puzzle. But he didn't press further. Instead, he nodded and took the piece of paper I held out to him. He folded it once more and put it in his pocket. Then he resumed his speech.

"Tomorrow you will put these insights about who you are meant to be into a flower arrangement. When one knows one's deepest desire, then one is more likely to act in alignment with it." Jenson fixed me with a surprisingly fierce gaze. "Do not go through life as a mystery to yourself."

I swallowed. My statement was fine. I didn't have to make it public. The less my cousins knew about my hopes and desires, the better.

"Who called the police?" said Tad, staring at the garden gate nearest to the parking lot, where a uniformed police officer stood.

Jenson shook his head as though the sight of the RCMP had somehow broken his flow.

"You are dismissed," he said. "When we meet tomorrow, we're going to talk about more fundamentals of flower arranging and how it relates to our dharma statements. Then I will tell you more about the next arranging task. In the meantime, I'll give you a few minutes to prepare before your movement session."

None of us moved as the officer approached.

Chapter 26

The cop was medium height, overweight, and he looked tired.

"Officer Rosedale?" said Helen.

"You must be Helen Thorpe," he said. He had that flat, slightly suspicious watchfulness police officers seem to develop as he surveyed Helen and the small group in the garden.

"Yes, that's correct," said Helen.

"They're taking a course?" he asked. "As part of your test?"

"The students are learning about floristry," said Helen, skipping the part about finding their life purpose through writing their own eulogies.

"I see," he said, surveying the people assembled in the garden. "These are the relatives you mentioned?"

"Four of them. The one in the apron is the instructor."

Whitney, Tad, Wills, and Rayvn kept glancing over at Helen and Officer Rosedale. They all looked guilty of something. This must be what Officer Rosedale saw when he looked at most people. It must be nearly impossible to keep a truly open mind when so many of the people you met feared you and lied to you. On the other hand, it was a bit like being a meditation teacher, though students tended not to know what they were trying to hide from themselves and their teachers. Delusion was everywhere.

"I have to leave almost right away. As I was driving off the ferry, I got a call about a series of armed robberies on Quadra Island."

"Oh dear," said Helen.

"It's no big mystery who did it. The guy uses a wooden broadsword as his weapon and goes into stores and takes all the stuff he thinks is too dangerous for regular people to use. He takes all the little Buddha and Jesus statues, all the incense. Singing bowls. Stuff like that. Happens every time he goes off his medication. No one is too scared because he's a small guy, not strong. He can barely lift the broadsword, much less hit someone with it. He just sort of drags it around. But we have to pick him up and take him to the hospital. Nice fella, otherwise."

"Oh," said Helen.

"I thought I'd pick up that note you mentioned and see if anything else has come up. I'm going to ask if we can take another look into Ms. Todd's death. I agree that some of it sounds peculiar."

Helen brought him into her office and took the death doula's letter from the locked drawer in her desk.

Then she told him about her conversation with Jared Weintraub.

"He said that he spoke to Edna about a month before her death. It's a bit odd, as she was on a silent retreat."

"I see," said Rosedale. He made a note in his small book. "You have contact information for Jared?"

She gave him the painter's phone number.

"I don't know what any of it means. But if she was speaking to Jared before her retreat was over, maybe she was speaking to other people. She may have had a case of yogi mind."

"What's that?"

"People on retreat can get hyper-focused or concentrated. They have a lot of what's known as samadhi. And that focus can land on peculiar things. Maybe Edna got a case of yogi mind that led her to start talking to people."

"And what did Jared and Ms. Todd talk about?" asked Rosedale. His face had changed again. His expression was open and curious. He seemed like a man who enjoyed his job, at least the part that involved asking questions.

"He wanted to know if he could borrow a painting that's on display here for an art show in Vancouver."

"And what was the answer?" Rosedale cocked his head and glanced up at Helen. The transformation in him was remarkable. He looked ten years younger and no longer tired. He was a man who'd found his purpose. No need to write his own eulogy.

"Edna agreed. She was always very supportive of the arts. She believed that being creative is a human right. She'd have loved to see Jared make enough money through his art to be able to paint full-time."

"Can you show me the painting on my way out?"

"Of course," said Helen.

"Did he say how she was? Mentally, I mean?" said Rosedale.

"He said she was in good spirits. That she sounded like herself but that she was not keeping silence."

"Was that unusual?" asked Rosedale.

"Not terribly. Three months is a very long time to be on retreat, especially a self-guided retreat. I imagine that Edna found ways of breaking the container that felt justifiable."

"What do you mean?"

"We call it the container of silence. It helps people on retreat stay protected from outside distractions. Edna was a bit of a greedy type."

Helen caught Rosedale's expression and explained. "To say someone is a greedy type is not an insult. It's just a description. According to the teachings, there are only a few basic personality types into which people fall. Most people are afflicted with greed, aversion, or delusion." Helen did not explain that some combination of those so-called defilements is said to be at the heart of human suffering. She didn't want to get too far in the Buddhist weeds with the police officer.

"So was she actually greedy?" he asked.

"What it means in this context is that she was eclectic in her spiritual practices and she liked beautiful things and distractions. She was fond of pleasure. It's hard for people like that to maintain the strict discipline of silence for a long time."

Rosedale looked out the window. "But you don't think that staying alone here would have made her crack?"

"No, I don't," said Helen.

"How much longer are you conducting the courses?"

"Just over a week. We started yesterday, but this is the first full day."

"Have any of them figured out why they're here?"

"I haven't told them," said Helen. "I think they assume that having them take the courses was just some whim of Edna's. And I suspect they hope they will be rewarded with money from the estate when it's all over."

"If I had some holidays left, some extra money, and was a completely different person, I might like to come here and learn about flower arranging."

"And dance and meditation," added Helen.

He laughed softly. "And them too."

He got to his feet, looking weighed down by his heavy pants and his belt loaded with policing accessories. "If you hear anything else that seems relevant, please call me."

She escorted him through the lodge, and on their way past the kitchen she asked if he would like some food for the ferry.

"That would be great," he said and patted his stomach.

Helen brought him into the kitchen, where lunch preparations were in progress.

Chef Leticia came over, wiping her hands on a towel before shaking the officer's hand.

"Chef," said Helen. "Could we send Officer Rosedale on his way with a brown bag lunch?"

"Of course," said the Leticia. "Ribollita soup, fennel and parmesan salad, beet salad, and Gruyère scones okay?"

Officer Rosedale's eyes grew large.

"I probably shouldn't," he said.

"We insist," said Helen.

"Thank you," he said. "That sounds great."

Chef Leticia smiled, obviously enchanting the police officer. Then she asked Nigel, who was doing dishes, to help her pack up the meal.

"What is ribollita soup?" Officer Rosedale asked Helen under his breath. "I didn't want to ask your cook and seem like I don't know anything about food."

"Vegetable bean soup. It's delicious. Everything Chef Leticia makes is delicious."

When Nigel brought the police officer the bag with his lunch in it and a single tulip stem sticking out the top, Officer Rosedale, who was probably in his mid-forties, looked as pleased as a teenager. All the impassiveness he'd had when he arrived seemed gone. He was now full of expressions and frank reactions.

When he stepped outside and saw Wayfarer leading the four students in free-form movements in the garden, he stopped in his tracks and stared. Wayfarer executed a magnificent deer-like leap into the air on the narrow path that led between the big kale bush and a peony. The students followed after her in single file and tried to copy her moves. Their jumps were more like those of malfunctioning jumping beans than deer.

Rosedale inclined his head toward Helen. "What's that?"

"Movement class. It will be followed with a longer dance class this evening."

"I'd pay good money to see some of my fellow officers doing that."

He was still full of gratitude when they got to the car. "This is just great," he repeated, after he got into his cruiser. "I'll be in touch with any news or if I have any questions. I'll let you know what the higher-ups say. And you let me know if anything comes up here that you think I should know."

"Thank you," said Helen.

He looked at the bagged lunch in the passenger seat beside him. "I feel like it should be illegal to accept food this nice."

"But it's not," said Helen. "You'll have a longer life and a more productive career if you accept nutritious donations."

Officer Rosedale looked through his open car window at the garden fence in front of them. "I hope you can keep this place going. It's quite something. Maybe we should hold a retreat here for us officers who work the Gulf Islands and remote communities."

"You should," said Helen. "It would give you a new perspective."

He nodded. "I believe it would."

Helen watched the car drive away.

"Helen?" Murray said behind her. She stood in the open gate of the garden.

Helen turned. "Yes?"

"I think someone is trying to get your attention." Murray indicated Nigel, who stood on the stairs of the lodge, gesturing. "Someone really needs to tell him not to wave at people like he's drowning," said Murray. "Silly young goof should come over here and whisper like a proper professional."

Helen laughed and walked back to the lodge with Murray.

"Call for you," said Nigel, when she got within earshot. "It's a *forensic farm*!" His voice was an awed whisper. "What even is that?"

"Thank you, Nigel," said Helen. She took the cordless phone from him and took it to her office.

Chapter 27

This is Helen Thorpe," said Helen, closing the door to her office. "I'm sorry for the wait."

"Yes, hello. It's Dr. Amanda Pfieffer. From the High Plains Forensic Centre." The voice sounded young, upbeat. Not like the voice of a person in charge of leaving bodies on mountaintops to be eaten by wild creatures. Or bodies in fields, to slowly decompose under a blanket of leaves. Or . . .

"Devon Lest asked me to call you," said Dr. Pfieffer. "He said you might have some questions. About your loved one's remains. Part of what I do here is liaise with families."

"Thank you. As I'm sure Mr. Lest mentioned, I'm the executor for Ms. Edna Todd's estate. It's a bit more complicated than that, actually. Some questions have come up about her death."

"Oh?" said Dr. Pfieffer, sounding less cheerful.

Helen ran a hand over the smooth expanse of Edna's wooden desk. Looked at the shelf containing her journals.

"The police and medical examiner determined that Edna took her own life. She belonged to a death positive club. She was a founding member."

"I see," said Dr. Pfieffer.

"She died using the, uh, medicines she'd obtained for that purpose. But some people in the community question the timing. Some think she wasn't ready to transition."

Dr. Pfieffer didn't speak.

"There are things here that don't add up. Her last journals are missing. She hadn't made plans for someone to take over the lodge she owned."

"Ah," said Dr. Pfieffer.

"To be honest, I'm not even sure what my question is. I guess I wonder if you saw any signs that would point to anything other than a natural death. I mean, an intentional natural death."

"We took samples of her blood and tissue. They are stored here in case we need to re-examine them as part of our analysis of her decomposition process. But we did not do an autopsy. That would have been done by the medical examiner. Have you spoken to the M.E.?"

"Yes. Dr. Dekker said the results came up positive for the drugs used in assisted suicide. The medicines found near her body. In other words, she said they were her drugs." Helen considered for a moment. "Is there any other way to tell if something is out of order? I mean, now that she's with you."

Dr. Pfieffer's voice dropped. "I'm afraid not. Her soft tissues are nearly gone. We can't tell any more than the doctor who examined her."

Helen remembered a story some of her favourite meditation teachers from Hawaii told her about a senior monk from Burma who had spent years doing the death meditation. When asked why, the monk said he did it so that when death came for him, it would not be a surprise. And then he would laugh uproariously. When the monk died, he was put in a glass coffin, which was placed in a cave where people could visit and see him decomposing. The teachers, with whom Helen had sat several retreats, said that those who visited had been humbled and exhilarated by the raw truth of his example.

People spend so much of life trying to avoid the reality that we will all die. Edna had tried to turn toward that reality. But why had she gone without telling anyone? It simply wasn't in her character. Then again, Helen didn't know everything about herself, much less Edna.

"I appreciate you calling me," said Helen to Dr. Pfieffer.

"Of course. I wonder if we should reclaim her from the mountain," said the doctor.

"Will that invalidate your research?"

"Yes. Anything that interrupts the natural process of decomposition invalidates the experiment."

"Just leave her, then," said Helen. She knew that even if Edna had been murdered, she would have wanted her body to be of use. And she'd have been overjoyed to know she had been taken into the sky, even if it was inside the belly of a bird.

There was a rustling sound and then Dr. Pfieffer spoke again. "Actually, there is one thing."

Helen waited.

"There's a note in the file. It seems that Ms. Todd said that if she knew the time of her death, she would call us and let us know we could expect her remains."

"But she didn't call."

"No. I would have been the one to take such a call."

Another anomaly.

"Should I let anyone know about this?" asked Dr. Pfieffer.

"I will tell the officer in charge of the case. His name is Rosedale. He may want to talk to you."

They said their goodbyes and hung up.

Maybe Edna's death would remain a mystery. They would never know why she'd chosen that time. They would never know what she'd done with her journals. Or why she hadn't called High Plains to let them know her body would be arriving soon. It was all very strange.

Helen got up and looked out the window at the whitecaps on the ocean. She was not finished asking questions. It was time to reach out to the other members of the Sutil Island Right to Die movement.

But before that, she needed to supervise lunch and get ready for her afternoon interviews.

Chapter 28

Helen sat in a folding chair in Dauber Cottage and felt the breeze from the small window tickle across her face. Dauber Cottage stood at the far edge of the orchard at the end of a stone path that went up and over a tiny arched bridge. It had a sod roof and was built in classic cob style, with thick, rounded walls punctuated by small windows. Almost every part of it was handmade, from the heavy, rounded wooden door to the heated hand-poured concrete floors. The cottage was used for some of the more esoteric spiritual practices that took place at the Institute.

Helen had spent countless hours meditating in Dauber Cottage and had conducted hundreds of interviews there over the years, as she was doing now.

There was a quiet knock on the door. All knocks on the Dauber door were quiet because it was so thick.

She waited in her seat and the door creaked open. There was a rustling noise, and Rayvn poked her head around the corner, hesitating before entering the small round room where Helen sat across from the empty chair.

"Oh, hey. Are you, uh, busy?" asked Rayvn, more diffident than Helen had seen her. The girl obviously felt the odd gravity of the place.

"Come in," said Helen. "Sit down."

Rayvn swept in. She wore a dirndl sort of affair that made her look like she should be serving beer at a German Oktoberfest.

She sat and looked around. "This place is so cool," she said.

"It is," said Helen.

"Does anyone stay in here? I mean, when the lodge is open?"

"No. It's used for activities. For individuals and small groups."

"I'd like to do a bouquet for it. For you while you talk to us here."

"That would be lovely," said Helen, noting Rayvn's impulse toward generosity.

Rayvn heaved a sigh. Helen watched her.

"How are you doing?" she asked.

Rayvn didn't answer right away. Instead, she cocked her head and considered. "Good, I think. I like it here."

"And how are the courses going?"

"I love them. I mean, I keep falling asleep in meditation and this morning I nearly slept in. So that's not great. But I like it."

"Falling asleep is quite common," said Helen. "Especially since you're all so busy. It's normal for people to feel exhausted when they step out of their everyday activities."

"I think tonight I'll eat less," said Rayvn. "That will make dance and meditation easier. But I don't want less food total, so I'll eat more before bed."

That would make getting up the next morning more difficult, but Helen didn't say anything. Students had to discover these things for themselves.

"I'm going to try to be on time for activities. Even though it's hard. Also, my cousins are not that nice. I don't think I'll be setting up any big family reunions with them when all this is over."

Helen listened.

"They make me nervous. I know I'm supposed to be talking to you about meditation, but the thing is, when I settle down without falling asleep, you know, like we're supposed to do in meditation, I notice that I'm sort of afraid of them."

"Is there some reason?"

"I mean, they're rude, but I work retail, so that's no big whup." She heaved a big sigh. "I wouldn't want to get between any of them and something they want. Tad has eyes like a serial-killing goat and Wills is just . . . off somehow. And I don't know *what* Whitney is. I can't get a handle on her at all."

Generally, when people came to an interview with a meditation teacher, they talked about their emotions. They mentioned old wounds that they were feeling. Almost everyone tried to sound more spiritual than they actually felt. Helen wasn't sure she'd heard someone speak as freely as Rayvn before.

"Yeah, so I guess I'm super into the courses, but I'm not going to try to win anything. Just in case."

Helen thought for a moment.

"If it helps, there is no way to win in any of the courses. Especially meditation. But students sometimes feel competitive. Particularly in some parts of the floral design course. Comparison is common."

"It's also a form of insanity," said Rayvn.

"You've heard that."

"Yeah. We talk about it in LARPing sometimes. And I believe it."

Helen nodded. She, too, believed that comparing oneself to others was the cause of great suffering.

When Rayvn got up to leave, Helen felt oddly reassured.

She waited quietly after blowing her nose and taking a sip of water.

Wills was due next, and he entered the cottage with surprising quietness. She barely heard the door open and close or his footsteps on the floor before his ruddy face appeared in the doorway.

"Should I just come in?" he asked.

"Yes, please. Take a seat."

He was a man who veered between hostility and deference. She'd heard him change his tone mid-sentence, depending on his sense of how he was being perceived. Helen sensed there was more to Wills than one might expect from looking at him or listening to him snipe at his brother. He had displayed an appreciation for beauty in his flower arrangements, and Jenson had reported that his dharmacize had been thoughtful and seemed honest. Perhaps it was an act. Time would tell.

She said none of this to Wills. And before she could ask him how things were going, he started.

"There's something I want to talk to you about," he said. His eyes were very blue and very pale, but not as otherworldly as his brother's.

"Okay," said Helen. His habit of unkind and thoughtless talk and his focus on material things led her to understand that he had a fragile sense of himself.

"I've been lying," he said and rubbed a hand over his slicked hair.

His words lingered in the air between them until she reached out and caught them.

"Oh?"

"More of an omission than an outright lie." He shook his head, small atop his wide shoulders, as though that would help him dislodge truer words. "Well, no, I guess it was actually an outright lie. I've visited here more recently than I admitted," he said.

"I see." Helen didn't want to interrupt his confession, if that's what this was.

"I came to see Aunt Edna. While she was on retreat."

Helen found herself leaning in.

"You know, she was getting older."

Edna had been getting older, of course, but only in the imperceptible way some vigorously healthy people do. Unless Edna had changed dramatically since the previous September, Helen couldn't imagine anyone looking at her and thinking that she was in decline.

"She emailed and asked me to come," he continued.

"During her retreat?" said Helen.

"I guess. I didn't know she was on an isolation kick. She said she was taking some time to think about some things. When I got here, she wanted to talk."

"When did this happen?"

"March," he said. "Mid-month."

"And how long did you stay?"

Helen was beginning to interrogate him and she needed to stop. But this was all so unexpected.

"Two nights. I think the idea was for me to stay longer, but she shut it down. The visit, I mean. To be honest," he said, words which are never a good sign for honesty, "I don't like to admit this. Especially not to you, since you're so—" He seemed to struggle to find the right words to describe just how Helen was. "Good," he said, finally. "And calm." He looked at her after he spoke, checking for her reaction.

Helen just waited. And watched. Let her mind be a clear sky.

"She said I should leave after I asked for some help. Financial help. She didn't like that."

Helen continued to wait.

"I think she might have asked me here to see what I'm like. Whether *I'm* good. And calm. That sort of thing."

His forehead had grown shiny and he rubbed it with the back of his hand.

"I think she decided that I'm not that good."

Helen believed him. The entire confession might not be true. But the part about what kind of person he thought he was was definitely true.

"I'm sorry," she said. "That must have been painful."

"I spent everything I had trying to get a yacht race off the ground. Things looked good and then—" He splayed out his fingers to indicate an explosion. "Then it all fell apart. I thought Aunt Edna could help. I said that if she planned to leave me something, it would be best if she gave it to me early."

"And she said no," said Helen.

"She said yacht races were for the idle rich and people should put that kind of time, money, and energy into helping refugees and stopping the climate crisis."

That sounded exactly like Edna. Spiritually oriented, but tough when she felt affronted. But Helen had to acknowledge to herself that as far as she knew, Edna hadn't done much for refugees herself. Or maybe she had and Helen just didn't know about it.

"So I left."

"Why are you telling me this?" asked Helen.

"Because it feels terrible to pretend. The flower-arranging course is doing something to me, I think. Or maybe it's that whacked-out dancing. Or maybe it's the meditation. Or this place. Maybe all of it."

Again she believed him.

"Why did you pretend you hadn't been here since you were a child?" she asked.

"Edna asked me not to say anything about the visit. To anyone," he said. "But she's gone and everything is incredibly weird and you seem like you might understand."

Helen found herself fascinated by those words. "Understand what?" she asked.

"That people are weak. They lie. They have visitors when they're not supposed to. They talk when they're supposed to be on silent retreats. They do the wrong thing, even when they don't mean to." She realized, with surprise, that he was talking not about himself, but about Edna. Helen studied his face. "Thank you for telling me," she said.

"Is this a shock to you?" he asked.

"It is," said Helen. "But I'm glad to know. Thank you again for your candour."

"I feel better," said Wills, getting to his feet abruptly. "My brother and I aren't anyone's favourites. We're just not. But we're garden-variety jerks. Nothing serious."

Helen got to her feet. And then she asked the question that had been nibbling at the edge of her consciousness since the conversation had begun. "Have any of the rest of you been here recently?"

Wills swept back his hair. "I think you should ask them."

She would do just that when she interviewed Whitney and Tad the next day. She sat in the stillness after Wills left and realized she hadn't asked him a single question about meditation.

Chapter 29

WILLS TODD

think the confession yesterday went well, all things considered. And the side benefit is that Helen never got around to asking me about meditation, which so far is just long spells of thinking about benzos or flower arranging, which makes me think about dying. Dance makes me think I'm damned out of shape for a sportsman.

I jumped the gun on the confession. We hadn't specified *who* would start to show the old spiritual advancement when. Always best to be first past the flag, I figure.

We endured each other at dinner and then survived our second bout of martial arts dancing with that absolute savage of a dance teacher. God, she's like an ancient Pict, with her Glaswegian accent and those biceps. But only if ancient Picts spent a lot of time getting spray tans and extensions in LA. This time bloody Tad didn't manage to get in any sneaky blows. Bastard.

I ate less at dinner so I wouldn't sleep through meditation. I noticed we all did that, even though the food was excellent. That chef they've laid in for our stay is not half bad. If I ever get my yacht club, I might give her a buzz, although our members will want sturdier fare.

They've stopped serving booze for some nebulous, spiritual reason. It's just as well. I need my wits about me to get through this in one piece.

We now have to get up at 5:45 a.m., which would be fine with me, except that I am having a surprising amount of trouble sleeping, especially considering there are people bobbing around on rafts in the North Atlantic right now who are getting less fresh air than we are. Hung in there through morning meditation. Helen didn't say much in the morning session. I understood bugger all that she said last night but did my best to give off a "listening intently" vibe before I fell asleep.

This morning after meditation and breakfast, we faced off against the floral educator again. He did his usual thing. The grand entrance. The staring at us with his hands behind his back.

I felt better than I had in a long time and like I might live to see thirty-five. I was even a little bit optimistic about the plan, in spite of cops showing up randomly and us having to read semi-realistic obituaries for ourselves.

Jenson talked about the task for the day but I couldn't focus. In spite of my increased sense of well-being, I was thinking about what I wouldn't give for a lorazepam. Even a half dose would be nice. Then I could be completely calm. Really show Helen and the rest of them my spiritual side.

"Are there any questions?" asked the florist. "If not, please get a container and any other supplies you might need and get to work. You'll want to give each other space. The arrangements will be more interesting if you each use different materials. And of course, the designs will be influenced by what you've learned about your dharma."

Jesus. I completely missed what we were supposed to do while I was fantasizing about benzos. I looked at the others. They seemed completely ready to go and do . . . whatever it was. Fuck.

Reluctantly, I put up my hand.

"Yes, Wills?" answered the teacher.

"I, uh," I said.

Tad elbowed me. "I'll go over it with you." In my defence, I've always had trouble listening or getting anything done after eating. I was famous for it back when we were in school. I was even tested for diabetes a number of times, but the tests came back negative, which confirmed Father's theory that I'm just inattentive and lazy.

"Have you got any recommendations?" I asked the teacher, hoping that was just open-ended enough to get him to recap everything he'd said. I didn't trust Tad not to lie to me.

"Recommendations?" asked Jenson.

"Like for what we should do?" I said, shame crawling up and down my skin.

Jenson stared hard at me. "I think you should do what your heart suggests."

"Right," I said. "Thanks. Will do."

"Nice one," Tad said, as we headed for the work table under the apple tree. The morning was brisk and unsettled. Tree trunks rubbed together and leaves rattled noisily as gusts of wind freight trained through. It was bloody unnerving, actually. I found myself looking around every time the rushing sound started, to make sure we weren't going to get squashed by some massive bloody tree. We were in the middle of the garden so we were safe. For now.

"He asked us to find a spot on the property and make a 'dharmarrangement' using whatever we find nearby," said Tad. "But don't take too much of it."

I gave him a suspicious look.

"Seriously. That's what we're supposed to do."

"And that stuff?" I asked, pointing at all the containers and tools on the work table. I kept my voice down so Jenson, who was standing nearby, wouldn't overhear me.

"Fill a bucket with whatever you need. Then go find a place by yourself to work. You need to make an arrangement that expresses your dharma. We're supposed to leave our arrangements where we made them and then Jenson's going to go around and assess them. I guess he'll assign us a grade, or whatever."

"Anything else?"

"Jesus, you really didn't listen, did you?"

We stopped talking when Rayvn swept up to speak to the flower teacher, her long skirts collecting wood chips from the path. She took a tarnished metal container shaped like a skull from her voluminous, scruffy velvet bag.

She showed the skull to Jenson Kiley, who turned it in his hands, apparently admiring the hideous thing.

"Bitch," muttered Tad.

"She's worryingly overachieving," I said, feeling more in need of tranquilizers than ever.

"It'll be fine," said Tad. "We've got a solid plan."

I wasn't so sure. Whitney joined Rayvn, holding up two containers and asking Jenson sincere-sounding questions. Bloody women.

I tried to remember what my life's purpose was supposed to be and wondered how I could express it in a flower arrangement, especially when I didn't have access to a flower shop or anything. Back when the trust fund was still producing, I ordered flowers from whatever shop my richest friends recommended. They were usually big, mounded bouquets with one kind of flower in them, something pricey, in a glass vase, tied with a matching ribbon. Fucking boring, now that I've seen Jenson whip up some magic with a few sticks and tulips.

Something told me Jenson isn't much for the all-one-thing arrangement, probably because one's dharma isn't all one thing.

I gave my head a little shake. Dharma. The concept was irritatingly vague. I barely understood what I wrote yesterday and don't know if it's true. What *is* my life's purpose? Maybe I should just stab myself in the throat with a good-looking branch and stick a flower up my nose and get it all over with. It would be a relief to stop trying. A sigh whooshed out of me like air from a slashed tire.

"There, there," said Jenson, who'd come up to stand beside me. "You'll be fine. I think you know more about yourself than you profess. Just try to pay attention to the here and now." He talked like he'd just been inside my head. It was eerie and his words made me feel finally, finally awake.

"Stop hiding. Let yourself emerge."

Did the little flower man know I'd been dreaming about benzos? That I am used to drinking myself into oblivion several times a week? That I'd been taking sleeping pills and tranquilizers and doing blow, as needed, since I was fifteen?

Of course not.

I nodded with what I hoped was a serious, receptive expression on my face but was probably more of a shame-filled grimace.

When Rayvn and Whitney had finished picking over everything and dithered their hearts out, I went to the table and took a pair of scissors, a spiky frog, adhesive, a branch cutter, and two porcelain containers. I put everything into a big white bucket. Then I added a large cranberry juice container filled with water.

Jenson smiled at me and put a hand on my shoulder. "Courage, brother," he said and smiled.

For some reason, this made me feel incredibly sad. I wished I had more courage. If wishes were horses . . . isn't that how it goes? Or is it if wishes were dollars? My wishes better be dollars because horses cost worse than boats.

When I came to again, everyone had disappeared. I stood in the middle of the garden, trying to decide where to go. To the woods? To the orchard? The shoreline?

Yes, that was it. I could do something near the beach. Everyone loves the goddamned beach. I turned and walked through the garden gate, heading around the lodge to the expanse of shoreline in front.

I walked along the rutted gravel road and passed a huge lavender bush so full of bees that it seemed to pulsate. I could do something with grass. Sand. I am a sailor, after all. A man of the sea. I even said so in my eulogy. I was about to walk across the lawn to the water when I saw Tad was already there. Bent over his bucket at the edge of the driftwood line.

A wave of resentment washed through me. *Bloody Tad*. But then something about the sight of my brother out there on the beach reminded me of when we were kids. We used to play. Make things. We used to be okay. What happened to us to turn us into moral failures who can't get along and who can never get enough?

"Christ," I muttered, knuckling my eyes. Then I headed for the orchard.

I walked up past the garden and onto a path that led through the woods parallel to the little road. There, in a small clearing, was Rayvn, with her supplies spread out across the path. Girl had to be crazy to be out there with the trees swaying all around her.

I turned back the way I'd come and took the main road to the orchard. *Good*, I thought as I reached the field. I could do something with an apple branch. That would come across as . . . fertile? Nourishing?

But no. There was goddamned Whitney. She had one of her endless supply of huge scarves spread out beside one of the gnarled old trees, the trunk of which was protected with a wire-covered wooden box to keep the deer away. She was on her knees, arranging her materials. Her floppy, grey felt hat made her look like an old painting. An annoying old painting that was in my fucking way.

As soon as I felt that resentment, I remembered Whitney as a little girl. So uncertain of herself, overwhelmed by that horrible, attention-seeking mother. Out from under her mother's eyes, she'd been rather sweet. Now she was this worried, fretful person who couldn't even share her own eulogy.

I gave my head a shake. The ocean was taken, the woods were taken, the orchard was taken. Maybe I should just go into the garden and cut all the tulips. Make a huge tulip arrangement. My dharma destiny: tulip hog.

Then I remembered that there was a pond on the property. I remembered it as a pretty place, surrounded by poplars. I hadn't been there since we were kids. I headed there via an old path that cut from the orchard through the woods above the lodge. Whitney sensed movement and looked over at me. I gave her a half wave, but she just stared.

The path had been raked. One of the butlers or that weird kid they had working here must have done it. Not a good use of time. Why rake a path no one travelled? Then again, why not? Maybe doing something like that showed care and thoughtfulness. Those things have never been my top priority.

I stopped to stare down at the rake marks on the path. Was it enjoyable to do a task for which you would never get credit? Maybe it was like maintaining a sailboat. I'd always liked to keep everything as pristine as it could be in the face of the ocean's relentless destructiveness.

Maybe, just maybe, if you made the time to rake an unwalked path, you were less likely to end up swilling gin and tonics at a club populated by people who would never notice a raked path. Or something.

I was filled with an unfamiliar feeling of gratitude for whomever had done the pointless raking.

Less unnerved now by the wind, I followed the path until it branched off. One direction led down to the lodge. The other headed up a small hill. At the top, the path opened onto a plateau, in the middle of which was a small pond, its surface covered with lily pads. A slender white tree had fallen across half the pond. A gleaming green-chested duck sat on the downed trunk.

I stopped. The small silvered leaves on the tall, pale trees shivered when the wind rose, and their trunks swayed back and forth.

The place was absurdly pretty. It would have suited Rayvn more than me. It was very much up her velvet-skirted, laced-bodice alley.

I felt like I was intruding on the duck's peaceful afternoon. "Sorry, guy," I said. And then I looked around, embarrassed. That's when I noticed the knee-high Buddha statue at the end of the small stone bridge that went over a creek that led into the pond.

"You too," I said. "I'm just doing a thing here."

Two benches faced each other across the pond, and I chose the nearest one. After laying a cloth down on the bench, I arranged the containers and supplies on top of it. Scissors in hand, I stood up and looked around. I didn't want to cut anything that was still standing. Anything that was alive.

I stood, arms behind my back, feeling ridiculous but also gripped by some strange mood. I was overly aware of my breathing. Too aware of the trees and the filtered sunlight and the shadows of birds flitting around in the branches. I stayed perfectly still until the sense that I didn't belong faded. I stayed like that until a design, an arrangement if you will, appeared in my mind.

And then I set to work.

Chapter 30

NIGEL OWENS

I went with Jenson Kiley when he inspected and took pictures of what he called the "in situ" arrangements. Each of the students had told him where to look when they were done. Wills was upset because he said someone or something threw rocks at him when he was walking back to the lodge after he made his arrangement.

Jenson asked if the objects might have been pine cones and Wills said no, he could tell the difference between rocks and fucking pine cones. He swore at the teacher! He said his scalp was still bleeding, though when he took his hand away from his head, there was no blood. He said he also got nailed in the back and that anyone who thought it was funny to throw rocks at a person was a total psychopath. Then he glared at his weird, white-haired brother, who told him to grow up. That made me a little nervous about going out there.

I had to carry the equipment so Jenson could take pictures. I'd have been helpless if rocks started flying because I was lugging around about twenty odd-shaped bags. The straps were around each of my shoulders and around my neck, and I had a bag in each hand. The stuff was pretty heavy, too. You'd have thought we were heading out to take pictures of the *Sports Illustrated* swimsuit issue. Is that still a thing? It's the most famous photography I'm familiar with. Don't get me wrong. I'm not *that* familiar with it or anything.

"Come along, come along!" Jenson said as he left the garden, all jazzy and brisk and unconcerned about bizarre rock attacks. He nearly shut the gate in my face, which was already overheated from trying to keep up with him. For an older guy, he's really energetic. He always seems like he's on the 2X speed setting.

I'm really feeling the whole floral design thing and starting to think maybe I could be a floral artist and do spiritual designs and make huge money decorating special events, like the Oscars or at least a wedding with a massive budget. When I go back to Port Alberni, I might see if any car dealership owners are getting married soon. Those are the richest people I know. Maybe my floral focus could be the automotive industry.

I'm also wondering if I should become a butler, like Helen and Murray and Gavin, but that would mean dealing with clients like Wills and Tad and Whitney.

It's interesting to me that the awfulness of the cousins doesn't seem to bother the butlers, especially Helen. She never rolls her eyes when they complain or say mean shit that no normal person would ever say except on the internet. And she doesn't scrunch up her face when one of them asks for some dumb-ass rich person thing, like when Whitney asked if someone could iron her scarves, or Tad asked if anyone had time to wash and vacuum his Land Rover. An hour later I saw Gavin cleaning it. And Gavin did it the way he does everything: like he really cares. I carried Whitney's scarves to her cabin after Murray ironed and folded them. The freaking things were as big as bed sheets. Man, that kind of stuff would make me crazy, so I probably shouldn't be a butler.

At least Rayvn's nice. Probably because she's not rich. That makes me want to help her out. I'd be happy to iron her velvet skirts or whatever.

"Please, darling," said Jenson. "A bit more careful with the camera equipment. It's banging around on you like pots on a tinker's pony."

"Sorry," I said, and tried to hold the jouncing bags against my body as I broke into a trot so I could keep up. "Are you worried about someone throwing rocks at us?"

Jenson laughed. "No. I think Mr. Todd was in a heightened state. A pine cone fell on him and it felt like a rock. Floral design is very intense."

I wasn't so sure but I didn't argue.

First, we went down to the beach.

Jenson Kiley stopped as we reached the tide line and lifted his nose as though he could sniff out the arrangement.

"Hmmm," he said, and then he turned and marched off toward something I couldn't see until we got closer.

"I see," said Jenson, when we reached it. He put his hands behind his back and slowed his pace. Head cocked to the side, he stared down.

"Tad Todd's," he said.

"Yes, sir," I said. It was a dramatic moment so I felt like I should be formal.

Jenson walked around it, viewing it from every possible direction. Then he got on his hands and knees and stared at it. It was fascinating to watch him.

And Tad's "dharmarrangement" was, I have to say, cool as shit.

Tad, who for my money is the nastiest cousin, had used a long, narrow tin shaped like a rectangle as his container. He'd half buried it in the sand behind a driftwood log. Then he'd made a little person and a little dog out of driftwood. And they were good. Totally recognizable. He carved little holes in the bodies to attach the limbs. The little man figure stood with one foot on the lip of the tin container, like he was about to walk out of it. The little wooden dog sat beside him. Tad had used a short, thick piece of wood for the dog's body and head, and it had a stick tail that had just the right amount of curve to it. The little man figure had a stick in his right hand and a hat made of a leaf, a seagrass beard, and seaweed clothes. It was hard to imagine Tad taking the time to make such a neat little driftwood doll. It made me feel some kind of way. Surprised and maybe sort of sad, though I don't know why.

The tin was mostly filled with sand and lined with small, round rocks. Tad put tiny clumps of frilly white stuff that looked like grass around the rocks. I remembered Tad talking at dinner about how their father wouldn't let them have a dog and how he'd always liked those Scottie dogs. He'd sounded sort of human when he said that.

The whole thing made me like Tad Todd a lot more than I had a few minutes ago. It probably wasn't great art, but there was something kind of sweet and cheerful about the little stick man walking on the beach with his loyal driftwood dog. They looked like they belonged right there and also like they were just passing through.

"I see," Jenson Kiley was saying, when I tuned back in. "I see. Duty, discipline, companionship. It's all here. So straightforwardly presented. My god, my god, the charm of it!"

I found myself nodding.

"He's cut tiny joints into the figure's limbs. I don't know how he managed it in the time available. Shows real skill as a woodworker. But nothing too invasive."

"The little guy looks like he's about to walk out of the container," I said. "No tin is going to stop him."

Jenson turned to look at me, and for a second, he didn't say anything. I wondered if I'd upset him. "That, young man, is a fine insight. What does it suggest to you?"

I shrugged and looked down at the tiny man and his walking stick. "It's like he's just taking a rest in there. He's definitely going to keep going, him and his dog. Forever, maybe."

"So good!" Jenson said in a voice so loud I jumped. "This is not a static design. It reflects the movement of the ocean. It's entirely suitable to its place and its maker. Excellent. Excellent! I did NOT see this coming." He clapped his hands.

"Please," he said. "Unpack my things. Let's capture this before a marauding seagull eats the little fellow's pants."

And soon he had me holding a huge silver reflective dish to hide shadows as he photographed the arrangement from all angles.

Chapter 31

Helen, Murray, and Gavin took a break after serving lunch and watched Jenson Kiley taking photos of something on the beach.

"Did your late mistress, Ms. Todd, take this class?" asked Gavin.

"Many times," said Helen. "She adored it. And she adored Jenson."

"And what was her purpose?" asked Murray.

"Her dharma statement was always the same," said Helen. "It never wavered as long as I knew her." Helen thought back to the letter Edna had left for her. In it she'd said that her greatest wish was that the Yatra Institute would continue to run in a way that honoured the earth and the goodness in all people. It could never be developed. It had to be kept safe to function as a place of deep spiritual and environmental development.

"Might we go around and see the arrangements later?" asked Gavin. "I'm quite intrigued."

"Lunch is over," said Murray. "And dinner prep is well in hand. I think we'll use the Minton china this time."

Helen nodded. "Certainly. You can visit the displays while the students are doing movement. I will warn you to stay out of Jenson's way. He'll be deep in his flow. Photographing and assessing."

"It's all so powerfully strange," said Murray. Gavin put a hand on her shoulder. "Like you, my dearest." Murray beamed up at him and Helen wondered what would become of the two of them. Neither had spoken aloud about their feelings. Gavin had briefly mentioned that he was taking a time-out on relationships. Helen had no idea whether he was gay or bisexual or straight. Gavin was the best-mannered, kindest, and most widely competent enigma Helen had encountered. And she was quite sure Murray was in love with him.

But Helen didn't ask questions. Their relationship would unfold in its own way and its own time without her getting involved.

"I need to go out later this evening," said Helen. "I'll be away after dinner."

They turned to her, surprised.

"I need to attend a meeting. Do you mind handling things?" Her question was a formality. They were trained butlers. The two of them could have handled dinner service for the G7 if necessary.

"Of course," said Gavin. Helen didn't want to have to explain that she was heading off to a meeting of the Death Positive Club. She'd discovered that their monthly meeting was being held that evening at the Sutil Fairgrounds at six. And though she felt faintly absurd about it, she was going to go and sound them out. For what, she didn't know. Discrepancies about Edna's death, she guessed. Concerns. Anything she could report to Officer Rosedale. She wasn't going to investigate, exactly. She would just help out by making use of the fact that she was a good listener and people liked to talk to her.

But before she could prepare for her visit to the Death Positive Club, she needed to interview Tad and Whitney.

And so, at 2:30, she was once again waiting in Dauber Cottage. Helen emanated calm in a way that was almost impossible to ignore. But even with her core emotional temperature so deeply regulated, she had to acknowledge that she was not looking forward to these interviews. She'd been charmed by Rayvn and found Wills quite surprising, but the thought of Tad and Whitney made her stomach clench. She sat still, paying attention to her breath and the subtleties of air and sound and sensation in and around her. She acknowledged her slight aversion to Tad and her discomfort with Whitney. She felt the borders of her resistance and they dissipated, so that when Tad Todd entered the cottage, bringing with him his own peculiar energy, her own steady-state equilibrium stayed intact.

"Uh, hello there?" he said, his voice slightly too loud for the soft contours of the space.

"Welcome," said Helen.

He left his jacket on and he entered the round room looking exceptionally uncomfortable. Come to think of it, Helen had never seen him looking comfortable anywhere, except a few times when she'd spotted him walking by himself outdoors.

"Take a seat," she said.

He sat down. In the deep stillness of the cottage, she saw clearly again that Tad Todd was a striking individual, with his refined features and exaggerated grace. How odd that his personality obscured his appearance to such a degree.

"How are you doing?" she asked.

"Fine."

"How are you finding your meditation practice?"

"Terrible," he said. "It's uncomfortable and boring. And strangely stressful."

She smiled. "Yes, it is sometimes."

"But I get the point of it. I mean, most of life is just trying to avoid how uncomfortable and stressful and boring everything is."

"That's a deep insight," she said.

"I guess this is where you tell me there's something on the other side? Like nirvana or bliss or something?"

"Sometimes. For some people."

"And for the rest of us? What's the point?"

"The point is to pay attention to what's actually happening. Most of us are not present for most of what happens in our lives."

"Mindfulness," he said. "Shoot me now."

She laughed. People who signed up voluntarily for meditation classes did not usually speak so candidly. They were too invested in putting a positive spin on things or at least trying to. His hostility was almost refreshing.

"If whatever is going on gets to be too much—physical pain for instance, or intrusive and repetitive thoughts—you can change the channel."

He stared.

"By that I mean, find a neutral place in your body. A place that doesn't hurt. A place that just is."

"Just is," he said.

"A place that feels settled. You can move your attention there. That will give you some rest. Then, when you feel ready, you can go back to your anchors."

"When I concentrate on my breath, I feel like I'm going to pass out."

"The breath is hard for many people. That's why I suggest you use sound or the feel of your hands instead of or in addition to the breath."

"Okay. I'll try it. I have no doubt this is good for me," he said, in the same tone one would use when about to eat a cold bowl of gruel.

"I encourage you to remain open. Have no expectations for what might happen. Try to greet whatever arises with curiosity. Friendliness. That's enough."

Tad exhaled, long and slow. "There's something I should mention. I mean, besides the meditation stuff. Now's probably as good a time as any."

Helen waited.

"I know Wills has told you about him coming here. We had a pact. We were going to keep it a secret. But Willy has never managed to keep a promise in his life. Why would he start now?"

"Why was it a secret?" she asked.

"Edna asked us not to say anything."

"You were also here earlier?" asked Helen.

"Yes," said Tad.

"Do you want to tell me about it?" she asked.

"Edna emailed. Asked if I could come and see her." A pause. "She asked me not to tell Wills or my parents or anyone what I was doing."

"I see. And how did it go?"

"A bit strange. Because it was Edna. She asked me a lot of questions about my life. About my values. Tried to get me to do yoga." He laughed softly at the memory. "The only thing I dislike more than yoga is dancing. And meditating, it turns out."

"Do you know why she invited you?"

"Oh, I assume she was trying to figure out whether to put me in her will. Or whether to cut me out. My parents said that our uncle Ned, her late husband, wanted to leave us something. Apparently he thought wealth was wasted on the old so he wanted the youngest generation to inherit from him. None of us have had kids, so we're the youngest generation, even though we aren't particularly young anymore."

The colour was high in his cheeks and so he looked less bloodless and sinister than usual. Or maybe it was just the soft light of the cottage.

"How did she seem?" asked Helen.

"My god, she was fit for someone her age. But so opinionated. I always wondered if she was"—he lowered his voice—"a little loony. You know, from all the strangeness around here."

"Did she appear cognitively impaired?" asked Helen.

"No. Sharp as a . . . well, sharp as she ever was. Given her starting point." He shifted in his seat, and his natural indolence asserted itself. He crossed one long leg over the other and brushed something invisible off his trousers.

"What happened?" asked Helen.

"You don't like me, do you?" he said.

Helen didn't answer.

"It's okay. No one does. It's my eyes. They're strange. Edna didn't like me either."

"She didn't?"

"I am not her sort of people. Going to see her was a useless exercise and a waste of my time."

"What do you do when you're not here?" asked Helen, suddenly curious.

Tad let his head fall to the side. "Nothing. But I do a lot of it. It has fallen to me to look after our parents and stop them from falling further into penury. No wonder the old lady didn't want to leave anything directly to them."

The old lady. How Edna would have hated that description.

"My parents have blown all their money or at least what was left after the crash in '08. And I have blown most of mine trying to keep them afloat. My mother has a penthouse apartment in West Vancouver. My father lives on a golf course in Palm Springs. I go between them trying to put out fires."

This was not at all what Helen had expected to hear. She'd assumed Tad spent his time going from cigar bars to private tennis clubs.

"Oh yes, we're right on the razor's edge. Willy too. But at least he didn't waste his money on the parentals. Oh no. He threw his in the ocean when he tried to get that regatta going. And Whitney. God, those people who birthed her make our parents look like responsible citizens." He sighed. "Is there anything sadder than poor rich folk? I think not."

"Whitney and her parents are not well-off?"

"God no. There are church mice that have healthier financial statements. Her father, the producer"—Tad surrounded the word with air quotes—"does nothing but cheat on her mother with women who think he can put them in his pathetic movies. And Whit's mother blew all *her* money trying to finance pictures that would give her a starring role. I'm surprised Whitney had the money to get herself here."

Helen took that in. "I'm sorry to hear things are challenging for you," she said, finally. And she was. She appreciated the honesty of his answer. Of his obvious need. And she honoured his commitment to his parents.

"I should not have let Edna know how disappointed I was that she planned to put this place in a trust."

"She told you that?"

"Yes. I suggested there were better, more lucrative options. One wouldn't have to turn it into a subdivision filled with McMansions, of course. But it could be made into a rather nice resort instead of . . . whatever it is now."

A centre for spiritual and environmental education, thought Helen, feeling protectiveness well up in her. She felt relief every time she remembered that the lodge and grounds were protected. Even if she chose the wrong person, the Institute could not be sold or turned into anything other than what it was. On the other hand, the wrong person could do a lot of damage in other ways.

"It was tacky of me. But when the money's gone, it's hard to even pretend to be anything other than a greedy little grub, isn't it?"

Helen, who'd never had much money to speak of, thought perhaps there were other responses available. Such as living within one's means. She often thought of the parable of the wealthy man who asked the Master why spirituality was important. "It will enrich you," the Master said, "by teaching you to want less."

She didn't share the story with Tad because he probably wouldn't enjoy it. In her career working for the very wealthy, she probably wouldn't get many chances to retell parables about the dangers of wealth. Nor would she be retelling many of the suttas about the Buddha and the rich householder, which were some of her favourites. Not for the first time, she reflected that she found herself in a strange career.

"Did you and Edna have an argument?" Helen asked.

"Like I said, I asked her what she planned to do with this place when she went. She told me it was going to be left in a trust. And I said it was my understanding that that was not what Uncle Ned would have wanted. And she informed me that Uncle Ned had been dead a long time and that she was following the spirit of his wishes. I asked how, exactly, she was doing that if she left the place in a trust to be run by the old hippies and communists on this island and not a blood relative. She made a face at me, and I guess it irked me. I said I might have to get a lawyer to see about her plans and she suggested I leave. Post-haste. Don't blame her, really. I'd have thrown me out too."

When he finished his inglorious account, Tad's narrow face appeared more relaxed and he slouched further into his chair. In that moment, Helen found herself almost liking him.

"This place is the only significant asset left in the family and we're not getting any part of it. Fine. I can get a job in finance or some god-damned thing. I know guys from school who'll find me something. Willy can go be a captain on a yacht. He won't care. And our parents are going to have to adjust their lifestyles. That's all there is for it."

"Tell me," said Helen. "If you knew she was not going to leave the Institute to you, why did you agree to come here and take the courses?"

He pursed his lips and made a little kissing noise. Ten minutes before, she would have found it distasteful. But now it seemed almost endearing. Tad Todd was a man under a lot of pressure and, like most people, he didn't seem to understand that he'd picked up his burdens and could put them down, if he chose.

"Just in case," he said, "she had changed her mind. Or she'd decided to give us another chance. I thought maybe she would leave us a few crumbs if we came and did what she wanted." He hesitated. "I didn't know anything about our mystery cousin. Did she come and see Edna? You should check into that. Maybe Rayvn doesn't care about the money. But you can be sure the rest of us do. Acutely."

"When did you last see Edna?" asked Helen.

"About three weeks before she died. Like I said, she looked extremely well, in that clean-living way of hers. Like she'd never met a probiotic she hadn't taken."

Then Helen found herself asking the question she hadn't planned on.

"What do you think about her death?"

"Totally bizarre. She always struck me as someone who would make a big deal about being comfortable with dying, but only because she assumed that she would live forever."

It was exactly what Helen thought. The medical examiner and police theory was that Edna had taken her life because she was in emotional distress after being alone and silent for too long. That theory was now in pieces. She hadn't been silent or alone.

"Do you think she took her own life?"

"How the hell do I know?" said Tad. "Lots of people you wouldn't expect do it. The world is completely fucked, if you're paying attention." He grimaced. "But I can't see why she would. She didn't like me or Willy much, but she seemed pretty happy with herself."

"Thank you for your candour," said Helen. Then a final question occurred to her.

"Did you see anyone else while you were here?"

He shook his head. "No. Just the ferry people. I brought my vehicle. Didn't get out of my car on the boat. And I was only here for one night before she decided I wasn't worth her time." He levelled his pale gaze at Helen and it was like two moons had settled their cold, twin lights on her. "I guess she wasn't such a dummy after all."

The self-loathing in his words made compassion for him well up in Helen's chest. As difficult as it was to be the target of his hostility, it was certainly much harder to be the one awash in so much anger and fear that it poured out of him. Only someone suffering a great deal behaved like Tad Todd did.

"We are all worthy of each other's time," she said. "And each other's care."

Tad Todd slowly closed his strange eyes. "Thank you," he said. "I guess I need to remember that. Maybe these courses will help."

Helen didn't answer.

"Our time is up," she said. "Thank you."

Whitney entered Dauber Cottage. Helen sat in the silence until she took off her shoes and hung up her coat before she appeared in the doorway, diffident as any new yogi.

"Welcome," said Helen and gestured for her to take a seat.

When the girl was settled, Helen asked how she was. Whitney's face crumpled and she began to cry.

Far from being concerned, Helen took this as a good sign. People engaged in spiritual pursuits were like flower buds. Sometimes they opened easily and sometimes they needed to stay closed until they were ready. Tears, in Helen's experience, were one manifestation of the heart's opening. Within reason, of course.

"I'm sorry," said Whitney, as she reached for the box of tissue Helen had placed between them. "This keeps happening."

Helen didn't say anything. She just waited.

Whitney blew her nose and looked around for a garbage can. Helen moved the small birchbark receptacle toward her.

"It's going fine," said Whitney, grabbing another tissue and balling it in her fist. "I don't know why I keep crying."

"Sometimes when we slow down, emotions arise," said Helen.

"And the floodgates open, apparently," said Whitney. "I guess all of this"—she gestured around the cottage—"it's got me thinking. Or feeling, rather. I am not living my best life."

Helen nodded.

"My mother is focused on success. A bitter irony considering the state of her career." She dabbed her eyes. "All of this, uh, work we're doing has made me feel how much pressure I'm under. *We're* under. Me and Tad and Wills, I mean. I don't know if Rayvn's parents are also needy and demanding."

Helen made herself as quiet as possible.

"I'm quite interested in becoming a librarian. Having a quiet, creative, *appreciative* life. This is a horrible disappointment to my mother. First, she sent me to finishing school in Switzerland. I was supposed to find a rich husband. No luck. I also failed to meet a wealthy partner during my undergraduate studies at university. So now—"

A knock at the door interrupted her flow of words. The heavy door opened, and seconds later Rayvn appeared, most of her obscured behind an enormous bouquet.

"Oops, sorry to interrupt," she said, peeking out from behind the splendid mass of greenery and blossoms. "I thought you'd be done! I just made this for you. For here. It's like, my gratitude offering. Anyway, I'll leave it over on this ledge." She did so and quickly shuffled away, her bare feet making a shushing noise against the concrete floor. Then the door opened and closed and she was gone.

The atmosphere in the interview had changed. So had Whitney. Her face had gone expressionless and Helen wondered what it had taken her to open up as she had.

"I'm sorry."

"Me too," said Whitney, in a flat voice.

"You were saying," prompted Helen.

"I was saying that my mother is starting to lose hope in me. And maybe that's okay."

The previous intensity was gone. The arrival of the bouquet had been fatal to the flow of the interview. Helen wondered if Rayvn had done it intentionally. And she wondered if Whitney had been stopped before she, too, could confess that Edna had invited her to Yatra.

With luck, Helen would find out at their next interview.

"Do you have any questions about meditation practice?" Helen asked.

Whitney shook her head. "I'm just trying to show up and be present for whatever happens."

That, Helen thought, was a fine answer.

Chapter 32

MURRAY CLEARY

At about three thirty, when some of the students were having their personal reflection time and Helen was doing interviews, I was trying to avoid reflecting on the fact that I had no job waiting for me when I finished here, but I did have massive student loans to take care of. Oh, and I was also avoiding the reflection that the end of our time at the Institute meant I would no longer be living with Helen and Gavin, which felt unbearably bleak.

A blessed distraction came in the form of Jenson Kiley striding through the garden, followed by Nigel, who laboured under the weight of various pieces of equipment while Jenson carried exactly nothing. Fair play to him.

Shortly after, Nigel came puffing into the lodge.

I put down a slender container filled with small, fuzzy-headed alliums on the coffee station table, and he burst into his story.

"Holy sh—, I mean, wow. You need to check it out. They're so . . . like soulful. I mean, considering."

"Pronoun references, my good man," said Gavin, who was sweeping the floor, making it look like dancing.

"The arrangements, I mean, dharmarrangements. They are, like, cool as hell. It's shocking."

I turned to Gavin. "Shall we dash out now and have a look?"

Gavin looked at his watch. "We have time. Where are they, Nigel? Save us hunting them down."

Nigel explained that one arrangement was on the beach, which we already knew. Another was up near some pond. A third was in the small clearing in the forest, and the fourth was in the orchard.

"If you can guess who did which one, I'll give you ten bucks," Nigel said.

"Are you good for such a princely sum?" I asked.

"After I get paid, I will be."

We took off our aprons and put on lightweight jackets. When we reached the beach arrangement, Gavin bent low to inspect it.

"Look at this," he said, admiringly.

I had to agree that it was lovely.

"Quite cunningly designed," said Gavin.

The little driftwood man and his dog rested in the half-buried tin container, standing firm in the face of persistent winds.

"Surpassingly charming," I said. "Who do you think made it?"

"I believe I saw Tad Todd working here. It must be his."

"What does it mean for his dharma?" I wondered. "That he wants to go for a walk with a dog?"

Gavin glanced up at me, not accusingly, but not precisely admiringly either. "I think it's more than that, probably. Something more meaningful. Loyalty, perhaps? Nature? Companionship?"

These were not things I'd have associated with the rude, translucent-skinned, and slightly eerie Tad Todd.

Gavin stood. "On to the next?"

"Yes," I said, taking his arm. "Let us go and see what other hidden depths these arrangements reveal about our guests."

I admit, it was heaven to walk with him.

We made our way up from the beach, past the lodge, and onto a trail behind it. "This way to the pond," he said. "I found it on a jog. It's tucked away, and surpassingly pretty."

What I wouldn't do for him to call *me* surpassingly pretty.

As we walked, light seemed to shift and the white trees around us swayed.

And there was the small pond, the sky and the trees reflected on its surface. Pond skaters jerked across the water and birds hopped from branch to branch in the encircling trees. A frog leapt into the pond with a plop when we approached, and a duck paddled placidly away.

I was too enchanted to speak. Then we both spotted the arrangement at the water's edge.

At the base of a slender tree that had fallen partway across the pond, stones had been placed to form a sort of platform that led up and onto the pale trunk. The rocks extended far out onto the trunk as it bridged the pond, and the procession ended with a simple, perfectly round stone. Petals from the flowering wild currant bushes that grew in profusion and fragranced the area had been scattered onto the stone platform and between the stones that led up to the fallen tree.

The designer had set two simple porcelain containers on either side of the stone platform. Each was filled with water and rocks, and the ends of flexible branches that had been woven together to create a curved archway.

"It looks like the setting for a fairy wedding procession," I said. "Exquisite."

"It really is," Gavin agreed, squatting down to take in every detail.

For reasons I didn't totally understand, I felt deeply moved and had to sit down on the old bench that faced the little arbour. Gavin joined me and we stared at the arrangement for a while.

And as we watched, a small bird landed on the rock platform and pecked at one of the petals. Then the bird flew through the woven bower, as though delighted at its own daring.

"I'm dying," I whispered. "Do you think whoever made this fell in trying to place the rocks? It's not a big tree."

"I imagine it was touch and go," said Gavin.

As gusts of wind blew through the clearing and rippled across the pond, pink petals fluttered up and then fell into the water, where they floated among the lily pads.

"Which one of the guests is half elf?" I wondered.

"Maybe Rayvn?" said Gavin. "Or Whitney? This is so delicate. But that's reductive, I suppose."

"Could you imagine if it was Wills's? Wouldn't that be a shock?"

Gavin nodded as we watched a pair of tiny songbirds flit through the archway.

I tried to imagine Wills Todd, so bulky and raw, crawling out onto the delicate white tree, placing small stones and petals as he went. I tried to visualize him weaving the branches into a bower. If he'd made this, he was nothing like the person I thought he was.

"And what does this say about the person's dharma?" I asked.

"That they love beauty," said Gavin. "That they appreciate delicacy. That they can take a lot of care."

"And that they are half elf," I added.

"Or troll," said Gavin.

With awareness of time passing and the dinner hour approaching, we got up and headed for the apple orchard. We saw no one on the path that we'd so carefully raked before the guests arrived. And I didn't see any of the rocks Wills reported being struck with as he was making his way back to the lodge.

When we emerged into the apple orchard, the tall grass swayed around the short, twisted fruit trees. Some of the branches were staked with lengths of lumber. Many of the trees were protected by wood and chicken wire frames to keep out . . . something.

Between two of the apple trees we found the third arrangement, hidden in the grass.

"Oh," said Gavin, and the single word captured what I felt.

The arrangement looked like a funeral pyre, waiting to be lit. Broken sticks and twigs formed a cone, out of which emerged a single apple branch, topped with three white blooms. The branch was broken about two-thirds of the way up, so the blooms hung down in a poignant way.

Was this arrangement expressing hope out of brokenness? Or despair?

Dead grass had been painstakingly tucked into the base of the arrangement. Some of it was woven around the sticks, some protruded at intervals in little grass tassels.

"Is there a vase under that?" Gavin knelt to get a better look.

I got down beside him.

"What does it mean, do you think?" asked Gavin, almost to himself.

"Bloom where you're planted?" I suggested, though I didn't mean it. "Which one made this?"

"Wills?" suggested Gavin.

"I have a feeling it's Whitney," I said.

"Why?"

"Just a hunch. Something about that broken branch reminds me of her."

Gavin glanced at his watch. "We need to go. We can stop in the clearing on the way back and look at the final one. They'll be coming in for drinks soon. Need a full diplomatic presence."

Gavin smiled at me and his lean face creased in a way that reminded me of a black-and-white photograph in a men's magazine. Classically handsome.

"Do things seem less tense between them the past day or so?" I asked. "Not saying that I don't think they are going to stab each other in the side with forks when we're not looking."

Gavin winced. And because he was always the consummate professional, even out here, in a windy orchard where no one could possibly overhear us, he didn't reply. But he also didn't make me feel as though he disapproved of my idle gossip, which I appreciated.

We walked over to the cabins closest to the orchard and then took a path that led through the lower woods toward the lodge. We rounded a corner and I saw a flash of movement. A person. Someone had turned and fled when they heard us.

"Hello?" I called to the person. Nothing.

Then I rushed to see who it was. Gavin hurried after, and we emerged into a clearing, the grass golf-course green.

No one was there.

"Did you see?" I asked.

I followed his gaze and saw a silver container shaped like a skull, cracked in two and tossed into a patch of ferns at the edge of the glade.

"Oh," I said, feeling rather disturbed by the violence against a helpless vase. "You don't think the brokenness is the point, do you? Like some postmodern deconstructionist thing?"

Gavin shook his head.

We inspected the broken vase. "There's the arrangement," he said, pointing to some flowers that had been thrown into the bushes.

"Should we try to fix it? Clean it up?"

Gavin looked pensive. "Let's talk to Helen first. And let's hope Jenson got photos before it was . . . destroyed."

"Seems wildly hostile to go around wrecking a person's flowers," I said. "Especially when they're meant to represent the person's life goals or dharma or whatever. Do you think the person who just ran away from us is responsible?"

"I don't know," said Gavin. He took my arm in a protective way, which I quite enjoyed, and we walked together out of the clearing. "I find it extremely suspicious."

"Maybe an animal wrecked it," I said. "Like a crow or magpie. They like shiny things. Do they have magpies in Canada?"

"I don't expect birds are quite so hostile," he said.

"Or a fox. Are foxes quite mischievous? Flower wreckers and whatnot?"

"I don't think they make a habit of breaking vases and throwing their contents into the woods, but I could be wrong," said Gavin.

"Skunks, then?" I said, lowering my voice as we entered the garden and waiting as Gavin carefully closed the gate behind us.

"What's this about skunks?" asked a gravelly female voice.

It was Wayfarer. As usual, she looked as though she might be about to scale a tall building. She really was amazing to look at, and I found myself checking to see whether Gavin was staring as much as I was. He wasn't.

"Do they have skunks here?"

"Ha," said Wayfarer. "I've nae seen one. But I'm no naturalist." She held an enormous glass of something brown in one hand and a brown egg in the other. "Got to refuel and it's a no carbs day."

"How was this morning's movement class?" asked Gavin politely.

"Oh ay, just fine. Hardly any violence. And tonight we are going to burn bright. Getting ready for the first performance."

I felt my eyes go wide. "They will be doing a public dance?"

"You won't believe your eyes," she said.

I suspected that no matter how it went, I wouldn't.

"I'm going for my nap after this. And then my stretching routine. Join me if you feel like it?" she said and I noticed she was looking at Gavin.

He smiled politely back and didn't commit. At least, I hope it was merely a polite smile.

Wayfarer swept off in a cloud of vanilla perfume and we continued toward the lodge.

"Now that is a magnificent Scotswoman," I said.

Gavin grinned and smoothed the front of his jacket in preparation to enter the lodge and begin service. We stopped on the porch just outside the deck.

"Are you dying of lust?" I asked, in spite of myself.

"I want to know her leg routine," said Gavin. "And you're right. She is very entertaining."

"More than me? I also have the remnants of an accent, if you hadn't noticed." Dear God, I was pathetic.

"You have the best accent in the world," said Gavin.

"Good," I said. I slipped my feet in the shoes I use for service. "I'm guessing she does squats while holding small cars over her head. Plus four to five thousand leg lifts per side."

"Hundreds of thousands of leg lifts per week, would be my estimate," agreed Gavin.

"Tonight, we can tell Helen and Jenson about the destroyed arrangement and discuss who might have done such a thing and why."

My heart nearly stopped when I spotted someone sitting on the small bench tucked to the side of a huge lavender bush just below us. The figure was motionless and seemed to be listening intently.

After a beat, I realized it was Tad Todd. He didn't look at us. Instead, he kept his gaze fixed on the garden.

Chapter 33

At 6:15 p.m., Helen drove onto the fairgrounds. It consisted of five acres of cleared, lumpy ground on which stood an uneven riding ring, a dilapidated rabbit barn, a tilting chicken shed, and a row of ramshackle horse stalls, as well as decrepit cow and sheep barns. The barns had been painted red to distract from the fact that they were not structurally sound. Everyone on Sutil knew that one good windstorm during the fall fair could take out every competitive farm animal on the island, which would have been sad, even to the people who loathed the concept of farm animals or animal objectification.

The Death Positive Club met in the 4-H building, a plywood-sided hut with a tin roof and no right angles. Inside were a peeling linoleum floor, a single portable heater, two folding tables, and stained folding chairs. On one wall was a poster detailing the reproductive system of the duck and on another was a poster listing the tenets of the death positive movement, which included a list of items, like *(1) I believe that by hiding death and dying behind closed doors, we do more harm than good to our society,* and *(3) I believe that talking about and engaging with my inevitable death is not morbid, but displays a natural curiosity about the human condition.* Helen couldn't argue with any of it.

Every head in the room turned to look at Helen when she entered.

"Look who it is!" said one.

"It's Helen!" cried Ronald Li. "She's come to help us die!" He stood outside of his casket, hammer in hand.

Ronald Li was a retired notary and the owner of the Sutil Island landfill. He'd given his notary business to his son and the day-to-day operations of the landfill to his daughter. He was at least eighty and still considered one of the best fiddlers in town, which was high praise because fiddlers were almost as common on Sutil Island as drummers.

"Helen! Check out my coffin," said Tanner, who was sitting in a graphically daring coffin that could have followed the Grateful Dead on tour if it had wheels.

Coffins, most of them with people inside, ran the length of the room.

"Hello, Tanner," said Helen, not terribly surprised to see him here rather than at the float plane dock. She'd assumed that most of the members of the Death Positive Club would be senior citizens, but Sutil Islanders were not ageist in their interests.

Tanner beamed from inside his brightly painted box. Her initial impression that the coffin looked like a jam band poster had been right. The name Phish was actually painted along the side of the coffin and she could see an inexpertly painted alien and a lot of flames stretching around the whole thing. The art was a little on the nose, but it was enthusiastic.

"After Edna died, I decided to check out the club," said Tanner, who looked like an angel sitting inside his casket. "Get myself ready for the inevitable. We're working on our coffins," he added, unnecessarily.

Ronald nodded. "Way more fun than building birdhouses." He gave his own coffin, made of what looked like a collection of spare bits of lumber from the dump, a kick and a piece fell off.

"More room to express oneself than a commercially made version," said a white-haired woman who looked like she should be greeting people in church, not emerging from a coffin like the world's most wholesome and grandmotherly vampire.

"Oh, hello, Mary," said Helen, going over to clasp her hands. "It's such a pleasure to see you again."

"Mary and I are just back from India," said Mary, beaming at Helen. She was a former Catholic nun who had left the Church when she was in her fifties so she could marry her wife, who was also called Mary. There were at least eight Marys on Sutil, but "Nun Mary" and her wife claimed the title of "the Marys." The Marys were almost as vigorous and involved in the community as Edna had been. Non-nun Mary, which was the name people used for Nun Mary's wife, was a fine furniture builder, which explained why their side-by-side coffins were beautifully constructed using dovetail joinery. As Helen approached, Non-nun-Mary sat up. She was dressed in Carhartt overalls with a handknitted cardigan overtop.

"I think we should line them both with dog blankets," she said.

Mary turned to look at her wife. "Why?"

"Because we've kept the dog blankets for every dog we've ever had. Couldn't bear to throw them away. That's clinging, right Helen?"

As usual, any question about attachment was directed to the Buddhist meditation teacher, even when there was a former Catholic nun in the room.

Helen allowed that it might be.

"I would like to be buried among the scent of our dead dogs," said Non-nun Mary, who had grown up in Texas and lived in Medicine Hat before coming to Sutil twenty-five years before.

"Fewer things for our executors to chuck out," said Nun Mary.

All the people sitting in coffins nodded.

Helen guessed that this sort of conversation was a big part of the appeal of being in the club. They came together to consider death in all its aspects, from the mundane to the spiritual and from coffin accessories to executors.

"I hope you don't mind me dropping in," said Helen, "but I have a few questions and thought it might be easier to talk to everyone together."

Nods from the people sitting upright in their boxes.

"I might need some help getting out of this," said Non-nun Mary. "I seem to have seized up."

"I wonder if anyone's ever been buried in a chair?" mused Tanner. "Like a super-comfy easy chair recliner? You could build a box around it?"

"Sounds like a lot of waste to me," came the voice of someone lying in their coffin.

More people started to sit up and extricate themselves.

"You'd have to go pretty deep to fit a chair in the ground," said a man with a lavish grey-and-white beard. "Ground around here's pretty rocky for that. Might need a rock chipper."

"Neighbours would complain about the noise," said another one.

"And you'd have to ask the crematorium about the size of the oven door if you're going the commercial cremains route," said a tiny woman who emerged from her coffin looking supremely rested.

"Be okay for an outdoor pyre," said Ronald. "But there are too many toxins in your average recliner."

Bless them, thought Helen. Her mind went to her teacher and the other monks who practised the death meditation. They spent months and sometimes years contemplating the nitty-gritty of things like decomposition into a human's component parts. She wondered if any members of the Death Positive Club had thought about having their remains put into a glass coffin and displayed. She suspected a few of them had. In that way, the club was obviously working for them. They were facing death head on. Or at least at an angle. Helen had a sudden vision of a row of decomposition boxes placed outside the local Legion to remind people going in and out of what awaited us all.

When the club members were settled onto the folding 4-H chairs or sitting up in their coffins, she smiled at the group.

"I'm sorry to interrupt," she said, again. "But I'm trying to understand Edna's death."

"Join the club," muttered someone. Helen thought it might have been Nun Mary.

"So are we," said Ronald. "We are concerned."

"It's bullshit is what it is," said the grey-bearded man. There were many nods of agreement.

"Oh," said Helen, surprised.

"She didn't do it," said Non-nun Mary. "She'd have told us. We're in this together."

"She'd have at least followed her plans," said Ronald.

"What did you know about her plans?" asked Helen. "For her transition, I mean."

"She was mostly focused on the sky burial," said Nun Mary. "We were all so happy for her when she found that place in the States. You helped her with that, right?"

Helen nodded.

"So exciting," said someone.

"I'm a bit jealous," said someone else.

"She was interested in making friends with the process," said Ronald. "Like the rest of us."

"She did keep quiet about some parts of her decision-making," said Nun Mary.

"Around estate planning and the lodge and that sort of thing," added Non-nun Mary.

"Witches like to keep things close to the chest," said the man with the beard. "Sort of secretive, I've noticed."

"I found it strange that she didn't discuss her estate," said Ronald. "The rest of us talk about it endlessly. And as a notary, I really encourage that."

"It *was* strange, considering she was our president," said the tiny, well-rested woman.

"Everyone plans at their own pace. One's death is no small matter," said Nun Mary.

More nods.

"Did any of you have any idea that she was planning to transition when she did or why?" asked Helen.

Club members exchanged looks. Helen saw concern in those glances, and suspicion.

"She hadn't been to meetings for a few months," said Ronald.

"She was on her retreat," added Non-nun Mary.

"Do you know who her death doula was?" asked Helen. "Was it anyone in your club?"

There were furtive glances but no one put up a hand.

"None of *us* is a qualified death guide," said Nun Mary.

"Well, you sort of are," said her wife. "In that you *were* a nun."

"So was Helen," said Nun Mary. "But there is specific training involved in companioning someone through their death."

"Do any of you have a death doula?" asked Helen.

Instead of lying, none of them answered. It was an honourable approach.

"My apologies if that's a rude question," she said.

"That's okay," said Ronald. "We used to use the term death midwife. But we stopped because of some trouble. The midwife's association frowned on it."

"All death guides, no matter what they're called, are viewed with suspicion by the damned bureaucrats," said another student.

Helen had a hard time believing that the midwives association was full of bureaucrats, but perhaps she was wrong. Maybe every organization had its share.

"It was the term midwife that was problematic," said Nun Mary.

Helen was having some trouble following.

"Death guides do important work at considerable risk to themselves. I'm sure the midwives recognized that," said Nun Mary.

"Do you have a death guide? Or a doula?"

Again, no answer.

"We're glad you came to see us, Helen," said Ronald. "I was going to come to see you. This saved me a trip."

"We're concerned," said Nun Mary and Non-nun Mary together.

"But we don't know what the hell to do about it," said the man with the beard.

"I called the police and they said they had no concerns," said the white-haired woman. "But we think something happened to Edna."

"Is it true that there are three butlers at the Institute right now?" asked Ronald.

"Yes. Two of my classmates have joined me to help with the . . . arrangements."

"If this was an Agatha Christie novel, one of the butlers would have had something to do with her death," said the white-haired woman. "But none of you were here when she died."

"I promise no butlers were responsible. I hope that sets your mind at ease," said Helen.

"It does," said the woman.

"Thank you for sharing your worries," said Helen, even though they'd been strangely reticent to give her helpful information. "If you think of anything else that might help me understand Edna's transition, please let me know. And congratulations on your coffins. They look like fine resting places."

"We have to take them home soon because the 4-H club needs the space back," said Ronald. "My wife's not excited about storing mine in the yard."

"You'll need to find a nice tarp. Or maybe build it a little shed," said someone.

And then they were off discussing where they planned to store their coffins until the big day when they were needed.

The visit had revealed very little, but Helen didn't regret it. She waved goodbye and headed out to the little lavender Smart Car with the Yatra Institute logo on the door. She closed the door and sat for a few moments, listening to her heartbeat and her breath. The knock on her window came as no surprise.

She lowered it.

Tanner stood there in his rough sweater, looking like a young Highlander. His face was tense.

"I think they're all planning to use the same doula. But they don't want to say anything because she's having problems with the midwives' association."

"Can you tell me her name?" asked Helen.

His normally unperturbed face became serious. "Greta Johannsen. She was, I mean, we were together for a while. But we're not now. We're not even talking. Well, she's not talking to me."

"Will Greta talk to me, do you think?"

He ran a hand through his curly hair. "I don't know. She's sort of paranoid. I think being a death midwife, sorry, doula, for half the people on the island is too much for someone her age. You know, even though she's hardcore emotionally balanced."

Helen gave him a sympathetic look.

"She thinks I'm not a serious person. That's partly why I joined the club. I wanted to show her that I think about death. That's important to her."

This was not a conversation Helen could imagine having anywhere else with a young man about his love life.

She thought of the riotously coloured Phish-logo coffin in the 4-H hut. Tanner's general zest and high spirits were not about to become sombre anytime soon.

"If I speak to her, I'll be discreet about where I got her name."

"That's okay. Tell her I told you. I don't want to be shady. She's already mad at me. But I don't think all this hiding is doing her any good. There's nothing illegal about what she does."

"Thank you, Tanner," said Helen. He handed her a piece of paper with an address on it. "Does the group know you're speaking with me?"

"Yeah," he said. "None of us are comfortable with what happened to Edna. But no one wants to betray Greta."

She thanked him again and drove slowly away.

Chapter 34

As the students settled in for their flower-arranging session the next morning, Helen excused herself and slipped away to visit Edna's death doula. She felt a pang of guilt as she did so. Things had moved into high gear with the classes. The next day the students would be showing off their floral design skills in public, a Yatra Institute tradition. Wayfarer had them practising for their first demonstration dance. And in meditation, they were all getting into it, meaning that many of them were beginning to suffer as their practice deepened. Helen felt, as she used to when she ran the Institute, that she was running as fast as she could along a high wire while balancing a stack of plates. It was a sensation she rather enjoyed, but it required intense focus. Adding her own private investigation of Edna's last days was a bit like adding water glasses on top of the teetering plates.

During the drive, she allowed her mind to plan. After speaking to Greta, she would step back and pass along what she'd learned to Officer Rosedale. He could follow up on the leads, if that's what the discrepancies were. *On the other hand . . .* , she thought, as her mind began to generate justification for continuing her hunt for the truth. She paused to imagine Durga, the many-armed Hindu warrior goddess. There was always another hand when one felt called to battle. Helen conjured the image of Durga riding her lion across a tightrope, stacked dishes in several hands, weapons in the other. The image reminded Helen of the tantric meditations that involved adding and adding to a visualization until it was a technicolour glory. Ah, the human mind was a splendid thing.

She settled her mind with a deep breath. She was not Durga or a tightrope walker. She was Helen. A butler. She was in charge of making things go smoothly. For the rest of the drive, she tried to be as present as possible. *Driving. Driving. Seeing. Hearing. Driving.*

GRETA JOHANNSEN LIVED in a tiny A-frame cottage, shingled from top to bottom with silvered cedar shakes. The front featured many windows of different sizes, and a strip of rockwork ran from the peak of the frame down to the deck. It appeared to be the work of someone just learning how to do rockwork. The width of the strip varied, and a number of the rocks had fallen out, leaving bits of insulation peeking out beneath.

Attached to the side of the cottage was a pinkish cob extension. It was too small to be a room. Perhaps it was for storage. It looked like a large piece of Hubba Bubba gum stuck to the side of the Brothers Grimm cottage.

The building was surrounded by the scrubby trees so common on Sutil Island, which had been logged at least twice before it was protected. The Yatra Institute grounds, the large provincial park nearby, and two or three other properties were the only other parts of the island with intact stands of old growth trees.

Helen had great affection for the people of modest means who made their homes on Sutil Island and who formed the backbone of the lively, if fractious, community.

Many were young, almost all were idealistic, and they, like their 1960s forebears, did things like put random cob additions onto their modest homes.

Dauber Cottage at the Institute was a masterful example of the form, the result of money and craftsmanship. This structure was the result of cob, hard labour, and likely an introductory how-to book.

Helen got out of the van and knocked on the warped front door. The yard contained a VW bug that didn't look as though it was drivable, but that didn't mean it wasn't driven. Sutil Island was full of vehicles that seemed like miracles every time they started and trundled their way down the narrow, winding roads.

The front door opened to reveal a slender girl with her hair in braids that were tucked into a single heavy ponytail.

"Greta?" asked Helen.

She'd never met the girl before, and Helen assumed she must be new on the island.

"Yes," said Greta. There was a calm about her that rivalled Helen's own. Like some sort of Madonna, the young woman held a baby goat in her arms. The girl looked exactly like the sort of person who should be cradling young creatures. She wore jean overalls, a plaid shirt, and several strings of beads around her neck. The scents of incense and woodsmoke and curry floated out of the little house like a tranquil back-to-the-land cloud.

"I'm sorry to bother you," said Helen. "But I'm hoping you will be able to answer some questions about a mutual friend."

Greta didn't answer but dropped her head to let the tiny black-and-white goat nuzzle her face.

Over the years Helen had met many people whose lack of attention to superficial niceties could make them seem almost rude. People who, once you got to know them, were as kind and generous as it was possible to be. They were often contemplatives, operating on a deeper level. Or maybe this girl was just a little stoned.

"I gather you knew my friend and former employer Edna Todd?"

At this, Greta looked into Helen's eyes, and Helen saw that the girl was perfectly sober.

She didn't respond.

"I'm concerned about what happened to her. Some things about her death don't make sense. I think you agree with me about that. So do the members of the Sutil Island Death Positive Club."

More silence.

"I don't want to cause you any difficulties," said Helen, "with anyone."

"Come in," said Greta and Helen followed her into the little house.

It was as pleasant and rustic inside as it was ramshackle outside. The plywood board floors were strewn with threadbare Persian carpets. The walls, some of wood, some of stained plywood, and some whitewashed drywall, were crowded with colourful paintings and wall hangings depicting Kali, the goddess of destruction, and White Tara, the Buddhist goddess of compassion who helped people cross to the other side. The furniture was old, covered in blankets and throws, and the overall impression was of ease and comfort.

A small loft ran half the length of the upper storey of the house, accessible by an upright ladder. Set away from the wall was a tiny red woodstove on which sat a copper kettle.

It was as Sutil Island as a home could be.

"This is lovely," said Helen, sincerely.

"My mother and I built most of this place ourselves. My brother came and helped when he could," said Greta. "That was before my mother crossed over."

"I'm sorry for your loss," said Helen, imagining the slight young woman and her mother working on the building, hammers in hand. It was an image to gladden the heart.

"Thank you."

"Have you been here long?" asked Helen.

"About two years," said Greta. "But it feels like forever."

Helen was surprised she hadn't met Greta before she moved away. But from June until September, when the lodge was in full swing, Helen didn't get much chance to be out in the community.

Helen waited until Greta invited her to sit at the small kitchen table, which was covered in tiny bottles.

"Essential oils," said Greta. "My own blends."

Helen nodded.

"Would you like some tea?" asked Greta, after putting the baby goat in a pen lined with blankets near the stove. Helen gratefully accepted. A dark-orange cat lay stretched along the back of an upholstered chair. The atmosphere in the little house, built by the little family, brought into sharp focus the stress she was under at the Institute.

For a fleeting moment she wished she could just hand all her responsibilities over to this girl.

After Greta served Helen loose-leaf tea in a shapeless mug, she sat down across from her.

"I appreciate you speaking with me," Helen said.

"I haven't spoken with you," Greta pointed out.

"Well, I hope you will."

"I was in Vancouver at a conference when Edna died," Greta said.

"I see. Do you know anything else about her plans?"

Greta didn't answer.

"I will try to keep anything you tell me confidential," said Helen.

Greta gave a tiny smile, and Helen realized that they both knew that was a promise she could not keep. If Greta knew anything about Edna's death, Helen would need to tell the police. Nothing could be kept secret. Helen regretted her words, but didn't try to take them back.

"Were you Edna's death doula?" Helen asked.

"I'm a certified midwife," said Greta. "Who told you about me?"

"I received a letter," said Helen. "I think it might have been from you."

"Did it mention my name?"

Helen allowed that it had not.

The goat, who'd been busily chewing on a fleece blanket, made a little noise that sounded strangely like a baby's cry. Greta turned her calm gaze on the kid. "Pepperpot," she said. It settled back into warm silence.

Helen decided it was best to be completely candid with this poised and rather guarded young woman.

"I went to see the Death Positive Club."

Greta's eyes narrowed. "So Tanner told you about me?"

"He's very fond of you," said Helen.

"I know," said Greta. "But I can't help you." She got to her feet.

Helen set down her homemade mug and rose from her chair. "Thank you," she said, at the doorway.

"Good luck," said Greta.

In the car on the way back to the Institute, Helen reflected that she was probably not cut out to be an amateur investigator if she couldn't coax information out of a gentle soul like Greta Johannsen.

Chapter 35

The next morning the students appeared more energetic, even for the first meditation sit. They didn't fidget, but a new current of excitement ran through them, probably at the prospect of leaving the property and going into public to show off their floral design skills. The day after that they would be giving their first dance performance.

When they came into the lodge for breakfast, Wills and Tad managed to be quite civil and Whitney wore a touch of colour, rather than her usual cloud-hued scheme. Rayvn had messily arranged her unruly hair.

They seemed to Helen almost like normal people as they poured coffee at the coffee bar and then lined up to get hard-boiled eggs and oatmeal with stewed rhubarb, which they took back to their shared round table.

They spoke in quieter voices than they had when they'd first arrived, and the poisonous hostility leaking from them seemed, for the time, to have been stoppered.

As the guests ate breakfast, Helen stood quietly in the doorway to the serving room and watched Nigel tenderly rearrange the kale blossoms that had been laid out between bowls of sugar and cinnamon. Murray walked briskly past him on her way into the kitchen, silver coffee canister in her hand, and gave him a gentle pat on the shoulder. Gavin, who was in the kitchen going over details for lunch with Chef Leticia, sensed Helen's gaze and looked up and smiled at her.

The entire lodge had that familiar bustle to it, warm and fragrant and full of purpose and growth. And underneath the bustle was her uncomfortable and growing conviction that something bad had transpired here.

Much as she wished she could just give her dhamma talks to these students and then get on with her life, she could not. Keeping such dark suspicions at bay would take much of her energy. Denial and delusion were demanding taskmasters and they stood firmly in the way of living an awakened life. No. She wouldn't pretend, no matter how much she wanted to.

She returned Gavin's smile before heading for the dining room. On her way she picked up a canister from the coffee station even though she knew Murray had just offered them top-ups.

"More coffee?" she asked.

Tad held out his cup without looking at her. "As I was telling Willy, a good regatta requires a dead sailor. It just does. At least, from an entertainment perspective."

"Did you hear any rustling last night? When we were walking back from the hall?" Rayvn asked Whitney, who was staring down at her porridge as though it might also start rustling.

"What is this?" asked Whitney.

"Slop," said Tad. "It's health slop. Of the sort you'd give to pigs."

"It was creepy. I'm sure I heard footsteps," continued Rayvn.

"It was probably Mother Teresa over here," said Tad, finally looking at Helen.

Helen poured the coffee, and for some reason, felt reassured. The Body Snatchers hadn't taken the nieces and nephews. They were present, full of bile, and accounted for.

Twenty minutes later, the four students were slouching around in the bright garden, where Gavin and Nigel were putting the finishing touches on the table full of supplies.

Helen stood some distance back and watched as the cousins took their seats. Her mind went to Rayvn's words. Steps behind her on the path. The staff walked back via the road, not the trail to the cabins. Then there was Rayvn's destroyed dharmarrangement. Who had done that?

It was time to keep a closer eye on Rayvn. If these incidents were disconcerting for Helen to hear, they must be quite frightening for Rayvn to experience.

And what of the rocks Wills swore someone had thrown at him? Was there a poltergeist at work?

Come back, Helen gently urged herself. *Here, now.*

She returned in time to see Jenson Kiley shoot out of the garden shed like a jack released from a box.

"Greetings! Greetings!" he said. He'd pinned a peony bloom to the lapel of his green tweed suit jacket, and it was so large it obscured his entire shoulder and brushed up against his chin when he bent his head. It was patently ridiculous and wonderful.

"A critical inflection point in our journey as floral artists is upon us!" he announced, making each word sound as though it ended in an exclamation point. "You have learned how your deepest selves can be expressed through flowers and foliage. You have gained a sense of who you are as floral designers and as soul vessels."

Helen suppressed a grin when she saw Tad and Wills wilt in dismayed unison.

Jenson Kiley, who had learned Ram Dass's lesson that one should love everyone *and* tell the truth, confronted them about their body language.

"Now, now," he said, staring at the slumped brothers. "Do not let your ego-driven self-protections send your true natures into retreat at this critical juncture! I know you are suspicious of the language of inner knowing. If you don't like the term *soul vessel*, I invite you to substitute *agents of your own destiny.*"

This drew nods from the brothers. Helen could sense Whitney and Rayvn's irritation at Jenson's pandering to the two men.

Jenson swept his arms at the work table under the blooming apple tree. "Today we will combine all that we have learned thus far." He paused for effect and stayed paused until the students leaned forward. "And we consider two more aspects of floral soul design." There was another long pause. In addition to being a floral educator, Jenson Kiley was something of a pause expert.

Finally, Tad put up his long, white hand like a schoolboy. "Yes?" he said. "And?"

Jenson, who had closed his eyes, so caught up in the moment he forgot where he was, slowly opened them.

"Audience and crass commerce." He grinned at his small class in their uncomfortable garden chairs, as well as the three butlers standing in the background, and Nigel, who might as well have been watching a spaceship launch.

"Until this point, you have had an audience of one. *Moi!*" Here,

Jenson stroked his enormous boutonniere, like a man showing off a pet cat. "Today, you create for the world!"

Pause.

"Who?" asked Wills.

"The world!" repeated Jenson. "You will create your works here with an eye to selling them to the highest bidder. We will set up a table at the Co-op and there you will sit, as artists must do from time to time, hoping that some patron will think highly enough of your work to actually pay for it. And let me say, that is no easy task on this island." He smiled benevolently.

Helen found herself nodding at Jenson's words. It was true that people on the island were not keen to pay for bouquets they could easily make at home.

The students began to radiate alarm.

Rayvn spoke without raising her hand. At least, Helen didn't think she'd raised it. The girl's hair was so wild that Helen couldn't see her arm. "Trying to sell them doesn't seem very artistic. It's sort of like selling our souls, isn't it?"

Jenson cocked his head like a robin considering a worm. "Our souls must sometimes venture out of the garden, and even the greatest floral artist does not live on petals alone."

And that was it for his explanation. "You have an hour and a half to create your arrangements," he said. "We'll bring a bagged lunch to the Co-op, where they are expecting us, and the rest of the afternoon's usual activities are cancelled."

Helen gestured to get Jenson's attention and made the little face she'd made many times before at exactly this point in the course. He nodded his understanding.

"Yes, of course. Thank you, Helen. Designers, I remind you not to denude the entire garden. There is abundance here, but let's be judicious. The containers are a modest size, so please keep that in mind. Walk about and consider your design before you cut anything. No pulling up entire plants by the roots. And even though we are moving into the capitalist realm of the hungry ghost today, no stealing from one another."

"What do people on this island like to buy?" asked Rayvn.

Jenson laughed merrily. "Nothing!" he said, and with that, he set them loose upon the garden.

Chapter 36

Helen drove everyone to the Co-op. The way the students sat silently, hands in their laps or at their sides, made her feel like a sergeant transporting troops to battle. Nigel kept casting nervous glances at the four arrangements carefully stored in boxes at his feet.

Birds flashed across the road in front of the van. Greenery crowded into her visual field, interrupted by small, flat black bodies of water.

Every so often, Helen glanced into the rear-view mirror at her passengers. Rayvn and Whitney stared out the windows. Wills kept his eyes closed and his face tight. And Tad's eyes met hers, which made her skin crawl.

Helen asked herself what Tad had done to make her so uncomfortable, other than be unpleasant, cold-handed, and odd-eyed. Well, he had lied about how recently he'd been at the lodge. But so had Wills, and she didn't have the same reaction to him.

Stay open, she counselled herself silently.

When they pulled into the gravel parking lot of the Co-op, clouds had turned the sky into a smudged charcoal sketch.

"What if it rains?" Nigel whispered to Gavin.

"There will be a tent," said Jenson cheerfully. "Because it almost always rains."

"Who's going to come out and bid on our flowers if it starts pouring?" asked Rayvn.

"Probably no one," said Jenson, beaming. "Wouldn't that be an artistic heartbreak? One year we got trapped in the biggest storm I've ever seen. As soon as we packed up, sunny skies for miles. A total loss."

"This is going to be hard on the ego," said Rayvn.

"Exactly!" said Jenson, elated at the idea of an unsuccessful auction.

Before the floral educator could scare his students any more, Gavin opened the back door, jumped out, and then went to open the side door.

Wills made a move to get out first, but when Jenson cleared his throat, Wills sat back down and let the teacher go ahead.

When they were all in the parking lot, Helen was pleased to see Tanner waiting for them. He'd set up the long folding table and the tent was half up.

He smiled. "Going to rain, I think. And they're saying the weather is going to kick up."

Nothing unusual about that. Sutil Island seemed to find itself directly in the path of every storm that came through.

Gavin and Murray soon helped him finish putting up the canopy. The table was covered in a flowered oilcloth, and four folding chairs were neatly arranged behind it. The students had taken their seats behind their arrangements.

Jenson stood in front of them, his hands behind his back.

"And now," he said, "your inner arrangements meet the world."

"I'm sorry, but what does that mean?" asked Tad, straining hard to remain polite.

"It means we have to sell our flowers," said Rayvn.

"Why can't he just *say* that?" said Tad.

Before they could discuss further, three women came out of the Co-op. They looked to be in their seventies, and they carried takeout coffees and paper bags with goodies from the bakery. Together the three of them probably topped out at two hundred pounds.

"It's the flower auction," said one, who somehow managed to light a cigarette even with both hands full.

They came over to inspect the arrangements. "Hey, Delilah!" said a red-haired white woman. "These are better than sometimes, eh?"

Her friend, an Indigenous woman with spiky hair, stared at Rayvn for a long time. "Where you from?" she asked.

"Nanaimo," said Rayvn, who had dressed up for the occasion in a green velvet jumpsuit with a gold vest that made her look like Maid Marian after a raid on Robin Hood's closet.

"What's your people's name?" asked the woman.

"She thinks she knows your face," explained her red-haired friend.

"Delilah's good with faces," said the smoker, another white woman, who blew a cloud of smoke at the floral artists. Tad wrinkled up his nose and waved a hand in front of his face.

"Rayvn. My last name's Wildwood."

"Huh," said Delilah. She turned to look at her friends. "She looks like that girl from the hairdresser's that time. 'Member when we went to Nanaimo to go shopping for Georgina's prom and she got her hair done in the mall?"

"That's my mom!" said Rayvn. "Fran Martine. She owns the Hair's To You salon!"

"Yeah, I see her in you," said Delilah.

"Delilah's real good with faces," said the smoker again. Her own face looked surprisingly soft and unlined for a woman who had likely been smoking for three times as long as Rayvn had been alive.

"Can we interest you in an arrangement?" asked Wills in a fake-polite voice.

"We're going to a prayer shawl meeting right now. Then bingo at the Legion," said the red-haired lady.

"These bunches look better than some years," said the smoker, as though the floral artists weren't sitting right in front of her. "But I would never pay for one of 'em."

"Say hi to your mother," said Delilah. "She did a real nice job on my granddaughter's hair." She paused for a beat. "And I think I like yours the best," she said, pointing to Rayvn's arrangement.

Rayvn's smile stretched from ear to ear.

"It's the daisies," said the smoker. "Delilah loves daisies."

"There's about two million of 'em on the side of the ditch," observed the red-haired lady, who wasn't much wider than a daisy herself.

Then the three of them tottered off toward the small church across the street, conveniently located next to the Legion hall.

"Can we just put in bids on each other's arrangements? Get this over with? I find this utterly humiliating," said Tad.

"I'm afraid not," said Jenson, with satisfaction.

"Is this to raise money for some kind of charity? I fail to understand the point," said Wills.

"I suspect we are meant to learn what it is to be an artist in a world that mostly doesn't care about art unless there's money in it," said Whitney.

"Sort of like being a goth in a world that doesn't appreciate velvet," added Rayvn wisely. "You can get bitter or you can embrace the pain."

"Make friends with the discomfort!" agreed Jenson. "Get to know your own ambition to escape pain!"

Tad rolled his pale eyes, and Wills's stocky body slumped further into his folding chair.

One of the cashiers came out of the store, vape in hand.

"Nigel!" she said, when she spotted him. "You still working at the Institute?"

Nigel nodded, looking bashful.

"I guess you showed my mom, huh?" said the cashier. "You're not a total deadbeat!"

Everyone looked at her.

"My mom got Nigel the job. She didn't think he'd even last a day. She's also waiting for me to get fired from this job. I'm staying, just to spite her. I'm not going to quit until I can get a ride to Vancouver with someone cool."

Nigel remembered his manners.

"Oh, uh, everyone? This is Amy. From camp? I was living at her parents' place before I got the job."

Amy, a dark, round-cheeked white girl with a short, bobbed haircut, smiled through vanilla-scented vape fumes.

"Those things are lethal for young people," said Tad, sourly. "I'm surprised that so many people smoke on this island."

Amy made big "check this guy out" eyes at Nigel.

"Definitely stay away from the flavours," said another voice. Helen looked and saw Greta pushing her bicycle toward them. She took off her helmet and her braids swung free. At the sight of her, Tanner's face lit up.

She wore loose jeans and an oversized sweater. The ring in her nose glinted as she grinned.

"Didn't want to miss the flower-off," she said, putting down her kickstand and making her way to the front of the table. "I've heard so much about it."

"Hey, Greta," said Amy, and the two girls hugged.

Tanner's delight in Greta was evident, and they appeared quite friendly with each other, even though he'd given Helen Greta's name. Helen wasn't sure what to make of that.

"You know Helen," he said and Greta nodded solemnly. "And Greta, this is Gavin and Murray. They work with Helen to the Institute." His voice dropped. "They're *all butlers.*"

"Three butlers? That seems like a lot," said Amy.

"Too many," said Tad. Everyone ignored him.

Tanner introduced Greta to Nigel and then pointed to the students at the table. "And they're taking the flower class."

Whitney and Rayvn held up hands in greeting. Wills nodded. Tad stared sullenly into the middle distance.

Greta began to inspect the arrangements with the air of someone who had spent a lifetime judging flowers. Amy joined her, holding her vape off to the side and waving the smoke away.

The two girls conferred about the arrangements and then took small pencils and pieces of paper to write their bids on, which they folded up and put into a carved wooden box.

While they were doing that, an old green Jaguar pulled slowly and erratically into the parking lot and came to a stop so it was maximally in the way.

A heavy door swung open and an older white woman with a

helmet of artfully arranged snowy hair began, with some difficulty, to get out of the car. Gavin materialized beside her and she took his arm in a way that suggested people had been helping her in and out of her Jag since forever.

Jenson hustled over to greet her.

"Mildred!" he said, bending down to give her a kiss on each heavily rouged cheek. "It is *wonderful* to see you."

"Thank you, dear. I have roused myself from my little nest to observe your latest efforts. It's strange to think Edna is gone. I feared we would never see another of these blood sport floral competitions at the local grocer's."

With Gavin at one elbow and Jenson Kiley at the other, Mildred, who was bent over in a painful way, made her way to the table.

"Mrs. Pyle," said Helen. "It's a pleasure to see you again. I hope you are well."

"Thank you, Helen," said Mrs. Pyle. "I am the pits. The absolute pits. I hate to leave my home and my plants. But seeing you brightens one's day."

She looked appraisingly at Murray. "Lovely," she said. "So neatly turned out." Then she stared at Nigel. "Ghastly costume, but a nice, bright eye on him. Not bleary with marijuana like so many of them. Please show me the arrangements. I've brought my chequebook."

"Of course," said Helen.

"Oh dear, I've forgotten my glass. Jenson, can you please help me retrieve it? Or perhaps this elegant young man would like to escort me?" She smiled flirtatiously at Gavin, who bowed ever so slightly. "Oh, aren't you heavenly. When we lived in Philadelphia, my parents had a dear friend with your grace. He was a former ballet dancer. Are you a ballet dancer?"

Mildred Pyle was a trifle deaf and so everything she said was too loud. Her voice was, Helen thought, uniquely bracing, as befit one of the wealthiest women not just on Sutil, but also in British Columbia.

Gavin allowed that he was not a ballet dancer.

"Have you thought of dancing?" she asked.

"No, madam," said Gavin.

"He does yoga," said Nigel.

"Quite so," said Mildred Pyle. "Yoga. Yes. It's what young people do now instead of ballet, isn't it?"

Jenson hurried back to Mildred, carrying her glass, a single magnifying lens on a short stick that she raised to her right eye as she turned to inspect the flowers. Each of the students straightened. Wills and Tad and Whitney because they probably sensed on a cellular level that they were in the presence of real wealth, and Rayvn because she had a well-developed sense of drama.

"Hmmmm." Mildred bent closer to Tad's bouquet of three lavish pink peonies, each just barely open, surrounded, unexpectedly, by the first tender sweet peas of the season in pink and purple and white. "*Enchanté.*"

She nodded gravely at Wills's square vase filled entirely with closed tulips. "An eye for colour and a good formal approach," she muttered.

Then she made her way to Whitney's arrangement of irises and tulips around a single slender apple branch, heavy with flowers.

"Ah," she said, getting closer to train her glass on the flowers. Satisfied that she'd gotten the sense of the thing, she nodded her head and moved to Rayvn's offering.

Meanwhile, people had begun to appear seemingly from nowhere. They lined up behind Mildred and were talking quietly among themselves. Helen was surprised to see so many people. The flower competition was never announced, so usually the only participants were those who happened to be at the Co-op or who chanced to be passing by. And of them, few bid on the bouquets, which were always enthusiastically arranged but of varying quality. But today a steady stream of people arrived as though summoned. They came on foot, by golf cart, squeezed into old cars, on bicycles, and at least one by skateboard.

They were a true cross-section of Sutil Islanders, which is to say there were people with home haircuts and homemade clothing, people in old work jackets and pants, Patagonia-clad city people visiting their Gulf Island place, and one or two architect types with angular spectacles, angular hairdos, and all-one-colour ensembles. Helen knew many of them.

As they joined the lineup, they gave Helen their condolences.

"We're going to miss Edna," said a preteen who had apparently never combed her mass of brown hair. "She was really cool." The preteen's mother, a handmade sort who home-schooled and knew all the good spots to pick wild mushrooms, nodded. "We wanted to pay our respects, and since there hasn't been a service, this seems like the only way."

"Thank you so much," said Helen.

"Edna always got so chippy when no one bid on the flowers. She said it reflected badly on the island and discouraged her students," said a skinny man named Elliot who'd coasted in on a reclining bicycle because of course he had. He wore a dented helmet with a dragon's ridges on top and elbow and knee pads painted to look like dragon scales. Helen was glad to see the extra protection. Elliot was the local physiotherapist. When he wasn't working his rigorous schedule of approximately three hours per month, he was causing many a near car crash as he navigated the twisty roads on whatever contraption he was currently trying out. His bike was adorned with the flags of British Columbia and Manchester United, and a weed flag in the colours of Jamaica. In his treatment room made of reclaimed glass and plywood, he was said to perform miracles, and he sold his CBD oil at cost.

Leon showed up and fist-bumped several people. He had brought with him two Elders from the Klahoose First Nation, Johnny and Yolanda Louie, who both spoke Klahoose and were in high demand to pass along their knowledge. They had the sort of calm, abiding energy infused with humour that Helen had seen in some of the monks she'd known. If Johnny and Yolanda were not fully realized beings, then she suspected they were close.

She went to pay her respects.

"You're back," said Yolanda.

"You don't look like you buttle rich people," said Johnny. "Thought you'd be wearing one of those penguin suits."

He and Yolanda laughed and so did Helen. "Not yet. Maybe in my next job."

"It's real good to see you," said Yolanda. "We wanted to come when Leon told us about this. Edna was a friend."

Edna had been a friend to many. This strange, impromptu gathering was a sign of that.

"We would have gone to her memorial, but Leon says Edna wanted some witch thing," said Yolanda.

"That's right," said Helen.

"She sure had her own ways," said Johnny. "Is it true she's over in Colorado getting eaten by the birds?"

"Yes," said Helen.

"That's good. Help science and the birds," said Johnny.

"We'll honour her in our way, too," said Yolanda.

"Thank you," said Helen. "She would appreciate that."

"We all want to know what's happening with the lodge. And the land," said Johnny in a more serious tone.

"I understand." A pang of anxiety shot through Helen's stomach. What happened to Yatra would affect everyone and everything on this island, particularly the people who had been here since before the settlers came.

"We don't want it turned into a Holiday Inn," said Yolanda. "Unless it's got a pool."

Helen laughed.

"You'll do what's right," Yolanda continued, taking Helen's hand. Helen felt a rush of gratitude for the older woman's faith.

"Even if you colonizers almost never do," said Leon, cheerfully.

Ronald Li arrived in his truck and was followed, soon after, by Nun Mary and Non-nun Mary, who also drove a truck. They were followed by other people from the Death Positive Club, who in turn were joined by wild-looking women from Edna's wiccan community, who all managed to look radiantly healthy and vaguely threatening for reasons Helen could never quite put her finger on.

"I've never seen anything like this," whispered Murray. "It's beautiful. Fair play to you all."

Helen nodded, standing back and taking in the community.

Gavin appeared at her side. "May I suggest that we offer a round of refreshments from the coffee shop? I'll tell the coffee shop we'll pick up the tab?"

"Yes," said Helen, gratefully. "I should have thought of that. Edna would have loved this. The spontaneity of it."

Ronald Li brought a fiddle out of his truck and began to play, and someone else pulled a pan flute from somewhere and joined him.

It was, Helen reflected, turning into a peak Sutil Island social event. When people had finished looking at and bidding on the flower arrangements, they gathered in small groups.

Soon Gavin and Murray were handing around date squares and soft chocolate chip cookies tucked into napkins, and people were holding paper cups of coffee and tea. A few people sipped from flasks. More musicians had joined Ronald Li and the flute player.

Tad, Wills, Whitney, and Rayvn had gotten up from the table and disappeared into the crowd. Rayvn was deep in conversation with Mildred, who'd been given a chair. Rayvn crouched on one side of her and Leon on the other side. Helen heard one of them say something about the care and feeding of Venus flytraps.

The manager of the Co-op, Olaf Haroldsen, came over and gave Helen a hug.

"This is good, eh," he said, in a Norwegian accent still slightly detectable after thirty years in Canada. "Everyone has been wanting to do something."

"Thank you," said Helen.

"We've missed you. How is it—to be a butler?"

She found herself shrugging. "I don't really know yet. We just graduated."

"If you decide to be a butler on the island, let me know. We'll get you a special discount. For butlers only. Maybe you should work for Mildred."

Helen laughed. Mildred Pyle was the only one on Sutil who could afford or need a butler, but she made do with part-time helpers.

Olaf, sixty, was an adventurer. When he wasn't running the grocery store, which was often, he embarked on extended sailing trips in strange, handmade vessels. He climbed remote peaks wearing just his shorts.

He biked absurdly long distances in countries under panicky-sounding travel advisories. He hunched over to look into Helen's face. "All is well, eh?" he asked.

"Mostly," she said. Helen had always been able to talk to Olaf, in part because he was so direct and sincere.

"What is not well?" he asked, glancing at the people gathered in the parking lot.

"I don't know why she did it," said Helen. It was a relief to speak the words to this man whose favourite activity was getting himself into situations where the main goal was not to die.

"Ya," Olaf agreed. "I thought Edna would be ordering special vitamin skin creams from France until she turned one hundred and ten."

"Did you or the delivery staff notice anything unusual toward the end? When you dropped off her supplies? Did anyone see her? Did she seem okay?"

Edna always ordered her groceries for her retreats in advance. They were delivered once a week and left on the front deck. If she had any special requests, she left a note. The Sutil Island Co-op was familiar with providing food for people on self-retreats.

Olaf, whose untidy blond hair was fading to white, rubbed a wrist against his weathered face. "No. The kids didn't say nothing about it. And I asked. But I was gone for the last month or so."

"Ah," said Helen.

"Ya, took the new lapstrake out. Was going to try for Alaska, but no," he said.

"No" was code for "I almost died."

"Next year, try again," he continued.

Helen said what everyone always said to him. "Be careful."

"Oh, ya," said Olaf.

He gazed out over the gathering, then added, "One thing, I guess. She ate more than usual."

Helen felt herself go still. Edna was a careful eater. Not disordered, but intensely focused on optimal digestion. She never ate too much. It was an article of faith.

"I heard she ordered some potato chips. Even white bread." He grinned. "Maybe three months not talking was too long, even for her." He inclined his head at Helen. "Not for you, though. You could do three months alone standing on your nose."

Olaf had invited Helen on his adventures several times. He seemed to have the impression that because she was calm, she was comfortable with danger. That was not the case and so she always declined. When he brought companions, they tended to be young islanders or grizzled outdoor types like himself.

Helen was confounded. White bread? Chips? The only chips Edna would have eaten were apple chips. What had she done with extra food? From their interviews, Helen gathered that Tad and Wills hadn't lasted long at Edna's. A few days at most. In the ten years Helen had worked for her, Edna had eaten exactly the same way. Mostly organic fruits and vegetables, never more than she needed. She avoided processed foods and sugar. She had none of the neuroses about food that afflicted so many modern people. There was nothing punitive or self-denying about the way Edna ate. She cherished every bite and rejoiced in every meal for the strength it gave her and for the work that went into producing it. She was remarkable in that way. Helen wished she had such a relationship to food.

This was another detail that seemed fundamentally off. All she could do was tell Officer Rosedale, who would probably just say the retreat had made Edna hungry.

Something caught her eye. Whitney was speaking with Jared, the watercolourist realtor. Only they weren't really talking. They were arguing. Jared was saying something and Whitney threw up a hand as though to make him stop. Whitney turned away, but Jared grabbed her arm.

Helen was already moving but Olaf was faster. Gavin was faster than both of them.

"Pardon me," he said, smoothly arriving beside Whitney and Jared like a wish conjured by a genie. Helen and Olaf were a few steps behind him.

Jared, whose face was white, immediately let go of Whitney's arm.

"Excuse me," said Whitney, and she hurried away.

Helen wanted to follow her, but she also wanted to know why Jared had put his hands on a girl he didn't know.

"What was that you were doing there?" asked Olaf, his voice loud enough to draw everyone's attention. There were some advantages to not being a polite butler.

Jared shrunk away. "I didn't mean to," he said. "She just misunderstood something I said."

"You touched her arm very rough," said Olaf.

"I'm sorry," said Jared. The colour was coming back to his face. Helen thought she smelled wine on his breath.

"Not okay," said Olaf. "Not okay."

Jared swallowed. "Of course. I was just . . ."

"What exactly did she misunderstand?" Helen asked.

Jared shook his head as though to dislodge his thoughts. "I didn't mean to be rude. I just asked about the property. When she would be taking over."

Helen, Gavin, and Olaf stared.

"She took offence. I really didn't mean to grab her. I meant to touch her shoulder. To let her know I knew. About the arrangement."

Helen's ears rang. "The arrangement?" she said. Then she noticed that everyone around them had quieted and seemed to be leaning in to listen.

"I need you to apologize to her for me," said Jared, and there was a strange quality to his voice.

"Let's go for a walk," Helen said. Gavin and Olaf hovered nearby, Olaf frowning at the slim realtor. Gavin maintained a perfectly neutral face. "It's fine," Helen told them and she gently manoeuvred Jared out of the crowd in the parking lot and down the road. They walked in silence for a few minutes and then turned up a side road. Helen was waiting for Jared to calm down, and just as she was about to gingerly ask how he was doing and what happened, something over the treeline caught her attention. Billowing smoke. More than could be explained by a burn barrel.

"Fire," she said. "Go get help. I'm going to see where it is."

Jared didn't move. He stared after her, open-mouthed, as she ran toward the source of the smoke twisting into the air like a grasping hand.

She was nearly there when she realized she was at Greta's house. Footsteps sounded behind her and Gavin appeared, sprinting effortlessly.

"How—?" she began, but didn't bother to finish the question. This was Gavin being Gavin.

They ran up the short driveway together.

Chapter 37

When they saw the grey-black smoke pouring from the back of the house, Helen and Gavin stopped and exchanged a look but didn't speak. Gavin ran for the big green cistern that sat beside the cob addition and began hooking up a hose.

Helen slowed her breathing, pulled off her jacket, and then ripped off her button-down shirt and plunged it into the rain bucket at the front of the house before using it to grab the front door handle. The knob turned and she took another breath of fresh air. Let it out. Then she inhaled deeply and went inside and closed the door behind her.

Helen had, in her time at the Yatra Institute, learned about her lung capacity through extensive breathwork training with different teachers. She'd once held her breath for almost four minutes, but in that instance, she'd been practising several times a day for months. And in those days, she'd warmed up by slow breathing for many minutes before she took a deep breath and held it. Today, there'd been no warm-up. She was panting from the run to the house and her breathing had been faster than optimal for most of the past several days. Still, she called on her old training.

Everything seemed to slow down as she looked around the smoke-filled space. It was hot, but not unbearable. She kept the wet shirt over her mouth and nose and peered around. The baby goat, the one Greta had been holding when Helen interviewed her, was still in the wire pen near the stove, bleating and running back and forth.

Helen reached in and picked it up. It struggled, but only for a second. Then its small black-and-white body went still in her arms.

The cat. Where was the dark orange cat?

Helen ignored the sounds of shouting that had started outside, barely audible over the noise of the fire consuming the back of the small house. She expelled some of her precious breath into the acrid air and called for the cat, keeping her voice reassuring.

"Come on, kitty! Kitty!" Then she put the shirt back over her nose and mouth.

Like a shadow, the cat crept out from under the old sofa. It looked at her, then at the front door, which Helen opened. It scampered outside, and, after she grabbed the framed photo of Greta with her mother and sister posed in front of their self-made house, Helen slipped outside too.

Gavin appeared to have dampened down much of the fire with water from the cistern. He was perfectly neat and dry, and someone else had taken over the hose. He nodded at her as she emerged and took the goat from her arms while discreetly handing over her jacket, which she put on and zipped up over her bra.

The volunteer fire department truck had arrived and the firefighters were setting up their pump truck. Other people were hurling buckets of water onto the back corner of the house and the trees surrounding it.

Helen took a breath, then another. Her lungs felt fine. She'd probably gone almost two minutes without taking in any new air, but she was unharmed and so was the little goat, which Gavin handed back to her. It bleated in her arms.

A burly firefighter stormed over, perhaps ready to yell at Helen for having gone inside the house, but as he got closer and took in Helen's unperturbed demeanour, he thought better of it. "You okay?" he asked.

Helen nodded. "Yes, thank you."

"Dangerous thing to do," he said.

Helen nodded.

"I guess you already know that," he said. "Did you breathe in any smoke?"

"I don't think so," she said.

"Well, okay. Nice goat." Then he left to begin hosing down the rest of the house and surrounding area.

As always, Helen was a rock in a river; other people, water.

Greta pushed through the crowd, followed by Tanner. "Oh my god," she said. "You have Pepperpot."

"She's fine," said Helen.

Greta peered around wildly. "Did you guys put out the fire?" she said, staring between Helen and Gavin.

"Gavin made a good start," said Helen.

"My cat?" asked Greta. Her face was tight.

"She ran out," said Helen. "When I opened the door."

"This must be why people have butlers," Greta said in wonder, as the panic seeped out and her natural centredness reasserted itself. "I had no idea."

Helen handed her the goat, which Greta folded into her arms.

"I don't understand how a fire could just start. It's been raining off and on for a month."

"That's probably why it wasn't worse," said Helen.

"It started outside," said Olaf, joining them. He'd donned his yellow firefighter's uniform, which he kept in his truck. "Did you have some flammables stacked on the back corner?"

Greta shook her head. "No. My woodpile is over there." She pointed at a tarp draped over a modest pile several yards from the house.

Someone said something about accelerant and Olaf went to investigate.

"I don't understand this," said Greta.

Helen looked over at the crowd of people who stood in the driveway and out on the road, watching. She spotted Wills and Tad, Whitney, Rayvn, and Jared. They all gazed intently at her. Or maybe they were staring beyond her at the house that was very much no longer on fire.

Chapter 38

Back at Yatra everyone was abuzz with the strange energies of the day. The students wandered around restlessly until they retired to their cabins.

Even Helen, usually equanimous in the face of other people's emotional upset, found it difficult to concentrate.

Her phone buzzed not long after they arrived back at the lodge and she looked down at a text from a strange number.

I have something to show you. Meet me at my house. The firefighters are gone.

Helen's heart sped up.

Greta.

"Nigel," Helen said as she headed into the kitchen where Nigel was helping Chef Leticia prepare for dinner.

"Yes, Coach?" he said, coming to the counter.

"The candles in Kalaivaani?"

"Yes."

"Could you please remove them all? Along with the matches?"

"Good move. Definitely don't need any more fires today."

Helen didn't even want electricity on right now. It felt strange to be in such an untrusting place.

"I have to step out for a little while. Please let Gavin and Murray know I'll be back as soon as I can," she said.

Fifteen minutes later she pulled into the driveway, where Greta stood, waiting. The driveway and yard were soaked and muddy.

"Thank you for saving Pepperpot and Pawpaw," said Greta without preamble.

"I was glad to do it," said Helen.

Greta gestured for Helen to follow her, and they went around to the back of the house and sat across from each other in two old lawn chairs in the small and scraggly yard, which was definitely the worse for wear from firefighters' boots. The back corner of the house was scorched black, as though a dragon had attacked it.

"I have changed my mind. About talking to you."

Helen let out a slow breath.

"Do you believe we should be able to die in our own time?" Greta asked, and Helen again appreciated her directness. She thought about the question. It was one Edna had never asked her, even though they had spoken extensively about Edna's wishes.

Helen had been a devout Buddhist for most of her adult life, so her thoughts on suicide were complicated. Some sects forbade it and considered it a form of aversion. Others counselled compassion for the person who wanted to end their life, but also believed that meditation and medication should be enough to keep a person mentally and spiritually able to cope with whatever situation arose. Many Buddhists thought that suicide prevented the working out of karma, which was the entire purpose of life. But there were a few suttas in which monks killed themselves and the Buddha seemed to approve.

Preventing harm, one of the firm tenets of most Buddhist traditions, included not causing harm to oneself.

And yet, the deepest part of Helen had tremendous sympathy for the Right to Die movement and she thought she would want the freedom to decide for herself, when the time came. She might not take it, but she wanted the option.

"I do," said Helen. "As long as great care is taken and every support is offered first."

Greta nodded. "I'm a certified midwife. And I believe that people who are dying need just as much help as people being born. My professional organization doesn't agree with me."

"I'm sorry," said Helen.

"I mean, they may agree in principle, but they didn't want me using the word *midwife*. They threatened to sue me and pull my licence. So now I say I'm a death doula instead. I feel more called to the end-of-life practice."

"Right," said Helen. "I received your note."

"What do you want to know?" asked Greta. Her fine-boned face was tired, but she was fully present in a way few people can be, particularly after a stressful experience.

"I would like to know more about Edna's end-of-life plans. I know she had them. So do the other members of the Death Positive Club."

"Why?" asked Greta.

"The plans might make the police pay attention if something untoward has happened."

Tanner had mentioned that Greta was paranoid. Helen sympathized. She was beginning to feel fairly paranoid herself. The girl was clearly sensitive and engaged in delicate and emotionally demanding work. Paranoia was a natural response.

"I already told them something wasn't right. Anonymously. It didn't help," Greta said.

"I have to ask. Has something, uh, illegal occurred?" asked Helen.

Greta shrugged. "No. I've stopped doing assis—" She abruptly stopped speaking and Helen knew then that the girl *had* helped people cross over by administering medicines. She was in legal jeopardy and was right to be careful.

Helen spoke carefully. "I don't need to know about anything that has happened in the past. I would just like to know Edna's plans. She and I only discussed what she wanted done with her body. She was in the process of deciding the rest of it when I left to go to school. If you had an agreement, to, uh, help at the end . . ."

"No," said Greta. "Nothing like that. I agreed to be with her and that's all."

If Greta *had* agreed to take a more active role in helping Edna die, they had wisely avoided documenting it.

Greta stared up into the flat, white sky.

Helen waited and saw the decision happen in the girl's body before she spoke. Her shoulders settled. Her hands relaxed.

"The police know even less about assisted death and the death positive movement than the midwife's association does. I want to help people, not end up in jail. A lot of people are still counting on me."

Greta got to her feet and fished a disposable face mask out of her pocket. "Here," she said. "You're going to need this."

She put on her own face mask and led Helen into the little house through the open front door. All the windows were open, but the house still reeked of smoke and there were scorch marks all along the back wall.

"I'm not really supposed to be in here until the insurance agents come over and inspect it. But oh well," she said.

She went to the old brass-trimmed chest that served as a coffee table, in front of the sagging velvet couch, and opened the lid. Inside the chest was a safe that Greta opened with a fingerprint.

It was full of manila files.

Greta leafed through them until she found the one she was looking for. She pulled it out and handed it to Helen.

"Here," she said.

Helen looked down at the yellow folder with Edna Todd's name printed neatly at the top.

"Maybe this"—Greta gestured at the folder—"will change how the police are thinking about Edna's death. There are reasons she might have transitioned so suddenly." Greta hesitated. "But I can't think of any good ones."

"I'll try to keep your name out of it," said Helen.

"I'll deal with whatever comes. I should have spoken with you earlier. But my work is important. I am worried I won't be able to keep doing it."

"It was nice to see you with Tanner," said Helen, changing the subject abruptly. She was not normally one to put herself in the middle of people's relationships, but she felt compelled in this case.

"It was nice to be with him. He's a good person. But sometimes I feel like I'm a thousand years old and he's thirteen."

"They say young people are the future," said Helen as they walked out of the little house.

Greta laughed, and all at once her own youth showed.

WHEN HELEN GOT back to the lodge, she went straight into the office. The students were still resting in their cabins and everyone else was preparing dinner.

She shut the office door and opened the folder. On the sheets, Edna had listed all of her personal information and then filled out a section labelled Death Preferences. As soon as Helen had read partway down the first page, she understood why people were suspicious about Edna's death.

Under Preferred Location, Edna had written that she wanted to die in the garden "on the bench, under the wisteria." She'd added that this location would keep any resultant messiness outside and her body would be close to the gate so the emergency services personnel wouldn't have far to walk from the parking lot. Edna was always very cognizant of back health for people of all ages.

She'd listed her doula and Helen as the people who would attend her transition.

There was a playlist of music she wanted during her transition and at her service, instructions about flower arrangements that varied by season, a speakers list for her service at Samhain, and clothes she wanted to wear for her final journey to the High Plains body farm.

If she'd changed her wishes, Helen was almost certain that she would have amended her list. Edna had stuck to her various programs for exercise and health and spiritual growth for decades. Changes were incorporated, but she was a consistent person. Her decision to have a secretive, uncelebrated death didn't fit.

Helen let out a long breath. She reached for the phone.

"Officer Rosedale here," said the policeman after the second ring.

"Hello, it's Helen Thorpe calling. From the Yatra Institute."

Some extra warmth came into his voice then, probably thanks to the memories of Chef Leticia's lunch. "Helen. How are things going there? Sorry I haven't been in touch. But you're on my list of people to see."

"There have been some developments."

"Oh?"

"I have come across Edna's final wishes. Her end-of-life plans."

"Uh-huh." He sounded like he was writing.

"The pages include details about how she planned to cross over, her memorial. All of it."

"Okay," said Officer Rosedale.

"Reading this, I feel concerned that nothing went according to plan. Edna loved a good plan."

"I see," he said again.

"The plans are *very* detailed and extensive. For instance, she wanted to do it in the garden so her body would be closer to the parking lot."

"People change their minds. Particularly when they are not in a good way mentally," he said, carefully.

Helen found herself nodding. "Yes," she said. "But Edna was . . . she . . ." She struggled to find the words. Edna hadn't figured out what to do with the lodge. That did not speak well of her planning abilities. The current situation suggested she was not a "dot every i" person.

But she was when it suited her. Inconsistency was a tricky quality in the living and the dead.

Against the silence from the receiver, Helen took note of birdsong outside.

"Did your late employer, Ms. Todd, always follow her own plans?"

"No, not always."

"Where did you find these plans?" asked Officer Rosedale. "Did you locate her missing journals?"

The big question.

Helen didn't want to lie, so she didn't answer him but instead said, "The plans are here in the lodge."

"You *found* them in the lodge?" he pressed.

Helen looked at the ocean. Thought of the slim, strong girl who'd given her the file. Who'd said she would deal with the fallout. "Not exactly."

"You are probably going to have to tell me. At some point. Can you store the papers securely until I can get there?"

Helen wished she had a fingerprint-protected safe, like Greta's, but the small lock on the office desk would have to do. "I will lock them in Edna's desk," she said.

"Is there any chance Edna was suffering from cognitive decline? Made worse by such a long period alone?" he asked.

"That's the other thing," she said. "She wasn't alone during her retreat. She didn't just see Jared. The one I told you about. She seems to have had a number of visitors during her retreat."

"Really." His voice grew sharp. "Who?"

"Two of her great-nephews visited. The two who are here right now."

"Do you think she had others?"

"I don't know."

"I will want to speak with them," he said, his pen scratching in the background. "Their names?"

Helen gave the police officer Tad's and Wills's full names.

"When were they there?" asked Rosedale.

"I'm not sure exactly. I think Edna was trying to determine whether they were suitable to take over the lodge."

"She was doing a version of what you're doing now?"

"Yes, only her version was a little more direct."

"And what did she decide? About them?"

"They told me that she sent them away. Their visits didn't go well."

"Huh," said Rosedale. "That's interesting. If she'd already decided who should run her lodge, why do you have to do this . . . test?"

"I think she died before she'd made her final decision. Or she forgot to write it down. Or she forgot to tell the lawyers. I don't know."

"Okay. I'll bring this to my supervisors. I think you're right. This bears some looking into. I'm in court for the next two days at least, but I hope to get there soon. I may bring another investigator with me."

"Also, we had a bit of excitement this afternoon," she said. "Someone set a house on fire. It was the house where Edna's death plans were kept." As she spoke, she realized that it would take Rosedale about two minutes to find out which Sutil Island house had been on fire today. She had not done a good job of keeping Greta's identity a secret.

"Helen, I've started recording this. Is that okay?"

She swallowed. "Yes," she said.

"How do you know the fire was intentional?"

"It started on an outside corner. I believe I overheard someone from the volunteer fire department say he saw signs of an accelerant."

"Can you send me his name and contact information?"

"I don't have that information," said Helen.

"It's okay. I can get it from someone," said Rosedale. "Why would someone want to set the house on fire?"

Her long training in right speech made it hard to speculate out loud, but she went ahead.

"Maybe someone was trying to get rid of the files."

"Wouldn't breaking in and stealing them be easier?" he said.

"I would have thought so," said Helen. "Using fire certainly says something about whoever lit the fire."

"Hmm."

She recalled a section of the Fire Sermon the Buddha had given to an audience of a thousand monks.

> Everything, monks, is burning. What, monks, is everything that is burning? The eye, monks, is burning, form is burning, eye-consciousness is burning, eye-contact is burning. The feeling that arises dependent on eye-contact, whether pleasant, unpleasant, or neutral, that also is burning.

In the Buddha's teachings, greed, delusion, and aversion are fires ignited by craving, and craving comes from hearing, seeing, feeling, tasting, smelling, and thinking. The goal of mindfulness is to recognize the moment of contact at the sense doors *before* craving arises. To become truly disenchanted with the senses is the only way to put out the fires. Whoever set Greta's house on fire was in thrall to craving. Was it a craving for some desired thing or a craving to escape some undesirable thing? What had they seen or heard that had set them off?

She said none of this to Officer Rosedale, who surely knew better than she did that all great harm comes from too much wanting.

She wondered if she should tell him about the incident between Jared and Whitney. But what *had* happened, really? She should wait until she understood better. Helen would speak to both of them as soon as possible. She'd already told Rosedale that Wills and Tad had been here more recently than they'd let on and that had felt like breaking a trust.

"I can't really put the rest of it into words. I have a feeling that there are things going on here that I don't understand. Or at least, there's a story here that I'm not seeing," Helen said.

Officer Rosedale gave a soft laugh. "Welcome to my life." He paused, then said, "I'll get over there in the next few days. The trial I'm testifying in is going to take longer than I thought. The other officer who would normally step in for me just had a baby. But if anything comes up, and I do mean anything, give me a call and I'll get someone over there. It looks like we've got some weather coming our way. That's what we're hearing. I'll try to get there beforehand."

Helen hadn't even glanced at the weather report. She sighed. It wasn't like her to miss such things.

"Thank you," said Helen. She realized that she was relieved that he wouldn't be there right away. It would be hard for the students to immerse themselves in their studies if they knew they were being investigated.

"I'm sure we'll be fine. There are more staff here than guests. It's an excellent ratio."

He chuckled. "Right. I'm talking to a butler."

Something about Rosedale's voice renewed her wish to speak to her teacher. Sayadaw U Nandisara would give her guidance. He should be back any day now from the spring retreat he taught each year. She would email tonight and try to arrange a call.

"Thank you, Officer," she said.

They hung up. She felt relief wash over her. It felt good to give the problem to an authority.

Helen realized she hadn't told him about the other matters— Rayvn's damaged arrangement, someone throwing rocks at Wills, Rayvn hearing footsteps behind her at night. Officer Rosedale would probably think *she* was experiencing cognitive decline. She sighed. So be it.

Then she remembered that there was a file cabinet inside the small reception building that had a sturdier lock than the one in Edna's office. So she left the lodge and headed there. She tried to keep the file folder at her side and out of sight of the students as she went through the garden.

She unlocked the back door to the reception building, turned on the lights, and went into the small office behind the front desk. She began trying keys in the tall cabinet.

None of them worked. Maybe she should take photos of the pages and email them to Officer Rosedale from her phone. Or she could go back into Edna's desk in the lodge to see if the key for the cabinet was tucked away in there.

"Hello?" said a voice, and Helen turned quickly around, instinctively pushing the folder out of sight behind her.

Tad stood in the dark entryway. He'd come in through the front door. She hadn't realized it was open.

"I was wondering if there were any extra paper clips in here?" he said.

"Of course," she said. She quickly left the office and closed the door behind her. Then she retrieved the clips from behind the counter, wondering why he hadn't asked Nigel or someone else for help. He seemed to enjoy ordering people around.

"How many do you need?"

Tad's goat eyes were fixed on hers. "Maybe six?" he said.

"Here you go." She slid the little metal clips over to him. When he reached out, his hand touched hers. It was so cold she nearly recoiled. "Can I help you with anything else?"

"No, that's fine." He stepped back from the desk, his strange gaze never wavering. "Wish me luck," he said, but didn't say with what.

"Luck," said Helen.

As soon as he was gone, she locked the back door and left by the front, locking it behind her. She would keep the file in Edna's desk for now.

In the garden the bouquets were arrayed on the table. They would be delivered to the top bidders the next morning.

Jenson was using a small brush to touch up a leaf. At least, that's what Helen thought he was doing.

"What an afternoon!" he said, without looking up. "So high-pitched!"

"That's an apt description," said Helen.

"I think I learned more about Edna at that little impromptu soiree than I did in all the years I worked with her."

"Oh?" said Helen.

"When I was helping Mrs. Pyle back to her car, she said something odd to me." Jenson turned to face Helen. His attention was like that of a small sun. Warm and a bit too intense. "She intimated to me that Ms. Edna was extremely well off."

"She did?" said Helen.

"I believe what she said was 'I wonder how many of these people understand that Edna could have bought and sold this entire island ten times.' Then she said it had always been humbling to have someone so much wealthier than herself in the same community." Jenson's eyebrows rose until they almost touched his perfect hairline. "Is it true? Was Edna fabulously wealthy?" he asked.

Helen opened her mind to the possibility. Other than the beautiful dishes in the pantry at the lodge, which she assumed had belonged to Edna's late husband, had she seen other evidence of great wealth? No, she didn't think she had.

Edna had been generous in some ways, and parsimonious in others. The lodge had not been a huge money-maker, but its finances were healthy enough that Edna never seemed to worry about it. Edna had some lovely clothes, but not many. Her kayak was of good quality and she kept the Institute vehicles well maintained. Helen always assumed that Edna was secure but no more than that.

"Perhaps Mildred is mistaken," said Helen.

Jenson shrugged. "In my experience, the very rich know each other." He lowered his voice. "These students, for example—"

Helen waited for him to continue.

Jenson brushed some non-existent dust from his lapels. "They are *not* wealthy. I have worked for some of the richest people in the world, and my big-money sense door is well developed."

Helen smiled at his terminology. She hadn't known there was a "sense door" specifically dedicated to detecting wealth. She thought of her interviews with Wills and Tad. Jenson was right about their financial situations.

She wanted to ask him what gave the students away, but Wayfarer entered the garden through the back gate. She was like a summer storm full of lightning, thunder, and random flashes of colour, blotting out even Jenson's small, overheated sun.

"Oh hello, then!" said the dance instructor as she approached. She wore a matte black leotard and tights with laser cut-outs here and there. The spandex was printed with what appeared to be galaxies and constellations.

"Do you like it?" Wayfarer asked them, running her hands down her leotard. "It's a new line. MY new line. Doing it with the Princess Hala. I've been training her for three years now. You would not BELIEVE that girl's figure under her chador." Wayfarer moved her hands, tipped with long, pointed nails, to show just how va-va-voom the princess's body was.

"It's timeless, darling," said Jenson. "Like space."

"You're sweet," said Wayfarer. "Obviously, space is the inspiration. The universal need to get tha ass in shape, yeah?"

Helen and Jenson nodded.

"How'd the auction go?" asked Wayfarer. "Who won?"

"It's a surprise. We're going to announce the results after dinner," said Jenson.

Before he could say more, Helen excused herself and slipped out of the garden.

Chapter 39

The walk was an opportunity for Helen to get settled and remember to breathe. Meditators sometimes called it dropping in, which meant leaving the thought-gripped state in which most people lived and becoming conscious of all facets of her awareness. Helen was experienced enough that she could calm her system quickly and easily, even after impromptu flower shows, wakes, fires, animal rescues, interviews, investigations, and phone calls.

The late afternoon was achingly perfect now. There was no sign of the weather Olaf had warned of. Clouds scudded by, leaving only faint cotton-batting traces against the blue-and-white ginger-jar sky.

Helen noted the sound of her feet crunching the gravel and the tickle of the air entering and leaving her nostrils.

By the time she stood before Whitney's door, she felt equal to the task in front of her.

She knocked and got no response. Maybe Whitney had gone for a walk before dinner. She tried again.

A shuffling noise sounded inside, and finally Whitney answered the door. She looked half asleep.

"I'm sorry to interrupt," said Helen. "But I wanted to check on you."

Whitney's eyes, behind the drooping hair that fell in front of her face, narrowed for an instant, then returned to their usual distracted expression.

"Oh, really? Well, thank you."

"May I come in?" asked Helen.

Whitney cast a quick glance over her shoulder. She'd declined to have her room tidied during her stay, so perhaps she was embarrassed by the mess.

But when she waved Helen in, the cabin looked undisturbed, except for a few books lying on the coffee table and a pair of mugs on the counter. If Whitney was untidy, she kept the disarray confined to her bedroom.

They stood in awkward silence until Helen gestured at the couch across from a large padded chair. "Shall we?"

"Oh, yes," said Whitney, as though sitting down was a novel approach.

Helen took the chair so Whitney could take the couch, which seemed to be where she did her reading. She glanced at the book titles. There was the Thich Nhat Hanh book and the rest were all children's books. One was beautifully bound and had elaborate lettering on the spine. Another had the word *Molecules* in the title.

Whitney noticed her curiosity and seemed to brighten. "I've already confessed that I have fantasies of becoming a children's librarian."

Helen thought Whitney would be a good one. Away from the

pressure of this situation and the dynamics with her cousins, she was probably quite thoughtful and deliberate. Around them, she seemed cowed and somewhat depressed. She was the only one who hadn't relaxed into the routine or the work. The only one who hadn't fallen asleep during meditation.

"That one looks interesting," said Helen, pointing to the book with the ornate cover.

"Ah, *The Assassination of Brangwain Spurge*. It's wonderful." The flash of enthusiasm in one so wan was touching.

"It's good?" asked Helen.

"Oh yes. It reminds me of classic children's stories. No pandering. Totally gripping."

Whitney looked like a different person when she talked about books. Her face brightened, her spine straightened. Helen was reminded how important it is to love things. Then, like cloud cover obscuring the sun, Whitney's face darkened. But she wasn't looking at Helen. She was looking out the window behind Helen, who turned to follow her gaze. She thought she saw movement, something disappearing out of sight. Someone?

"Is there someone out there?" asked Helen.

"No," said Whitney, quickly. "A bird flew by. It was big."

Helen was certain she was lying but she couldn't tell why.

"Sorry, I get distracted easily," said Whitney. "Anyway, my mother thinks me becoming a librarian is ridiculous. You'd think I wanted to join a monastery or something."

Helen smiled. "It doesn't sound ridiculous to me," she said. "But then again, I have joined a monastery."

Whitney gave a short laugh. "Oh, that's right! I forgot. It must have been interesting. To feel so committed to something."

"I think everyone has doubt, at least sometimes, no matter how clear the path."

Whitney ran her hand over the stack of books like she was stroking a cat. "I think I would be happy to stay in this cabin reading for the rest of my life." She glanced at Helen. "Though I am willing to be interrupted for the wonderful meals."

"I'm glad you're enjoying the food and accommodations. I don't mean to pry, but I noticed the incident at the Co-op today. Between you and Jared."

Whitney stiffened.

"Is everything all right?" asked Helen. "There seemed to be some sort of altercation. He grabbed your arm."

There was another long beat, and then Whitney seemed to realize she was expected to respond.

"You know Jared?" Helen asked.

"No. I mean, not really. He introduced himself. The last time I was here. And then I saw him again at the Co-op. Today."

"The last time you were here?" said Helen.

Whitney hesitated. "A few years ago. I came camping. Visited Auntie Edna briefly. I just stopped in to say hello."

Helen was in charge of the lodge a few years ago. She didn't remember Whitney visiting. And why hadn't Whitney mentioned this before? Like Wills and Tad, she'd given the impression that she hadn't visited since she was a child.

"I camp sometimes. By myself. When I need time alone, you know." Another beat. "I like to go to islands."

"You saw Edna during that trip?"

"For maybe five minutes. She was in the middle of something. A big group was coming in for a program. She told me to come back later, but I didn't."

"And Jared?" said Helen.

Whitney, who was unlikely to be recruited by the CIA or become a professional poker player, wrinkled her nose and coughed and looked as uncomfortable as it is possible to look.

"I met him at his gallery when I did a tour of the local art studios. You know, there's that list they give you?"

Helen did know. A pamphlet listing all the artists and artisans on the island was prominently displayed on the ferry and handed out at the local information centre. People were encouraged to visit all the studios, chequebook in hand. Preferably twice.

"I see," she said.

"We talked. I liked his work. It's really quite good. I think I told him he could be an amazing children's picture-book artist. There's something quite fresh and strange about his work."

Jared painted enormous landscapes, and his work leaned heavily to dark forests and stormy, wind-tossed seas. His work had power, yes. Childlike wonder? Not so much. But Whitney was probably a better judge of art than she was.

To Helen's surprise, Whitney picked up on her train of thought. "Oh, I know his big pieces are quite moody. But when I visited, he'd just completed a series of tiny paintings of birds and woodland creatures. Voles and moles and mice and so on. Each little creature was tucked in amongst flowering bushes and red berries. Incredibly pretty. I bought them all. They were quite undervalued."

Helen was surprised to hear Whitney had enough money to buy original art, even if it was underpriced. Everyone seemed to think she was in dire financial straits. Everything about her suggested unmet need. Tad's comments about Whitney's family being poor as church mice rang in her head.

"Did you keep in touch with him?" Helen asked.

"Jared? Once he came to the city and we went to an art show. But we live in different worlds."

"How so?" asked Helen.

"I felt bad for him. He's so talented, but he has to work in real estate because he can't make a living from his art. That's a hard place to be."

"Maybe not so different from wanting to become a children's librarian," commented Helen.

"I suppose," said Whitney, though she didn't seem convinced.

"And you saw him again at the Co-op?"

The girl seemed startled, as though she thought the conversation was over.

"Yes, he came up to me and we talked. About art and Edna. And then he asked if I was going to take over the Institute. And I told him no. I don't think he meant to grab me. He said he had something else he needed to tell me and he reached out. He wasn't being rough or anything."

She rubbed her forearm as though checking to make sure it was still there. "And that's it. There was the fire and we came back here."

"Did you know that Wills and Tad were called here by Edna not long before she died?"

Whitney stared at her book pile.

"Were you also summoned by her?" Helen asked.

"I . . . I promised Edna not to tell." The silence stretched on until

Whitney made her decision. "I think she felt like she was cheating during her retreat."

"When did you visit?"

"About a month ago."

Helen watched her. "And how was your visit?"

"Fine," said Whitney. "We got along well."

"I see," said Helen.

Did that mean that Edna planned to turn over care of the Institute to Whitney? Had she been deemed the most appropriate candidate?

"Did Wills and Tad tell you that she asked them to leave?" said Whitney abruptly.

"They did."

"I'm surprised. They are not usually so forthright. Then again, neither am I."

The last point felt like the truest thing Whitney had said yet.

"Did Edna explain why she invited you for a visit?" asked Helen.

"Not really. I assume she was trying to decide whether to put me in her will or not."

"And?"

"No idea. Just like I have no idea what's happening here now. I'm just showing up."

"Fair enough," said Helen. "We are all trying to follow Edna's wishes."

"You are taking very good care of us." Whitney glanced at Helen. Her grey eyes, which had formerly seemed so soft, now glinted like steel. A slow blink and the hard gaze disappeared behind the veil of hair.

"Thank you for speaking with me," said Helen. "See you at dinner."

Whitney said no more as she saw Helen out.

On the walk back to the lodge, Helen reflected that she needed to speak to her meditation teacher. She felt confused and full of doubt. She also needed to speak to Jared. She would contact him in the morning. When she got back to the office she tried Jared and received no answer. If she didn't hear back, she would stop by his house the next day. Unless he was showing a property, he was never very far from his studio.

Then she headed downstairs to help with dinner.

Chapter 40

Helen was staring out an upstairs window of the lodge after dinner when Nigel appeared in the doorway.

"It's time," he said. He looked relatively well groomed in a clean, white—white!—button-down shirt and dark jeans under one of the dark denim aprons she'd ordered for all the staff as a sort of uniform. She'd heard Gavin gently counselling Nigel in the art of not offending the eye, and judging by his current ensemble, the project was going well. While part of her had enjoyed Nigel's flamboyantly bad dress sense, the more practical part of her knew Gavin was right to try to give him the Eliza Doolittle treatment. Nigel liked and had an aptitude for domestic service, but he would need to learn to blend in if he was to fulfill his potential.

As a former nun, made intentionally nondescript by baldness and robes, she preferred not to stand out, but she was intrigued by those who took the opposite approach. Toning it down wouldn't be easy for Nigel. He kept glancing down at himself as though he'd lost something.

Some people's dress sense was foundational to their character. Avoiding such constructions of the self was why monastics wore a uniform.

"Thank you, Nigel," she said.

He didn't move.

"Yes?"

"Whatcha doing?" he asked.

"Just thinking." And hearing, and feeling, and seeing, in order to get a break from all the thinking.

"Okay." He didn't move.

"I'll be downstairs in a minute."

"Um, Helen?"

Helen felt a small sense of irritation rise in her and she let it flutter up and out.

"Yes, Nigel?"

"I like it here."

Warmth replaced annoyance. "Good."

"It's just great."

"It is."

"But . . ."

She waited for him to finish. He buzzed with the energy of unspoken words.

"I hope you give this place to someone good. Some of these people—" Nigel made a face like he'd just bitten into a slug.

Helen saw only earnestness in his face.

"I will do my best."

EVERYONE WAS ASSEMBLED in the garden in their usual places. Jenson had not yet made his dramatic entrance from the garden shed.

Helen slipped in beside Murray, who gave her a little grin of excitement. Just as the wait was becoming uncomfortable, Jenson strode out of the shed.

This evening he wore the green tweed suit that made him look like a tall leprechaun with a good tailor. He could have been born in the garden, perhaps under a hosta. Helen imagined him, four inches tall, emerging from under a large green leaf with a bouquet of lily of the valley clutched in his arms, like a bride. A wave of affection for the floral educator swept through her.

"Darlings," said Jenson. A long, pregnant-with-triplets pause. "I am so proud of you."

Whitney stifled a small cough.

"Today's performance at the Co-op was the result of so much work and deep inner reflection. Thus far we have explored your inner flowers. We've gone deep. You've learned the skills so you can show the world who you are and who you aspire to be. And you will learn more skills in the coming days.

"Today you did one of the hardest things an artist can do. You cast your pearls before the public, come what may!" Jenson clutched his chest and bowed his head to show what a brave and honourable thing he felt that was.

"Now I suppose you want to know which of your arrangements got the highest bid?" he said.

Helen loved this part of the performance.

"And you want to know what the winning bid was for each?"

"Well, yes," said Tad. "Obviously. It was a competition."

"Ah, but can there really be a competition to determine whose inner arrangement is best?" Jenson turned and suddenly windmilled his arms. "NO!"

"Oh my god," whispered Murray.

"What does this feel like? This wanting to know?" Jenson demanded, staring from student to student.

"It feels like what the hell are you talking about?" said Tad.

Wills agreed. "It feels like could you please just get on with it."

But there was no sting in their voices. None of the usual venom.

"It feels like impatience," said Rayvn. "Like wanting."

"Yes!" crowed Jenson. "Wanting! Wanting! Wanting!"

"Worry," said Whitney.

"And worry!" said Jenson. "But you're not actually worried about the outcome, other than from an ego perspective, which doesn't seem to be that strong in *most* of you right now. You're worried about the wanting, wanting, wanting never stopping. Very unpleasant to never stop wanting!"

The students nodded.

"Don't worry," said Jenson. "I will tell you the results. But when you put your true and deep self into the world, wanting and fearing will twist your perspective. Keep the purity of your original intention!"

As the truth of this landed, the students seemed to heave a huge breath.

These were profound teachings Jenson was dropping on them. Helen wondered if they understood that.

"What I'm saying is that you are perfect just the way you are, and you could use a little improvement!" he added, using the old Suzuki Roshi maxim.

He removed a folded piece of paper from his coat jacket, tipped his glasses down his nose, and peered at the writing.

"The florist whose bouquet received the most bids is . . ." The trailing off was so dramatic Helen could just about hear the dot-dot-dots.

"Rayvn Wildwood's arrangement of daisies, grasses, and crocosmia."

Rayvn looked back at the butlers and gave them a huge smile. Her white and red and green arrangement was very beautiful and Helen wasn't surprised it had been so popular. Rayvn had chosen a variety of tall grasses with fresh seed heads for interest. They were the perfect accompaniment to the rows of nodding crimson crocosmia blooms on their long stems. The white daisies turned the whole thing into a natural gardenscape in a narrow black-and-white vase with flat sides.

"Congratulations, Rayvn. I was glad to see your good work recognized by so many." He bowed at her and then continued.

"The arrangement that received the highest bid, by quite some margin, was Whitney Varga's." He stepped back and flourished his arm over Whitney's display of irises, tulips, and the single blossom-covered apple branch. "Congratulations," he said.

"This is sexist," muttered Wills.

"Ah, but I'm not finished!" said Jenson. "There are two more categories! The winner of the Best Classic Design is Wills Todd for his formal purple-and-white tulip display. And the winner of the Colour Award is Tad Todd."

All the students sat up straight. Jenson had a gift for coming up with enough categories so that each student won something. He understood that experiencing a public loss during a self-discovery course was not good for a person's motivation or dhammic momentum.

"You have all shown yourselves to be not only gifted floral artists, but also insightful and well-intentioned people. You are now ready to go deeper and become more contemplative in your floral arts studies."

He dropped his hands and his head, a conductor worn out after a seminal concert.

Rayvn and Whitney clapped vigorously and Tad and Wills reluctantly joined in. Helen, Gavin, Murray, and Nigel joined them.

Nigel shuffled over until he was beside Murray. "Who actually won?" he whispered. "I couldn't tell from that."

"I think they all did," Murray said. "It's all very lovely, isn't it? Like a school for ungifted children."

Helen pretended she hadn't heard the exchange. The students, unprepossessing as they were, had proven more creative and intuitive than she'd expected. The four of them were no longer lashing out at each other. The Yatra Institute was working its magic on them as it did on everyone.

Helen had seen it happen with even the most raucous groups, like the time the wiccan quilters had come for the weekend. Then the entire property had been dotted with bits of silk and velvet in ruby red and a thousand shades of black. During the day the women hooted and cackled as they sat at rickety foldaway tables in the orchard, running their sewing machines using long, long extension cords. At night, naked silver-haired women ran through the trees under a full moon, carrying heavy, quilted banners. By the end of the retreat, the formerly voluble quilters might have been at a church service, so calm and focused they had become, like a flock of birds settling in at dusk.

Edna always said the place "aligned people."

Aligned or not, would Helen hand over operations to any of the great-nieces or -nephews? No, she wasn't ready to do that. Perhaps the dance course would reveal something meaningful. Or her next round of interviews would tell her something to reassure her that one of them was the right choice to run the lodge. And there was the question of what had happened to Edna and whether any of them were responsible. Interviews felt to Helen like a sacred trust, but there was no legal expectation of privacy, unlike Catholic confessions. If someone said something incriminating, she would have to tell the police. She looked forward to handing over to the authorities the burden of sorting out what had happened. Murder investigations were not her calling.

Wills and Tad and Whitney left the garden. Rayvn followed Gavin and Murray back into the lodge. Helen approached Jenson Kiley, who stood alone by the work table, humming to himself.

"What do you think?" she asked.

The performance fell away from the florist's face, leaving him clear-eyed and wonderfully present.

"I think these are tricky people," he said. "They all have a feel for beauty. Remarkable, really. And I believe their dharma revelations to be true, at least as far as they know. But I could swear there is something else going on with all of them. I'm sorry, Helen. It's a flower-arranging course. I can't be more definitive. Maybe the next half of the course will reveal more about who they are under all those defences. Their eulogies were revealing, although Whitney didn't actually read hers aloud. But what she wrote felt generic but honest."

"Do you have a sense of how Edna might have felt about them?" asked Helen, on a whim.

He frowned slightly. "My guess is that they would have been different people around Edna. They are like actors. Skilled ones. Who can tell what part of their performance is real?"

Helen was startled by his insight, which captured a thought she hadn't been able to put into words. "Who are they performing for?"

"I'm not sure," he said. "Me. Each other." He fixed his eyes on her, and she saw that his face, usually so mobile, so moisturized, showed signs of his age. "If I had to guess, I'd say they were putting on a show for you."

Helen nodded. She'd been afraid of that.

Chapter 41

When the evening's dance session was done, Helen watched quietly as Wayfarer, dripping sweat, led the students through their stretches and told them to go outside and cool off before the last sit. They staggered around, seeming a little drunk.

"That was good, Whitney," said Wayfarer as the girl put her oversized sweater back on and slumped out of the hall. Whitney swept her wet hair back from her face. She looked shell-shocked at her own performance, which had been surprising for its vigour. "Thank you," she said, simply.

Rayvn stopped in front of the dance teacher, and for a moment, it seemed the girl was going to embrace her. "Thank you," said Rayvn. "I loved that so much. Also, you are the total hotness to end all hotnesses and I am stoked to be in your presence."

Wayfarer, whose darkly spray-tanned skin glowed, smiled. "Ach, you're lovely. Good work tonight. You know your body and it shows."

Rayvn's smile was huge. "I LOVE my body," she said. "In fact, I love everything."

"Endorphins," said Wayfarer. "Nothing like Devi Dancing to get them pumping."

Rayvn put her hands into a prayer position and bowed to the dance teacher. "Your worship," she said. And walked out into the night like she owned it.

Wills and Tad had lined up behind Rayvn.

"Sorry about the little scrap," said Wills, sounding quite sincere.

"We used to fight like that when we were kids," added Tad. "Now we do it every single night."

"He's always loved a good sneak attack," said Wills.

His brother, whose normally pale face was flushed a strange shade of pink, pointed a finger at his brother.

"I'm a sneak?" he said. "You should talk." But their voices were bordering on affectionate.

"You are both bringing tremendous power to our sessions," said Wayfarer. "A little violent, perhaps, but nothing we don't see every night in Glasgow."

"Oh god, now we're like Scottish thugs," said Tad.

"Some of the absolute best dancers are thugs," said Wayfarer, who seemed not to care at all what the brothers said. Instead, she watched their bodies, scanning them up and down as though using an energy detector. "Thugs and dancers are physical people, yeah?"

"Okay, well, thank you," said Wills. "I feel odd. Sort of cleansed. I mean, except for my sore stomach where he punched me." And with that, he inclined his head at the teacher and left to walk around the hall. Soon, the bell would announce the meditation session.

Tad was the only guest left inside. "Thank you," he said stiffly to

Wayfarer. "This dancing is extremely bizarre and I always feel embarrassed afterwards."

"You'll get over it," said Wayfarer.

"But I do feel strong. And open, I guess. It's remarkable what dancing like your favourite animal can do for a person. I would like to be a panther all the time."

Helen thought about Tad's performance. They'd been asked to express their inner animals. Tad skulked around, swaying from side to side, taking swipes with his hands, which she now realized were meant to be claws. Rayvn seemed to be mimicking a bird of some kind with her arms outstretched and her great leaps. Wills was a bear or maybe a stork? Helen couldn't tell. There was shambling, then periods of stillness followed by lunges at the ground. And Whitney had pretended to prance. Each dancer had gotten so immersed that they forgot they were being watched. Their unselfconsciousness was beautiful to see.

Tomorrow afternoon's "public" performance promised to be quite a show stopper even though only Helen, Gavin, Murray, and Nigel would be in the audience.

"Your performances tomorrow might just blow a hole in your psyche that will change you forever," said Wayfarer, and Tad made a face that indicated he would prefer his psyche, such as it was, intact.

Fifteen minutes later Nigel went outside and rang the bell, and the students settled into their meditation nests. The hall filled with a gentle rustling, and a sense of shared protection for the quietude took shape.

Helen walked to the front of the room, bowed, and took her seat, reflecting that it had been a long and busy day.

"We have talked about metta, or loving-kindness. And we have explored karuna, or compassion. Tonight we consider mudita, or empathetic joy."

Before her, the students sat in their usual places and were quiet and unmoving, but for the smoothing of a scarf, or a small cough. Rayvn's quiet seemed to go deep and so, surprisingly, did Wills's. Sometimes meditators with a deep practice stabilized those around them with their calm energy. Wills's and Rayvn's practice already had that quality.

Whitney's energy was more splintery and there was something strangely alert in how Tad sat. It was hard to describe, but Helen had sat with groups of people and led students in meditation for so many years that she could read expression in the way people sat.

She explained to them how one might access mudita. "Think of a time," she said, "when you felt great joy for another being. What was that feeling? Where did it live in the body?"

She let them know that it was fine if they could not feel joy in that moment. If not, they should simply sit, making soft mental notes of what was happening and where their attention was called.

"Mudita is sometimes compared to the joy of a parent seeing a child succeed through character and hard work. Or a mother cow gazing upon her newborn calf. It is different from an attached love. Or a joy based on luck. This is pure pleasure because of the goodness of another."

Helen surveyed the hall. The four students sat on their cushions or chairs in front of her and the three staff members in their chairs at the back of the hall. Jenson and Wayfarer sat off to the side. And she could feel that at least some of them were accessing that great selfless pleasure that is empathetic joy. But not everyone. When Helen looked at Tad Todd, he wasn't meditating. Instead, he was staring at her with his strange eyes. And when their eyes met, he didn't look away. For every desirable state, there are opposing states. Some, known as "near enemies," *look* like the positive states but are imposters. The "far enemies" are true inversions. The near enemies of mudita were comparison, hypocrisy, insincerity, and happiness for others tainted with attachment and over-identification, as in the case of the hockey parent jubilant over their child's ability to smash other kids into the boards. The far enemy of mudita was envy. Before Tad Todd finally closed his eyes again, Helen wondered which of the enemies was afflicting him. Was it near or far?

Chapter 42

Because Helen's root teacher, Sayadaw U Nandisara, had just returned to Nova Scotia after teaching his regular three-month retreat in Thailand, there would be a long list of people waiting to speak with him. The people in charge of his correspondence at the monastery would pass along messages in the order they deemed most important. A vaguely worded request from a former nun would not be at the top of that list, so Helen felt a bit guilty for jumping the queue by WhatsApping him early the next morning.

For some unfathomable reason, Sayadaw U Nandisara fiercely loved the encrypted program and it was the fastest way to get in touch with him. She sat in the office with her phone on the desk in front of her and decided what to write. She would make sure to include a photo she'd taken of the garden. Sayadaw loved gardens almost as much as he loved WhatsApp. Then again, he also loved dogs, cats, insects, clouds, dirt, cars, and the colours on bits of discarded packaging. Perhaps it was more accurate to say that Sayadaw loved.

Helen remembered walking the narrow roads near the monastery with him when he was recovering from knee surgery. Her job was to prevent him from getting so interested in something that he wandered into the path of an oncoming car.

She would pick up garbage, beer cans mostly, but also the odd chip bag or chocolate bar wrapper, and tuck the items into the plastic bag she wore at her waist.

"Oh!" U Nandisara would exclaim, pointing at the object. "Wonderful!" She knew he meant the graphic design on the package, or perhaps the way the garbage was shaped: the half-crushed can, the discarded school assignment. To U Nandisara these things were treasures. He would cradle the run-over beer can in his hand and comment at how symmetrical it was. He would stare down at the McDonald's fish sandwich wrapper and nod appreciatively at the simplicity of it. "Good packaging!" he would say. "Just right."

And she in turn would feel that she was handling treasure when she put it into her little garbage sack.

It was the same with people. Sayadaw U Nandisara was thrilled with almost all of them. The whiniest, most neurotic student was met with deep appreciation. And as a result, even the most challenging students seemed to transform in his presence.

Sayadaw U Nandisara should be handling this task, thought Helen. She feared she was starting to see only the shadow side of things.

Hello, honoured teacher.

After she typed the words, she attached the photo and hit send.

There was almost no pause before the reply appeared in the little bubble.

Helen! How fortunate it is to hear you on this!

Welcome back from your retreat. I hope it went very well. I wonder if I could talk with you. There are matters I hope to discuss.

Oh yes! I would be so happy to do this!

This was how Sayadaw U Nandisara was. Eager to see students. It was also why the senior monks, who handled the requests to speak to him, wished he wasn't quite so keen on WhatsApp. Requests coming in via bits of paper left on the bulletin board outside the dining room at the monastery or sent via email could be easily managed. But Sayadaw would eagerly agree to visits via WhatsApp with little or no notice.

Thank you, Sayadaw. What time and day would be good for you?

Let us say to talk now!

She called, using the video application.

Moments later, the teacher, who was said to have reached the third stage of awakening, appeared on the screen of her phone. Even on the small screen and from so far away, his eyes shone with a warmth that instantly soothed.

"It is Helen," he said, grinning widely.

She bowed, which felt awkward with one hand holding the phone.

"You are well?" he asked, peering so intently and so close to the screen that she could only see his eyes and nose.

"I am. And you?"

"It's a good day," he said, his face suffused with joy.

Helen's breath, which had been growing shallower by the day, steadied and deepened.

She explained where she was and what she was supposed to do, and he listened with a quality of attention she'd never encountered in another person.

Helen tried to keep it simple: she was supposed to choose someone to take over the lodge. There was no need to get into the rest of it. His time was so precious.

"You see, I want to do as my late boss asked and give her life's work to the right person. And I'm afraid I'll make a mistake."

She felt exposed after the words left her mouth.

He stared into her eyes, and she felt her own eyes well up in return. This was also typical. Being in the presence of someone with Sayadaw U Nandisara's power made many people cry.

"You know we miss you at the monastery," he said. "And that I would never suggest there is any higher calling."

"Yes," she said.

"But I do see a role for you outside in the world."

This was not what she'd expected.

"You do?" she said.

He hadn't asked if she was going to take up the robes again after her mother passed and she'd always wondered why.

"Oh yes!" His eyes twinkled.

She had to admit her doubts to him. "Is it because my pāramīs are not strong?"

The pāramīs are the ten Buddhist perfections of generosity, morality, renunciation, insight, energy, patience, truthfulness, resolution, loving-kindness, and, Helen's personal favourite, equanimity. These were the qualities well developed in enlightened beings. Even before she left the monastery, Helen had been sure she possessed them in inadequate quantities.

To her surprise, U Nandisara laughed, loudly and happily.

"Ha ha!" His white teeth shone in the screen as he threw back his head. "Ha ha ha!" Then his eyes came into view. "It is my mistake. I should have assured you that your pāramīs are quite fine and developed."

He had receded into his usual simmering, shimmering joy, evident even over a video chat.

"So . . . ?" she asked. Why hadn't he encouraged her to come back? Why was she not sitting in the meditation hall at the monastery right now? Arranging the altar? Oh, how she had loved to arrange the altar and sweep the steps.

"Even as I was sorry for you to go, I could see another path for you. One of importance."

She stared harder at her beloved teacher, wishing for the thousandth time that he was just a tiny bit clearer.

"You make people feel good. You have very strong equilibrium and discernment."

"I know I'm an aversive type," she said.

He nodded solemnly. "We all have our inclinations," he said. "You have a gift for clear seeing, dear Helen. And for helping people who do not at first seem to need or even deserve it. You will remember the student from Toronto in Ontario who came to us?"

Helen did. The fiftyish heiress, married to a much younger man, had been going through a divorce, the kind that involves being replaced by a younger woman and being asked to support the two of them. She'd arrived by private jet at the nearest airport, where Helen had met her. The woman's face was taut with recent cosmetic procedures. She had a cloud of dyed-black hair and a whipcord body, and she quivered all over with dissatisfaction.

When Helen brought her to the monastery and showed her to her quarters—a wooden kuti the size of a small garden shed furnished with a space heater and a single mattress made up with a sheet, a blanket, and a single pillow—the thin woman stared in amazement.

"Are you serious?" she'd said. "Is the bathroom hiding somewhere?"

"The communal washrooms for guests are behind us. I'll show you those afterwards."

"Communal washrooms," she'd said, wonderingly. "Did the website mention this?"

Details about the bathroom facilities were clearly laid out on the website and in the guest confirmation emails, so Helen only smiled.

"God," said the woman, who looked very much in need of a sandwich and big bowl of hearty soup. "I haven't shared a bathroom since boarding school." She put down her cream-coloured leather travel case on the plank floor and stared at it. With some difficulty, Helen manoeuvred the large matching case beside it. Both pieces of luggage were pristine. Even the tan leather straps were unscuffed.

"It's a Globe-Trotter," said the woman.

"I'm sure it is," said Helen, thinking the woman was describing her travel habits.

"I mean the luggage is *Globe-Trotter*. Made in England. The small one probably costs more than this"—she gestured around, trying to come up with a description—"shed."

"Ah," said Helen. "It's very beautiful."

Then the woman remembered her manners. "Thank you. I will need another blanket. Do you have one with only natural fibres?"

"I'll see what I can do," Helen said. And then she handed Raquel the schedule for her stay. "The first meditation is at five."

"In the morning?" said Raquel.

"Yes."

"What have I done?" The tiny, brittle woman suddenly sagged onto the small bed and clutched her knees. "This isn't a good way to get back at him, is it?"

"No, but it might get you back," said Helen.

It was not uncommon for complete beginners to sign up for lengthy retreats and then be startled and sometimes aghast at what they'd done.

For the first few days of the silent retreat, Raquel spent her free time writing notes to Helen. "Might I get some Desert Lime Numi Tea?" "Would it be possible to get another heater? That one seems to be burning dust and is causing me to wheeze." "Would it be possible to get some FIRM tofu in my soup this evening? Soft tofu has such an unpleasant texture."

Helen did her best to care for the high-maintenance woman. She got her another blanket, old, but a hundred percent cotton. She ordered in regular lemon tea. She replaced her space heater with the exact same make and model. The soft tofu remained soft. Helen did these things because it seemed to help the woman, who was clearly suffering. And Helen stayed close to her, supporting Raquel's practice in the ways she knew how. And for her part, Raquel undertook the practice with a diligence that surprised everyone. She went to every sit, even the one at 4:00 a.m. She did the walking meditations, which were often the hardest part for new people, who found themselves wanting to *go* somewhere instead of slowly walking back and forth and being present for every step.

And as Raquel sank into stillness and the practice, she also opened up, a process that was painful for her, as it is for most people. She wept silently during sits, at dinner, and on her own, sitting on the front step of her kuti, seeming more alone than anyone else.

Raquel had been assigned to see one of the senior monks for her interviews, but she sent a note to the retreat manager asking if she could talk to Helen instead.

Sayadaw approved the change and so Helen listened to Raquel for fifteen minutes a day as Raquel poured out the pain in her body and in her mind.

"This is so horrible," she would say, her pretty, too-tight face struggling with the waves of churning emotion. "I feel so incredibly bad. It's torture. Why am I doing this? Why does anyone do this?"

Helen agreed that the feelings were hard and that sometimes the present moment was a nightmare river of endless wanting and aversion.

"No wonder I shop. I hate everyone in the meditation hall. Especially that woman next to me. She keeps BREATHING. She's actually breathing at me. I'm going crazy," sobbed Raquel.

"My hips are killing me," she went on. "I think I might need back surgery. And my shoulders. They're also on fire. What's wrong with my body?"

Helen reassured Raquel that she simply wasn't used to paying attention to her body. That there were likely other, more pleasant things going on alongside the pain. Could she try to notice them?

"But there's that man with the *appalling* hair. He slurps his soup. It's enough to make me throw up. And he also drags his fork over his plate. He's being intentionally aggressive!"

And on and on. Sometimes Helen suggested Raquel go for a non-meditative, slightly brisker walk, and afterwards she would see the tiny woman nearly jogging around and around the hayfield at the edge of the property. Or Helen would catch sight of her speedwalking through the maze that had been cut into the tall grass at the edge of the lake.

But in spite of her oft-repeated wish to leave the retreat, Raquel didn't. The flood of complaints eased and finally stopped. Sometimes she didn't cry. She continued to go to every sit.

A couple of weeks into the retreat, Raquel told Helen that this was her third divorce and that she kept getting married because she thought only a legal bond would make someone stay with her. She believed her husbands had all married her for her money and that she'd never tried to know them and they'd never really known her. She was sure no one had ever really loved her.

Helen listened.

The one-month retreat was thirty days longer than Raquel had ever retreated before, and throughout, she stayed close to Helen, like an oxpecker bird to an elephant. And by the time it was over, she was transformed. Gone was the perfect hair, the gleaming makeup, the constant complaining. Her parting dana was enough to sustain the monastery and all the monastics in it for a year.

"What did you do with that student?" Sayadaw U Nandisara asked Helen over the phone screen.

Helen considered. "I tried to see what she really needed. And I listened."

"Yes! Exactly so! What she really needed, you gave. And she realized that much of what she thought she was requiring was unnecessary. It is a gift rare and beautiful to be able to work with the privileged. Buddha was such a one. The rich have so much to overcome. Many of us prefer to avoid them." He smiled as he said it, and she knew he was speaking the truth. Many of the meditation teachers she knew dreaded extremely wealthy students who were new to the practice and even some who were not. She found she rather liked them. They were so grateful for any morsel of genuine peace without conditions. And they usually had lovely luggage.

Understanding settled over Helen and the ache in her heart lifted. Sayadaw did not think her unworthy of taking the vows.

"This is why I was pleased to see you go to the Yatra. And now I am happy for you to be a butler. It is so funny!" he said, and burst into laughter.

She laughed too.

"How good it is!" he said, when he'd recovered a bit. "You will help those trapped in privilege and delusion. Maybe the Buddha could have used a butler such as you. Would have saved him some of the harshest ascetic practices. Maybe he would reach enlightenment sooner."

Buddha had been a princeling, protected by his father from all difficulties, including the knowledge of pain and death. Discovering the reality of sickness, old age, poverty, and death had been a terrible shock for him and had set him on the path to awakening. Before he found the middle way between the extremes of asceticism and self-indulgence, he'd tried all sorts of harsh practices in his effort to get free of greed, hatred, and delusion. None had worked.

"Thank you," said Helen.

Sayadaw U Nandisara clasped his hands in front of his face, which filled the frame. "My eyes are happy to see you, Helen."

"But what should I do about these people? And this place?"

"You will know."

Helen let out a long breath. She hesitated, then launched in. "There's one more thing. I—" She paused, considering how to say it. "I think that, I mean, I worry that Edna was murdered." Then she corrected herself. "There is worry. About that."

He gazed at her and she felt reassured by his steadiness.

"There is concern that one of these candidates might have killed her."

Sayadaw's face grew serious and she knew he had put his hand to his heart.

She told him, as quickly and clearly as she could, her suspicions.

He listened quietly.

"You have informed the police?" he asked.

"I have. But they have not yet come."

U Nandisara nodded, then closed his eyes for several seconds.

"I think you will help find out," he said.

"Excuse me?"

"You will investigate and help the police."

"But I'm not—"

"You are," he said. The shining optimism was back in his eyes. "Investigate, and find out what happened to your beloved mentor. She trusted in you?"

"Yes," said Helen.

"Now it is time for *you* to trust in you. But keep a careful eye on those ones!" He held up a warning finger. "If what you fear is correct, some may be hanging out in the lower realms. Hungry ghosts! You will set things right."

And then he was gone, taking his Yoda-like wisdom with him.

The lower realms, thought Helen. Also known as the hell realms. Naraka in Sanskrit. Niraya in Pali. In the Buddhist lexicon, the hell realms were places of heat and cold and suffering, adultery and violence and torture and greed. The thought caused a shiver to run through her body. Sayadaw thought she could handle the situation and the people, no matter what realm they inhabited. He thought she should investigate.

So she would.

Chapter 43

WILLS TODD

Sweat ran down my back as I did lunges around the garden. A couple of times I narrowly missed Rayvn, who was twirling in circles. If I had to guess, I'd say the animal she'd picked as her inspiration for tonight's performance was some sort of creature that likes to go around in circles. Maybe one of those purebred dogs, like bull terriers, that get that form of epilepsy that makes them chase their own tails until they die.

Personally, I'm pretending to be a charging rhino, which requires a lot of quad strength, hence the lunges. Fuck, I can't believe I am doing this. Two weeks ago, you could not have convinced me I'd be seriously thinking about how to look more like a charging rhino in a dance performance meant to show off my true physical nature. Then again, two weeks ago, you probably couldn't have woken me up.

Whitney was easy to avoid because she'd chosen to stay in one spot, waving her arms around like a tree in a stiff wind. Trust Whitney to confuse a tree with an animal. That's not going to get her any points with Wayfarer, who is all about the animal essences. And the quads.

The main thing I had to do was keep a good distance from Tad in order to avoid some Tonya Harding–style attack that could take me out before the competition.

Technically, we weren't supposed to be practising our dances. We were supposed to be doing what Wayfarer called "morning interpretations" in the garden. I think we were supposed to be using our bodies to mimic the garden? Or the experience of being in the garden? Maybe Whitney had it right with her tree impersonation after all. All I know is that I'll be damned glad when this part of the course is over. Between being put on display at the flower show yesterday and having to do dance solos tonight, we seem to be deep in the public humiliation part of the program.

Tad was barely even pretending to try. He was just going around the garden with his arms folded, giving his foot a little shake after each step, like he'd gotten some dog shit on it. The expression on his face was enough to kill all the plants. I noticed that he was keeping an eye on Wayfarer, and when she looked his way, he flapped out a hand like he was waving flies away. Not much of a dance move but better than the dog-shit foot thing.

We'd been doing "morning interpretations" for half an hour already, and the sun was getting hotter and I was getting more and more tired. It didn't help that I'd spent an hour this morning after the meditation session arguing with Tad about how to proceed. Tad was still pissed off that I did my confession early, which forced him to do *his* early. And Whitney was furious we hadn't told her we'd already done ours, and that Helen had asked her directly about visiting Edna. Well, maybe Witless should have been more on the ball for her interviews with Helen. She's always had poor timing.

When we were working on the plan, Whitney said it was too complex. Baroque, she'd called it. She was probably right. And Rayvn, who was an authentic person in spite of the fact that she dresses up like a "maiden of yore," had screwed everything up. Had Edna secretly interviewed her, too? There was no way for us to know. We had to proceed as though Edna didn't know about her. And Rayvn is at least candid about being incompetent. She's usually late for the morning sits, and I can't see Helen being into that even though this place glorifies incompetent people and pointless activities.

Would our plans work? I doubt it. We were supposed to slowly reveal ourselves to be deep and thoughtful types, capable of the kind of personal growth Edna was into. How hard could that be? After all, we aren't *that* bad, at least I'm not. Shallow, preoccupied, impatient, and a little mean, yes. But isn't just about everyone that way? During some of the flower-arranging exercises, I felt stirrings of . . . something. That eulogy for myself had cracked me open a bit. The thought of it made me give my head a shake. When I looked up, Wayfarer was staring at me so I lunged a little harder and tried to get a bit more rhino-ish before going back to my thoughts. Then I remembered we were supposed to be reflecting on the garden, so I tried to make my lunges a little bit more bird- and less rhino-like by doing some hop-lunging. Birds are more common in gardens than charging rhinos and thank fuck for that.

The truth is that Tad and Whitney and I are the children of our parents. Snappy and unhappy. Bitter, closed, and suspicious. We aren't great, but we're about as good as we could be, given our circumstances. We're six days into the course and I bet Helen wouldn't let one of us borrow a bike, never mind give us even part of Edna's estate.

Maybe we could have fooled some people, but goddamned Helen

has those butler eyes. She sees everything, including us.

I will be very glad when she's not looking at me anymore. I'll be happy not to do any more interviews with her. I prefer not to be seen quite so clearly.

Also, this dance course is killing me. It's exhilarating and makes me feel powerful, and it's also one of the most embarrassing things I've ever done. When I'm not hopped up on the endorphins, I feel like an asshole. I think we all do, except for Rayvn, who is only too keen to go flailing around the place at the drop of a goddamned hat, hair flying, arms tendrilling this way and that.

My legs were about to quit on me, so I gestured to the kid who was helping the butlers. "Can you get me a glass of water?"

"Yes, sir," said the kid, who looked practically normal today in a long-sleeved white shirt under a dark denim apron. His hideously dyed hair was growing out and a soft brown colour peeked out at the roots. He was still doughy, though, like a perogy left in the water too long.

"Okay!" yelled Wayfarer. Her accent would be sexy if she didn't always seem on the verge of shot-putting someone about five hundred yards over a fence. "That's good, then. You've got the blood pumping. Now you can go inside for breakfast. I know the schedule is different today for the show and that might throw you off. You'll no want to overeat. We've a big night with your first performance, yeah?"

We filed into the lodge and I made sure to be last in line so Tad didn't get behind me.

Tad was muttering some complaint to Whitney as they filed into the serving room, and then he came to a screeching halt.

"What is this?" he asked.

Helen, the two other butlers, the chef, and the kid, who had my water glass on a tray, stood staring at him. On the serving table I could see four large glasses of something greenish-brown and a bowl of boiled eggs.

"Where. Is. Our. Breakfast?" demanded Tad, volume going up with each word.

"Wayfarer prefers dancers to have a cleansing diet on performance days," said Helen. The other two butlers moved aside to let us into the serving room.

Tad stomped up to the table and held up a large glass of thick liquid. "We've been up for hours meditating and physically exerting ourselves," he said. "And you serve us this *swill?*"

"I like smoothies," said Whitney.

"Suckhole," said Tad, savagely turning on her.

This, I reflected happily, was not going to convince anyone that Tad was a changed man.

"What's in it?" asked Rayvn, studying the sludge. "It's pretty brown."

The chef cleared her throat and stood up straighter. She was a pretty woman with clear, thoughtful eyes. "It's a recipe Wayfarer has provided," she said.

Rayvn, whose hair was even wilder than usual this morning, pushed past Tad, who was still rigid with outrage, and grabbed her glass and an egg, which she disappeared into a pocket of her skirt.

"Okay, then. Tits up, girls," she said, before sailing into the dining room.

Whitney quietly took her drink and left her egg on the table. She took the time to thank the chef and the butlers. *Bitch.*

I sidled past Tad, took my glass, and put an egg on one of the small white plates. I was about to leave the room when I heard Tad inform the chef that he'd like eggs Benedict for breakfast.

I stopped walking. I recognized his tone.

"I am a guest here," Tad said, barely keeping his voice under control. "I'm being made to take these courses for no discernible reason and I WAS PROMISED PROPER SUSTENANCE!" He jabbed a finger in Helen's direction. "BY YOU!"

I watched, fascinated. I fully expected her to give in. Tad was a terror when he got like this. But Helen the butler, Helen the Buddhist, didn't give an inch. Instead, she seemed to turn into an oak tree.

"At Edna's request, you have been invited to take these courses in the same way that all students take the courses. If you'd prefer not to participate, we will make arrangements for you to leave."

No apologies. No negotiating. What Tad should have finally understood then was that Helen Thorpe was not there for us. She was working for Edna.

Maybe he did get it because he collapsed in on himself.

"Ridiculous," he muttered. "Dinner had better be something substantial. At minimum, there needs to be a serious snack before bed."

He turned and grabbed the smoothie and two eggs, which he dropped onto the plain white plate. Predictably, both skittered off the plate and rolled off the table and onto the floor. Tad just left them. He picked up two more eggs from the bowl and stomped past me and out of the room.

When he'd been gone for a beat or two, I got my chance.

"My brother has always been sensitive about food. Fussy. Demanding." I took an ostentatiously large sip of the drink, which was surprisingly tasty for something that looked like a backed-up toilet. "This is really quite delicious. Thanks for all your hard work."

Then I went to the dining room, where I took a seat with Rayvn and Whitney, ignoring Tad, who was glaring out the window and throwing a warm egg from hand to hand like a grenade he was thinking about lobbing.

Chapter 44

When Helen drove to Mildred Pyle's home after breakfast, she considered what she knew and what she needed to know. The course was more than half over and she still had no idea who should take over the lodge. Rayvn was the most natural fit but she had tremendous difficulty getting up in the morning. She napped extensively and was often late to activities.

And Helen didn't know what to make of the others. They showed flashes of candour and openness followed by pique, jealousy, combativeness, and greed.

Wills, Tad, and Whitney had all been to see Edna during her supposedly silent self-retreat. She'd obviously tried to execute Plan A—meaning she'd tried to decide which of them should take over the lodge.

Wills and Tad had been sent away by their own admission. Helen didn't know whether Edna had even been aware of Rayvn's existence. Edna's journals, in which she might have recorded her decisions, were missing.

Yes, Helen would happily hand it all over to Officer Rosedale, but first she would do as U Nandisara had suggested and investigate. She would speak to Mildred, then Jared. She would do what she could. She would find out whether Edna had been wealthy and what had happened between Whitney and Jared. What else? What else?

Helen was so caught in her many questions that she hadn't taken a mindful breath in what felt like hours. How could one investigate a mystery without getting caught up in mental busywork? Thinking was the whole game. Or was it? She had five other sense doors to work with.

She let out a long, slow breath and tried to wake up to the world around her. She noticed the sound of the tiny car's tires humming along the pavement. Outside, the flat white sky hovered over the trees as the uncertain day tried to decide what it would be.

Flashes of light and dark, hands firm on the wheel. Her breath rising and falling.

Why had Wills and Tad confessed? Did they decide to get honest because the courses were opening their hearts? Or was something else going on?

She gave herself a metaphorical pat on the head. Mindfulness was going to be a stretch as long as she was playing the world's most unlikely amateur detective.

The turnoff to Mildred Pyle's house was marked with a simple black iron gate, which was always left open because this was Sutil Island and even the wealthy, who so often felt under threat, felt safe here.

The long driveway was large enough to accommodate two cars passing side by side, unusual on the island. The road was not paved, but it was perfectly maintained with gravel and there were no ruts, which was also extremely unusual.

The wide drive opened up to reveal what was known locally as the

Pyle. It was large, but not ridiculously so, modern, but not aggressively, and surrounded by thirty acres of old growth forest and another five acres of lawns and show gardens.

The lawns were beautifully maintained, but not medicated, so they were mossy and lush instead of bright green and strange. In summer the lawns were allowed to be dormant. On one side of the house was a mature rhododendron garden, which was festive with purple, pink, red, orange, and white blooms. On the other side of the house was a half-acre Japanese moss and water garden, complete with a small pond, a pagoda, and intricately bent trees.

Mildred's three greenhouses, arranged from small to large, had been designed to suit the style of the house. There was one for orchids and carnivorous plants, another for flowers, and a third for vegetables.

Helen had been to Mildred's many times over the years with Edna. The two older women got along well despite their differences. Mildred didn't hold with nonsense (her words) and she clearly thought most of what went on at the Yatra Institute was utter nonsense. She advocated for calisthenics over yoga (not that she was known to do any exercising other than gardening), and she ate meat with every evening meal. She liked canned tomato soup for lunch. She'd once invited Edna and Helen to a luncheon at which she'd served tomato aspic with olives in it, which Helen had never seen before and hoped never to see again.

But, like Edna, Mildred was fierce and independent, and Helen admired her.

Helen parked the car and approached the front door, admiring the spotless windows, which were covered in many places with bird silhouettes to stop birds from flying into them.

The extra tall and wide front door swung open before she could reach it.

Leon stood in the doorway.

He grinned at her.

"Madam," he said.

"Oh, hello. I was expecting . . ." Helen stopped. She'd been expecting one of Mildred's "girls," as Mildred called her employees, who were usually competent middle-aged women with experience working in remote camps as cooks or labourers. Most had an epic capacity for hard work. It wasn't that Mildred was a severe taskmaster, but she couldn't bear softness in her employees or any mention of work–life balance, a primary consideration for most Sutil Islanders.

Leon laughed. "Yeah, I'm just filling in until school starts. Mildred's my homie, least when it comes to plants. Come in."

He held the door open for Helen.

When she was inside and had removed her shoes, he looked at her, gestured around the house, and whispered, "Holy shit, eh?"

Helen grinned. Holy shit was right. The house was not massive by the standards of the very rich, but it was spacious and it was exceedingly well designed.

The entire front of the house was made of glass so that it seemed to extend right into the ocean. The walls were stark, flat white, which helped to accentuate the modernist masterpieces that hung on them.

The furniture was not fussy, but was of a similar excellent and understated quality.

The Pyle was like an extremely welcoming and comfortable museum.

Leon was dressed as usual in a T-shirt and jeans. The shirt bore the logo of the Klahoose Nation and he had on a pair of what looked like Edna's slippers.

"I love your slippers," said Helen.

"Thanks. Don't worry. I still have my gumboots."

Helen laughed. The Klahoose people were famously fond of gumboots. The first thing people who came home from away were asked was where their boots were.

Leon pointed to a pair of yellow gumboots arranged neatly beside the door. "My sisters say my boots are too cityish. I might have to get some of the regular kind with the red soles just to stop the teasing. Least I don't roll mine down."

"They're nice boots," said Helen.

He looked comfortable and at home in the space. Helen wondered if *he* had ever considered a career in butlering.

"I'll take you to Mildred," he said.

"Thank you."

"I guess you're used to rich-people places like this."

"Not yet," said Helen. "I've just completed my training."

They walked into a kitchen at least twice the size of the commercial kitchen at Yatra. No Mildred.

"She must have gone to the greenhouse," said Leon.

A flagstone path led from a door at the back of the kitchen to the first and smallest greenhouse, which had a post-and-beam frame and floor-to-ceiling windows. Leon invited Helen into the humid space filled with the sound of trickling water.

The door closed and they were in a vaguely oppressive jungle. Ferns and unidentifiable tropical plants hung from the rafters and lined the shelves and tables that crowded the space.

Mildred was seated at a dark, wooden table on which was arrayed a collection of very small plants. She had a syringe in one hand and was carefully squeezing out droplets onto the plants.

"Mildred? Helen's here," said Leon.

"Ah, hello, dear," said Mildred, not looking up. She wore the wealthy woman's uniform of neat khaki slacks and blue button-down shirt with pearls. Over the shirt she had on a white apron. Her hair, a firm set she had redone each week by the village hairstylist who came to visit her, looked like a white wave cresting over her head.

"I'm just feeding my pitcher plants, dear. There are no fungus gnats in here for these poor dear Sarracenia."

She added a droplet to the tip of one leaf. "I expect this sundew is absolutely ravenous."

The plants looked like a 1970s film version of alien life forms. Fleshy, veined cups rose out of the soil. Some were covered in creeping tendrils. Others seemed to have tiny jaws at the ends of their stems.

Helen glanced at Leon, who made a face like he was about to be sick, which made her want to laugh.

"Now, Leon," said Mildred. "Don't be ridiculous. You know you love the carnivores! Do not try to pretend you aren't fascinated, you silly thing."

"It's true," said Leon. "They are cool, even if they are a giant hassle. Mildred got me into them a while ago, and now I spend about two hours a day trying to catch live flies to give them. I'm like an unsuccessful frog."

"Not unsuccessful," chided Mildred. "Inexperienced! And you are not the first to catch the bug of carnivorous plants—"

"Don't do it!" cried Leon.

"Too late, dear," said Mildred. "The pun has been launched. As I was saying, Leon is not the first to catch the carnivorous plant bug, thanks to my bog table."

Leon nodded. "It's true. She's like a flytrap dealer over here."

Mildred pretended to squirt him with her syringe. "That's enough out of you."

"Okay. Can I bring you guys anything?" asked Leon.

"No dear, but thank you."

And with that, Leon left the hot, fuggy little room.

"I'm sorry to bother you," said Helen, who walked closer in order to see more clearly what Mildred was doing with the plants.

"Not at all. I'm pleased to see you, Helen," said Mildred. "I'll offer you tea when I finish here. The poor things have been waiting for me to finish with the orchids."

Helen didn't know what Mildred had been doing with her orchids but imagined that it was something painstaking and magnificently fiddly.

"I'm here to ask about some comments you made."

"Oh?" said Mildred, peering over her half-size lenses.

"Jenson Kiley said you suggested to him that Edna was quite well-off."

Helen didn't like to gossip about other people, and the line of questioning felt uncomfortable.

"She was," said Mildred.

"Can you tell me more?" asked Helen.

"Edna was one of those who kept her wealth a secret, perhaps to remove that barrier that great wealth puts between those who have it and those who don't. She wanted to live on the same plane as others, or whatever plane it is that people with bizarre beliefs inhabit.

"One had to admire her for her discretion," Mildred continued. "I imagine it's much less isolating than to show one's wealth. I mean, look at me. I'm a veritable circus attraction on this island."

"You're an important and valued member of the community," said Helen.

"People never feel they can be themselves around people with real money. There are exceptions, of course. People like you. But most cannot abide the discrepancy in circumstances. I'm sure that's why Edna hid her financial position."

Helen listened, rapt.

"Her late husband was a Todd. But *he* wasn't the one with the serious money. Edna was an Endicote. An only child. The Endicotes owned copper mines, originally. Then oil and gas. I believe they owned a significant part of downtown Toronto. When her parents died, she inherited everything."

Helen was unable to hide her amazement.

"When did her parents die?" she asked.

"Perhaps thirty-five years ago. Edna was already widowed. She was here, running the Institute."

"I see," said Helen.

"I believe she sold most of her holdings and has given away a large part of the proceeds. Quietly, you understand. But with a fortune that size, it's hard."

"So how wealthy was she?" asked Helen.

"Oh, she was certainly a billionaire at a time when that meant something. But no longer. I believe she whittled it down to the last seventy-five million or so. That's the last I heard, anyway."

"Seventy-five million," repeated Helen.

"The very rich like to talk about giving it all away, but one still needs a bit of mad money."

Mad money. The words rattled around in Helen's head.

"How many people knew her financial situation?" asked Helen. "And are you *sure* she had that much money?"

"Quite sure," said Mildred. "We talked about it now and then. She could hardly speak about it with anyone else now, could she? People would be at her constantly, wanting things. But some people had to know. Word gets around even from the most discreet law firms. Trust managers talk. Relatives speculate."

Helen considered for a moment. "Did she tell you what she wanted to do with the money? I mean, separate from who should run Yatra?"

"Oh, I imagine she made plans for it. But no, she didn't tell me."

Helen hoped those plans were more solid than the plans Edna had made for the Institute. And she gave silent thanks for the fact that she was in charge only of determining who should manage the lodge.

Finally, Mildred looked up from her flesh-eating plants, syringe between her fingers like a mad doctor.

"You seem upset to learn this. Do you oppose wealth?" Her face, with its beautifully soft and nearly wrinkle-free skin, was impassive.

"Not at all," said Helen. "It just changes things. Or maybe it doesn't."

"Money changes everything," said Mildred. "Everything but death. That, it can't change."

Too much money or not enough, Helen thought, could probably accelerate a person's death.

She turned down Mildred's offer of tea and saw that the older woman was relieved not to have to leave her plants.

On her way out she poked her head into the huge kitchen where Leon was polishing a large collection of copper pans.

"I have no idea what I'm doing here," he said, holding up a large, gleaming saucepan. "This pot costs twelve hundred dollars. I know because I looked it up to find out how to polish it properly. I can't imagine paying that much for a pot." He shook his head in wonder and amusement.

"They're very beautiful," replied Helen.

"Yeah, but it's enough of a pain in the ass having to clean pots and pans after you use 'em. I don't get the point of having ones you have to clean even when you don't use 'em."

"It's a different approach," said Helen.

"But I guess butlering teaches you a lot of useless stuff."

"We take great pride in knowing a lot about useless things."

"Hmmmffff," said Leon, looking over the collection of copper pots stacked one atop another. It *was* a rather daunting sight. Then he looked back at her. "Everything okay over there at the lodge?"

"I really don't know," said Helen.

"Yeah. I sort of got that feeling." He rubbed the back of his wrist across his forehead so as not to get copper cleaner on his face. "Lot of tension over there."

"Agreed."

"The love birds pecking at each other again?" asked Leon.

"I'm sorry?" said Helen.

"You know, Jared and that one with the hair in her face. Every time I see her, I want to give her a hair clip or something."

"You're saying they are . . ." Helen waited for Leon to explain.

"In love-hate with each other?" he said. "Yeah, pretty much."

"How do you know this?" asked Helen.

"I saw 'em walking a few times this spring. One time they were arguing. And the day the courses started, like early that morning, I was in the garden planting some sweet peas and he came hustling down the path, mad as a—well, mad as a realtor. I figured they had an argument."

Helen frowned and tried to remember what Whitney had said about her relationship with Jared. She had certainly *not* mentioned that he'd been to see her since she'd arrived.

Another lie.

"When did you see them walking?" asked Helen.

"I'm not sure, exactly. Edna was on her retreat. Five or six weeks ago maybe?"

"Do you know what they were arguing about?"

Leon's handsome face was serious.

"No. They didn't see me. I was clearing some brush up by the pond. Figured I'd let them have some privacy."

Helen sighed. Why were Whitney and Jared being so unforthcoming? And why was Whitney hiding their relationship?

"Good luck with whatever you're doing with those people," said Leon.

"Thank you."

"And if the one who dresses like she's living in King Arthur times starts shooting the other ones with a bow and arrow, you should call the cops."

Helen laughed. "Thank you, Leon. I will."

Chapter 45

'll be back before the dance performance," said Helen to Murray in the kitchen of the lodge a few hours after she'd returned from Mildred's. She'd been anxious to speak to Jared since her conversations with Mildred and Leon. "Looks like we're in for a storm, so we may need to change the venue from Kalaivaani. We don't want anyone walking those paths if the wind is really blowing."

Murray nodded seriously and made a note on a small pad she carried with her everywhere.

The girl had, to Helen's delight, settled beautifully into the demanding routine. She seemed unfazed by the peculiar nature of the tasks and the guests. And she'd demonstrated a great gift for efficiency.

Back at the North American Butler Academy, Helen had sometimes wondered whether Murray was cut out for a life of service. She had seemed to quietly resent some of the clients and had come back from her practicum rattled and even somewhat depressed. Plus, there was her tendency to drink too much and her obvious crush on Gavin, who'd been quite clear that he was in a period of celibacy but unclear about who he might date when it was over.

Helen was a carer, not a worrier, but if she'd worried about anyone, it would have been Murray, who for all her wit and charm seemed somewhat tender. Or she had until she'd started work at the Institute, where she bloomed like one of the peonies in the garden.

She undertook every task with calm competence and anticipated most of Helen's requests and those of the guests. Her happiness in Gavin's presence was lovely to behold. For a moment, Helen contrasted Murray's journey at the Institute to Tad Todd's. His transformation from jerk, to disarmingly honest confessor, back to entitled jerk had been disorienting and suggested that things were not going easily for him as he opened and then closed back up.

She'd seen it before. The flower-arranging course coaxed self-discovery and deep reflection from participants. Devi Dance yanked inner knowledge out of them and not everyone handled it well. The body, as Helen knew well, houses human beings' deepest emotions and experiences. That was why most experienced meditators begin each sit with a body scan. People who are in touch with their mental states are also attuned to their bodies.

"Helen?" said Murray, interrupting Helen's reverie. "Where are you going?"

They stood in the foyer near the pass-through to the dish pit where Nigel was loading the dishwasher.

Helen looked around, aware that she was being paranoid.

"I'm going to see someone," she said.

"Very mysterious," said Murray.

"I'm sorry. I have some questions I need to ask someone."

"I see!" said Murray. The fact that she didn't see hung in the air.

"I won't say more right now," said Helen, feeling ridiculous.

Sayadaw U Nandisara might think she would make a good investigator but that was because he hadn't seen her investigating.

"I'll see you soon," Helen added as she slipped on her raincoat.

She drove to Jared's studio in the ominously dark late afternoon. The day had gone from bright and hot to cold and overcast, and the air was filled with the promise of rain. Helen's body felt tight. Old injuries were speaking up. A sure sign that she was stressed. Small wonder. She was not an investigator and she had no idea what she would say to Jared. Was she really going to quiz him about his love life? To what end?

Helen thought again of how Tad, Wills, Whitney, and Rayvn sometimes came across as human embodiments of the hindrances— ill will, sensuous desire, restlessness and worry, doubt, and sloth and torpor—but also as people capable of accessing finer feelings. There was Tad talking about caring (with maximum resentment) for his parents, and his acid tongue, set against his first arrangement of the man and the dog on the beach. Loyalty and service. His cruelty and pique. His sometimes-creepy comments and his unsettling and intimidating affect. If Tad was a hindrance, it was ill will. But no one was all one thing.

Wills also seemed well supplied with ill will, but he was also greedy. Why would anyone try to start a regatta for rich people to race boats? That money could fund a refugee camp for years. Sensory desire could be every bit as destructive as pure ill will. Just ask any drug addict. But as with his brother, Wills had other facets. Helen thought of the design of Wills's bentwood archway with its scattered petals and carefully placed stones. It had been so beautiful and generous.

Then there was Whitney. If Helen had to guess, she'd say the girl was drowning in doubt, about herself and everything else. She seemed afflicted with restlessness and worry. Doubt and its companions were tricky. Until you truly knew someone, it was impossible to know what their doubts were. For meditators, doubt showed up as a lack of faith in the path, in the principles of Buddhism, and fear that the practice of meditation itself was pointless and true spiritual growth was impossible. Helen thought Whitney might also be the kind of introvert who secretly despised those who were not. They seemed outwardly calm but contained vast amounts of resentment they'd been quietly stewing over.

Then there was Ferdinand, the cousin who declined to attend. Wills and Tad had referred to him as being lazy as a stuffed duck. His hindrance was apparently sloth and torpor. Or was Rayvn, who had trouble getting up, the one most afflicted with sloth?

Edna would have loved Rayvn: her velvet bodices, her charming frankness, and her strange hobbies. Edna appreciated anyone who managed to be unconcerned about what other people thought. Perhaps Rayvn was racked with delusion, but perhaps not. She seemed very clear-eyed about things. Rayvn seemed to shine with the four immeasurables of loving-kindness, empathetic joy, compassion, and equanimity. They came easy to the girl, as they had to Edna, who had lived a fortunate life.

And there was the rub. Helen believed that there was nobility in working with one's hindrances with grace and honesty. It was moving to see someone try to reckon with their all-too-common human weaknesses.

How would people uninjured by conditions and blessed with balanced personalities behave when life got difficult? It was hard to know.

This, Helen knew, was why the students were being put through the courses. Edna could not make them take Navy Seal training, but in her world, flower arranging, dance, and meditation courses tested a person's mettle in a deep and fundamental way.

Helen's job was to watch, stay open, and investigate the students for signs of change as well as manifestations of their true natures. But for now she would intrude on Jared to ask about his personal life.

She pulled up to his cottage and got out of the van. Jared's silver Lexus was parked in front and she immediately noticed that the potted flowers near his front door, usually so well-tended and welcoming, were dying. The geraniums and salvia and pansies had turned into sticks and wilted bits of velvet.

An uneasy feeling stirred deep within her.

She walked to the front door and knocked. There was no answer. Then, unable to help herself, she picked up the watering can at the edge of the porch stairs and gave all the plants a drink.

After that, she made her way to the side of the cottage to Jared's studio. Both cottage and studio were timber framed with matching whitewashed exteriors and cedar shake roofs.

There were no lights on inside and the glass door was closed, but Helen peered inside.

His canvases lay on the floor, not stacked, but as though they'd been thrown.

There was no way Jared had left his paintings, which were beginning to command good prices, in such disarray. His fastidiousness in all things extended to his art.

Helen went to the door and tried the handle. The door opened.

She stepped into the small studio, which smelled of wood and faintly of chemicals and something else, and reached for the light. The sky outside was so dark that in spite of all the windows the interior was gloomy.

The space was a shambles. Easels knocked over. Huge canvases toppled and small ones piled on top. Brushes spilled onto the floor and counters. Helen took another step into the room. Had someone broken in and vandalized it?

She took two steps further and carefully lifted a large canvas that rested precariously against the counter with its stained sink and array of jars and cans, most of which had been knocked over. She lifted the picture and couldn't quite figure out what she was seeing. Why had someone broken in and left their pants in the studio? No. Not just pants. A person. After a beat, her mind admitted what her heart already knew: someone lay beneath the painting. She'd exposed his pant leg. The rest of him was hidden under other toppled canvases.

"Oh," she said, softly. She pulled two more canvases off Jared Weintraub and then knelt beside him.

He lay in fetal position. His feet, clad only in socks, looked strangely vulnerable.

He was dead, and it looked like he had been for some time.

She knew she shouldn't touch anything else, but she felt she had to touch him. He had died and been left alone in this place that should have been his sanctuary. To leave him untouched would be cruel. He was so alone, and that aloneness was the ache at the root of everything.

Helen put a hand to Jared's brow. It was cold, but she made sure not to pull away. She stayed like that for a long, long moment, sending all the metta she could to the young man before her. Then she backed out of the studio. And felt the shaking begin.

Chapter 46

Rain began to slant down and Helen retreated into the van. She sat staring at the little cottage and studio through the fogged windshield and then took out her phone. No reception.

She pulled her rain hood over her head, got out, walked to the end of the driveway, and tried again.

It worked. She called 911 and reported what she'd found with some difficulty over the crackly line. When she hung up, she called the lodge and Gavin answered. He sounded like he was on the moon and the line kept cutting out.

Helen told him she would be late getting back and that they should hold the dance performance in the lodge rather than Kalaivaani. She also tried to explain where she was and what she'd discovered.

"Shall I come?" he asked. Then he said something else she didn't hear.

"I think you should stay there," she said. "Just in case."

She couldn't hear his response.

"I'm not sure what's happened, but I think we need to be very careful."

"You think," he said, followed by some garbled words, then, "is responsible?"

"I don't know what I think. But please try to keep everyone there together."

"I understand." Another bit of static. "The weather is getting quite—"

"Please take good care," she said. "I'll be back as soon as I can."

"Stay safe and—" The line went dead.

Helen tried to call Office Rosedale. The phone rang and rang. The sky seemed to open up and a clap of thunder boomed directly over-head, and in her jumpy state, she dropped the phone and it skittered into a puddle.

"Oh no!" she said, pulling the device out of the dirty water and giving it a shake. It was only in there a few seconds. Hopefully, it was okay. She'd call Officer Rosedale from the lodge, where there was a landline. Or maybe the 911 dispatcher had called him.

Helen had retreated back to the van when Olaf pulled up behind her in the red Sutil Island Volunteer Fire Department truck. The 911 operator must have dispatched him.

He appeared at her window.

"Is it Jared?"

"It is," she said.

"He's in there?" Olaf's tall, lanky body was draped in a worn slicker and his lined face and deep-set eyes were almost invisible inside his hood. The rain pounded down around them. "He's dead?"

She nodded.

Olaf muttered a curse. Then he adjusted his hood and water cascaded out of the folds.

"The ferries are all cancelled with this wind. RCMP can't get a helicopter out either. They asked me to stay on the scene until they can get someone here. Stan will be here in the ambulance pretty soon. There's no doctor on the island right now. Not even Dr. Dubinsky. She's in Mexico."

"It's too late for an ambulance," said Helen.

"Me and Stan can watch until the cops get here and do their thing. Unless we get called away. Lotta wind. Might be accidents."

"How long is this storm supposed to last?" she asked.

"Might be a while. Supposed to get up to twenty-five knots by this evening. I think we're going to get hammered."

Helen thought of how the monks sometimes sat with bodies, overnight. But they weren't generally sitting with the bodies of murder victims whose killers were still on the loose.

"I'll head back to the lodge and you can pull up closer."

"Ya, okay," said Olaf, sounding more Danish with every word. "That is good."

Helen reversed out of Jared's driveway so Olaf could move the truck in front of the door.

The afternoon had turned dark as night, and the rain seemed to change directions every few seconds, like the planet was tilting on its axis. After Helen had been driving for a few minutes, she pulled over and tried Murray.

"Hello?" she said. "Can you hear me?"

There was a response, but Helen couldn't make it out. Was the phone messed up from getting wet or was she in another cell dead zone?

"Can you ask Chef to put together some food for two people who have to watch a house tonight?" she asked. "And coffee? They will be there all night, most likely, so I'd like to feed them. I need someone to drop it off at Jared Weintraub's studio. It's Number 6 in the Sutil Art Guide. The food is for the people inside the red truck parked outside. Someone has been killed. The police will be coming."

Helen thought she heard Murray exclaim and then say okay. But before she or Murray could say anything else, the call was dropped. She stared at her phone and then set it aside.

When she pulled the van back onto the road, the water sluiced out of the sky and Helen couldn't see out the windshield. She steadied herself and pulled over again, listening to the sound of the downpour echo in the empty interior of the van. Strong gusts of wind made the big vehicle tilt, as though unseen hands were trying to push it over.

Soon there would be trees down all over the island, including across the roads. She should have thought of that. She tried to call Murray and tell her not to come, but she couldn't get through.

Helen gave herself the pep talk she used when fear arose. *Never again this moment.* In normal circumstances, it was a reminder to stay present, but in this situation, the mantra felt like a threat. Then she started the van and headed to Yatra.

Chapter 47

NIGEL OWENS

'm not sure when everything got so fucked up, but somewhere along the line, the job at Yatra had gone from cool and unusual to bizarre and borderline scary. The tension was so high in the lodge, where we were all hiding from that mother of a storm, that I was getting blood pressure issues. The guests were like leaky nuclear reactors blasting radioactively hostile vibes at each other, not that I know shit about nuclear reactors.

The lodge seemed big in the daytime. Or at least it did in the *regular* daytime when the sky was clear and the rain wasn't pounding down and the wind wasn't driving so hard that the whole building groaned. A few times I made the mistake of looking outside and seeing the trees bend way over one way and then back. It was a miracle any of them were still in the ground. Now the lodge seemed cramped. With the black storm outside and the guests giving each other the hate stares, the place felt like a one-bedroom apartment with four feuding gangs in it.

I was trying to stay out of the dining and sitting rooms, where the guests were, but I kept having to go get stuff for the asshole brothers. Wayfarer, who looks like she was born in a storm just like this one, stood in the middle of the dining room, by herself, doing some kind of show-offy stretching. Which obviously would have been awesome if everything else wasn't so terrifying. Chef was quietly making bread and preparing dinner. She had headphones in and was listening to her audiobook. "This place is bumming me out right now. I need to listen to something fun," she said, when I asked what she was listening to. "It's about swingers. You'd love it." And then she went back to kneading the bread.

Tad came into the kitchen and asked me for a gin and tonic, even though the guests weren't supposed to drink during the courses. I wasn't about to say no. The guy's a pressure cooker.

I brought it out to Tad and heard Wills complaining. "For god's sake! Look at it out there. And I don't feel like dancing right now. Performance or no performance, I'm going to my cabin. I can't stand being in here anymore."

Gavin was trying to explain that the cabins were off-limits until the winds died down when Wayfarer appeared at his side.

"The dance goes on," said Wayfarer. "You should ask yourself what the powers of nature can do for you and your performance before you decline the invitation our glorious goddess Mother Earth has given you, yeah?"

As she spoke, Wayfarer went up on her toes like she was going to rocket up, up, up into the air. Then the power went out and we were in darkness.

"Damn!" came the faint cry from somewhere.

"Pardon me," said Gavin, moving past us. "I'll see about the generator."

Whitney stared pointlessly at the book in front of her. "It's too dark to read."

"Who gives a shit?" said Tad. "How about you stop reading for ten seconds and help me convince these people to cancel the dance performance. If we all refuse, they might actually listen."

"It's not cancelled for me," said Rayvn, getting to her feet and twirling around. "I love a good storm."

"Shocker," muttered Tad.

Wayfarer smiled at Rayvn. Then she turned to Tad. Her smile was gone and her high cheekbones were like stone.

"The requirements for the class are clear. Helen explained it to all of you at the beginning. If you no want to continue, you can quit. It's fine. But we do it when I say we do it. This is not shuffleboard. If you don't do it, you're out."

I felt my eyes bulging out of my head. I imagined Wayfarer brutalizing dancers around the world to get the most out of them. I respected her even though I was glad she wasn't trying to make *me* dance during a massive and dangerous storm and power outage.

Wayfarer whirled around and clapped her hands several times. "We'll clear all the tables and chairs so you'll have plenty of room. You'll need to spread out as much as you can. Let's see your physicality in action, yeah? We're calling on the dark gods for this one."

And seconds later, I was helping push the tables to the sides and carry the chairs into the foyer. We were in the middle of this when the lights flickered back on, powered by the humming generator. Gavin rejoined us and was greeted with applause, at least from me and Rayvn, who seemed to be enjoying herself thoroughly. Then the lights went out again.

"Oh dear," said Gavin. "Helen mentioned that the generator is somewhat temperamental."

"Ach, it's nothing," said Wayfarer. "We'll create our own electricity."

I was starting to think she might be a little nuts, but I wasn't about to say that, since I have approximately one one-hundredth of her muscle mass.

Rayvn made a big show of going outside, saying again how she, too, loved a good storm, and she started her own dance warm-up on the deck consisting of not very high kicks and some wobbly twirls—until she was nearly hit in the head with a falling branch and came scurrying back inside, where she stood dripping onto the floor and talking about how exhilarating it had been to be "one with the elements."

Wayfarer was showing me where to shove the last pieces of furniture when Murray showed up in the doorway and signalled to me. She had on a red rain slicker and pants.

"You help Gavin keep the peace while I'm out."

I tried to read the serious expression on her face.

"Helen's asked me to drop off food for some people who are watching a house tonight. She should be back soon."

"Are you sure it's safe for you to go out in this?" I said.

She shrugged. "Helen wouldn't have asked if it wasn't. Shouldn't take long."

She must have noticed that I was borderline freaking out.

"It's fine. Just keep your wits about you, okay?"

"This is all pretty intense, isn't it?"

"It is," agreed Murray, who held a big insulated bag in one hand and a massive Thermos in the other. "But even us atheists are in god's hands in weather like this."

It was not quite five o'clock in the afternoon. But with the storm blotting out the light, the ocean thrashing around in front of us, and the trees heaving back and forth, it felt like deep night. A deep, bad night.

"Enjoy the dancing, then. And help Gavin keep an eye on them."
I nodded and swallowed.

Murray ducked out the door, letting in a blast of wind. Then she was gone into the storm. I wanted to call her back. But I didn't. I straightened, feeling glad I had changed into a proper shirt with some colour and flare, even if it was a bit tight and the collar was sort of flappy. When things go bad, a person needs to be comfortable. Then I went to see Chef because I find her relaxing. And she always has food.

Chapter 48

Helen was able to drive around the first two trees, but the third, a good-sized Douglas fir, blocked the entire road. It wasn't going anywhere until someone came along with a chainsaw and cut it into pieces.

She put the van in reverse and parked it as far off to the side of the narrow shoulder of the road as she could get it. She doubted many other drivers would be out.

After the engine was off, Helen considered the situation. The storm seemed to have settled into a rhythm of long sighs followed by screams of wind. Rain pounded, then softened for a few moments before raging back.

Helen had experienced many storms on Sutil Island. This was an order of magnitude worse than any other she'd seen.

It would take her at least twenty minutes to walk the rest of the way back to the lodge. She'd be safer in the van, but she felt called back to the lodge. Helen summoned the image of Sayadaw U Nandisara and his eyes, so full of joy. She thought of his confidence in her and the curiosity and equilibrium he'd bring to this situation. She would try to live up to his example.

Calm settled over her rattled nervous system and she got out of the van and closed the door. She sent compassion to the fallen tree. It was sad to see it sprawled across the rain-soaked pavement, its green branches, so recently alive, now broken and smashed. The tree was dead but its branches had not yet gotten the message.

Helen climbed carefully over the tree, making sure not to impale herself on the protruding branches. And then she began her trek, keeping to the middle of the road so that she was less likely to be struck by falling branches or another tree. With luck she would hear any cars approaching before they could hit her.

As she walked, she kept her head turtled deep inside her rain jacket. Alone in the tumult, her thoughts began to rise and fall like waves. She noted the sensation of thinking, but paid no more attention to her thoughts than to her other senses. She was mindful of the bottoms of her feet as they rose and fell. Sensations of all kinds came and went. In the midst of the storm, she felt pure calm and deep concentration.

A sense of rapture rose, unbidden, and her breathing became almost imperceptible. There was no boundary between her and the elements. She was empty and she was not. She was the wind and the trees and the rain.

Thinking fell away entirely and the initial ecstatic quality subsided and spread until she felt stretched as long as the road. She was as wide as the storm and as deep as the ocean that surrounded the island. The being called Helen was no more for a time.

So who moved along the narrow, black road littered with branches and leaves? A constellation of conditions, a spaciousness without end.

Consciousness and preconsciousness. From this wondrous state that may have lasted seconds or minutes, Helen came gently back into her body and back into awareness of the various likes and dislikes and history that had formed her. Newly added to the mix was a strong intuition about what had happened to Jared and perhaps to Edna.

Helen didn't push this awareness away or grab tightly onto it. She just allowed it to filter into her conscious mind. That's what she was doing when a pair of headlights, very close together, appeared out of the rain in front of her.

Chapter 49

MURRAY CLEARY

hadn't driven for a long time but surely I could manage the little Smart Car. I'd have been much more nervous in the big van. Luckily the island is so small I wouldn't get myself permanently lost, in spite of the horrendous weather. Eventually, I'd end up at the ocean, which would be my cue to stop. Gavin had written out the directions. The cell service on this island is extremely patchy so Google maps was not an option.

After a fortifying drink of tea I headed out, repeating the instructions to myself. Go down the driveway and turn right onto the slightly bigger road. Stay on that road for four and a half kilometres, take a left at the first road past the big red barn, drive for another kilometre. Pull in at the house with the red fire truck in the driveway. Give food to the man in the truck because he would be spending the night there because the house had to be watched until the police arrived, which might not be until the next day. At least, that's what Gavin thought Helen had said to him. He'd had trouble understanding her call.

I'd have given a lot to know why a firefighter had to spend the night in front of someone's house. It was probably something insane and islandish. Someone's pet peacock was on a crime spree and was expected to attack the place at any moment.

As soon as I was in the parking lot, I realized that this wasn't just rotten weather. It was like something you'd see on the news out of Florida during hurricane season. I hurried to the car and fished around in the deep pocket of my red raincoat, looking for the keys. When I couldn't find them at first, I put down the insulated bag Chef had handed me and set the large Thermos on the sopping ground. Even with the enormous hood pulled all the way over my head, rain lashed into my face when I stood up. That's when the odd feeling hit. It was somehow both hard to understand and oddly unmistakable. Had I ever felt such a thing? No, I had not. Time seemed to judder off its tracks, and I remembered being fifteen and in the operating room to have my appendix out. Count back from ten, the anesthesiologist had said. I'd made it all the way to four. I remembered the look of alarm on his face as I kept counting and counting.

Later, he told my mother that I hadn't "gone down easy." "No indeed," my mother had replied. "She never has. She's a strong girl. Wilful to her last bone." That was true enough.

The feeling got stronger, blocking out the storm and everything else. I felt the ground rush up to meet me.

Get up, I told myself. *Get back in the house. Get Gavin. Get Helen. Yes, Helen. Helen would know what to do. And tell Gavin that you—*

But I had turned to lead and ashes, and so I stayed there on the ground beside the bag of food. I sensed someone approach and knew they were rooting through my pockets, and then I didn't know anything.

Chapter 50

NIGEL OWENS

I stood in the entryway to the dining room and tried to mimic Gavin's calm attitude. It was hard, because I wasn't calm, like, at all.

The students didn't want to stay together. First Whitney had to go to the bathroom, then Rayvn said she had to go. Then Wills said he was heading outside to look for a "break in the weather." He kept mentioning that he was a sailor, so he was really good at weather. Tad stomped into the kitchen every ten seconds, asking for food or for another gin and tonic, and I tried to keep him away from Chef, who didn't need hassles from him.

If only Wayfarer would do something. She had the—What's the word? Gravitas? Ferociousness? What I mean is that she was tough enough to make them do as she said. But no. She kept messing around with her phone and the speaker.

Jenson had moved into a corner of the dark dining room, his legs crossed, like he was waiting for someone to tell him his car and driver had arrived.

"Ready?" Gavin asked Wayfarer, and I was pretty sure I could hear a tiny speck of impatience. Not that Wayfarer cared.

"When the time is right. Dance is intuitive, yeah?"

"Certainly," said Gavin, perfectly polite again.

Wayfarer finished fiddling with her phone and then she nodded at Gavin.

"Okay," said Wayfarer. She put a hand to her perfectly flat belly. "The root chakra drives this dance. It's the source of the earth energies. It's aligned to your deepest physicality, which is what dance should be. All energies poured into your inspiration animal."

It was so dark it was hard to tell who was who, but that made everything all the more dramatic.

Wayfarer held up a hand and Gavin hit play on the music, and she began to sway.

The music actually did sound like the earth moving, although I'm no expert on music or the earth. It was deep and rhythmic, like a planet being born, I thought, feeling a bit poetic in spite of my terror.

It got louder, so it cut through the roar of the storm battering the lodge. Wayfarer started doing . . . something. I stared. Everyone stared. She was elemental, if that's the word. Was that the tango? Her black hair snapped back and forth. One leg drew up, impossibly high, then came down. The other one flicked out the back.

I wouldn't have wanted to be the student who had to dance after her.

Big preggo pause. Then BOOM.

The entire lodge gave a huge jerk and people screamed. All of a sudden, the storm seemed to be inside with us. Gavin cut the music and put out his arms. "Everyone, please get into the middle of the room. I think something may have fallen on us."

Everyone did as he said. Now all we could hear was the screaming wind. I thought I could even *feel* the wind.

"I can help," said Wills, I guess because of his experience with weather.

"Thank you, sir. I appreciate that, but I'm going to ask that you wait here. Your safety is of paramount concern. Nigel? Come with me," said Gavin.

That was super disappointing. I've never valued bravery, due to my belief that it invites danger and injury, but I went with him anyway. Gavin gave me a rain jacket and we went out the door nearest to the kitchen, on the ocean-facing side of the lodge. As soon as we stepped outside, the wind started shoving us around and driving sheets of rain into our faces.

"Come along," cried Gavin. I could hardly hear him, but I followed his yellow coat as he went down the steep stairs.

As soon as we rounded the corner, we saw that a huge tree had fallen. It had crushed the reception building and the top of it lay on the top floor of the lodge. Actually, it was inside the top of the lodge.

I stood beside Gavin, surveying the damage.

Gavin looked like he wanted to say a prayer, but he didn't.

"Not ideal," he said instead, using his best butlerish understatement. "But at least it won't be joined by any others. The rest of the trees appear to be out of range of the building. *This* building, at least."

"What are we supposed to do?" I asked. I hoped the answer was to curl up in a ball and wait for someone else to come and fix everything.

"The guests," said Gavin, simply. "We tend to the guests first and the property second."

I had no idea what that meant and was afraid to ask.

"When the storm is over, we'll put up a tarp, if we can. The tree may continue to descend further into the lodge, so we'll move everyone away from that part of the building. As soon as it's safe to go outside, we'll move into another building. I'll make sure the power is out and the water has been turned off."

"The tree is right over one of the upstairs bedrooms and the back of the kitchen," I said, pointing at where the tree had fallen.

"Quite so," said Gavin. "As soon as phone service has been restored, we're going to need a professional tree service and the insurance company. But for now, we wait and stay out of harm's way."

As though to demonstrate that plenty of harm was still possible, there was a loud crack in the forest behind the lodge and a swooshing thump as another tree toppled. A beat. And then another crack and swoosh.

"It's like a war zone," I said, because I have seen some war movies and the sound of falling trees reminded me of the sound effects.

Gavin stared at me from under his oversized hood.

"Depends which war," he said, shortly, in a voice I'd never heard from him before. Then he continued in a more normal voice. "There are some tarps in the mechanical shed. I'm going to dash over there. We can try to cover the upstairs floor and furnishings."

"I'll come," I said, shocked at my own words.

"Quickly, then." Gavin walked toward the shed where all the equipment was stored. It was on the edge of the parking lot, just a few yards from where the huge tree had come down. I was so close behind him that when he stopped abruptly, I ran right into his back.

Before I could ask why he'd stopped, he bolted.

Then I saw the lump of red in the parking lot. It took me a second to realize it was a person in a red coat.

I threw back my hood to see better and got drenched. But in

the second before the rain washed away my vision, I saw that it was Murray on the ground. I'd never seen a dead person before but I was pretty sure I was seeing one now. Then Gavin was crouched over her, his head bent down to listen to her breathing.

"We need to call an ambulance!" Gavin shouted back at me.

I'd left my phone inside and there was no reception, anyway. "Okay," I said, but I didn't move. Murray's face was this oceanic blue colour, like she had frozen to death.

"Move," said Gavin, but not in a mean way. "Try to call. And ask whether anyone inside has first aid training."

I ran as fast as I could.

Chapter 51

You can't race boats without knowing what to do when things go to hell. Half the races I've been in felt like a crisis from start to finish.

When the chubby kid with the bad hair came running in, yelling for help, I put my hand up.

"It's Murray. She's outside. She's . . . fallen," panted the kid, who had all the aerobic conditioning of a bag of chips, not that I'm much better these days. "I think she might be dying. Or she's . . ."

I didn't ask any questions. Maybe she'd been hit by the tree that had obviously come down on the lodge. In that case, my training wasn't going to be worth much. I ran over and asked the cook if there was a first aid kit in the kitchen.

She nodded, her face gone pale.

"Bring it outside," I said, and then I ran after the kid, who was waiting with the door open. We went down the stairs, around the side of the lodge, and into the parking lot where the butler lay. She hadn't been struck by the tree, which had crushed the little building and hit the top of the lodge. The tall butler was doing something to her. Maybe he was just trying to block some of the rain.

The fuck?

The kid turned to me and I realized I'd spoken out loud.

When he saw me, the butler gave me the first glance I'd ever seen from him that was not completely polite and professional. It was a suspicious glance, and god knows I deserved it.

"I've got some medical training," I said. "Can I have a look?"

Gavin, that was his name, frowned but he let me get closer. I knew instantly what was wrong with her.

"She do drugs?" I asked.

The butler looked confused. "No. Not that I've seen. I . . ."

"This looks like an OD."

"How do you . . . ?"

"You don't want to know," I said. I grabbed her shoulders and gave her a shake. "Wake up! Wake up!" She didn't move. I unzipped her coat and knuckled her sternum. She was limp.

"Hey!" I looked at Gavin. "What's her name again?"

"Murray," he said.

I turned back to her. "Murray! Murray! We've called 911."

Nothing.

"You got the bag?" I asked the cook, who'd arrived and was standing beside Nigel. She hadn't even taken the time to put on a coat.

The cook nodded and handed it over.

I unzipped it and rooted around inside, looking for the distinctive black-and-red container. There it was. Thank Christ. "The things you find at the modern meditation centre," I muttered.

I swiftly unzipped it, pulled out the syringe, uncapped it, and injected the Narcan through her pants and into her quadricep. Then

I listened for her breath. It was very, very slow. But it was still there.

"Okay," I whispered after checking whether a minute had passed. "Let's try this again." I uncapped another syringe and shot it into her other thigh.

The butler held his coat over us.

I was just about to start rescue breathing on her when she arched her back and gave a cry, sucking air and water into her lungs and beginning to sputter.

"She might fight a little," I said. "They don't like being woken up. Let's get her into the lodge."

The girl was trying to get up. Her head moved from side to side and she tried to speak.

"Come on, Miss M," said the butler, his face stricken. "Let's get you inside."

"Gavin?" said the girl, and her voice sounded like it was coming from a well. It occurred to me that this was the first time I'd thought of either of them as anything other than staff.

I felt strangely ashamed. I wanted to hang back. Go to my cabin. But I didn't. "Let's get you inside."

"I don't want to—" she said and then forgot what she didn't want. She was wobbly and spent, the way they always are, unless they wake up in a white-hot rage because you ruined their high.

I've seen people revived. I've even done it for people a few times. This girl, Murray, was more co-operative than most. But they all wake up not wanting something. They don't want to be straight. They don't want to be alive. Who knows what she didn't want?

I looked at her and thought the butler, Gavin, was probably right. Murray wasn't a junkie. But somehow she'd OD'd in a parking lot.

What a crazy goddamned time to try hard drugs. Or maybe it wasn't. "Come on," I said and took one of her arms, while Gavin reached for the other one.

When she was on her feet, swaying back and forth, she said, "Stop."

She was staring at the parking lot.

"Who took the car?" she asked, her voice muzzy beneath the storm and the overdose.

Chapter 52

NIGEL OWENS

Gavin and Wills got Murray inside, which left me feeling sort of useless.

In the two minutes it took to get Murray to the lodge, the sky seemed to have lightened and the rain let up. It looked more like a regular west coast storm instead of a sizzler reel of extreme events on the Weather Channel.

Gavin put Murray on the couch in the sitting room and made her put her feet up. She started apologizing like every drunk girl I've ever tried to help, which is a lot because I'm the kind of guy who makes sure drunk girls stay safe, even though they always ended up puking in my mother's Kia.

Gavin was helping Murray get her rain gear off and he managed to make it look like a completely normal thing to do.

While he was getting Murray's right arm out of her sleeve, he looked up and caught me watching.

"Can you go check on everyone, please? Remind people to stay together. I'm worried about that tree coming further into the building."

Wills showed up in the doorway that led into the dining room.

"They're missing," he said, his face still wet from the storm and red from all the excitement.

"I'm sorry," said Gavin. "Who's missing?"

"The rest of them. My brother. Whits. Rayvn."

Gavin finished removing Murray's jacket and she fell back on the cushions. "Chef? Would you mind making sure she doesn't go to sleep?" he said. Then he walked into the dining room where Wayfarer and Jenson Kiley sat side by side in separate chairs. They had so much energy around them I could feel it in my chest. They were like a couple of heart attack clappers.

"Pardon me," said Gavin, who looked completely calm even though he was soaked, there was a tree on the lodge, and he'd just barely avoided losing his friend and fellow butler to an overdose. "Where has everyone gone?"

Wayfarer adjusted one of her long eyelash extensions with a painted fingernail. She turned to Jenson. "Do you want to explain?"

"We asked them to stay, and they said no. And then they left. Does that cover it?" Jenson asked Wayfarer.

"Yeah, that's it. We reminded them that we were all to stay together for safety and that, and they didn't give one-tenth of a shit. Went off on their own straightaway."

Both teachers were angry. Small wonder. They were used to being obeyed without question.

"We couldn't exactly hold them against their will. Well, this one probably could," added Jenson Kiley, gingerly patting one of Wayfarer's biceps like he was afraid it might bite him.

"I could, but I wouldn't. No being paid enough to tackle uncooperative students."

Wayfarer's tone was entirely matter-of-fact. Just because someone had told her to keep an eye on someone else didn't mean she'd lose sight of all her worth. That made her even more magnificent in my eyes, due to how I have almost no sense of what my worth is.

"If it helps, they went through tha door," said Wayfarer, pointing to the door at the end of the dining room. It was on the opposite side of the building from the fallen tree and the parking lot where we found Murray.

Gavin considered for a moment. "We need to find all of them and bring everyone back together. We will reassemble at Kalaivaani Hall. I'd like to get everyone out of the lodge until we know the tree isn't going to come in further."

He got busy issuing orders. "Wayfarer? May I ask you and Chef to help Murray to the hall. Nigel? Can you find Rayvn? Jenson, if you could look for Whitney, please. Wills? Would you mind finding your brother? I'm sure everyone has had enough of being in a building hit by a tree. It's unsettling. I'll make sure nothing here is about to explode, and I'll protect what I can and then I'll be over, too."

I felt a little sick thinking about walking near those huge trees to get to Rayvn's cabin and then to Kalaivaani Hall. It occurred to me that I didn't want to work here anymore. Not even for a few more hours, no matter how much I admire Helen and the other two butlers. No matter how fascinating I find Jenson and Wayfarer. Or how much I want to learn to cook like Chef. I would tender my resignation, effective immediately. The place had gone a bit nightmare-y so I was going to bow out, and I, for one, didn't blame me.

I opened my mouth to tell Gavin but stopped when I saw his expression. I could tell that it hadn't even occurred to him that I might bail. He was looking at me with this . . . confidence? Had anyone ever looked at me with confidence before? I mean, other than my parents' confidence that I would never do anything with my life? No. I don't believe anyone has.

So instead of quitting, I just nodded. "I'll check Rayvn's cabin," I said.

I was halfway there when it occurred to me that Gavin might have just pulled some butler voodoo on me. If so, it was super effective and I want to learn how to do that myself.

Chapter 53

WILLS TODD

On the walk to my brother's cabin, I was shivering in my six-hundred-dollar rain jacket, as much from adrenalin as from cold. I saw the fat kid heading down the trail toward Rayvn's cabin and the florist heading down another trail, on his way to find Whitney. The sky was clearing fast, the way it sometimes does after a storm. It was hard to tell what was rain from the remaining clouds and what was just water dripping off the trees.

I tried not to think about what I'd say to Tad when I found him. Should I tell him to stop killing people? Because I was pretty sure that's what he'd done. He killed Edna and then he tried to kill the young butler, for some reason only a psychopath like him could understand.

I muttered a curse. Chances are, if I said anything, Tad would take me out, too.

Could a person go to jail for knowing their brother was a killer and not doing anything about it? *Would* Tad get away with it?

The whole thing was a complete cock-up. Edna had hated all of us, although she'd probably have liked Rayvn if she'd met her. That girl was born for a place like this. But Tad and Whitney and I are a different story.

We should've just left it alone after she told us to get lost. The old woman didn't like us. Wasn't going to leave us anything. Fine. Other people come back from the financial brink. Though of course, I'm not actually on the brink. I fell off the brink a while back and I'm now at the bottom of a chasm, financially speaking. And if Tad had done what I think he did, it was for nothing.

Try as we might, we couldn't even pretend to be the kind of people who should own and operate this place. I would bet my last dollar that she'd tied it up in about three trusts with four codicils plus another eight restrictions so we wouldn't be able to sell it or do anything useful with it. And frankly, money aside, I don't want to see the place turned into anything other than what it is. The courses and the people who take them are a pain in my ass, but at least it's intact. It's a goddamned gorgeous piece of land. There are not enough beautiful places left unspoiled. My brother can fuck off. I'm not going to help him or cover for him.

I reached Tad's cabin, which was, of course, newer and quite a bit bigger than mine, and knocked on the door, trying to ignore the burn in my stomach. I was probably getting ulcers. Wasn't fair, since I was living clean at the moment.

I knocked again when there was no answer. There were no lights showing in the crack between the cloth curtains. I looked behind me and turned the doorknob. The door opened.

Tad's place was neat. No snacks, because Tad was always watching his weight. Not even a coffee cup. I stepped further inside. Maybe Tad had conveniently left a confessional note that I could take to the authorities. But no.

There was a copy of *Dwell* magazine.

I wanted to toss the place, but (a) I didn't know how, and (b) my brother never forgets a slight or a betrayal.

I backed out of the cabin, fighting the urge to wipe away my fingerprints, and I walked back to the main path, where I looked around. Where could he be?

Then an idea occurred to me and I headed back the way I'd come. One side of the reception building had been sheared off by the tree. The other part of the building stood like nothing had happened. I entered through the door that the guests used for check-in. It was surreal to enter and find myself right next to a great bloody tree. The smell of fresh cedar was overpowering. Branches lay across the counter. When I approached, I saw my brother going through a filing cabinet in the office behind the desk area.

He didn't notice me.

"Hey," I called. "What are you doing?"

He didn't even look around. Such a goddamned sociopath.

"Looking for something," he said.

"Someone is going to notice," I said, feeling incredibly lame.

At this, Tad turned and came to the door of the office. The fallen tree was right beside him. He shoved a few branches out of the way.

"I highly doubt it," he said. "The situation is a little chaotic. And no one except me, and I guess you, is crazy enough to come in here. This whole building could fall on us." He sounded untroubled by the prospect.

Now that he mentioned it, I realized he was right. The ceiling overhead listed inward.

"You know, don't you?" said Tad, sweeping his lank blond hair back from his head.

"I think so," I said, not wanting to be the first to say it.

"You *think so*," said Tad, his tone acid. "You *think so*."

"I know you're trying to hide your tracks."

Tad tilted his head, which made him look even more like a sled dog than usual. "What did you say?"

I felt incredibly tired right then. Like a narcoleptic. Or a drug addict.

"Why would *I* hide? You're the one who did it," he said. "You were here with her last."

That woke me up. "No, I didn—"

"For god's sake, of course I know you didn't kill the old lady, you boob. Neither did I. What do you think I am?"

A murderer, I thought. But I didn't say it. After all, I did not want to be next on his victim list. As I stood there, I realized I'd been worried my brother would kill me ever since I could remember. Had I ever met a more malevolent person? I thought not.

"She threw you out, just like she did me, and Whitney. And you came back and . . ." I said.

Now Tad just looked annoyed. Like he could hardly be bothered to listen. And now that I thought about it, had my brother ever *really* done anything to me other than say nasty things and act as though I was the world's biggest inconvenience? Sure, he'd ratted me out to our parents a few times, and made it clear he would never be a source of emotional or financial support. But he hadn't *done* anything to me, per se.

"Do you ever get tired of being wrong?" asked Tad. Which reminded me why I thought my brother was the devil incarnate. Maybe he was a minor devil. Not a major, murdering devil.

"What are you doing, then?" I asked. "You're up to something."

"You think?" said Tad. "Wills, you moron, she had a lot more than this lodge. Did you know that?"

I felt myself gawping at my brother.

"Yes," continued Tad. "She was worth a fortune and not a small one. Generational wealth. And do you *know* where it's all going?"

I fervently wished I was on a boat. And I also fervently wished I was getting a call to let me know that my naturally deceased late great-aunt had left me A LOT of money. What an exceptionally good phone call that would be.

"How much?" I asked, ignoring his questions and keeping an eye on the massive tree. It seemed pretty stable, but I'd heard that fallen trees could shift sometimes. Trap people underneath them.

"Not sure," said Tad. "It seems she's already given most of it away. But she died before she could get rid of all of it. I know people in the financial industry. Someone gave me a ballpark figure and it was a fuck-ton. But rumour has it that there may be up to a hundred million left."

A fine sweat broke out all over my body, like I'd been burned with a laser. My mind raced as I thought about what had happened. We'd come here, at Edna's invitation, and I'd grubbed around thinking I could get a few hundred grand out of her. And she was sitting on not just this property, but tens of millions of dollars. Why hadn't she just given us some? Dispensed with all the nonsense?

"Are we here to try to win the lodge or the money?" I asked. "Or both?"

"Who the hell knows? I imagine the butler, Helen, has an idea. But I can tell you that this place is in a trust. The realtor, Jared, told me that. No one is getting a penny out of this place that doesn't come from running it exactly as it has always been run. My guess is we're doing all this to find out which of us, if any, should run it. Can you think of a worse thing to do? Maybe our performance in these courses is going to determine how much we inherit."

"Shouldn't we be doing a better job, then?" I said, and what I meant was shouldn't *you* be doing a better job.

"It may surprise you to learn this, but I'm doing the best I can," said Tad, with painful dignity.

I could think of many worse fates than operating this lodge. In fact, I thought that looking after our useless parents—like Tad did —would be worse, but I didn't say that. But I could also think of a hundred things I'd rather do than run the lodge.

"I still don't understand what you're up to," I said instead, pointing past him to the filing cabinet.

"I took a few journals when I was here last," he said. "Including the one where she wrote about our visits. Mine. Yours. She didn't say anything about Whitney's. I guess that visit was later. She definitely wasn't impressed with the two of us. But she didn't say anything about her will. All she said was that she thinks we are useless sacks of leaf litter. In your case, that was her exact description."

Tad raised his hand and I saw he held a journal.

"She wrote in books like this one. Every night. I have taken the liberty of recreating the journal where she wrote about us. I've written new accounts of our visits," said Tad. "In her handwriting. This journal says that while we are not suitable to run the Institute because we are unspiritual clods, we should inherit most of her money because that's all we understand, and she owes it to her late husband to support us because we are so utterly useless."

Something in me fluttered at my brother's words. Hope. Yes, that's what it was.

"I've spent about five hundred hours getting her handwriting correct," said Tad. "And working on the tone. It was tricky because she was such a foolish bloody woman. Of course, it would be far too convenient for one of *us* to find this thing. I need to make one of the butlers find it. The book has got to hold up in court in case her will stipulates that we get nothing. I think Helen will be useful for that. She's big on doing what Edna wanted."

A thought crossed my mind.

"All of us?" I said. "You're including all of us in this diary entry?"

Tad sighed. "Yes, of course. People might get suspicious if she left it all to her favourite nephew, Tad Todd. I mean, to Tad and Wills Todd," he said after getting a glimpse of my face. "I wrote that all of the great-nieces and -nephews will share equally in her estate. Didn't name us all, even though it pains me to think of Ferdinand getting even richer. And I hate to cut Whit and the appliance salesgirl in. I hope to god she didn't write another one where she gave everything to Whitney. I don't think so. Whit said she struck out, too."

"Didn't Edna notice her diary was gone?" I said, edging up to the real subject.

"She filed them by size and colour. It was just our luck that she finished the one about our visits right before I left. I saw her put it away in the middle of a full shelf. By accident, of course. It was the only one with this cover. I went into her office a few nights after she asked me to leave and retrieved it." The cover of the book he held up looked like a reproduction of a Hawaiian shirt pattern.

I thought of my brother staying on the island and creeping into the lodge at night while Edna was upstairs. What would he have done if she'd caught him?

The only way that stealing and recreating her diary would work was if she died before informing her lawyers of her wishes. Had he done something to make sure she didn't have time to tell her lawyers about her decision?

"What was your . . ." I didn't finish. I didn't want to sound too accusatory.

"Plan?" he said. "I hoped she'd never notice. She's so . . ." He fluttered his fingers next to his head. "I have to tell you, taking these courses while trying to rewrite this diary has been exhausting."

"I still don't understand how this is supposed to work."

"Of course you don't," said Tad, with maximum condescension. "I thought I'd come back in a month or two. Apologize. Show my spiritual side or something. Maybe get her to change her will. And if she didn't, I'd sneak the faked diary onto the shelf with the others and arrange for it to be found after her death. In the meantime, if she found out someone had forged her diary, she couldn't prove it was me. This is a retreat centre. Packed full of weirdos for months on end. It's probably not even that illegal to commit diary fraud. At least, not that I'm aware of.

"I've been trying to figure out how to get this"—Tad held up the journal—"into Helen's hands in a way that doesn't make her suspicious. I wondered if I should knock over this cabinet and have the journal sort of poking out?"

"What if she discussed her plans in a later journal?" I said. "Or told her lawyer her actual desires?"

"Call me a gambler," said Tad, shortly. "I planned to come back and get any journal with contradictory information. All I want is to create some grounds to contest her will and make our claim. It's the best I could come up with."

I appreciated that apparently he'd chosen forgery and diary theft over homicide.

"Let me see it," I said.

"Don't get your fingerprints all over it," said Tad, whose fingerprints were all over it. But he handed it to me and watched as I flipped through it.

"You didn't, uh, help her along, did you?" he asked, as though he'd been waiting for his chance.

I suddenly realized that my brother thought *I* had something to do with Edna's death.

"No," I said. "I didn't. I kind of liked her. Even though she treated me like a vacuum salesman. I left when she told me to and that was it."

"Are you *sure*?" said Tad. "Not that I'd criticize if you were responsible."

"I would never. Not for any amount of money."

Something passed over Tad's face. Relief? Disappointment? "Well, she didn't completely hate you," said Tad. "At least, not compared to me."

"But she didn't leave me anything?"

"She did not."

Each page was filled with neat, faked handwriting. It was quite impressive in its way.

"You're going to leave this in here?"

Tad nodded. "Surely they'll have to go through this cabinet for the insurers. And I can't leave this in the office in the lodge. Helen knows the diary is missing. I heard her mention it to the cop."

"You better hope she finds it," I said. "A lot of wasted effort if she doesn't."

"I did nothing wrong," he said. "We need the money more than some charity for old cats."

Chapter 54

Nearly blinded by the rain, Helen ducked into the tiny car and closed the door. She'd assumed either Gavin or Murray would be driving the food to Olaf. But when her eyes adjusted to the dim light, Helen realized that it wasn't Gavin or Murray sitting inches away from her. It was Whitney.

She was surprised but she wasn't afraid. After the powerful opening she'd experienced on the road, her mind felt expansive and full of possibilities. She felt ready for whatever might happen.

"Oh, hello," she said. "It's amazing that you made it this far. The roads are very bad. I had to stop for a fallen tree."

The girl's face was a pale smudge inside the dark cabin of the car.

"Wild storm," Whitney said. "Dangerous."

Helen now thought she knew what the girl had done, even if she didn't understand why. Whitney's cousins, Wills and Tad, were much easier to read. They wanted money. Their reasons for wanting that money were individual, but their desires were simple. Whitney's weren't.

Whitney didn't move. She kept the car in drive, her foot on the brake.

"If you do a three-point turn here, we can head back. There are trees down everywhere. I don't want us to get hit. I had to leave the van back there."

Whitney didn't reply. The energy emanating from her was the kind Helen associated with distress. The countless hours she'd spent in silence with others meant she understood how people who have never exchanged a word grow to dislike or even hate each other. And how they come to find comfort and solace in each other without even exchanging a glance.

In the tight confines of the miniature car, Whitney had the kind of dark, frantic energy that made other people get up and move in a meditation hall. Her intensity was like that of a small, panicked creature.

Helen knew she had to be able to hold some of whatever furies were driving Whitney. No matter what the girl had planned for her.

Never again this moment.

Whatever happened, Helen could be present for all of it.

"Where have you been?" asked Whitney.

"There has been an . . . emergency in the village."

"Oh, too bad," said Whitney. She put the tiny car roughly into reverse and backed it up jerkily across the road, not looking where she was going until the rear tires sank into the ditch. Then she slammed the gear shift into drive, yanked the wheel around, and began to speed down the road toward the Institute.

"That's really too bad," she repeated.

The car was going much too fast, and when they hit water pooled on the narrow, curving road, it began to hydroplane sideways, but Whitney kept them on the road.

"Please slow down," said Helen, who somehow felt deep peace at the prospect of these being her last moments of life in her current form. The girl was a bird trapped in a tiny box. The only way to save them both was to open the box somehow.

"Oh, sorry," said Whitney. And this time she looked at Helen, her thin face made ghastly by what she had done.

"Yes," said Helen. "I know you are."

Another glance. "What? Why do you say that?"

"Would you like to pull over?" asked Helen. "So we can talk?"

Instead, Whitney made a hard right onto a small side road. Then she turned right again, and she drove them up a narrow gravel track. They climbed and climbed, and the car bumped in and out of ruts.

Helen didn't speak. When Whitney finally stopped the car, they were in a clearing at the top of a hill. Fallen trees were stacked in piles on one side of the bare lot being prepared for a new house. A new house that would overlook the ocean. A new house perched high atop a sheer cliff.

Orange plastic safety netting had been strung up in front of the drop-off so no careless machine operators would accidentally back over the edge. But the flimsy fencing offered no safety at all for anyone who intended to go over.

Helen bowed her head. She felt momentary sadness rise in her, but mostly she felt ready.

Whitney kept the car in drive, her foot on the brake. "I guess you know," she said.

"Why don't you tell me," said Helen. "It's your story." And like all stories, it had confined the girl and limited her perspective.

Whitney puffed out a breath. "It's always about stories with you Buddhists, isn't it? You people spend all your time trying not to get caught in your own stories. Isn't that the goal? You call it mental activity and ignore it?"

"That's right," said Helen. "At least, partly."

Whitney nodded. "Aunt Edna wasn't a very good Buddhist."

Helen didn't answer. It was true. Edna had not been a Buddhist of great attainment and she'd always seemed fine with that, which itself was an attainment of sorts. She was also a wiccan and, by her own admission, a somewhat self-involved wild woman. Like most people, Edna had contained multitudes. Unlike most people, she'd been quite fond of all the facets of herself.

"She made cruel judgments about people. Without having all the facts," said Whitney.

"Yes, that did happen," said Helen. Edna, for all her eclectic spiritual seeking, had been prone to hasty conclusions and trusted her own opinions too much.

"At first she liked me," said Whitney, defensively.

Helen could just get out of the car. She didn't need to sit here with this girl. She could run into the woods and Whitney probably wouldn't be able to catch her. She thought that if she got out and ran, there would be no Whitney anymore. Just a lavender Smart Car half submerged in the waves and smashing against rocks below. And there would be a slender body shifting back and forth in time with the currents. If Helen didn't get out of the car, there would be two bodies.

So be it. She would stay and listen.

"Did she?" asked Helen.

"At first she said I was intuitive. We had a lot of good talks. She thought it was great that I wanted to be a children's librarian. Obviously, I *knew* she'd like something like that. She even ordered me junk food when I mentioned I was craving it. That's when I knew she liked me. For the record, I don't eat junk food."

Whitney stared straight ahead. The rain had slowed so that the view through the windshield was clearer. The oppressive black and grey sky was lifting to reveal shards of evening light.

"It was going well. It really was. But then I asked the wrong question. Maybe a couple of wrong questions. I had to. My mother would have killed me if I didn't find out where I stood, inheritance-wise. She thinks I'm too passive."

"I see," said Helen.

"I just asked about the estate. What Edna planned to do with it. Jared already told me it was in a trust. I was curious about that. I also asked about her finances even though I knew my parents weren't getting anything. They are such a financial disaster. That's why they're at me all the time about money."

"I'm sorry," said Helen. "About your parents."

Whitney gave no indication she'd heard Helen. "I wasn't trying to get anything from her. I wouldn't have turned money down if she offered, obviously. Everyone thinks we're well off. My mother puts on such a show. But we aren't. Haven't been for years. Jared was sure I came from money." She gave a brittle laugh.

Helen thought of the young man's body under the stacks of canvases.

"You and Jared were friends," said Helen.

"If you want to call it that. We spent some time together. He had a hard time when I told him I was leaving. And probably not coming back."

Helen said nothing. She could imagine the handsome young painter wanting this girl, and compassion vibrated in her heart. He had always seemed lonely, trapped in his in-between life of painting and real estate sales. Living on an island he loved and hated the same way he probably loved and hated his mother.

"He's the reason no one knew what I did," said Whitney. "To Edna." Now the girl's cheeks were flushed in the dim light as though she was burning with a fever, brought on by the truth.

"Edna said some things to me. That last afternoon. After I thought she understood me. Understood that I'm decent. That I have *worthwhile priorities*."

"That must have been upsetting," said Helen.

"A person can't just *say* things to other people. A person can't call another person greedy. That was the word she used. She said I was just like Tad and Wills. That all I cared about was money. But that's not true." Whitney's voice rose, became shrill. "All my *mother and father* care about is money. And attention. And money is all Tad and Wills care about. None of them care about me. But I really did love this place. I even sort of loved Edna. I'm not shallow. Or greedy. I have qualities beyond what people see when they look at me. I know I do. She should not have said that."

Helen kept still. And she stayed open. "It must have hurt a great deal."

"I used to think I'd rather die than ask anyone for anything," said Whitney. "But then I thought, well, maybe someone else should die if I'm being forced to ask for things."

Whitney's words made Helen feel momentarily weightless and unmoored.

Edna had always been too quick to decide who was worthy and who wasn't. It was a shortcoming she'd worked on. Now Helen understood that it was connected to the vast sums of money she hid from everyone. Paranoia about that wealth was a side effect of her vast, hidden fortune.

Whitney touched the back of a finger against her nose.

"No one understands the pressure," she said. "Wills and Tad do, maybe. When your parents run through their cash and think you can fix it for them. It's supposed to be the other way around."

Helen nodded. The three cousins were staggering under the weight of their parents' expectations. That weight was deforming all three of them.

"Edna had told me all about her Death Positive Club. All about the drugs she had stashed in case she decided to go and there was no doctor available to help her. She had a special cocktail created for her by a doctor in Stockholm. Apparently, it contains some drug it's almost impossible to get now, plus a sedative, and a muscle relaxant. She got enough of it to give some to other people in her death club. Pretty reckless, if you ask me. She told me that she kept enough for herself to kill herself four times over. She didn't want there to be any mishaps when the time came. She wanted it over in a few minutes. I knew that she took her liquid vitamins every night. I found her drugs and I did what I did. Guess I'm not so useless after all."

Helen didn't respond.

"Look, I never thought she'd *die*. I assumed she'd taste it and spit it out."

This, Helen knew, was not true.

"That night, after I put the medicine in her vitamins, I was supposed to go to Jared's. I was going to say goodbye. Tell him things hadn't worked out. But I really didn't feel like it. Instead, I just got on the ferry and went home. And I took the rest of Edna's drugs with me."

Whitney stared through the windshield at the place where the evening sky met the cliff's edge. She reminded Helen of someone performing a one-woman show she doesn't care for.

"For the next while, I couldn't understand why I wasn't arrested. You know, for attempted poisoning." She shot a look at Helen from under her bangs. "Or murder, after my mother told me Edna had died. I didn't do anything to cover my tracks. I didn't even wipe my fingerprints off the bottle before I put the rest of the drugs into another container. Only Jared knew I'd been there. And my mother, but she would never suspect me of doing anything so forceful."

Helen listened, absorbed by this confession and by what Whitney was saying and what she was not saying. In her years of doing interviews with retreat participants, she'd listened to many people who felt very bad about the things they'd done and hadn't done. A doctor who'd misdiagnosed cancer, a man who let his husband, who was in the last stages of Alzheimer's, choke to death. But this was the first time she'd heard a murder confession like this. But she didn't flinch away. Instead, she listened with everything she had.

"It was Jared who saved me," said Whitney. "When I didn't come by, he went to the lodge to find me. It was night by then. He found Edna. He said she was already gone. He knew right away what I'd done and he knew I was going to get caught. He wiped off the empty bottle I left behind and put it on her side table. Put out all the death literature she kept in her bedside table. He even went down to the office and removed the journal she'd been writing in, in case it mentioned my visit. Everyone knows about her journaling. She thought keeping a record of her life was *very significant*."

Whitney seemed to sense Helen's question. "I'd told him all about the Death Positive Club. About how Edna planned to kill herself if it came to that. As *if* she'd ever do it. Edna was too wrapped up in herself."

The girl spoke with a spiteful resentment that was painful for its lack of self-awareness and for its truth.

"Why did you do it?" asked Helen finally.

"Why?" demanded Whitney. "I already told you—because she hurt my feelings. Because she should have seen that I didn't have a choice other than to ask her for money." She gave a little laugh. "One time, this boy I was seeing broke up with me by text. And when I complained, he said they were just hurt feelings and I'd get over them. But the thing is: What is there besides feelings?" She turned to stare at Helen. "I don't think I've ever gotten over a hurt feeling or a resentment in my whole life. That's all I've got room for in here, now." Whitney pointed a thin finger at the side of her head.

"And your heart?" said Helen. "What's in there?"

"Nothing," said Whitney.

Helen looked into the girl's flat grey eyes and saw that it was true.

"That's what Jared didn't understand. He covered up for me because he loved me. Or he thought he did. He probably just wanted to have a rich girlfriend. But he misunderestimated me."

The word play was the first joke Helen had heard Whitney make. The timing of it caused another wave of sadness to pass over her.

"And Jared?" asked Helen.

"He shouldn't have tried to force me to talk to him about things when I didn't want to." She paused. In the dim interior of the car, her pale face was grim. "He shouldn't have expected me to be grateful. And he shouldn't have hinted he might tell someone. He didn't think I was capable of hurting him. Ridiculous. I went to his place and I asked him for the journal and he said there was nothing important in it. I said I wanted to see it anyway. He wanted me to have a glass of wine with him. He was quite into his wine, you know. I think he was on track to end up like his mother. Maybe I saved him from that."

Helen willed herself back into her body and listened.

"I put some of Edna's drugs in his glass when he went to get the journal. After he drank the wine, he flailed around for a while. Knocked over a few canvases. Made a mess. After he went down, I hid him under some canvases so no one would notice him if they looked inside."

She sounded as though she was talking about hiding an old shoe on a whim.

"He was right about the journal. There was nothing important in it. She'd only filled in a few pages and she hadn't written about me at all. Edna really was incredibly thoughtless." Whitney brushed her hair out of her face and then looked sidelong at Helen. "I worried there wouldn't be enough of the cocktail left for anyone else. But there was." She smiled.

"Who did you poison?" asked Helen.

"How do you think I got the car to come and get you? I gave someone else a taste of Edna's cocktail. Maybe I should have saved it for you, Helen. Turns out it was barely enough for three people."

Helen's sense of equilibrium held, but she felt her mouth go dry. Who else had Whitney killed or attempted to kill? It must have been whoever had, at Helen's request, headed to Jared's with food for Olaf. Gavin? Murray? Poor Nigel?

"You should have left well enough alone. You shouldn't have kept asking questions. Making calls. Watching all of us. Judging."

Helen sensed that more questions in that moment might prove fatal.

Now the girl was still as a blade. Then she sniffed. "Jared seemed to think I was going to take over the lodge. Get a big inheritance. And we could live there together. He could paint full-time. I guess I was supposed to work the bloody front desk."

The silence between Helen and Whitney drowned out the noise of the ocean.

"What's the plan?" said Helen, her heart sore for this girl and for Jared, who'd had the misfortune to love her. And for Edna and for the third person Whitney had poisoned.

"I guess we'll go now," said Whitney. "It's over. Please take off your seatbelt."

"I'm sorry?" said Helen.

"Take it off. You won't need it."

Helen did as she was told, aware and somewhat surprised to find that she was still not afraid. Instead, she felt deeply concentrated.

Whitney put the car in reverse, backed it across the construction site, and turned so they were pointed the way they'd come from. Helen, beside her, was pure stillness.

The car suddenly began to accelerate until the engine whined. Whitney aimed the passenger side of the car at a huge tree that had been left standing at the edge of the lot. Helen saw what was about to happen and reacted without thinking. She threw open the door and jumped out, rolling, rolling along the wet ground. Helen sensed rather than saw Whitney turning to stare at the empty space where Helen had been. Then the car hit the tree.

The car bounced off the tree trunk and began to roll over and over until it came to a stop on its side.

Helen got to her feet, realized she was unhurt, but muddy, and approached the car. Whitney hung upside down, suspended from her seatbelt, trapped in place by her airbag.

"You've got to help me," Whitney said in a weak voice. "Get me out of here."

Helen stepped around the car and saw that the passenger door had been smashed in and a branch of the tree had gone right through the window where her face had been seconds before.

"Are you seriously injured?" she asked the girl, whose face was a mask of bloodly hair pinned in place by the balloon.

"No. I don't think so. I'm just stuck."

"Okay. Well, for now you can stay there," said Helen, her voice firm, but kind. "I think that's probably for the best."

Chapter 55

The aftermath was a mess that required all three butlers and a butler trainee.

When she called the lodge after phoning the police, Helen was profoundly relieved to hear that Whitney had not, in fact, managed to kill anyone else. Everyone was alive. She waited calmly in the clearing for over an hour until the police arrived in two vehicles, having helicoptered over from Campbell River. By nine o'clock that night, two of the officers were on their way back to the helicopter with a bruised but otherwise unharmed Whitney. There was no jail on Sutil Island, so they'd decided to take her off the island right away. Two other officers drove Helen back to the lodge.

Those officers, who'd been assigned to stay behind on the island, took Helen's statement in the dining room, which they determined would be safe, in spite of the tree lying on the roof over the kitchen. Gavin, Murray, Nigel, and Chef had all left the lodge at the request of the officer who interviewed Helen. The guests and teachers had also been asked to stay in their cabins. The pair of investigators were staying at a bed and breakfast, and when they finished speaking to her, they told her they would be back the next morning with other officers, who would be arriving by ferry to begin further interviews with everyone else.

When the police were gone it was after eleven at night and Helen fell, exhausted, onto the small sofa in the sitting room. Chef slipped back into the lodge and brought her a mug of hot chocolate that she'd apparently made in her cabin and covered Helen in a blanket.

"Nigel has prepared Flicker Cottage for you when you're ready," she said.

Helen was so grateful that she could barely speak. Then Chef went back to her own cabin.

Helen had just taken a sip of the luxurious hot chocolate when the nearest door opened and a dishevelled head poked into the sitting room.

"Where is she?" demanded the woman.

It took Helen a moment to recognize who she was looking at and a further moment to remember her name. "I . . ." she said, blinking. Whitney's mother, Meredith Varga, looked as though she'd been living in the woods for a month. Her hair was wild, and not the sort of carefully tended wild hair that suggested artistic impulses, but the kind that suggested vermin had moved in.

"Ms. Varga," said Helen, sitting upright and nearly spilling the chocolate on her lap as the blanket fell to the floor.

"Where is she? Why didn't she go back to her cabin when the others went?" said Meredith. Her face seemed to have aged fifteen years in the week since Helen had last seen her. "I've been waiting. Outside, naturally. Since I am forbidden from being here. Which is ridiculous."

Helen tried to gather her thoughts. "But you're—"

"I have been here to support my daughter and to ensure that her best interests are . . . served."

"Did Whitney know you were here?" asked Helen, carefully.

"Of course not," said Meredith in an offended voice. "She felt up to the task of proving herself worthy of inheriting this place. Well, that made one of us." She sniffed. "And I'm staying at the worst Airbnb you can imagine. It's one of those tiny house things. Like a chicken coop, for god's sake."

"What have you . . ."

"I have been monitoring the proceedings," said Meredith, who'd calmed herself enough to begin brushing things off her bedraggled jacket. "In the pouring rain. I've been watching Whitney showing zero signs of floral design talent. Virtually no ability in dance. And no spiritual qualities. What. So. Ever.

"And now she's left the competition in one of her huffs. I swear to god, no more Mrs. Nice Guy," said Meredith, who sounded about as far from a nice guy as it was possible to sound. "If she wants to pursue some pathetic little career in whatever"—she rolled her eyes wildly to underscore her point—"and go around with a talentless man who lives in a veritable shack, well. That's not my problem. Did you kick her out or did she quit on her own?"

Helen realized her mouth was hanging open.

"I'm afraid your daughter—" she began.

But Meredith wasn't listening. "This latest failure is the last straw. After what her papa and I have tried to do for her."

"Your daughter has been arrested," said Helen.

"She has what?" said Meredith, suddenly alert.

"She has been arrested on suspicion of murder," said Helen.

She waited for Meredith Varga to crumple.

Instead, Meredith tilted her head back and seemed to make some sort of fast calculation.

"She may be responsible for, um, taking another's life. Two lives, actually," Helen continued.

"Well," breathed Meredith. "That *is* a surprise." But it didn't sound as though it was an unwelcome one. "Who is she accused of killing?"

"Her great-aunt Edna. And Jared Weintraub."

"Really!" said Meredith, sounding not at all dismayed. "Why ever would she do such a thing?"

Helen was not about to tell her, and so she said that was all she knew.

"I do believe that my daughter has finally managed to surprise me," said Meredith Varga.

"I'm sorry, it must be a shock," said Helen.

But Meredith Varga was not listening. She had her phone out. "I need to call my husband."

"Would you like . . ."

Meredith ignored her. "Darling? You won't believe it. Whitney has been arrested. I don't know the details. But I think you need to call your agent. This is going to be a big story. We need to get out in front of it. Control the narrative. There is going to be a lot of interest in the press. I think Ros Davison would be the perfect person to handle the PR." Meredith was still speaking as she left the lodge, with Helen staring in her wake.

After it became clear that Meredith Varga was not coming back, Helen got heavily to her feet and went to the office, where she dialled the number for the officers who were still on Sutil Island. She told the one who answered about Whitney's mother. There was a long pause.

"Her mother has been here the whole time?" he said. "Did she see anything?"

"I don't think so," said Helen. "She's not very . . . observant." At least she wasn't when it came to actually seeing her daughter.

He sighed into the receiver. "Okay. We'll track her down at the Airbnb. See you in the morning," he said.

"Yes, thank you."

In the aftermath of one of the most disconcerting and depressing conversations she'd ever had, Helen needed to be with good people. She walked down the path to Gavin's cabin, hoping he was still up.

She knocked on the door and saw that Murray and Nigel were gathered inside, and she felt instantly better.

"I was so afraid for all of you," she said simply, standing in the doorway.

"It was a close thing," said Gavin, getting to his feet. "If we hadn't found this girl when we did . . ."

The thought made Helen feel sick.

Gavin ushered Helen inside and got her settled in a comfortable chair and then he went to check on Murray's temperature.

"Now you," said Murray, who did not get up. "I'm fine. But I don't understand why Whitney tried to hurt you and why she poisoned me."

"Perhaps she drugged you because she overheard our phone call," Helen said. "She said she did it because she wanted the car. She knew I'd found Jared but she wasn't *sure* what I knew. She decided to pick me up and fake an accident in which only I would die. I have no idea how she thought that was going to help her. She was not thinking clearly."

"Maybe she thought that without you, the lawyers would decide to give the operation of the lodge to her?"

"I don't think so," said Helen. "Other people knew she'd been seeing Jared. She would be the main suspect in his death. I think she was just angry. With me, with Edna. With Jared. With anyone who made her feel judged and inadequate."

Then she told them about the scene with Meredith Varga.

"My god," said Gavin.

"Parent of the year award does not go to Whitney's mom," said Murray.

"Do you think she's the one who threw rocks at Wills?" asked Gavin.

"And I bet she's the one who ruined Rayvn's arrangement. Can you imagine doing something like that for your adult child?"

"My mom wouldn't even come to my plays," said Nigel. "Said she was allergic to musicals."

Murray reached over and patted his shoulder.

"So Whitney killed her boyfriend? And then she tried to kill me?"

Helen nodded. "So it seems."

"What about Edna?" asked Gavin.

"Yes, she killed her, too. Over hurt feelings at not being given the lodge," said Helen.

"Maybe she was, in some deeply twisted way, trying to impress her mother. From what you say, it sounds like her mother is actually pleased," said Gavin.

Helen paused. "You're right," she said. "Perhaps Whitney was getting back at those who doubted her and proving to her mother that she was capable of . . . strong action."

Murray gave a shudder. "Can you imagine? Having a mother who thinks you're more interesting if you kill someone?"

Helen had met enough meditation students terribly damaged by narcissists that she could easily imagine it.

She explained how Whitney had killed Edna and how Jared had covered up for her. When Jared had tried to re-establish the relationship by telling Whitney what he'd done for her, she'd killed him, too.

Nigel's eyes were huge as he listened. "That's the most messed up thing I ever heard," he said.

"So tell us, how did you get away from her?" asked Gavin from the couch across from Helen.

"I could see that she planned to ram my side of the car into a tree and so I jumped out."

"While it was moving?" said Murray. "Like an action hero?"

"Yes," said Helen.

"Oh, fair play to you," said Murray. "You Buddhists are full of surprise talents."

"And this happened right after the big confession?" said Gavin.

"That's right."

"I still don't get it," said Murray.

"I think she was in terrible distress, and in those circumstances, people do unfathomable things."

"Did she light Greta's house on fire?" asked Nigel.

"Wait a moment," said Gavin and he gestured at a tin on the table. Helen nodded and he took out a neatly wrapped joint. Gavin was the most gracious man alive, but he did enjoy his pot.

"Oh thank god," said Murray. "But I guess I shouldn't partake after having an overdose so recently."

Nigel, clearly stunned at the story and at the sight of Gavin about to smoke pot, stared from person to person.

Gavin smiled back.

"I thought you were, you know," said Nigel, "clean living."

"I am. But today has been a bloody hard day." Gavin inhaled and then offered the joint to Helen, who declined. As always.

"So did she?" repeated Murray, fascinated. "Start the fire?"

"I don't know," said Helen. "I expect so. She knew about Edna's plans and that Greta was her death doula. Apparently, she and Edna talked about all of it before Whitney was sent away."

In spite of the grim day past and the subject matter, something about the present scene reminded Helen of butler school. Her two dear friends smoking pot and relaxing. Her enjoying their company. As the Buddha himself said, good friends are the whole of the holy life.

Gavin put out the joint without offering any to Nigel, who looked disappointed and relieved. He'd been glancing at Helen repeatedly, probably remembering what she'd said about not getting high while he was working at the lodge.

"It's all very sad and surreal," said Gavin. He closed his eyes and lay his head back against a pillow.

The four of them sat in silence for several minutes. Gavin took Murray's socked feet in her hands and began to rub them.

"Well, I think I'm going to bed," said Helen finally.

"What's going to happen?" said Murray.

"I have no idea," said Helen. "But I need to sleep."

"Me too. I'm beat," said Nigel. "Being a domestic professional is way more dramatic than I ever imagined."

"Not usually," said Helen. "It should be drama-free if you're doing your job well."

Gavin sat up slightly. "Where will you sleep?" he asked Helen.

"In Flicker Cottage. Chef tells me that Nigel has already kindly moved my things there. I didn't even have to ask. This young man understands that when a tree has fallen through your sleeping quarters, other arrangements must be made." She smiled at Nigel and he lit up.

"He's got good instincts," said Gavin.

Helen and Nigel put on their shoes at the door. "You want me to walk you back to your cabin?" Nigel asked Murray.

"She's staying with me for a spell. I need to make sure she's suffered no ill effects," said Gavin.

Then Helen and Nigel were off, using their headlamps to light the way.

Chapter 56

MURRAY CLEARY

As soon as the door closed, Gavin sat up and took my hands.

"You," he said. "I thought I lost you."

You could have popped the tension between us with a seafood fork.

I thought about saying something like "I didn't know you cared." Just so he would say he cared.

But then, maybe because we were in the middle of a moment, I went for it. "Gav, I don't have a job," I said.

He paused, head cocked to the side.

"I'm sorry, what?"

"I need you to know that I didn't get a position after the Academy."

His expression was pure confusion.

"You remember when I got that hotel internship? And I was in charge of the penthouse?"

"Yes," he said. He'd done an internship with a famous fashion designer who'd asked him to model his fall line. Gavin had declined, saying he felt he was more a behind-the-scenes person.

"Well, on my last night, a family arrived. They had a son. Maybe nineteen? Or twenty? Anyway, I arranged for his parents to go to this new restaurant. I had to work all my connections to get them the reservation. I wanted them to be impressed, you know? I wanted them to rave about me to the hotel managers, so they would tell the Academy, so I would get a fabulous post. Like you and Helen."

"Okay."

"Well, I went up to ask the son if I could get him anything, since he didn't want to go out for dinner. And he was a little drunk. And he made a, um, pass."

Gavin's face went hard, but he didn't speak.

"He said some stupid things and I tried to keep it professional. But then he, uh, touched me."

Any softness the weed had brought to Gavin was gone.

"And I took his finger and broke it."

Gavin blinked.

"I broke it and told him if he said anything else, I'd break all his fingers. One by one."

Gavin's eyes were huge. "Jesus."

"Neither of us said anything about what happened. I got the hotel doctor up there for his finger. Said he'd had an accident. But his family told the hotel I was a terrible butler. Worst they'd ever had. And the Academy didn't give me a recommendation. And I didn't get a position."

Gavin rubbed his hands over his face. "I'm sorry," he said. "I would very much like to break one of his fingers too."

"No need," I said. "I can break any fingers that need breaking."

He stared at me. And then he said, "You know I love you, right?"

You could have knocked me over with a flower petal.

"No," I said. "I didn't know that."

"Well, I do."

And then we said something along the lines of "what are we going to do about it." And then we did something about it.

Chapter 57

Helen slowly made her way back to Kalaivaani Hall the next morning after walking around the whole property. The roads and paths were covered in branches but no major trees had come down. Most of the fallen trees were on a hillside up behind the lodge.

She took off her shoes outside and set them down in the foyer. Inside, the hall was warm with the fire she'd asked Nigel to start. She'd only had a few hours of sleep but felt calm and perfectly rested.

She felt even warmer when she saw the three students on their mats in front of the stage. Behind them were the staff and teachers.

Helen approached the dais and bowed three times before the Buddha. Then she turned and settled herself in front of the remaining students.

"We normally sit in silence in the morning," she said. "But this morning, I want to tell you about upekkha, or equanimity. From upekkha we find freedom and wisdom. And it stabilizes us to love without attachment."

The three remaining students were very quiet this morning, in spite of all that had gone on the day before.

"Equanimity is based on the knowledge that everything changes and will always change and that is okay. We find equanimity only by paying close attention to what is happening in the moment."

She felt herself smiling at the students and feeling great affection for everyone in the hall.

"We find equanimity everywhere in the teachings. It's the result of good practice and preparation for awakening. It can be hard to feel equanimous in the face of upheaval. If it's not present, that's okay. Be curious about what is present. But don't get lost in the story."

And with that, she led them through the sit.

After she rang the bell to indicate that the meditation was over, she watched them open their eyes.

"Today," she said, "we have some things to discuss."

Tad, Wills, and Rayvn straightened and glanced at one another.

"Yesterday was a difficult day. Today will also be challenging. The police will want to speak to all of us. I imagine they will be here on the first ferry. That means we won't be able to proceed as scheduled with the courses."

More glances.

"If you'd like to stop now and go home after your interviews, I understand."

Rayvn put up her hand. "What if we want to finish?"

"In that case, the teachers have agreed to finish the last two days of the courses as soon as we are able to resume normal programming.

No one will think less of anyone who wants to leave."

"I'm definitely staying," said Rayvn.

"Are we going to talk about Whitney?" asked Wills. "About what happened?"

"Not before we have our interviews with the police," said Helen. "However, I have decided that it's time to speak candidly to you about what you're doing here. You deserve to know what is going on before you decide whether to go or stay. As some of you have probably gathered, you are taking these courses so I can determine whether any of you are suitable to take over the day-to-day running of the Institute. Edna has already stipulated that the centre must continue in its current form. I believe she also stipulated that a board be formed to oversee the management of the centre, meaning whoever takes the place over will have to report to a board."

Tad seemed about to say something, but Helen held up a hand.

"That is all I know. The lawyers will have more information when the courses are over. I agreed several years ago to do this for Edna if she couldn't decide what to do with the lodge and the campus. And even though she seems to have interviewed most of you, she left no record of her thoughts."

At this, Rayvn tilted her head.

"I'm sorry, Rayvn. I don't think she knew about you."

"Good thing, too," said Wills, "or she probably would have given it all to you. You would have been very much up her alley."

Rayvn looked pleased at his comments.

"If we decide to stay, what are we going to do?" asked Tad. "When we aren't being interviewed by the police."

"There will be floral arranging and dancing and meditating. And eating and walking and breathing."

"I'm in!" cried Rayvn.

"Me too," said Wills.

"I suppose I'll stay too. But please, do not make us drink brown liquid during this difficult time," grumbled Tad.

Helen smiled at them.

"Full breakfasts are in order this morning, I think. But Chef is going to be cooking out of one of the cabins until the tree is off the lodge."

With that, everyone got up, and perhaps because of the shared trauma or just the renewed sense of commitment, the group seemed more cohesive than she had seen it before.

The following two days were full of interviews. Everyone was spoken to multiple times by Officer Rosedale and the other detectives.

The police revealed little of what they knew to Helen or anyone else, but that was okay. She knew what had happened and she knew why. Rosedale revealed that they'd found the remnants of Edna's final journal partly burned in the woodstove in Whitney's cabin. Helen did not mention that Edna had purchased a lethal cocktail of drugs from a doctor in the Netherlands and had given some to other members of the Death Positive Club.

Meredith's mother had been caught on her way off the island the next morning and taken briefly into custody. She was apparently already in talks with a literary agent about a book, and her husband wanted to do a documentary.

"Do you think *she* had anything to do with Edna's death?" Officer Rosedale asked Helen in the large cabin where the interviews were being conducted.

"I don't know," said Helen. "But she seems to have applied a lot of pressure to Whitney to succeed. No matter what."

"Hmmm," said Rosedale. "Do you want to press charges? For

trespassing? We might also be able to get her on mischief charges or assault, if she was the one who threw rocks at one of your guests."

"No, thank you," said Helen. "Being Meredith Varga is probably punishment enough."

Rosedale gave a dry little laugh. "You know," he said, "I believe you may be right about that. That woman is something else."

While the interviews were taking place, a local faller and his crew removed the tree from on top of the lodge and reception building. Even though Chef was cooking out of a much smaller kitchen, there was no noticeable difference in the quality of her offerings.

"Because she's a genius," said Gavin.

On the third day after the storm, the contractor came to assess the damage to the reception building and top floor, and the roofers got to work on repairs to the lodge. Meanwhile, the students went back to their regularly scheduled programming. They made more floral designs that reflected their inner destinies, they danced like animals and then like "inner flames" for the staff. They sat in silence with Helen. They undertook every activity with a seriousness that suggested they might all want to take over the lodge.

And when it was over, Helen gathered them together in the garden, where she thanked them and the teachers.

"Thank you all for persisting," she said. "It has been beautiful to see you grow."

Wills patted his stomach, which was bigger than it had been. "Bread," he said simply. "I really love it."

At this, Chef Leticia grinned.

Birds twittered all around them and the wind moved like silk around the garden.

"Ms. Edna's lawyers have asked me to not only tell you the results of this, uh, experience," Helen said, loath to use the word *competition*. "They also asked me to read out the terms of her will."

The three students leaned forward. So did the teachers and staff.

Helen carefully unsealed the letter that Lest and Associates had couriered to her.

She read over the first few lines and then got to the particulars.

"Edna Todd leaves each of her grand-nieces and -nephews the sum of three million dollars. She does not specify names, which means that all of you are included."

Wills seemed to slump over, so great was his relief. Rayvn's mouth was stuck in an O shape like she was about to scream.

Only Tad seemed like he was still waiting for something.

Helen read on. "Wayfarer and Jenson have each been left the sum of one million dollars and a standing invitation to teach your courses here as long as you'd like."

Helen did not mention to the assembled that she, too, had been left three million dollars because it did not seem quite real. But she knew she would find uses for it. There was much need in the world.

She looked at the group, who seemed in a state of shock. And she saw the expressions on Nigel and Chef Leticia's faces. She suddenly knew where some of her money would be going.

She cleared her throat. "The lawyers will explain to you when the funds will be available.

"Now for the results of the courses. Edna asked me to decide whether any of you had the qualities that would make you good at running the Institute. And I have decided that I should just ask if any of you would *like* to take over. Perhaps I should have done that from the beginning."

Wills and Tad looked at one another. Neither moved or spoke.

Rayvn looked at the brothers and put up her hand. "I'd like to try. If it's okay with . . . everyone."

Helen nodded and felt pleased.

"But I know jack squat about hospitality and stuff. Also, I hate getting up in the morning." She said this in spite of the fact that she was no longer late to every morning sit. "I kind of hate to give up my old job. I was good at it. I thought I was going to be a businesswoman like my mom. Two generations of businesswomen. That's cool, right? Plus, my friends are all back in Nanaimo. But I love it here. And maybe I could be good at this, too."

Helen did not point out that the Yatra Institute was also a business, even if it didn't feel like one at the moment. Rayvn would come to that realization soon enough.

"I wonder if anyone else might like to stay to help?" asked Helen, after a moment's consideration.

Murray glanced at Gavin. "Maybe I could," she said.

"I would like to join you," he said. "For a time."

"What about your position?" asked Murray.

"There will be others," he said. "I'm rather employable, you know."

The look on Murray's face was beautiful to behold.

"Me too," said Nigel. "I want to stay."

"Very good," said Helen. "Rayvn, you will take over the lodge and Murray and Gavin and Nigel will assist as long as they would like and as long as you would like them to. I'll let you work out the terms between you."

With that decided, the day seemed even fairer than before.

Chapter 58

Later that afternoon, Helen watched a work crew carrying things out of the destroyed reception centre.

The forewoman walked over. "You want anything out of there?" she said, pointing at the filing cabinet two workers had just shoved into the back of a truck.

"No," said Helen. "We mostly stored old programs and calendars in there. All the guest information and anything of value has been computerized."

Helen imagined that the new reception building might look a bit more like a medieval thatched hut than the old one had, but that would be fine. Rayvn had already announced that she wanted to host a LARPing conference in August.

Behind Helen the carpenters and roofers were working on the roof of the lodge. Rayvn was hard at work planning for the season that would open in just over three weeks. Edna had prepped everything for the season, but after she died, Helen had put a pause on all the reservations.

As soon as the website formally announced the season at Yatra would go ahead as planned, the phone would ring non-stop.

Now Rayvn and her team of butlers and Nigel were already confirming staff and teachers and doing the million and one things that needed to be done before the Institute opened.

Nigel had thanked Helen at least twenty times for the twenty-five thousand dollars she'd promised him when she got her inheritance. "You can use it for school," she said. "Or whatever you want."

"Oh my god," he'd said. "I'm tempted to blow it on clothes, but I'm not going to."

She laughed.

Helen gave Chef Leticia the same amount and received a warm hug in return. "You are a benefactor," she said. She'd agreed to stay on for the summer and Helen felt glad for everyone that they would get to enjoy her food. The Yatra Institute was in good hands.

They were all happy in their work and Helen was happy for them.

Wills and Tad had offered to drive her to Campbell River, where she had a flight booked to Vancouver, and then she would be off to the Levines' home in San Jose, where she would start her job as their butler. She'd declined the brothers' offer, saying she would be going over on a float plane. Tad did not seem offended.

"Gotcha," he said. The red Land Rover was packed up and Tad had been in an exceptionally jaunty mood since she'd told everyone the terms of the will. The brothers seemed happy to be leaving Rayvn in charge of Yatra. Perhaps they felt they'd escaped. But Helen thought there was often great satisfaction in taking on an obligation willingly.

Tad spotted the truck filled with debris and office equipment slowly backing away from the ruined reception building and heading down the driveway. He stared at it for a long time.

"Everything okay?" Helen said.

He started, like she'd woken him out of a dream.

"Yeah. Sure," he said. "Everything is just fine. I'd say it couldn't be better, but you know, that's not true. It can always be better. Right, Wills?"

Wills stood beside his brother and also watched the truck disappear around the corner. "Things are fine," he said. "Better than we deserve."

Soon the two brothers were gone, having been waved off by everyone.

And then it was Helen's turn. Gavin drove, and Murray sat beside him. Helen noticed how often they looked at each other and touched when there were no guests around. It brought her great joy and it made her feel lonely in a way that was quite familiar.

Tanner greeted them at the float plane dock, and he carried her modest suitcase and stored it in the pontoon of the float plane.

Gavin and Murray each hugged her. "You call us if you need anything," said Gavin.

"We will come running. Rescue butlers!" said Murray.

"I hope the next time we meet, we'll all be on holiday," said Helen. "No more high-stakes work problems." As she said it, she realized the next time they met would probably be at Whitney's trial, if there was one.

Then, feeling deep appreciation for her friends, she headed down the plank.

"Dude, we're all going to miss the shit out of you," said Tanner.

"Well, thank you," said Helen. "I feel the same."

"Greta says hi."

"You two are . . . ?"

"We're good. She liked my coffin."

"I'm not surprised," said Helen. "It's quite something."

"Yeah," he said. "I'm down with death. But like not quite yet, you know?"

"I know," said Helen.

And then she climbed onto the plane and waited to take off.

Acknowledgements

Many people made this book possible. Thank you to Mia Tremblay, who, along with Sandra Thomson, introduced me to the practice of Buddhism. Both women are radiant examples of the dhamma in action. Thanks also to my Nanaimo sangha, and my teachers at Vipassana Hawaii: Steven Smith, Michele McDonald, Jesse Maceo Vega-Frey, Pari Ruengvisesh, Darine Monroy. An extra measure of gratitude to Jesse, who was kind enough to advise on many matters pertaining to Buddhism and read an earlier draft of this novel. Eternal thanks to Troy Barnes, who generously consulted about ɬoq̓ qaymıxʷ content, and to Sheena Robinson, who made that connection possible. Massive thanks also to Délani Valin, who helped in myriad ways.

I worked on this book for well over five years and I'm glad my agent, Hilary McMahon, didn't give up on me. Thanks to my magnificent editor, Iris Tupholme, for believing in it. I'm grateful to everyone at HarperCollins, including Canaan Chu, Julia McDowell, Catherine Dorton, Lesley Fraser, and Natalie Meditsky.

And as always, thank you to my trusted readers: Susin Nielsen, Andrew Gray, and Bill Juby, and to the rest of my family, who make it possible for me to be a spaced-out writer.

The eulogy exercise on page 168 was loosely based on *The Four Desires: Creating a Life of Purpose, Happiness, Prosperity, and Freedom* by Rod Stryker (Delacorte Press, 2011). If you are interested in learning more about your deeper purpose (and not just as it pertains to floral design), this is a useful book. The parable on page 229 comes from the great Anthony de Mello's *One Minute Wisdom* (Doubleday, 1986), a marvel of concise and profound teachings. The extract of the Fire Sermon on page 295 was translated by David Dale Holmes and is from https://www.buddhistdoor.net/features/the-fire-sermon-the-third-sermon-of-the-buddha. I should also thank the countless writers and spiritual thinkers who share so freely their insights and teachings in books and on the grand landscape of the internet for the benefit of us all.

A final note: the Yatra Institute was inspired by Hollyhock Leadership Learning Centre on Cortes Island in B.C. Hollyhock is one of the most beautiful places on earth and I have spent many intense periods of reflection and enjoyment there. But there is no Edna at Hollyhock and no character in this book is based on a real person. Sutil Island is a made-up place. The courses at the Yatra Institute are entirely the product of my fevered imagination. But I encourage everyone to visit Hollyhock. You'll never be the same.